Touched by Magic

DORANNA DURGIN

TOUCHED BY MAGIC

Copyright © 1996 by Doranna Durgin

A Baen Books Original

Baen Publishing Enterprises
P.O. Box 1403
Riverdale, NY 10471

ISBN: 0-671-87737-2

Cover art by Darrell K. Sweet

First printing, August 1996

Distributed by Simon & Schuster
1230 Avenue of the Americas
New York, NY 10020

Printed in the United States of America

Baen Books by Doranna Durgin
Touched by Magic
Dun Lady's Jess
Changespell (*forthcoming*)

THE ENDING

Rethia woke to wild hoofbeats. Frightened, she pressed herself against the ground. When she gathered the courage to peer up, all she could make out was flashing legs and leaping bodies—and all the while, the unmistakable tingle of magic coursed through her body.

Imperceptibly at first, the pounding diminished and the tickling magic intensified. The creatures were leaving, and a glimpse showed her they weren't just running away. They were bounding into the air and never landing. And when there was only one set of hoofbeats left, walking toward her, Rethia trembled with the knowledge that she was witnessing great magic in a world that was drifting free of such things, and forgot to be afraid.

The hooves stopped in front of her basket. Not a horse. She knew that even before she looked up to see the horn.

Rethia pulled herself upright and looked straight into the face of the unicorn, her deep blue gaze unflinching. It was a heavy boned face, with ridges etched in darkest walnut, and with odd icy eyes that abruptly reminded her that unicorns were not Tame. When the beast did not react to her impudence, she lifted a small trembling hand to touch the thick, tangled mane and forelock, so long they brushed her face even as the animal raised its head. It looked around the trampled, abandoned meadow, and blew out a huff of air. When it looked back down at her, its icy gaze warmed, catching the blue of her eyes, staining them with the reflection of its walnut features. It dropped its head to again accept her touch.

She had no idea it would be a trade.

◆   ◆   ◆

"I loved *Touched by Magic* and I was sorry when it came to an end." —S.M. Stirling

Once Upon A Time
there were two wild horsewomen on Mullins
Ridge.
This book is dedicated to the *other* one—

and
to John and Beth,
mountain caretakers

The Ending

Rethia sat at the edge of the meadow and arranged her morning harvest. Herbs and wild flowers, lichens and mosses—they all jumbled together in her basket despite her best efforts. The sorting was a game, and the hot midday sun brought out earthy scents as she organized the plants, making neat rows of color and shape in a never-ending process that pleased her six—but almost seven!—year-old's penchant for play.

The meadow was old pasture land gone poor, now thick with sturdy wild flowers and patches of briar, and the woods crowded close around it, offering refuge from the sun. Finally tiring of the game, Rethia stretched out on her stomach, lay her head down on her arms, and peered into the slat basket to admire the wilted results. The sun was well up, and the shade of the leafy maple beside her dappled her tunic, screening her just enough to keep the heat from becoming unpleasant.

Of course she fell asleep.

She woke to wild hoofbeats. Frightened, she pressed herself against the ground. The earth shook beneath her and the noise filled her ears, and though she should have crawled to safety in the woods, all she could do was quiver in front of her basket, her fright tinged with a trace of outrage. This was *her* meadow, her sanctuary and playground. It was her *safe* place, where no bulls were kept nor horses pastured. Still the beasts ran, circling the meadow, whipping through the wiry, long-stemmed flowers and trampling the briars without heed. The dust they raised floated in the sunlight. When Rethia gathered the courage to peer through the thick fall of her light hair, all she could make out was flashing legs and leaping bodies—and all the while, the unmistakable tingle of magic coursed through her body.

Imperceptibly at first, the pounding diminished and the tickling magic intensified. The creatures were leaving, and a glimpse showed her they weren't just running away. They were bounding into the air and never landing. Disappearing. Vanishing in a flash of not-being. And when there was only one set of hoofbeats left, solid and deliberate and walking toward her, Rethia trembled with the knowledge that she was witnessing great magic in a world that was drifting free of such things, and forgot to be afraid of the beast itself.

The hooves stopped in front of her basket, strong round hooves with heavy-boned, clean-lined legs rising from them. Not a horse. She knew that even before she looked up to see the horn. The unicorn dropped a brown-glazed muzzle into her basket, its lips twitching as it lipped and explored the pungent herbs. It wrinkled its nose and snorted mightily, leaving the plants in complete disarray, half of them blown entirely out of the basket.

"Hey!" Rethia protested, forgetting her fear. She pulled herself upright and looked straight into the face of the unicorn, her deep blue gaze unflinching. It was a heavy-boned face, with ridges etched in darkest walnut instead of gleaming highlights, and with odd, icy eyes that abruptly reminded her that unicorns were not Tame. Wild magic, free always, of what man might intend or wish for it. When the beast did not react to her impudence, she lifted a small trembling hand to touch the thick, tangled mane and forelock, so long they brushed her face even as the animal raised its head. It looked around the trampled, abandoned meadow, and blew out a huff of air. When it looked back down at her, its icy gaze warmed, catching the blue of her eyes, staining them with the reflection of its walnut features. It dropped its head to again accept her touch.

She had no idea it would be a trade.

Touched By Mystery

Chapter 1

Reandn crouched at the base of a rocky outcrop, poking his finger in the damp blemish that showed through otherwise crisp brown and gold leaves. The print in the underlying dirt showed the pad and claw marks of a fox instead of the scuff from a child's soft boot, and he stood with a scowl. The boy Reandn sought was as lost as ever.

A single spatter of cold rain hit the ground, then another. Reandn regarded the marks dourly, and had to remind himself that the fostered Highborn's son had not started his unicorn hunt with the intention of rousting all three shifts of King's Keep Wolves for a boy hunt instead. Even the Hounds, internal security for the Keep, were out in the fitful weather, driven by the importance of this particular child. He came from the north, the Resiore valleys—and although he was ostensibly fostered here at King's Keep as a favor to his Highborn father, the arrangement was also a reminder to the Highborn of the remote Resiores, a message of their ties and fealty to King's Keep.

A gust of wind penetrated Reandn's wool jacket, and the cold rain hitting his cheek was mindful of snow. *Get moving*, he told himself. *Find the boy before he freezes to death.* But he'd only taken a step when he felt an odd tickle behind his jawbones, the one that had plagued him on and off since late summer. It felt like he had a sneeze caught in the wrong place, and he'd learned to ignore it.

But this time it took him by surprise, moving up into his ears to hum with an edge that was as jarring as listening to sharpened steel scrape against rock. He shook his head, hard—once, twice—

And suddenly realized he had hit the ground, had been so disoriented he'd fallen without even noticing. When the noise faded and the tickle as well, it left only Reandn, stunned, on his knees with the cold seeping through his trousers and an even colder realization clutching his chest.

It was getting worse. Whatever it was, it was getting worse. And he was a Wolf—Wolf *First*—and not someone who could afford odd, unpredictable fits of dizziness.

He wondered how long he could hide it from the other Wolves. He didn't even want to think about Adela's reaction—after ten years as his wife, she'd well understand the danger he was putting himself in by continuing to ride patrol.

But life as Wolf First was what he knew. It was what he'd *earned*, fighting his way up from abandonment and life as a keep pot scrubber. The Wolves were the elite force that patrolled the area around King's Keep, just as the Hounds handled internal security, and the Foxes moved silently throughout the Keep—or anywhere else in Keland—without anyone quite knowing who they were.

Being a Wolf meant he didn't have to deal with the Highborn, who had as little tolerance for Reandn as he had for them. The Highborn—those born into lives of privilege and position—demanded respect they seldom earned and Reandn could not fake. They, in turn, seemed to regard him as threatening, no matter how benign his mood. Just as well he seldom made it to the main hall, but instead spent his shift supervising his patrol—the deep night patrol. Being Wolf First meant he was second in command, answering only to Saxe, the Pack Leader, and Prime Ethne. It would take a lot more than a few odd spells with his ears to wrench him away from it.

Carefully, one leg at a time, Reandn got to his feet. There was no vestige of dizziness, no oddness behind his jaws. He took a deep breath and set out down the faint deer trail he'd been following. A few more strides and he was deep in concentration again, dizzy spell forgotten as he scanned the thin golden-brown leaf layer—bounty from the stunted oaks and lean poplars that fought for a place among the dark green, bristle-needled pines that thrived here—for the slightest sign of recent disturbance.

The deer trail joined a main path that ran nearly parallel to the road, an informal trail created by both roadmen and the Wolf patrols that hunted, among other things, the roadmen. Reandn strode along it more briskly, his quick, practiced gaze searching the ground ahead. The boy, he knew, was likely to have been through here if he'd been heading for the clear waterhole the children called Unicorn Spring.

He stopped short. There, out of nowhere, there were boot prints—but those of an adult—a man—and not a child. Reandn's dark brows frowned over clear grey-blue eyes as he paced alongside the prints. They were evenly spaced, not too far apart, not too deep. Slow walking. They eventually met and mixed with hoofprints, a round platter-foot like those of the large pony the boy had ridden. The prints moved together a short distance, and Reandn slowed, unhappy with what he was seeing. If the boy had met an adult, he should be home by now—unless the adult was trouble.

Abruptly, the trail proved him right. Both sets of tracks

veered to the side and ceased in the midst of an area so scuffled no amount of skill would decipher the story. The disturbance spilled into the woods, tearing through an area of baby pines whose damaged, spicy scent still hung sharp in the air, a teasing reminder that he was too late for whatever had happened here.

Reandn scowled at the inexplicable scene, and at the faint hum that made him work his jaw without thinking. It was back, then. *Ignore it.* In the spitting rain, he paced the width and breadth of the disturbed sight, found nothing, and ranged outward, delving into the woods. Almost immediately he found a horseshoe, still bearing the six soft nails that had secured it to the pony's foot. A short distance away, essential to any unicorn hunt, was a metal halter, its carefully fashioned links almost buried in the leaves. He picked it up, hefting it thoughtfully in his hand. He had no doubt the boy was dead, and couldn't stop the next thought before it ran through his mind. *What if it had been Kavan?*

But it hadn't been, and he had a job to do. As much as he'd like to comb the area for some clue of exactly what had happened, right now that job meant getting back to the Keep, and reporting to Saxe. The boy was as found as he was going to get, and the only thing alive was the mystery of what had happened. Reandn gave the area one last glance, absently working his jaw, and turned his back to head for the Keep.

The Keep was built on a granite hillside, its grounds carefully leveled and, inside the tall stone keep wall, paved. The Keep itself was stone and wood, boards from the tall, plentiful pines of the area. It was built for defense, but placed deep inside the Northwest quadrant of Keland, where the risk from its neighbors—the smaller countries of Taffoa and Rolernia, all but inaccessible through rugged mountains on the west and north, and sea access from and south and east—was mitigated.

Inside the keep walls, along with the stone-walled barns and the small formal garden, there was room for the crowded, wood-framed buildings that housed the unmarried Hounds and Wolves. The Foxes were who knows where, and the Dragons, Keland's armed troops, were bunked in a separate area, just north and uphill of the Keep.

South was the Keeptown, almost a mile from the Keep itself, with thick rocky woods filling the area between them. This was the most densely patrolled area, and it was where Reandn picked up the main road back to the Keep, walking past the horse and troop training grounds just outside the south walls and through the main entrance.

Saxe waited in the Wolf barracks ready room. Saxe, with his dark hair cut short, neat, never ruffled. Sturdier than Reandn, but not as tall, and always more deliberate, more thoughtful with his reactions. His manner and skill had earned him the position of Wolf Leader four years earlier, and Reandn, his former partner, had been his First ever since, in command of his own patrol and the other patrol leaders—only two others right now, as low a number as it had ever been.

Caleb, the long-boned, rusty-haired Hound First, stood with Saxe by the squat iron stove at the far end of the long room, where they both warmed their hands and appeared dissatisfied with the situation in general.

Reandn walked along the bench rows to join them at the stove. "How'd you manage to pull duty in here instead of out with the rest of your patrol?" he asked Caleb. For *this* search, both Wolves and Hounds were combing the woods.

Caleb shrugged, as if the situation had taken no maneuvering at all, which Reandn knew to be untrue. "I'm coordinating for the Hounds. Brant's with Ethne"
—the Prime, who oversaw all the Keep security forces—

"trying to get the Hounds off the hook for this blunder. After all, it was one of your trainees who somehow let the boy out—Wace, right?"

Wace. One of Ser's Yearlings, a young man whose body's growth had outstripped his mind's. Stubborn at best, he took correction poorly and responsibility lightly. He was on training duty at the gate early that morning—all the Wolves trained to substitute at vital defense points of the keep—and had let the boy through without checking with the experienced gateman backing him.

Saxe cleared his throat. "Best remember where you are, Caleb." *Wolf* barracks, no place for a Hound to get careless with his words, not even when they came from a friend. "Reandn, what's the news?"

Reandn held out a clinking handful of halter. "Found this in Second Sector East, not far from the strangest set of tracks I've hit in a long time. Got a shoe from the pony, too." He fished it out of his belt and dropped it on one of the long benches.

"You didn't track him down?" Saxe raised incredulous eyebrows.

"Nothing to track—trail just disappeared."

Saxe clearly didn't believe it, and Reandn shook his head. "Don't look at *me* like that, Saxe—go look at the tracks. If I were you I'd get our best tracker—who is it now, that old fellow in Faline's patrol?—and go see for yourself."

"I did hold him back from the search," Saxe admitted. "But I never expected to have to send him in after your work."

"And I never expected to run into anything like what I found," Reandn said, not hiding his concern. He unfastened his jacket ties and moved closer to the stove. "I don't think you're going to discover any answers out there, Saxe, top tracker or not. If we're lucky, we'll convince the Resiores the boy was killed by a hill cat."

"But he wasn't," Saxe said flatly.

"No."

Saxe eyed his First for a moment. The missing boy was an up-pass boy from the Resiores, an area of wide valleys replete with the resources rocky King's Keep didn't have. Up-pass, where the Highborn moved in their own separate circles, created their own cycles of social whims, and for the most part cared little what happened at King's Keep. Isolated by mountains, cut off from the sea by formidable cliffs, and tied to the rest of Keland by one seasonal pass, the Resiores chafed at the chains that bound them to Keland, and to Keland's commerce and Highborn diversions.

Diversions like Tenaebra's Eve, the celebration building to a head at the Keep right now. The one last traditional fling before the goddess Tenaebra ascended in prominence over her sister Ardrith and began a harsh winter rule—and, for King Hawley and his advisors, a key point in relations with the Resiore folk.

It was not a good time to lose one of their children.

Finally Saxe gave a short nod. "All right. We'll have a look."

"It's right where you'd split off the road to go to Unicorn Spring," Reandn told him. "I'm going to grab some sleep or I'll be going into patrol tonight without any. For that matter, any of my patrol you can send back to the barracks would be appreciated."

"I'll recall them first thing," Saxe allowed.

"Too late for me," Caleb said mournfully. "Evening shift for Hound First."

"Which means you got your regular sleep last night," Reandn scoffed, roughly scrubbing his hand across his friend's head to destroy what little order there was to Caleb's rusty brown hair.

Caleb futilely tried to finger his hair back in place. "Like your trainee apparently got his, this morning."

"Wace is *Ser's* trainee—he's not in my patrol. For that matter, I hope Saxe lets him search the North sector all day. After this, I wonder if he'll ever scratch his way out of the litter. I'm not sure how he ever got *in*."

Caleb dismissed the shirker with a shrug. "What about the boy? What do you really think?" He snagged his jacket from the wall pegs and accompanied Reandn outside.

"What I found didn't make any sense to me," Reandn said. "A metal halter, one horseshoe and the biggest mess of tracks you've ever seen. That's all."

Caleb shrugged. "How about the obvious? The boy dropped the halter. The pony stepped on its own shoe and pulled it."

"A shoe gets torn off, it's twisted." Reandn said flatly, scrunching his shoulders against the cold raindrop that had somehow found its way down his neck. He stopped at the thick wooden door set in the base of the squat wizard's tower, where the overhang protected him from the drizzle. "I think I'm going to pretend you didn't imply I had missed the trail of a blundering pony."

"Never," Caleb quickly denied, looking askance at the wet sky as his rusty hair turned dark and limp. "Brant won't need me for another couple bells. I'm for the *Muzzled Fang*—how 'bout you?"

Reandn shook his head with a smile. "It's sleep for me," he said, thinking more about Adela than the bed. But as he reached for the door, it swung outward at him, and Kavan poked his head outside. At the sight of Reandn, his usually solemn little face brightened, and he ran the short distance between them. "Hey there," Reandn said, scooping Kavan up beneath the arms—at seven, Kavan was slight for his age—and taking in Kavan's quick hug before letting him slide to the ground again.

"Hey, Kavan," Caleb said, and the humor in his light blue eyes told Reandn his friend knew sleep now was out of the question, at least for the moment. "Good patrol tonight, Reandn," he said, reaching around Reandn to muss the boy's hair much as Reandn had recently done to him. "I'm off."

"Good patrol," Reandn said to his retreating back. Then he turned to Kavan. "What's got you out and about so early?"

Kavan didn't answer right away. Falling back into his pattern of quiet shyness, he pressed his face against Reandn's side instead. Six months earlier, he'd arrived at King's Keep, assigned as an apprentice to Ronsin— the last King's Wizard in a world where there was no longer any magic. It was a gesture of respect to an old man whose avocation was a thing of the past, and if nothing else the boy would learn his letters and numbers. But Kavan turned out to be a pale, undersized orphan whose fears and timidity at first interfered with anything he might learn. And the wizard was so far removed from children he had no idea how to deal with the withdrawn boy.

But Adela did. Although her own role in the keep— a combination of overseeing the wizard's tower and doing low-level training of the Wolf patrol leaders' mounts— kept her more than busy, she stayed with Kavan as the boy learned Ronsin's routines and gained confidence in the simple tasks he was required to carry out. Adela could hardly resist—for the boy craved love and she and Reandn, childless after ten years of partnership, craved a child. She was twenty-seven, three years younger than Reandn, and they both knew better than to hope for their own any longer.

So they made Kavan their own. And now Reandn knew him well enough to do nothing more than rest his hand on top of the boy's head and wait, ignoring the spitting rain.

Finally Kavan murmured, "Dela said you had a new horse. She said it needed to be petted."

Ah, Willow. The four-year-old gelding who was as uncertain of the world as Kavan, but was also as eager to please—as long as he didn't feel threatened. Making him comfortable in his new stable was Adela's priority. "She's right," Reandn said. "He feels like you did when you first arrived. Let's go see what we can do to make him happier."

He offered his hand to the boy, and Kavan took it with a confidence that made Reandn smile, and forget how tired he was.

The third-shift bells woke Reandn into the darkness of late evening, after putting off sleep until late afternoon. Adela had come to bed some time earlier, and was snuggled closely against him to ward of the chill of a night turned abruptly cold. Good. He hoped it would dig in and take hold—cold weather would dampen Tenaebra Eve mischief more surely than the evident Hounds, Wolves, and Dragons, even if it would be necessary to patrol for drunken Highborn who had underestimated the danger outdoors and fallen asleep in the grip of cold and the potent Eve wines.

A waxing moon lit the room just enough to navigate in without lighting a lamp—which meant there was enough light to lie there, snug under the covers, and simply look at Adela. During their years together, hard work had set some grey strands in her dark hair and the hint of lines around her mouth, and somehow they served only to make his eyes linger longer. He watched her for a moment, mentally tracing the night-blurred lines of her face—smooth, gentle features that blended roundly into one another, encompassing eyes set too widely for perfection and a mouth whose generous lower lip fit nicely above a barely clefted chin.

She'd given up a good position as Lady Cosette's attendant when they'd partnered, for it wasn't considered proper for young Highborn ladies to have married aides. But rather than dwell in town with the rest of the Packs' families, Adela had found a new, light-duty position with Ronsin—and then, when it became evident how well she worked with the young patrol mounts, she was assigned to the stable as well, where she and Reandn worked together.

It was a situation Reandn found eminently satisfying.

None of which made it any easier to remove Adela's arm from across his chest and slide out of the warm bed. He turned to her, offering a gentle kiss to her forehead through the lace of loose hair that covered it— and froze as he pulled away. *Not again.*

But it was. He stiffened as the new noise scraped along his nerves, humming in through ears that weren't actually *hearing* anything. *Get used to it.* He fought it, trying to maintain awareness of balance and position, and almost missed Adela's sleepy voice.

"Reandn?"

He couldn't answer fast enough to keep her from brushing the hair out of her face and peering up at him through the darkness. "What's wrong?"

"Nothing," he said, finally forcing the words out past the interference in his head. It could be done, then— even if he *was* lying to the most important person in his life. "I'm having a hard time leaving this bed—and you—and going out into the cold."

"Graces, can't blame you for that," she murmured, settling back down.

No. But he could blame himself for the lie—and did.

Somehow after that it was easier to brave the cold of the night, and Reandn dressed quickly, slipping out to the short landing in the stairway that curved around the inside of the tower.

Candlelight was bouncing off the walls above him, flickering wildly with the movement of the man who carried it, and Reandn looked up in surprise. Ronsin was usually long to his bed by this time of night, and certainly not just then descending from his work room at the top of the tower to his small sleeping chamber above Reandn's own.

The old man was hardly robust; although Reandn seldom crossed paths with the wizard, he had a clear image in his mind of a man stooped with age, giving the impression of frailty hidden beneath perpetually loose clothing, his thinning grey hair brushed back on his skull to skitter around his collar.

A door creaked, and the candlelight disappeared. Reandn found himself in the cold stone stairway, working his jaw against the discomfort in his ears and wondering, for an absurd moment, what the old man was up to. But he shook the odd mood off like a dog shaking off water, and went to brief his patrol.

That night the frigid air settled around King's Keep, and it stayed there. During the two days Prime Ethne and King Hawley soothed the missing boy's grieving relatives—who had arrived for a celebration and discovered a funeral—the ice crept firmly to the center of the keep pond, a sure sign of miserable cold. The cold kept all factions of the king's forces too concerned with staying warm on patrol to cause trouble amongst themselves, another common Eve problem. Saxe became noticeably more cheerful despite the unexplained loss of the Resiore boy, and Reandn added yet another layer between his leather vest and wide-sleeved, wool-lined jacket and cloak.

Even so, at the morning debriefing of Tenaebra's Eve, Reandn detected definite undercurrents of boredom in his patrol; they expected more from a pre-Eve week, and even continued extra half-shifts, wariness after the mystery of the Resiore boy's disappearance, weren't

enough to keep them occupied. He had dismissed them
and was toying with the idea of sending them back on
wide patrol rather than the tight Eve patrols when Caleb
came into the ready room, stomping his feet and rubbing
his arms. His face was wrapped in a scarf and the only
real sign that Caleb was within lay in the rusty hair that
escaped the red-dyed weave.

"Ah," Reandn groaned. "Get another scarf, or don't
put that one so close to your hair. Looks awful."

"Does it?" Caleb asked cheerfully. "That's the advantage
to being color-blind, I suppose. Though I didn't brave
the cold to hear about it."

"Huh," Reandn said. "I didn't think you did. It takes
something monumental to drag one of you Hounds away
from your arduous duty inside that nice warm keep."

"You've got it all wrong," Caleb said, unwrapping the
scarf enough to reveal a serious expression. "We're just
so indispensable the Prime doesn't dare let us out."

Reandn laughed, short and loud. "I'm for breakfast,
Caleb. You coming?"

"Can't," Caleb shook his head with true regret. "We
really do have a lot of last minute plans to finalize, with
all those Highborn who're gonna stay inside to keep their
toes warm. Makes your job easier, I know, but doesn't
do much for the Hounds. I really came to see if you
were going to be there tonight."

"Don't know, Caleb." Reandn hooked his jacket from
the wall peg and shrugged into it. "Dela's going; whether
I make it depends on how things are going with patrols.
They might need me out there early."

"Think about it, Dan," Caleb said, one of the few
who ever used Reandn's nickname. "I doubt Saxe's said
anything, since he knows how you feel about hanging
around a Highborn crowd, but tensions have been
running high among the Highborn—especially since
we lost that boy to the, er, hill cat. Ethne's encouraging

any of the off-duty patrol folk—Hound *and* Wolf—to be in attendance. Eve is open to townsfolk, too, so it's not like you'll stick out."

Reandn eyed him askance, and Caleb responded with a shrug.

"Well, so you *don't* blend into that kind of crowd. We could still use you." He hesitated. "I'd feel better if we had a few First-level folk around."

It was as close to an actual request that Caleb would come. Reandn tightened the jacket ties and flung his cloak over one shoulder. "I'll do my best," he allowed. "Already promised Dela that much."

Caleb grinned at him. "Good," he said. "See you there." And he wrapped his offensive red scarf back around his face and left, the grin on his face making it perfectly clear he knew just how horrible the color looked against his hair, color-blind or not.

Adela looked forward to the goddess Eve Celebrations. She was more devout than Reandn, who figured Tenaebra already had him marked for some sort of violent death, given the way his life had started and now the path it had taken. But Adela—Kavan in tow—gave Tenaebra her due, and then twice weekly visited the Ardrite faith house to pay homage, in search of a long, peaceful life and a quiet, painless death.

So after a day of overseeing the farrier at work on his three mounts and the irascible Willow, and very little time for sleep, Reandn found himself standing outside Elyn's door, waiting for Adela. Elyn, several years younger than Adela, had nonetheless turned out to be a good friend—and more than that, she was the same dress size. Although she was betrothed, she was attending Lady Cosette until the marriage, and her wardrobe was full of celebration dresses. Adela was within, fussing with some last minute adjustment to her borrowed clothing—or so Reandn had gathered from the muffled, giggle-interrupted reply to his knock.

He would be all but invisible next to her, he knew, in nothing more exciting than his most recently issued uniform. Knowing the Great Hall would be stuffy with bodies, Reandn restricted himself to one loose-sleeved, sturdy broadcloth shirt under the leather vest that bore the laced pattern of his Pack, Patrol, and rank. The trousers he pulled on were new and stiff, and the soft half-chaps meant to protect his legs from brush and equine sweat were unused. Though all the guests at the celebration would be unarmed, Reandn had thoughtfully tucked away his boot knife. On an occasion like this its obvious hilt could be a subtle—or not so subtle—reminder to the rowdy young men that they should behave.

"Are you ready? We're coming out!" Adela called from within Elyn's tiny room—Reandn often wondered how the two of them managed to dress in there at once—and he stepped aside so they could come out into the corridor and be properly admired. They burst out of the room, a splash of color and scent against the dim stone of the keep.

"A stunningly beautiful pair, as always, my ladies," Reandn told them, bringing his lightly fisted hand to the base of his throat in a Wolf salute.

Adela told him, "That's what you always say," but she was smiling.

"It's always true," Reandn said; reasonably, he thought. And it was. The current fashion was a closely tailored bodice over a full skirt, covered with a gauze weight, long-sleeved tunic with just enough tailoring and strategically placed slashes to give hints of the shape beneath. Adela wore deep sky blue edged with black, and it brought out the natural blush of her face against the black of her hair—and Reandn knew the shape beneath the blouse of the tunic. "Are you sure you want to go to this celebration?" he asked, assuming an innocent air. "I think I remember something in our room that needs taking care of."

"*You*," Elyn said dryly, sweeping past him in a rustle of deep green skirts, flipping her long blond hair over her shoulder. "*We're* dancing."

Adela merely gave him a sly smile and held out her hand, which Reandn took as they trailed Elyn to the Great Hall. At the wide-arched entrance, he hesitated; imminently faced with frolicking Highborn, he recalled Caleb's concerns. "Dela . . ."

"I know. They're likely to be rowdy tonight, and you're going to be doing as much crowd patrolling as you are dancing with me." She gave him a quick smile. "Just you keep an eye out, in case one of them happens to forget I'm married."

He scowled at her, which was what she wanted. "No one," he warned, "had better be that bold." Then he kissed her in plain sight of anyone in the Hall, which was also what she wanted, and let her move off with Elyn while he stepped aside of the entrance and surveyed the Hall.

Automatically, his gaze ticked off the Hounds, finding them scattered around the entrances and heavily peppered at the back end of the colorfully decorated Hall, next to the raised platform from which King Hawley, his Queen, and their toddler son would preside. The balcony along the back end of the room, strung with banners and a huge tapestry of the goddess Tenaebra— warmly dressed and surrounded by the fruits of the fall, crossed sword and knife in each corner as a reminder of her power—stretched over the throne dais. There were a few Hounds there as well, made less conspicuous than Reandn in tailored, slashed-sleeve shirts and tunics that blended with the crowd. Only the proliferation of certain color combinations made it clear that these men and women were on duty; Reandn's Wolf uniform was much more practical, designed for patrol and looking like just what it was.

Movement from behind Reandn captured his attention and he caught a glimpse of rusty hair. "Caleb," he said, without turning around.

"Ah," Caleb said in a disappointed greeting. "I'll catch you out one of these days, Reandn."

"The day you do, I'll join the Hounds," Reandn responded.

"Then best for us if I don't," Caleb rejoined without hesitation. He stepped up beside Reandn to consider the growing crowd, wincing slightly as one of the musicians made a slip on his pipes. "They'll be dancing soon," he said. "That's good. The Keepmaster always wants them plied with plenty of wine before the dance tunes begin, so they won't be so shy about getting out there. Myself, I think the practice causes more trouble than it's worth. Gets the young rowdies all full of glee and no outlet for it."

Reandn thought about Adela and glowered.

"Where's Dela?" Caleb said, as if he could read his friend's mind. "Ah, there. And you let her out there unescorted looking like that? Shame, Reandn."

"She's with Elyn," Reandn said, almost a growl. "And I'll be with her soon enough."

Caleb grinned at him, no doubt pleased at getting a rise from his friend. "I'm grateful you're here, Reandn. Go dance with her now, before it gets too crowded."

It was already plenty crowded, but Reandn went. The musicians had found their stride and the dances began in earnest—first the complicated group steps that Reandn's feet had never followed very well, but it amused him to try, and then the more loosely structured couples dances. By then Adela was ready for a rest and something to drink; Reandn escorted her to the food tables, made sure there were no troublemakers in sight—although frankly he felt Adela could fend well for herself—and went to prowl the edges of the hall. His obvious uniform took some of the wild out of the young men's eyes as he passed the small groups that might have been building themselves up to trouble.

But the stuffy air, redolent with the odor of food, humanity, and clashing perfumes, became unexpectedly overwhelming. Reandn drifted to the darker recesses of the Hall, watching the interplay of the Highborn, staying out of the way of couples that had chosen the darker areas for a few whispered endearments—and realizing it was not the air at all. It was his ears, humming with such wicked subtlety that the music had obscured the sound, leaving him only with a distinct unease.

Damn. He closed his eyes against sudden dizziness. Fresh air, quiet—he suddenly yearned for it. With only a quick glance to find Adela involved in conversation, her expression animated and her color high, he escaped the Hall by way of the tower that rounded off the back corner, climbing to the level of the curtain wall.

Breathing deeply, moving resolutely, Reandn walked the short length of the wall to the arch over the pond, trailing smokey breath behind him. Above the arch keystone, the dizziness eased, despite the underlying noise in his head. Relieved, he leaned against the cold stone to watch two slightly drunken young men try to navigate the frozen pond, slipping and sliding and laughing loudly at their own clumsy endeavors, mimicking their own blue-on-silver shadows in the moonlight. They slid under the arch and back, traveling beneath the stone in an unimpeded echo of sound.

The cold was just beginning to penetrate the warmth he'd carried with him from the hall when he spotted a patch of darkness in the sleek ice, at the artificially deepened edge where the children swam in the summer. After only a moment's hesitation, Reandn swung his leg over the inside wall and searched for the snow-slick footstones he knew were there. The skaters had wandered off into the courtyard and he was alone when he inspected the thin skim on the recently broached ice.

If someone had fallen through, it was far too late to save them. Grimly, he returned to the revelry to search out Caleb.

Adela met him in a rush of whirling skirts, with Elyn on her heels. "You left at the most important part, Danny," she said breathlessly, and he wondered if she'd been searching since he'd slipped out.

"I was about to say the same," added a dry voice beside him, where Caleb suddenly stood, face flushed as brightly as Adela's, though with effort instead of excitement. "That's a Wolf for you—always off sniffing around when you need them the most."

"What happened?" Reandn asked, not a little befuddled by his reception. The celebration was in a pause as musicians changed places, and it all looked normal enough to him.

"An Up-pass Minor's son took umbrage at one of our locals, is all," Caleb said, rolling his eyes slightly; Reandn knew why. The Minors wielded a lot of power in their own territories, and always tried to prove it when they came to the Keep. "We got them separated quick enough, but our local boy's a real scrapper and the Minor's son . . ." he grimaced. "Well, he lost. He's in with the Prime and the Keepmaster right now, pulling rank and trying to get the local a stiff penalty."

"Who started it?"

"That's not what I meant," Adela objected almost simultaneously. She gave Caleb a startled glance, but gestured for him to continue.

"Sorry, Dela," he said. "It doesn't matter who started it, Reandn, not to some of these Highborn. I sure wish you'd been here, though. He was all fists and too slick to get a hand on. You're used to that kind of scrapping."

Reandn gave his friend a warning glance. Caleb knew well enough he had little love of his struggling days in the kitchen, and even less love of reminders. "Go check the pond, Caleb. Looks like someone's fallen through."

"Tenaebra's ti—" Caleb started explosively, but stopped in mid curse with a quick glance at Adela. "I mean, just what we need. I'll go have a look at it. Better put out an alert to see if anyone's missing—not that even half this bunch is sober enough to consider present."

"Thought you'd be interested," Reandn said, placing his hand over Adela's on his upper arm and giving it a squeeze. "I've got to go, Dela—probably be late for patrol as it is. Come walk with me a ways."

She readily took his arm, and matched his leisurely pace out of the hall. "You missed Ronsin's appearance," she said, when they were far enough away to talk quietly. "You missed his magic!"

"There isn't any magic."

"He made colors in flame, Danny," she said, irritation sparking behind that excitement. "He took a torch and made it burn the most glorious colors. I'm so sorry Kavan missed it."

"There're powders that'll do as much."

She made a face. "I know everyone else thinks so, but—this wasn't powders! Danny, I work with this man. I saw the look on his face and there *were no powders*. Ronsin worked real magic tonight."

Reandn shook his head. "No such thing anymore. No more dragons, no more spells. Last unicorn was seen when I was a boy." It was more than no more dragons or spells, though—thinking of the trouble with the Resiores, he was forced to realize that. At one time, in full magic, King's Keep extended its influence throughout all of Keland with unquestioned authority. If trouble started, the current king had known immediately through magical resources, and reacted instantly. Now, trouble could brew for weeks—or longer—before King's Keep knew about it, even with the extensive Fox placements. And it was even longer before the response took effect.

Losing magic had changed the way Keland needed to be managed, and King's Keep hadn't quite caught on. The king—the current monarch's father—and his advisors had withdrawn the forces they could no longer easily communicate with, as if no one quite realized the rest of Keland needed that presence in order to maintain the Keep's influence.

"Reandn, listen to me!" Adela's sharp tone surprised him, and brought him right back to the conversation he'd already dismissed. "I saw what I saw. He may be a little soft in the head, but he would never stoop to using powders."

"He'd do anything to get back some of the prestige he used to have," Reandn said. "Even if it meant thinking up a new way to cheat with powders." He held up a hand as she drew breath to protest, her deep brown eyes flashing irritation. "No—I'm sorry. Compromise. I'll believe *you* believe in what you saw—and you understand that I can't believe it without seeing it."

"Fair enough," she said, although he could tell she wasn't entirely happy with it. They stopped, preparing to separate. "You be careful out there tonight—and don't freeze off any important parts!"

"I'll do my best," he assured her. "And when I get back, maybe I'll wake you up and prove it."

A sly expression crept over her face, part of the game. "I dare you," she said. She gave him a quick, hard kiss, and left him with a whirl of blue material, her tightly-fitting bodice peeking out from the loose tunic. Reandn would have sworn she'd planned it that way. He watched her walked back down the hall and shook his head with a smile. *Patrol*, he thought. *Keep your mind on patrol.*

Chapter 2

Reandn's patrol, twenty paired Wolves and a few Yearling trainees, was waiting for him at the ready room, grouped around the hearth for a few last moments of warmth while he reminded them that the regular army, the Dragons, had a watch out this night as well—although the troops were keeping to the main road between King's Keep and its town. Avoiding the Dragons through stealth was the most exercise the Wolves were likely to get on this cold evening, aside from pulling wayward Highborn out of the snow, and Reandn suggested that they consider it a drill.

They took it for the challenge he meant it to be, and went out into the cold making bets on each other. Reandn withdrew to the back of the room to stay out of the way while the evening patrol straggled in, tired and chilled, followed by the Wolf Third, a spare figure of a woman named Faline. Tying his warm fur-lined jacket closed and lacing up his half-chaps, he listened to the debriefing long enough to assure himself nothing unusual had happened, and went to the stables to collect Cloud, the greyed-to-white horse that would be waiting for him.

White, so he could be seen by his patrol as he made his circuit, a regular pattern on both road and rough trails that enabled them to report to him. Tonight, as he ducked low-hanging branches whose sting seemed magnified on his cold skin, none of his patrol signalled him to stop, which came as no surprise. He'd as much assured it, barring a real emergency, when he'd warned them not to be seen by the Dragons. For the general populace the solstice celebrations meant revelry and socializing; for the Wolves it meant watching over large numbers of vulnerable celebrants. For the Dragons it meant extra duty—and that made them something to avoid.

But, Reandn mused with a sigh, halfway through his shift, if you're walking down the road on a white horse, there's not a lot you can do to avoid detection, not even with the full moon hidden behind the trees.

"Patrol leader?" grunted one of the vague, unmounted shapes that met him on the road, ones that made the faint rattling noises of fully geared army men.

"Pack First," Reandn affirmed, settling his weight back in the saddle as Cloud snorted steam into the cold.

"Blue First," the other responded; Reandn's counterpart in one of the Dragon units. His voice was more abrasive than it was congenial. "Tenaebra's tits, it's a cold one tonight. Glad we don't have to do this all the time. Lucky your men are back in the barracks by the fire, ey?"

"My men," Reandn said, responding to the insult in the tone despite himself, "include women. They, like me, would probably appreciate a good fire right know. They're all out on patrol, just like yours." *Don't let it get to you*, he told himself. Not even if the man's as smug as they come. *Wolf First sets the example*.

The First snorted half a laugh and muttered a comment to his unidentified companion. "Maybe you'd better trot back to the barracks and check," he suggested. " 'Cause they're not out here."

Reandn hooked a leg over the pommel of the saddle. "They are indeed, and grateful to your men as well. It's nice to have so many noisy bodies blundering around. It gives the Wolves plenty of cover. Why, the Eve weeks are the most productive of the year for us—we always catch a poacher or two sneaking away from you Dragons."

"In a Lonely Hell," the man replied promptly. "More'n likely they've found themselves one of your Wolf bitches and made a little den under some tree."

Swiftly regaining his seat, Reandn leaned over, grabbed a handful of the startled man's jacket and jerked him in close. "My Wolves," Reandn said into the man's face, close enough to watch surprise turn to anger, "can out-stalk, out-trail, and out-think your Blues any time they choose. That doesn't give you an excuse to slut-talk them." He released the Dragon with a shove, and Cloud snorted, prancing away.

"You butt-sniffing son-of-a—" the Dragon First exclaimed, breaking the stillness of the night and the quiet of the previously muted conversation. The figure behind the Dragon put a hand on his shoulder and muttered the Prime's name. Ethne. A warning to both Blue First and Reandn.

Reandn said nothing, his breath wreathing cold steam before him, his temper hovering between wisdom and flare. At last the Dragon First reluctantly stepped back, growling something insulting. Reandn swung Cloud around and put him into a canter, removing himself from temptation.

Cloud snorted, unhappy, too cold to move out comfortably, and Reandn drew him back to a walk. *Wolf First sets the example.* Right. He knew there'd been at least one Wolf close enough to have observed the encounter, and that therefore all of them would know, before the night was over. Wonderful. He'd have to do something about that temper.

Until the next time someone threatened or insulted his own.

The rest of the night was uneventful, and debriefing was quick. When his patrol filed out of the stuffy room, Reandn took possession of one of the benches, stretching out face down for a few moments to clear his head before returning to the tower. The only noise in the barracks came from the adjoining men's quarters room, where two of his Wolves were in quiet conversation.

Footsteps approached and arrived at the doorway of the ready room, paused, and traced the aisle between the benches to come to a stop before Reandn. He knew the boots, as well as he knew the walk. Saxe. Reandn grunted an unintelligible greeting.

"Got to talk to you," Saxe said.

Grunt.

"Listen up, Reandn."

Knowing the slight edge of irritation spoke volumes in his even-tempered Pack Leader, Reandn rolled off the bench and stood in a tired slouch against the wall. "Uneventful patrol," he said with a yawn, "Considering Tenaebra's Eve."

"Uneventful," Saxe repeated dryly.

Abruptly realizing what the conversation was about, Reandn felt his own touch of irritation. "It wasn't anything."

"You laid hands on the Blue First. If the Prime hears about it, you can bet she'll be at my throat. Defense cooperation during the Eves is our biggest priority and you know it."

"Saxe, I won't have my people foul-mouthed."

"The Dragons, especially the Blues, talk that way about *every*body not in their unit." Impatience flared in the dark hazel eyes.

"Not about anyone in my patrol. Not in front of me."

"You're not even sorry." Exasperated, Saxe leaned his smaller, more solid bulk against the wall next to Reandn, a more companionable stance. "Once a week I'm apologizing for you, and you're not even sorry."

"Of course I am," Reandn said. "The trouble is never meant for you."

"One of these days Ethne's going to see us both replaced."

"No, she won't," Reandn countered. "We're both too good to lose."

Saxe turned to his former partner with a wry grin, a shake of his head that barely stirred his short-cropped, almost-black hair. "The young are always coming in, Danny. Someday they'll find someone to replace us both. There's always Wace."

Reandn snorted expressively, although he recognized Saxe's dry humor. "Oh, come on. The only reason that pup's still in training is the fact his father is a retired Dragon with more honors than he knows what to do with. What's really bothering you? It's not the Blue First's ego."

Saxe sighed. "Maybe not. The broken ice you found . . . there's a boy missing from the kitchen. Since everyone else seems to be accounted for, consensus is, the boy made that hole in the ice."

"A boy was heavy enough to fall through that ice? After the weather we've had?" Reandn said skeptically.

"It's the only thing that fits, so far. There are bets that it was some townie we haven't heard about yet. But the Hounds figure when spring comes, we'll find that boy in the thaw."

"Anyone checking with the boy's family? Maybe he got homesick and went creeping home." From the look on Saxe's face, he knew what the Pack Leader was thinking. The second boy missing, in a matter of weeks. Children died, accidents happened . . . but there were unanswered questions about these two events that left Reandn unsettled, and Saxe clearly felt the same.

"One of the Foxes is going to check out his family for us, but she's back at the Keep after a little altercation on assignment and won't be prepared to leave for over a week. And you know what travel's like this time of year—it'll take her a while to reach East River. It's more likely we'll find him in the thaw before we get an answer from East River."

"*If* he's in the pond," Reandn said darkly. "We could end up with another permanent mystery."

"I don't even want to think about that," Saxe said. "I'd rather think about what I'm going to do about you and your . . . let's call it *impulsiveness*."

"Let's," Reandn agreed. He pushed himself away from the wall, tightening his jacket ties. "Offhand, I think we're going to learn to live with it. At least anytime the Dragons get mouthy."

Saxe rolled his eyes. "If you weren't so good out there . . ."

Reandn flashed Saxe a deliberately cocky grin. "But I am," he said, and left before Saxe could think of a suitably scathing reply.

Breakfast was a quick affair in the commons, where Reandn scrupulously avoided the glares of the Dragons in blue diamond-marked cloaks; he ate his breakfast with Faline, Wolf Third, who also knew of the incident and seemed to consider the Blue First had gotten what he deserved.

Normally mornings meant training—either Yearlings or horses, with Dela—but Eve schedules were always out of whack, and Reandn was just as glad to go straight to their room and catch some sleep. Out of the eating hall, behind the kitchen in the seldom traveled hall that led to Ronsin's tower, Reandn mounted the stairs that led to their room—a little wedge of a space, sparely furnished with a wardrobe and clothespress, the wide, heavily blanketed bed and one ancient rocking chair. One of Adela's works, a small unicorn hunt tapestry, hung above the bed, and a smaller embroidery of delicate roses offset the shuttered window. The room was empty, chilly despite the banked fire that he paused to build up before pulling off his boots.

As he dropped his heavy wool jacket on the clothespress, someone fumbled at the latch of the old wooden door; he opened it to find Adela, laden with droopy potted plants. His attempt to lighten her burden involved juggling, lost dirt, an "oops" and Adela's giggle. Back inside, Reandn balanced on one leg and pushed the coat off the press with his foot, setting the plants in its place.

"What's all this?" he asked, as Adela straightened from depositing her armful to survey the greenery.

"Very sad looking plants," Adela said. "Ronsin insists on having them around but something up there disagrees with them. I'm going to see if I can't fix them up a little."

"It's winter," Reandn said with some surprise. "What does he expect?"

"Green plants," Adela said. She turned her scrutiny from the plants to his face. "You look tired, Danny."

"You should, too," he responded, and threw himself crosswise on the bed.

"I got extra sleep this morning—Ronsin told me last night that we'd start late today."

"Lazy," he mumbled into the bed covers. "What would your high-placed friends think."

"They'd gasp at the thought of getting up as early as I did," she said cheerfully. "Take off your clothes before you fall asleep, and give me a chance to get them to the laundry."

"I love it when you talk like that," he said, not moving.

She loosened the chap laces and tugged off his boots. "That's all the help you get. Now off with the rest—I want to take advantage of the morning while I've still got it."

"Umph," he said, eyeing her over his shoulder. "You want 'em off, you take 'em off."

So she did.

❖   ❖   ❖

Adela sat at Ronsin's workbench with Kavan beside her, the workbook open before them. *A . . . D . . . E . . .* she traced in the wax tablet they shared. But Kavan seemed stuck on *K.* "K-a-v-a-n," she prompted him gently, having just learned to spell the name the week before, herself. She'd memorized Danny's name first, and was working on her own name now, glad for the chance to learn at all. It meant time away from the horses, but Danny was as enthusiastic about having a reader in the family as she was, and had been taking up the slack.

Enthusiasm eluded Kavan this morning, however. Usually he was a cooperative little boy, glad for all the attention he could get, but since Ronsin had given them the morning's brief lesson and retired to his private study—he'd done a lot of that since the Eve festivities the week before—Kavan had done nothing but fiddle with the knotted string necklet his sister had given him before they were separated.

"Would you prefer to check the plants now?" she asked him, laying a casual hand along his cheek in case he had a fever.

His black eyes darted fearfully to the closed door of Ronsin's study, and when he spoke it was in an earnest, carefully lowered voice. "*He'll* just kill them. I don't like him."

Surprised, Adela considered the unexpected answer. Never before had Kavan ventured an opinion about the man who now controlled his life. "It's true the plants don't do well here, but Ronsin doesn't kill them. He wants them here. That's why we have to take such good care of them." As she spoke, his features molded into subtle stubbornness. She knew he wouldn't argue with her, but he didn't agree, either. "Kavan, has he done something to frighten you? Has he hurt you?"

Her obvious concern melted a little of his defensiveness. "No," the boy said, "but he acts strange, and I don't like it." His voice stayed a murmur, and he watched Ronsin's door rather than look at Adela.

"Ah," she said, with understanding. "He's had a hard life, Kavan, and he's getting older." Unconsciously she pitched the level of her voice to match the boy's. "Sometimes, when people are older, they do things the rest of us don't always understand."

"That's *different*," Kavan insisted. He looked directly at her, an unusual wheedling tone creeping into his voice. "De-ela, can I stay with you and Dan? Please? I can water the plants and fetch stuff and everything, even if I sleep downstairs."

Slowly, she shook her head, and the little boy slumped back into himself. "Kavan, you and I can't make decisions like that. I can discuss it with Ronsin and Dan, if you'd like, but I think it's important to Ronsin to have you here. I understand that you don't like it, and I'm sorry."

Kavan heaved a big sigh. "I know," he said, and unfolded himself to give her a hug.

She squeezed him tight and kissed his head, then set him back. "What about those plants, then?"

He hopped off the bench and fetched the little tin bucket—all he could carry when it was full—and dipped it into the larger tub that collected rainwater from a roof drain tile. Sticking his finger in the soil of each plant, Kavan gave the dry plants a dipper of water, speaking encouragingly to the saddest looking ones and tossing a smile back at Adela every now and then. In the past Adela had walked the room with him, double checking each plant before he watered, but she was trying to wean Kavan off such dependence so today she sat on the bench and watched. When Ronsin emerged from his room, she was in a perfect position to see the child's smile fade; he worked in somber silence, keeping his back to the wizard.

Adela looked at the old man, wondering—not for

the first time—just how old he was, for the impression
of frailty he gave didn't quite match his relatively
seamless face, a face that might have looked younger
yet if his white hair had been cut and combed. Ronsin,
in turn, watched the boy, his expression pensive and
not, she thought, entirely benign.

Now where did that thought come from? She caught
the tone of her thoughts and deliberately cut herself
short. *Absurd.* When Ronsin looked at her she smiled a
greeting and rose from the bench. She'd make a quick
stop in Ronsin's quarters to collect his laundry, and then
scoot on to the barn to do some groundwork with Willow.
She'd named the new horse Willow Wisp for the
imaginary visions he conjured for himself, but sometimes
she wasn't sure who needed the most reassurance about
life, the horse or the boy.

It didn't matter. She had enough of it for them both.

Chapter 3

There was no sign of the two missing boys, and over the weeks, Prime Ethne eased the pressure to solve the mysteries. It was something the Wolves and Hounds still talked about in undertones, and for the first half of the season, the Keep was filled with frustrated children who didn't understand why they'd suddenly lost some of their freedom.

Reandn knew why. It was the same reason he made sure Kavan told him or Adela every time he left the tower, even if it was only to visit Willow in the barn.

But nothing else untoward happened, and as Deep Winter Night passed and Ardrith's Eve drew near, people began to relax. The winter season was a slow one for all the Keep's forces. The unusual cold held, keeping most of the poachers and other miscreants inside by their fires. At first Reandn welcomed the respite, for it gave him time to adjust to the spells of noise inside his head, to learn to function through them. He could do it, if he set himself to it, and he thought he was even getting better at it.

He didn't tell Adela about the disorienting episodes. One of them worrying about it was enough.

But the slack time soon showed itself to be a liability. While he and the other patrol leaders had plenty to keep them busy, the main pack of the Wolves grew restless. The Yearlings, just graduated from trainee Pups and driven to prove themselves, had already caused several incidents with the Dragons.

Today, Reandn thought, traversing the distance between his tower and the barracks, the chill was missing from the morning air. With only a month to go until Ardrith's Eve and spring, a thaw was bound to bring out troublemakers in force, trying to make up for a slow winter. Time to put the Yearlings to the test. And afterward, he knew, grinning inside, it would be a long time before they complained of a lax season.

He was alone in the long, narrow ready room, rubbing waterproofing grease into his boots against the slushy snow, when Saxe's step, heavier than usual, brought his head up from his work. "What's wrong?"

Saxe stood in the doorway. "Politics," he said. "*A wolf has no need of tact, just a quiet foot and a quick eye.* I wish someone had warned me that wasn't entirely true for the Pack Leader."

"It could be worse," Reandn offered. "*I* could be Pack Leader."

"No . . . I've always had the feeling you were meant for other things," Saxe said, with a quiet seriousness that took Reandn by surprise. Then he snorted. "And there're reasons you're *not* heading this pack—I'm *still* soothing the Blue Dragon Leader."

"That was months ago. They must be as bored as our Yearlings, to make trouble over it."

Saxe didn't answer right away; Reandn wasn't sure he'd really been listening. Saxe paced to the long wall of the ready room, where the small window was unshuttered to let out the extra heat of the stove; one hand rubbed the back of his neck. "The Fox that Ethne sent to the East River is back. It looks like our kitchen boy ended up in the pond after all." Briefly, he stared out at the view; past Ronsin's tower the dark finger of the pond was visible, even in the fading light.

"It'll be thawed soon, maybe in a few days," Reandn offered, not questioning the change of subject. "I don't envy the Dragons who'll have to do the dredging."

"It's a tense time," Saxe agreed, turning his attention back inside. "The boy was no cast-off; he was training for cook. His family has relatives with influence, and the King has already sent an emissary and several Foxes to keep an eye on things."

"Surely there's not much to worry about," Reandn said confidently, capping his little pot of grease and shoving his foot into the boot. "A tragedy, yes, but it was an accident, and the boy's family can't be too highly placed or he wouldn't have started out as a pot scrubber."

"True," Saxe conceded. "But none of us needed it, not with the trouble the Resiores have been giving us."

"Just a lot of fuss and bother," Reandn grunted, stomping his foot a couple times to settle his heel into the boot and standing up. "You want to keep your mind off it, I'm sure I can come up with something—"

"Oh, no," Saxe said, holding his hand up to stop the thought in its tracks. "I've got enough troubles without your *help*. Wait'll you hear what Faline tried last week—"

But Reandn was not listening. The grating noise behind his jaws had blossomed with an unprecedented intensity, snatching away his alignment to the world, immersing him in misery. He staggered, knocking a bench over, and came down hard on his knees. Fighting to keep from drowning in the roar within him, he barely noticed Saxe's hands on his shoulders, keeping him upright.

The pressure finally faded, making way for Saxe's voice. "—Dan! *Danny!*" The hold on his shoulders tightened, shook him slightly.

Reandn opened tear-blurry eyes and discovered he was staring at the window, and had even managed to move in that direction. Pulling out of Saxe's grip, he climbed gracelessly to his feet and stumbled over to the window. Nothing. Nothing but the tower, where shutter-leaked light glowed in the deepening dusk.

"Danny!" Saxe repeated, not for the first time. "What in the Lonely Hells happened?"

Reandn turned, blinked at him, and took a deep breath through a chest that seemed suddenly tight. "I don't know. I mean," he added, regaining most of his wits and seeing the depth of Saxe's concern, "it's happened before—never this bad. But I've been to the surgeon. . . ." He trailed off and added lamely, "He couldn't do anything. He thought maybe I'd taken one too many blows to the head."

"A Wolf with dizzy spells isn't safe out there," Saxe said, his voice hard as he waved a hand that somehow encompassed the rocky, pine-laden territory beyond the Keep.

"It's not dizzy spells," Reandn averred. "It's . . . different somehow. Almost like being inside one of those long minstrel's horns on a low note." He grinned, but didn't even convince himself.

"Don't dodge me, Dan. You get one of these out on horseback, or in the middle of a scuffle, and you're dead just the same."

"I know." Reandn met his friend's hazel eyes for a long moment, saying all the things he couldn't put into words. *I'm a Wolf. It's who I am, what I do.* "They don't happen very often."

"Adela doesn't know, does she," Saxe said, and then gave a short laugh. "Of course she doesn't, or you wouldn't be going out in the woods tonight. And you won't be, yet, unless I get your honor you'll tell me if this gets worse."

Reandn ducked his head, scrubbing a hand through his thick, dark tawny hair. "Wolf's honor," he said quietly, at last.

❖   ❖   ❖

Where was he? Adela paced in the confines of their small room, moving with nervous energy, knowing that to stop would mean she would fall apart into useless tears. She was dressed for the stable, in long, lined split winter skirts and high fleeced boots, but she'd never made it, at least not for training. She'd gone up to Ronsin's rooms to make sure Kavan was started in his day, and discovered him gone—and Ronsin snarling about it.

Gone. Just like the other two—

No. She pulled herself up short on the thought. Kavan had been so good, so obedient, it was simply taking them all by surprise that for once he wasn't where he was supposed to be. And since she wasn't in the practice of searching him out, it was no wonder she couldn't figure out where he might have gone—although she'd looked in all the places that should have drawn him. When he wasn't with the horses, she'd come back here to wait for Danny. And where was *he*, late on this morning of all mornings . . .

At last. His tread was too habitually silent to clue her as he climbed the stairs, but even a Wolf couldn't turn that creaky old door handle without making noise. She was across the room in an instant, and had just enough time to see the surprise on his face as when she threw her arms around him. "I can't find him!"

"Dela, what—?" he said, his arms closing around her, the strength in them somehow making her feel stronger, too.

She pulled back just enough to look at his face. "Kavan," she said. "I can't find him anywhere."

He just looked at her a moment, digesting her words. "We've been trying to give him confidence for months. Maybe he's finally gotten enough to turn rascally on us. It'd be a good sign, I think." But he didn't fool her completely. She knew that look, the tiny down-quirk at the corner of his mouth, the way his brows drew minutely closer together.

Adela stepped away from him, giving him the space to enter the room and close the door. Worrying her betrothal ring with her thumb, she said slowly, "I don't think so. I . . . I'm not given to flights of fancy, Danny, or hysteria. I'm worried. He's been gone for hours— and *no* one's seen him."

"I know," Danny said—*I know you're not hysterical, I share your worry*—and sat heavily on the bed, reaching for the laces on his half-chaps. Adela suddenly realized how tired he looked—worn, as though he'd been over-worked for some time, despite the slow winter. She stepped back from her tightly wound worry and watched him a moment, twisting her ring on her finger. His dark blond hair was getting long, shaggy enough to tumble beyond his collar in the back, and fall into his eyes in front. She'd always enjoyed his face, an oval face delineated by a well-defined jawline. The contrast of his grey eyes against dark brows—darker than his hair—gave him a wild-eyed appearance, and even when he was obviously tired, he still seemed leashed, as though behind some restraint there was an untamed creature within.

She'd seen that untamed creature before, when he'd been forced to defend his own—his keep, his Wolves, and occasionally, herself. She knew it would come out for Kavan, that he would find the boy if anyone could.

"Ronsin's having fits," she said. She wasn't prepared for his reaction, the look on his face as he stopped unlacing his chaps and set his jaw. He'd never had any animosity toward the old man before, never seemed to care about him one way or the other. But now she saw anger, although he tried to swallow it, and went back to removing his chaps.

"I'm not sure about him lately," was all he said, his voice even.

Adela hesitated. "He's been a little preoccupied since Tenaebra's Eve, it's true," she said. "I think he's frustrated—he worked that little bit of magic, but I haven't seen anything since. And he must be feeling the pressure to come up with something impressive for Ardrith's Eve." And no wonder. They'd be getting the Ardrith's Eve tapestry out soon, with the goddess depicted among wildly sprouting vines and crops, her dress the sleeveless style that had been considered borderline scandalous when the tapestry had been made, and the honey blond hair and sweet features that always reminded Adela of her friend Elyn.

Danny snorted softly, drawing her back to the black despair the day had brought her. "Magic," he said. "Crazy old man."

"Kind of sad, actually." Adela did not remind him that she'd *seen* the magic he was scoffing at, last fall. "He's desperate, Danny. It's not his fault the magic left us. But . . . you may be right in a way. I think . . . he may be failing. He smiles to himself. He's using a huge amount of herbs, and there're wasted parchments all over his desk, all covered with that scribbley writing of his."

Danny tossed the half-chaps across the room to land neatly in the corner, and said nothing.

"Try looking at his life from his point of view," Adela said. "What if you spent your entire life being the best Wolf you could be—then, at the height of your career, the entire world changes, and all of a sudden no one wants any Wolves any more. All your skills are useless."

"That'd never happen," Danny said, harshly enough to startle her. Sometimes when he was stressed, when he was intense, his voice left its normal, slightly graveled baritone and hit a deeper register, bottoming out. It meant trouble. Adela wondered what hidden sore spot she'd hit, but when he left the bed to stare out the window, leaning out over the wide sill, she followed, unintimidated, but gentle.

"Suppose it did. Can you say you'd be any different than Ronsin? You might even be worse. You'd do anything to try to regain the past."

Danny shook his head without looking at her, and said nothing. She slid in behind him, wrapping her arms around him. She suddenly felt like they were alone in this world, that all they had was one another, and that she had to hold on tight.

He must have felt the quiver in her arms, for he twisted to face her, and lifted her, his hands strong at her waist; he set her down on the sill. And then he held her close and kissed her hard, and she knew he'd caught it too, that moment of intensity where being together was the only thing they had that they could call their own, and never doubt.

Ronsin dismissed Adela for the entire day, with an injunction to find Kavan—which suited both Reandn and Adela perfectly. She was alerting the Hounds through Caleb, and the families in the Highborn quarters who had children of Kavan's age—and visiting both goddess faith houses as well, with prayers of intervention to Ardrith, and prayers that Tenaebra keep the child's death quick and painless, if someone had indeed taken him. Reandn searched the yards, and put the word out to the Keep shepherds and groundsmen. In the back of his mind, he felt like he was just going through the motions—but his heart wouldn't even think about it yet.

He arrived at the Wolf barracks to find them steamy from the soggy clothes strung around the three stoves warming the long, narrow building. Wet, thawing snow was never kind to the patrols, but the odor of wet woolens was a balm compared to the heavy perfume of the Highborn men and women that Adela was facing, as far as Reandn was concerned.

He walked the narrow aisle between the cots that lined

the walls and stopped at the doorway to the common room. A big square space, roomy if chillier than the sleeping room, it connected the men's and women's quarters. In the common, there were tables of games and cards, and one whole corner of the room given over to inspection, cleaning, and sharpening of gear. Most of the Wolves were gathered around a noisy arm-wrestling contest, and he waited for its completion before moving in to question them about Kavan. No one had seen him, not even those on Keep perimeter watch—which meant he was likely still in the Keep. He asked them to keep an eye out for the boy and went to check the barn—again. He was in the hayloft when Adela called from below. "Reandn? Are you here?"

"Up here," he told her, sticking his head over the edge.

"You've got hay in your hair," she said, absently. She was back in her stable clothes, wearing her oldest, heaviest tunic—the one that should have hidden her shapeliness but didn't. "I've looked everywhere. I don't know what else to do . . . I can't stop thinking about it."

"Come to work Willow, then?" Reandn approved. He needed a little distraction, himself. "I think one of the Yearlings has him out, but whoever it is'll probably be glad to hand him over. He's difficult for most of them."

"I'll find him, then. Will you be coming out?"

He nodded. "There are a few more corners to check. . . ." No point in saying that if Kavan was all right, he'd have heard them talking from those corners. Adela gave him a look that said she'd heard the unspoken words anyway, and left for the round pens.

Good or bad, the boy was not to be found in the loft. Reandn climbed down, brushing bits of seed and stalk from his light jacket, and discovered Saxe standing before Specks' stall.

"You and Dela are married now," Saxe said wryly. He

reached in to scratch the gelding's upper neck, who curled his upper lip in pleasure. "No need to go sneaking around in the loft."

"Married or not, a loft has its attractions," Reandn said. "But if I'd been with Dela, I wouldn't have been caught out."

"Probably not," Saxe grinned, but sobered. "Still looking for your lad? I heard the Hounds are checking in town." He hesitated. "I'm sorry, Reandn. Kavan seemed like a good kid." Another pause, and he gave the gelding a last pat and moved away from the stall. "Three of them in the same season. I don't like it. And we were premature to suppose we knew what happened to the kitchen boy. The Dragons worked the pond this morning—what they found was one of those little statues from the public gardens."

"Tenaebra's Eve pranks," Reandn said. "If that boy is a pile of bones on the road to East River, we'll never solve *that* puzzle."

"I don't like trails that can't be unraveled," Saxe grumbled.

Reandn shook his head. "If—*if*— we lose Kavan, you can be sure I'll unravel *that* one." He headed for the back door of the stable.

Saxe walked with him into the bright afternoon sunshine, admitting to a certain curiosity about the idiosyncratic Willow. Together they headed for the horse corrals. The air was chill in the pleasant kind of spring day that gives horses an excuse to act up, and Reandn was glad Adela was there to work the gelding instead of one of the Yearlings.

The cobbles of the courtyard turned to packed dirt as they passed through the curtain portal to the wide, flat area of fenced training rings. The center oval—the high fenced ring that used to hold unicorns—was currently littered with debris: a substantial tree trunk, an area of rocks, a short bridge that went over nothing, and two constructed jumps.

All three rings were occupied, but Willow—his greying, dappled coat bright in the sunshine—was easy to pick out. Reandn frowned as he saw the horse was standing in place, prancing nervously. In the center of the ring, two figures argued loudly enough to send snatches of angry syllables out to Reandn's ears.

"That's Adela," he said shortly, and lengthened his steps.

It *was* Adela, and Wace, as well. Reandn's temper immediately rose a notch. Ser had had trouble with this trainee all season, and he wasn't about to let the pup harass Adela. But when he reached the round pen gate, he reluctantly halted, knowing Adela wouldn't appreciate the interference. Saxe stopped beside him, reinforcing temperance merely with his presence. From the gate, they could hear the discussion clearly— although as soon as Reandn got a good look at Willow, he knew what it was about.

The horse jigged, his hindquarters bunched and ready to propel him across the ring and through the fence if necessary; his ears were flat back and his head was high, protesting the chain across his sensitive nose. Adela, hands on hips and expression unrelenting, glared up at the big Yearling.

"I'm not taking it off," Wace said, the training whip forgotten at his feet, the coiled longe rope clenched in his fist.

Adela's voice was icy. "You're hurting him. If you can't handle him without it, then leave him to me."

"I'm handling him just fine," Wace retorted.

"You're *abusing* him just fine, you mean." Adela stepped between man and horse, taking hold of the rope where it swung between Willow and the Yearling. Wace's neck and face turned a fine shade of red. Reandn reached for the gate latch, still hesitating. *Let her handle it.*

"Let go," Wace snarled. "Just because you're the First's woman doesn't mean you can walk in here and order a Wolf around." He tore the rope from Adela's grasp; at the other end, Willow grunted angrily and half-reared at the slap against his tender nose.

Adela closed on the Yearling, her face dark. "I've got all the authority in the world when it comes to Willow. Now give me that rope, or you'll find I've *learned* a thing or two from being a First's woman!" She jerked the rope back out of his hands, careful to protect Willow from the whiplash. Wace took her completely by surprise; his temper popped and he hit her, knocking her down hard.

Reandn didn't bother with the gate; he vaulted the fence and sprinted for Wace. Willow reared, pulling back hard on the longe line and nearly taking Wace with him; the Yearling dug his heels in, fighting the grey's panic. When the horse leapt forward, bolting away from the pain, Wace jumped out of Willow's path and into Reandn's, a solid collision that left them a fallen tangle of limbs.

Stunned by two separate attacks where none was expected, Wace managed to struggle to his knees before Reandn dragged him back down again, savagely scrambling to get a hold on the bigger Yearling. In seconds his hands were locked around the bigger man's neck; rage coursed him, lending his fingers strength. Wace's eyes widened with panic as Reandn ignored Saxe's pull on his shoulders—

And then internal chaos hit him, and hit him hard. Suddenly face down in the dirt of the round pen, with grit on his lips and teeth and Wace squirming beneath him, Reandn felt his chest tighten; his jaws clenched against a muted roar. *Not this time.* Not with Dela at stake. Wace had wriggled out from beneath him, was not within reach; Reandn focused on Adela, the only thing that could pull hard enough to keep him going through this sensory assault.

Somehow he'd gotten tangled in the longe rope and it tugged erratically at him as he sought Adela, still sprawled in the center of the ring. Behind him, Willow raced back and forth, throwing dust at the end of each short run. As Reandn reached Adela, Willow jerked him back off his knees; angrily, Reandn grabbed his knife to slash himself free, finally moving more easily as the noise in his head faded. Then the hoofbeats became a tattoo of sound that encircled them while he anxiously, carefully reached Adela and moved the scattered curtain of hair away from her face.

She was staring at him in horror, one side of her face reddened and already swelling. "Danny," she whispered. "*What happened to you?*"

He wasn't going to answer her, not right away. He looked more stunned than she felt, his face pale and strained, his eyes wild. Adela gathered her shaky feet beneath her and slowly stood, taking in Wace, who was breathing in hoarse gasps beyond Danny, with Saxe beside him. But the Pack Leader was looking at Danny, not Wace, and his face was grim. Around them galloped the grey gelding, frantically trying to run away within the confines of the round pen.

Oh, poor Willow! She ran on uncertain legs to intercept the gelding, standing in his path to hold her arms out wide, making a barrier of herself and her confidence.

He could have gone around, but he dropped his haunches to take the weight of the sudden halt and then trembled before her. In one derisive movement she tore the halter and chain from his head and flung it at Wace, who had recovered enough to sit back on his heels, plainly dazed. "Get that pup out of here," Adela said, with a snarl in her own voice she'd never heard before.

Saxe gave the Yearling a hand up, pausing to give the

shaken young man a critical eye. "Go on over to the surgeon's," he said. "Maybe he can give you a poultice to keep the bruising down. Then wait for me in my office."

"He tried to kill me," Wace said, his voice rasping. "My father—"

"*Now*, Yearling!" Saxe snapped, and Wace straightened his shoulders, his steps uneven as he walked away.

Satisfied, Adela turned to Willow. "You stand easy," she said, her voice low and soothing. "I'll take care of you in a minute." But first, she had to know Danny was all right.

He was on his feet now, looking no less strained than he had when she left him. When she caught his eye, he looked away, and it spoke volumes. This was not new. This was something he'd kept hidden from her. She stopped and stood across from him, a mere foot away, offering no quarter. "Tell me."

Saxe joined her, and she suddenly realized he didn't seem at all surprised, just upset. "You *knew*," she said. "You knew about this. Does anyone else know? Am I the only one who doesn't?"

"The surgeon knows," Danny said, his voice low. "He just wasn't any help."

"What *is* it?" she asked, pursuing relentlessly, even though the lost look on his face suddenly made her want to put her arms around him instead.

He took a deep breath. "It's . . . he thought maybe I'd taken too many blows to the head."

Adela said with asperity, "The heavens know you've had enough of them."

"I just . . . get lost for a moment." He glanced at her—trying to judge how she was taking it, she knew. "My head gets filled with noise, and I . . . just can't think past it. No, that's not entirely true. I'm learning to."

Saxe's grim expression had not lightened. "And you'll have plenty of time to work on it, after this."

Danny's head snapped up; his voice hit gravel. "You can't do that."

"The hells I can't. What I *can't* do is send you out on patrol, knowing this could happen at any time."

"I'm *dealing* with it, Saxe. If you take me off patrol, you *know* what kinds of rumors are going to start. My people will never know if they can trust me again!"

"Can they trust you now?" Saxe said, biting the words off.

Danny looked away from him. Looked defeated. "I've never been hit on patrol, Saxe. Never. It doesn't seem to happen in deep night."

Saxe just stared at him a moment, as though he wasn't sure he could trust his First any more. Finally he said, "You'll tell me if it does."

Danny glanced at Adela, drawing her into the promise. "I'll tell you."

With a heavy sigh, Saxe nodded. "All right. For now." He looked after Wace, who was barely visible against the weathered wood of the barn. "He's not so lucky. Politics be damned, the pup is out of the Wolves. Not even Ethne's going to argue with me on this one."

"No," Danny agreed, some of the fire coming back into his voice. "And he'd better stay damned clear of me."

Saxe turned to leave them, but not without one last glance at Danny, a hesitation . . . but something he decided not to say. He looked, Adela thought, watching his shoulders as he walked away, as tired as she suddenly felt.

Danny was offering her his hand; instead of taking it, she put her arms around him like she'd wanted to do before. "There's more than one surgeon in this world. We'll keep asking."

"Yes," he said, sounding unconvinced.

"Danny," she said, "just how long has this been going on? Has it always been this bad?"

His voice, although it was coming from a mouth that was so close to her ear, sounded distant. "It's not usually this bad at all," he said. "Most of the time I can just go right through it. It started . . . just before we lost the Resiore boy."

She drew back and gave him a somber look. "Then we lost more than that boy last fall."

He took her chin, a gentle grip, and looked down into her eyes, his own grey gaze still looking a little bereft. "I'm going to figure out what happened to Kavan, Dela."

"I know," she said. *And if you don't, I will.*

Chapter 4

The king made it his business to ensure the rocky, pine scrub acres around the Keep and town were free of night wanderers, and of the trappers that surreptitiously laid their traplines in forbidden areas. There was too much stock, too many dogs working sheep and goats over the rocky pastures, to chance losing one to a trap, something a hungry hunter found easy to overlook or ignore. Night patrol was when the roadmen emerged, when people got lost, when trouble of all sorts crept to the surface. It was busy, and Reandn reveled in it. Usually.

But that night's patrol turned out to be a long and frustrating experience. Reandn kept a constant scrutiny inside his head, until he was no longer sure what was *normal*, and what wasn't. At one point, on the furthest arc of his ride from the Keep, he was certain he felt something, certain he'd swayed in the saddle; even Specks swiveled his flea-bitten ears in the darkness, as if to ask Reandn what was going on up there. But it faded, and he decided he'd been mistaken. He was merely too caught up in himself—and no Wolf could function like that. A Wolf had to believe in himself, and trust in himself and his abilities. With a murmured oath even Specks recognized as trouble, he refused to think about it any longer.

Instead he thought about Kavan. Perhaps the Hounds had found him by now. Even finding the boy dead,

Reandn thought desperately, was better than wondering for months what had happened to him. By the time he rode Specks to the barn and stalked into the ready room to await the arrival of his patrol for debriefing, he was in a dangerous mood.

Finding Saxe and Caleb there waiting for him did nothing to lighten it. He stopped short, looking from Saxe's somber expression to Caleb's harried one. Reandn didn't hesitate. "What in the Lonely Hells has happened now?"

Saxe was blunt. "Lady Cosette's favorite lady-in-waiting is missing. Adela's friend Elyn."

Reandn closed his eyes and took a deep breath.

"No one's seen her since yesterday evening," Caleb said. "Ethne and Brant have every single Hound in King's Keep searching—for both Elyn *and* Kavan." He snorted. "As if we might find some convenient bit of ribbon or torn lace to show us where she went."

"Elyn's fiancé was a Hound trainee, if I heard right," Saxe said.

Caleb nodded. "He's as frantic as Lady Cosette. Brant wants to know if the Wolves are doing a grounds search."

"We've got one started. But I don't expect to find her," Saxe said candidly. "There's been too many gone missing this winter with no explanation."

"It happens, Saxe," Caleb said. "The boy in the woods, the kitchen apprentice who was homesick—those were both months ago, just random things."

"Kavan?" Saxe said sharply. "And Elyn? Elyn was an intelligent young woman, Caleb. Not given to getting herself into trouble."

Reandn nodded—Saxe was right—but his thoughts were on Adela. Elyn. Kavan. Far too many missing.

"We're going to take some heat for this," Caleb said ruefully. "Ardrith's Eve is in just over a week. King Hawley's enticed the Northern Highborn through the pass early, with promise of social activity, and housing here at the keep." He gave an exaggerated shudder. "All this fuss, extra responsibility, all in hopes of a few Northies catching the eye of our local breed of Highborn, a few more alliances to hold it all together. Elyn couldn't have picked a worse time to disappear."

"I doubt she *chose* to disappear at all," Reandn said, giving Caleb a frown. Worrying about the nobles was a Hound's life. They sometimes lost track, in the complexities of the court, of the true nature of a problem. Let the Highborn be a little nervous. There was more at stake here than their frolicking.

Caleb made a placating gesture. "Right, right. Of course not." But his expression remained troubled. "We're closer to the court than you Wolves. Hells, we're *in* the court. Spend a couple of days in my boots, and you'll understand why I said what I did. Last fall, the Resiores were grumbling about seceding. They're pretty much self-supporting in those mountains, aside from luxuries—while at the same time they have resources we need." He gestured at the stove. "We'd get mighty cold if they *do* break away, and start charging exorbitant prices for their coal. Now they've been more or less cut off from us all winter, with plenty of time to think about breaking away."

Reandn just looked at his friend a moment; from Caleb's pale blue eyes to his wide, thin-lipped mouth and all the red freckles in between, there was nothing but grim sincerity. He asked, "It's gotten that bad?"

Caleb nodded; beside him, Saxe was doing the same. "I've heard as much," the Pack Leader said. "We just can't maintain contact with them the way we used to. For what it's worth, I don't think their stab at independence will last too long. From what the Foxes tell Ethne, they haven't heard a thing from Taffoa or Rolernia since years before the magic left us."

"Their magic was never as strong as ours," Caleb said. "As soon as the Resiores realize how lonely their little niche in the mountains really is, and just how much our Keland *luxuries* make their lives easier, they'll be sweet-talking us again." He gave an exaggerated shiver. "But Tenaebra's tits, I sure want to keep them—and their coal and timber and alsania wool—with us as long as possible!"

Reandn couldn't argue with that, although his heart was going out to Elyn—and Dela. The three men stood silently a moment, and then Caleb sighed. "I've heard rumors that Ronsin actually performed real magic at Tenaebra's Eve. He's going to have to come up with something *really* spectacular to distract people on Ardrith's."

Reandn had to agree.

Reandn cut patrol debriefing short, once he assured himself that no one had seen anything that would relate to either Elyn or Kavan. He skipped breakfast and went straight to the tower, hoping to catch Adela before she went out to the barn—while Kavan was gone, there was much less for her to do up in the wizard's rooms.

Their room was empty, but Adela's riding clothes were still in the wardrobe. She'd be back. Reandn pulled off his half-chaps and sat in their creaky old rocking chair to wait for her.

He didn't have long to wait. She burst into the room, pulling up short at the sight of him.

"You're home early," she said, surprise on her face. More circumspectly, she closed the door behind her, and leaned against it. In her hand she cradled . . . something. He couldn't tell, only that she held it like it was important to her. "I was just coming out to find you— I've been talking with Ronsin."

Reandn hesitated. There was no point to hitting her

with Elyn's death until she'd told him what she'd wanted to. "What'd the old man have to say?"

A faintly regretful expression crossed her face. "He's thinking about leaving, after Ardrith's Eve. I don't think he expects to get Kavan back . . . and he doesn't think they'll give him another apprentice, since so few people believed he really performed magic at Tenaebra's. He's feeling old, I think. He's talking about going to Solace. It's still a teaching city, even if the schools don't center around magic. He thinks he might be more useful there."

Reandn didn't say anything right away. Adela leaned against the door, looking tired, her eyes a little red-rimmed. Finally he ventured, "You could put in more time with the horses. You enjoy that, and it'd be better for the horses than relying on Yearlings to take up the slack."

"I know," Adela said, biting her generous lower lip as she looked down into her cupped hand. "It's just . . . well, I guess I'll miss him. Even if he *is* mostly gruff and bother."

"What've you got?"

She looked up, a tear trembling on the edge of her lashes. "It's Kavan's. I found it up in Ronsin's study. It must have fallen off, the last time Kavan was there." She uncurled her fingers enough for Reandn to see the little scrunch of dyed, knotted string that had been Kavan's necklet. "It was getting pretty worn."

Ardrith's graces, how am I going to tell her? "That it was," he said, rather inanely.

Nodding, she wiped a quick finger under her eye. He gestured at her to come join him in the chair, a tilt of his chin, and she sat sideways in his lap, a combination they were well used to—and she settled against his chest, breathing softly against his neck, her eyes and lashes damp against his skin. He put his hand over hers, where her fingers ran along the length of Kavan's necklet.

"The Hounds and Wolves are everywhere," she said. "Are they looking for him?"

"No. They're looking for someone else."

He felt her expression change. "Not another one!"

"Looks that way." He sighed. There was no easy way to do this. "Dela, it's Elyn."

She stiffened. "No."

"I'm sorry." How useless it sounded. "I'm sorry, love, but she's gone."

Her body was tense against his, her voice reduced to a disbelieving whisper. "She was here just last night . . ."

"She was?"

Adela nodded slowly. "She heard about Kavan. She came to be with me awhile."

"She stayed the whole night?"

"No . . . she left an hour or so after midnight. I'm not sure how long after the shift bells rang . . ." She was stiff within his arms, but he knew her, knew she was still fighting the horror of it. He rested one hand on her thigh while the other curved around her back, waiting for the tears.

And he knew Elyn had been killed—or taken— between their room and hers.

Reandn held Adela until she cried, and then while she cried herself into exhaustion—which she did as she did everything, wholeheartedly. Then, exhausted himself—he'd caught only a few hours' sleep the day before—he carried her to the bed and lay down beside her, not bothering to do anything more than kick off his boots as he stretched out on top of the quilt. As he was falling asleep, he felt her beside him, her hands running the length of Kavan's worn little necklet over and over again.

When he woke, it was to the sound of evening shift bells, which were deeper, and swung on shorter arcs than the hour bells. His stomach growled, reprimanding him for missing breakfast, but he lay where he was a moment. Adela was gone; when he glanced at the depression where she'd been, he discovered only Kavan's necklet. He'd find her for supper, he decided, and then spend the evening learning what he could about Elyn's disappearance.

Maybe, he told himself, as he sat, rubbed his hands over his face, and reached for his boots, Elyn was even back where she belonged, and embarrassed over causing so much concern. Maybe.

He was rinsing his mouth by the pitcher and bowl when he thought he heard Adela's voice, raised in anger. From above? He spat the water out the barrel-vaulted window and stood, listening, still holding the pitcher.

There—there it was again. Definitely in this tower somewhere. That meant Ronsin's rooms . . . but what in Ardrith's name would make her raise her voice at the wizard? And—had that been a touch of fear he'd heard? *Yes*.

But his dizziness struck, and the pitcher hit the floor with a clatter of tin, with Reandn right behind it, almost gagging from the chaos in his head. *No! Not* now—*not when Adela needed him*—

Reandn climbed to his feet, pulling himself up the door, fumbling it open, reeling through. As his body began to function again, adjusting to the pressure between his ears—*in* his ears—he heard Adela clearly, the buzz masking her words but not her definite fear. He bounded up the stairs, stumbling but never falling, and when he reached the top, she was silent again.

Reandn flung himself at Ronsin's door, bursting into the wizard's study, a room overflowing with shelves of strange dried things and precious metal contraptions, drooping greenery and pages of thickly scripted vellum. Reandn had seen it before and none of it drew his attention away from Adela, who stood, frozen, her face drawn with fear. She was clutching a forbidden metal-cased workbook in an arrested, off-balance stance that should have tipped her over—but didn't. Ronsin stood behind a cluttered table, annoyance on his face. *Ronsin.* Adela's insistent words rang in his memory, *He worked magic.* Even now, his fingers moved, his gaze skipped from Adela to a thick page of careful notes sitting on the table.

"Dela," Reandn breathed, and turned on the wizard, swaying, working his jaw and suddenly aware of the tightness in his chest. "Stop it, damn you. Whatever you're doing, *stop it.*"

"How could I be doing anything?" Ronsin said, resentment souring his voice. He looked away from his notes, his hands stilled like an orator staving off applause—or the completion of a spell. "I'm an old man. My magic has disappeared, and the king allows me my place here out of pity. That's what they say, isn't it?"

That's what they say. But they were all wrong, *he* was wrong. *Elyn disappeared here, and Kavan disappeared here, and the kitchen's not far at all*—and Adela stood frozen in time, one of the wizard's forbidden workbooks in her arms, workbooks she'd just barely learned to read. "It was you," he said, his voice dropping into the growl of its lower registers, struggling to function past the assault on his body. *And somehow, you're doing this to me.*

Ronsin tipped his head in acknowledgement. "Your lovely wife figured it out first—I knew I was too bold with the woman last night. But she shouldn't have come snooping around, and with Ardrith's Eve coming up, I needed what she gave me. And now that I've had time to prepare, I'll take the same from Adela."

"Not before I send you to the Lonely Hells," Reandn grated in fury, reaching for his knife. Barely rational, he fought for breath, fought his fear for Dela and the way his knees simply wanted to surrender and fold.

"Ah, Wolf Justice, is that it?" Ronsin stood taller, seemed oddly . . . different. "I'll show you justice, pup. Justice called up by an old man whose life was stolen away." His eyes glittered beneath their wrinkled folds. "Justice," Ronsin hissed, "is return of power."

The humming in his ears increased almost beyond tolerance; Reandn staggered, clutching the edge of the table—and then he saw the change in Adela.

Did she waver, like the shimmer of heat over hot cobbles? Did she fade, like dissipating steam? Reandn's hand spasmed on the knife hilt as her features oscillated—and suddenly he could see the crowded shelves behind her, through her. Her skirts turned to mere veils and then disappeared, showing nothing left beneath. The last he saw of her was her frightened face, her eyes. And then—gone. The book clattered to the floor, the pressure behind his jaws sighed away to the vestige of its former strength.

And Adela's betrothal ring dropped to the stone floor, metal singing in a short dance that ended at Reandn's feet.

Grief roared in his ears instead of magic. Reandn launched himself at the wizard and the roar turned to cacophony; a force slammed around him in midair, and he knew he was as good as dead, as dead as Adela.

But his greying vision never blackened, just smeared the room into colors he tasted vividly. The noise pressed in against his skin, he smelled the movement of his body—his entire being rebelled, seeking relief against a bizarre assault of senses it had never been meant to handle, and the scream of his agony reverberated impossibly against his skin.

A blink, and the world was normal again. Reandn had time for nothing more than an impression of a steamy

bright interior before he was shooting forward, still
lunging after a wizard who was no longer there.
Something, someone, had a firm hold on his leg, and it
brought him up short; he fell hard. Adela's ring filled
his sight, sitting on slick wet wood in front of his nose.

Exclamations surrounded him, scurried away, and
hushed to distressed murmurs. Bleary and muddled, he
raised his head to discover a group of partially clad women
huddled together, gasping and gaping. Astonishingly
enough, he seemed to be just inside the doorway at some
sort of woman's wash. He was seeing things, he had to
be seeing things, but there was no time to blink it straight,
not when something held his leg so tightly—frantically,
futilely, he tried to yank it free.

But when he rolled back to look he discovered nothing
but a doorway, the structure of which ran straight and
true to the ground despite the fact that the outer edge
of his boot and lower pant leg merged into it. Looking,
in disbelief, back to the ladies' horrified faces, he saw
that they, too, had noticed his impossible intersection
with the wood. Their gawking presence suddenly seemed
ludicrous; he grinned, a challenge: to the ladies, to Ronsin,
to the door frame. Then he pitched forward on his face.

Touched By Sorrow

Chapter 5

That brief moment of clarity was to be Reandn's last for what might have been forever. The world returned to its confusing state of jumbled senses, where undecipherable sounds beat against him, sights came to rest on his confused tongue, and darkness was a blessing that he learned to seek.

The disorientation had its interruptions. Snatches of authentic sensations teased him—a voice in his ear, a touch on his arm—and disappeared. He lurched back into reality when the distinct ring of magic thrummed in his head, and he erupted into violence against the infinite number of hands that materialized to hold him down—but lost that battle, too.

Eventually he found a darkness he was more familiar with—the faintly uneven, washed out blankness of his eyelids closed against light. He ached fiercely, and breathed carefully against it, waiting to fall back into the insanity he'd clawed his way out of.

It didn't happen. Wearily, he took a deep breath and tried to learn what he could about his location without giving away the fact that he was awake. It was warm, far warmer than King's Keep in early spring. There was

security in the feel of rough wool beneath him, and in
the feather bed that embraced him. He heard murmuring
voices, but they were far enough away that they did not
disturb him, gentle enough in tone they did not alarm
him. The faint odor of bread only served to complete
the impression of home and contentment. He could,
he thought, stay this way forever, if Adela were by his
side.

Adela. Danger and death. His eyes snapped open; he
rolled off the mattress, trying for his feet but finding
himself on his knees, a tangle of bed covers and legs.
Wincing at the bright daylight, he stared at the looming
shape of a teenage girl, trying to make her fit into
circumstances that made sense, and failing.

"Nice try, but you're not going anywhere," she said,
her strong accent only vaguely familiar and her eyes
averted in a gesture that clashed with her self-confident
words. "Get back in bed, and I'll get you something to
eat."

"Where am I?" Reandn demanded.

Her gaze lit on his and then darted away again; her
mouth struggled against a smile. "You're on the floor in
front of my brother's bed. And you're not wearing very
much. Now will you get back before my mother comes
in here and yells at me?"

True enough, the air moved freely against his bare
skin. Reandn glanced down to see that he wore only an
unfamiliar undergarment, and then inspected his
surroundings. He was in a small sleeping alcove, while
a rumpled bedroll beside the fireplace bespoke its
displaced occupant. A blackened, steaming pot swung
from a kettle hook at the same fire, while the door of
the chimney baking oven sat open, awaiting the bread
the girl must have abandoned for him. The elongated
room boasted another bed inset in the opposite wall;
there was a smaller cot next to it. Several trunks and a

wardrobe neatly lined the wall across from the fireplace, and a door broke the center. It was half closed, and Reandn got glimpses of figures moving in the next room. It was from there that most of the light came, there and the window by his head.

It all looked innocuous enough; the only immediate threat seemed to be this bossy child, who was still waiting for him to get back in bed, her fisted hands set against her hips.

Gathering the covers around himself, Reandn pushed himself back up to the bed, not without effort. With a satisfied nod, the girl left him and attended to the bread.

He'd thought he'd been killed; he'd certainly seen Adela die . . . hadn't he? By all rights he should be with her, in Tenaebra's realm for violent deaths . . . though . . . . the wizard had *prepared* the spell for her, and not for Reandn.

At the least, he expected to be in enemy hands—after all, the enemy had sent him here, and Reandn well remembered the pressure of magic in his ears, the hands that had held him after he'd arrived. And . . . what had that business been in the women's bath?

The bath. He stuck his foot out from under the covers and checked to see if it'd been left in the door frame along with his boot.

"You're all there," the girl said brusquely, from the middle of the room, where she was surrounded by several chairs and heaps of material. "Now will you please just lie quiet until Pa-farren comes back?"

Not with so many questions left unanswered. His eyes narrowed. "Where's Adela?"

She merely shook her head. "I don't know what you're talking about."

If he wasn't dead . . . was she? He grappled with his muddled memory, trying to sort through the details, remembering more clearly than anything the look on

Adela's face as she had faded to nothingness before him. Had he done the same, just faded out of the Keep and into . . . this place? But he remembered her ring, on the wood floor in front of him—and he'd had his knife, while she'd left metal behind. Reandn scowled, trying to make sense of it, and knowing he'd never be able.

"You got an awful fierce look for someone who just fell out of bed," the girl commented, irreverent of his thoughts. She sat in one of the chairs, observing him, her knees drawn up and her chin on her fist. Her face was open and cheerful—although he wondered if that wasn't just an impression, given by her round eyes and a generous splattering of freckles. Her hair was thick and dark, and not a bit longer than his. Below the short tunic sleeves her arms were plump and just as freckled as her face; the feet that poked out from her skirts were dusty bare.

Reandn stared back, an expression far from the benign interest on her face. She seemed unimpressed. Abruptly, he grinned intimidation at her, telling her *he* wasn't taken in by any of this apparent harmlessness. Startled, she dropped her gaze and watched her toes wiggle for a moment, and after that snuck only surreptitious glances at him.

For the moment, then, it seemed he was safe, which was just as well, since he was obviously too weak to do anything about it even if he hadn't been. He wasn't going to get any answers from the girl, whoever she was. All he had was questions, then. Wearily, Reandn closed his eyes to wait for Pa-farren, whoever *he* was. And though he was confused and hurting, with no idea which enemy had him now and what they would do with him, the only clear thought in the tangle of his mind was the desire to know Adela's fate. He was alive. Was she?

✧   ✧   ✧

He fell asleep, of course, unable to fight the demands of his body. Deeply asleep, past dreaming—but suddenly, Adela was there. She was a *presence*, she was with him and around him, full of laughter, her face flushed, her eye bright, her dark hair swirling about her shoulders and his. With a need too great to question, he reached for her, tried to pull her close . . . but his fingers always closed on empty air.

In a rush of spirit, she circled him, gently chiding. *No. Listen.* He felt a warmth then, a rush of energy tickling into the corners of his being. And then it was Adela's eyes he looked through, Adela's thoughts, her memories, running easily through his head.

∞   ∞

In the dim late afternoon light that filtered into their chambers, Adela wriggled closer to Danny's body as he slept. She gently ran her hand along the lean muscle of his side, a proprietary gesture. Danny stirred and shifted to his back, and she opened her eyes to watch him in the dim firelight, studying features she already knew by heart. She reaffirmed the fact that his nose, appearing straight from most angles, actually held a slight curve. She followed the angle of his jaw and its strong chin, and then, as always, she ended her inspections at his eyes. Even closed, they held her attention, with thick dark lashes that contrasted so strongly against the intense grey irises she could bring to her mind's eye at any given moment. She rested her head along his shoulder, enjoying the warmth he radiated, more content than any one woman deserved to be, just feeling him breathe against her.

∞   ∞

Adela held Danny's hand as they walked into the great hall for a song-fest, not surprised at the expression she caught on one young Highborn face. No doubt the youth had felt Danny's teeth as Wolf First. He could be arrogant, she knew, especially with the Highborn, and was sometimes too easily pushed into violence. She didn't know how anyone could expect else of him, coming to this keep small for his age and stuck in the kitchen, unprotected from the older, higher-born boys who needed something to do with themselves. Her own first sight of him had come by chance, as he fought off two older boys.

He'd won that fight, and maybe a bit of her heart as well. She'd been somehow captivated by the scruffy youth, at the time far below her own not-so-lofty status as attendant-in-training. The next time she'd seen him, he'd been in the Wolf Yearling uniform, a giant step for one of his social standing. The Wolves had been pulling back into central Keland, and openings were few, so she presumed someone had gone out on a limb for him. Even then she knew he was worth it.

ఞ   ౧

Adela watched him stoke the fire . . . joined in his silly guessing game with Kavan . . . helped him tease young Willow out of his sulk with a treat of molasses-soaked oats, laughing with him as the horse stopped playing deaf and dumb and flipped his nose up and down in impatience *give me, give me* . . . Adela tumbled onto their chamber floor with him as horseplay gave way to passion . . .

ఞ   ౧

Adela, giving him back his own eyes, his own thoughts. Surrounding him with her essence, leaving the touch of her lips on his mouth, his throat, the strong line of his collarbone. Leaving the sound of her voice in his ear, a murmur of affection, a murmur of reassurance— *I have Kavan, we are together*.

And a murmur of farewell.

ఞ   ౧

Reandn jerked awake, gasping with the impact of what had been much more than a dream. Even now, he felt the fading ambience of Adela's presence, and the impact of her farewell. No one had to tell him she was dead, not now. He knew.

He took his air in great gulps, feeling the burn of a tear on its way down the side of his face. And he felt, too, the stirring of new feelings, new desires. *Find Ronsin. Kill him.*

When Reandn woke again, it was to the muted light of evening, and the sound of a whispering voice, straining with the effort to be quiet—though not quiet enough to keep him from eavesdropping. Aching, wary of his environment, he listened with his eyes closed.

"You weren't here." The voice was a woman's. "I was in the doorway—I saw the look he gave Maurinne. I don't know where he came from, but I'm not altogether sure it was civilized!"

"He didn't act uncivilized to me." There, that was the girl, Maurinne, and sounding uncertain.

The woman ignored her input. "Find somewhere else to keep him!" That meant there was someone else in the room. Pa-farren, perhaps?

"Please, Lina," a third voice said. It was a mellow voice, worn with age. "He is no threat to us. And I *must* keep him here—you know that."

"I thought you left your wizardry behind you," the woman said, rather sullenly.

The man chided gently, "The art of magic is something you can never put aside."

Reandn could not help but stiffen. He'd been right. Ronsin had sent him into the hands of another wizard.

"Translocation is a powerful spell," the old man was saying. "Someone's discovered a way to tap into magic— and I *must* find out who."

"Even the women from the bath knew enough to come to Pa-farren, Mam," Maurinne said, treading carefully

on the edge of disrespect. "They could see it was magic.
Wouldn't it be fine to come across some magic?"

"There were plenty who abused it," the woman
muttered.

"All the more reason to find out who is wielding it
now," Pa-farren said with finality. "I repeat, this man is
no threat to us—even if he weren't so weak he couldn't
swat a fly dead."

"And just what makes you so sure?" Lina demanded.

"You've never had the opportunity to see the crest
he wears. This man's one of the King's Wolves. Considering their current scarcity, I imagine he's straight
from King's Keep—the ring, too, whoever it belongs to.
It's not his—it's a woman's ring." His voice rose. "How
much of that have I got right?"

"Where's the ring?" Reandn demanded, opening his
eyes to meet the bright blue gaze of the man looking
across the room at him.

"I am not the enemy," Farren said. "I prefer not to
be treated like one."

Reandn hitched back on his elbows, doing his best to
hide the effort it took. "You're a wizard," he said flatly.

"I was." The man stepped closer, and his bearing made
it apparent that although he was aging, he was by no
means aged. As he neared, Reandn could see streaks of
sandy hair holding out against the grey. "And you, it seems,
have a reason to fear wizards."

"Not fear," Reandn said steadily, veiling the threat very
little.

A smile crossed Pa-farren's face, and lingered. "Indeed,"
he said. "You see, Lina, there *is* good reason to try to
find out who has this stray bit of magic."

The expression on her face dismissed every concern
the old man might have had and replaced it with her
own. A strange man, the stern lines around her mouth
said. One who has threatened us, echoed the engraved

worry marks above her dark eyes, below hair that was both as dark and as short as the girl's. Though there were no freckles in evidence and her features were not padded with plumpness, the slightly crooked nose was a replica of the girl's—and the man's.

"The ring," Reandn said, trying to keep his voice level. After a moment's thoughtful fishing in his trouser pocket, Pa-farren extended Adela's betrothal ring.

Reandn took it with trembling fingers, though it was not weakness that plagued him now. With care, he inspected the gold, a plain band gone satin smooth with constant wear. Finally he closed his fingers around it, shaken by the evidence that his jumbled memories were correct, his startling dream had been real. Adela's flesh, suddenly evanescent, had faded away, and left only this ring behind her. And somehow, he'd brought it *with* him.

Until Pa-farren spoke, he didn't realize how long they'd been waiting for him. "Son?" said the older man, in a way that made it clear he'd gleaned some of Reandn's grief.

Reandn shoved the ring on his little finger, closed his eyes and took a deep breath. "I'm a Wolf," he said, answering that first question. "I'm from King's Keep." He looked directly at the woman and added, "You're all perfectly safe, as long as you keep your distance."

Her reaction hovered between relief and indignation. "He's as rude as a barbarian," she muttered to Pa-farren.

Unruffled, the old man spoke almost cheerfully. "Wolves have no need for tact—only a quiet foot and a quick eye."

Reandn gave him a sharp look at the training phrase. Only time at the Keep would have exposed him to it—although in the past there had been Wolves assigned to other areas of Keland. Possibly this man was old enough to have heard it from a Wolf stationed here.

The old man moved aside as Maurinne nudged her

way past him, carrying a tray with broth and toast. "You'll get more when you've gotten your stomach used to food again," she told him pertly, but her voice was not as bossy as it had been.

Pa-farren evidently noticed a difference in her, for he gave Reandn a thoughtful look as she left, and helped himself to a seat at the edge of the bed. "I need to know," he said, "how you come to be here. I need to know everything about it."

"Do you, now," Reandn said, swallowing his first bite and managing to burn his tongue. He didn't much like the man's tone of voice, his easy assumption that Reandn would be happy to comply.

"Bring a mug of water," the older man requested, not looking away from his more or less captive subject. The slap of bare feet on the board floor attested to the girl's response, and she soon came just close enough to hand a mug to Reandn.

Reandn held a mouthful of the water on his tongue. Held it while he pondered what to tell this old man whom he didn't trust. It was Keep business, anyway, and belonged between Saxe and the Prime Ethne, between the king and the Hounds and the Wolves—and, mostly, between Reandn and Ronsin.

"I'd like to know what you *really* did to her," Pa-farren grunted, glancing back at the girl. "Last time I saw someone set her back, she was ten. It's good for her."

Reandn attended to his broth. Then, as the old man turned back to repeat his first question, Reandn cut him off. "I asked her where I was, when I woke up. She said you'd tell me."

Pa-farren hesitated. "If you're from King's Keep, it's going to take quite a while to get you straightened around. We're in Maurant—or, on the edges of it, anyhow. Near the outer markets."

"Maurant?" Reandn repeated blankly. He'd seen

enough maps of the Keland to know Maurant was the southernmost boundary. Lined by the sea, it was the least dependent on goods from the north and stocked with a most independent crew of Minors, Keland's top town officials. *Maurant?*

"Don't take it too hard, son," Pa-farren said, his bright eyes crinkling at their edges in his humor. "You're a long way from home, it's true, and it's happened rather abruptly, but aside from part of a boot, you've made it in one piece. And that includes," he added more soberly, "the condition of your mind, although it's taken two weeks to get you to this point. Not many who take the Wizard's Road without preparation come through it sane."

Wizards again. Reandn wasn't all that sure he *was* sane, not with the loss of Kavan and Adela lingering like a terrible aftertaste in his mind. And how much could a wizard make a man believe? Perhaps, at this very moment, he was trapped in the tower, while Adela stood beside him, her frozen expression pleading through the silence.

He stared at the broth, and the coolness of the ring on his little finger brought him out of his uncertainty. He had seen her die, had known the truth despite his initial hope. The cry of grief and helplessness he'd felt at the moment this very ring dropped to the ground was something Ronsin could never produce in him. This ring was real. This bed was real, and so was the old man who sat at the edge of it.

The enemy, clothed in kindness.

Reandn realized he'd done it again. Fallen asleep, without the faintest intent to do so. *Some Wolf.* He lay twisted around the light cover sheeting, and the formerly comfortable air was heavy with heat. Cracking his eyes open, he found he was alone in the room except for the woman Lina, who sat in one of the chairs with a bundle of material in her lap, a needle flashing. In the next room,

an animated conversation started, and she tilted her head
to catch the words.

In the alcove, Reandn could hear none of it. His
strongest impulse was to curl up around his still-aching
body and go back to sleep, but his wistful stomach
reminded him of the unfinished broth. And . . . it was
time to find out just how things stood around here.

The conversation faded; the woman resumed her
relaxed posture with a sigh, and a small shake of her
head. The ever-active needle now slowed, and came to
rest halfway through a stitch. She was watching him,
Reandn realized. Instead of the distrust and anger that
had settled on her face while she argued with Pa-farren,
Lina was watching him with concern, and something
close to pity. Reandn lowered his cracked lids, shutting
out the sight while he tried to interpret it. Failing, he
feigned waking with a stretch his muscles begged for,
rotating the elbow that bothered him the most. When
he opened his eyes again, she was sewing.

"Do you want something to eat?" she asked, not looking
up.

"I'd rather have my clothes back, and make use of
your facilities," Reandn answered, swinging his legs over
the edge of the bed and deliberately not thinking about
who had attended those personal needs while he'd been
sick. At her nod, he found his clothes folded neatly on
the floor beside the bed, and he went through the
awkward process of dressing while she looked pointedly
at her sewing. When he stood, she stood, too, watching
as he swayed like a sapling in the wind. "If you'll return
my knife, I'll get out of your way. I know you'd rather
be quit of me, and I have things to do." Important things.

She hesitated, weighing her words. "It's hard enough,
keeping this wanderlust family together without something
like you popping in to stir them up," she said. "But Pa-farren
wants you to stay for a while. So get you out back to the

little building and then come in for a meal and a shave."

Reflexively, Reandn ran his hand along the bristles of his chin, finding proof enough that he had indeed been here more than a few days. But as his hand dropped back to his side, he lifted his head and said, "I won't be held here."

She snorted, stabbing the needle into the fabric to punctuate her feelings. "That's just the sort of thing I'd expect from someone like you," she said, laying the fabric atop the trunk that sat between chairs. "We take you in, care for you, and when Pa-farren needs you to stay and answer some questions, you get rude. We're just simple folk, here, meir Wolf, and we treat one another civilly. That does not mean scaring my daughter or threatening Pa-farren—or me." Chin set, she stared at him, waiting for his reaction.

Perhaps she expected him to act like a scolded child; she probably had that kind of control over her family. Reandn stared coldly back. "I'm grateful for your help," he said. "But I won't stay."

She was silent for a moment as she reached over to rearrange a fold of the fabric. She said quietly, "Think you can take care of yourself, do you."

After that he could hardly ask for more specific directions to the correct outbuilding. His back stiff and straight, he headed for the darkened corner that was the back door.

The house was surrounded on both sides by nearly identical dwellings. Back behind the outhouse, the yard faded into scraggly bushes; beyond them loomed high pines, and no sign of any attempt to tame the land. The culture here was a fishing one, he reminded himself. This close to the shore, farming was limited to the likes of the large garden he walked beside. Even now, a whiff of breeze in the otherwise leaden air brought him the scent of the sea.

The houses were set too closely together to see between them to the street in front. The long, narrow yards were unfenced, merging peacefully into adjoining lots, and the houses were uniformly low, each with a door under the obtuse angle of the roof peak that led out onto a second-story porch. Circled by a carefully carved railing, the platforms extended beyond the houses, creating pillar-strewn caves beneath. Glancing at the sun, Reandn realized these southern dwellers had become expert at creating their own shade, and opportunities to catch the breeze.

Reandn suddenly felt the heat of the sun on his shoulders, the warmth at the top of his dark blond head. Sweat was already trickling down the side of his face, and he finished his little expedition without wasting any more time. Back inside, the relative coolness of the building washed over him, and he paused to let his eyes adjust.

Lina was gone, but a glint of metal resided in her former seat. Reandn prowled in to discover his knife, which he replaced at his side with dispatch. Beside the chair stood his boots, the soft sides folding neatly down over hard leather toes and soles.

It merely confirmed his memories to find that the left boot was cut in half, rendering it without heel or half its sole. Wonderful. He was more than half a country away from King's Keep, and he had no boots—and just enough coin for a meal or two. Earning enough for provisions would keep him here much longer than he even wanted to think about.

He retrieved his boot knife, comforted by the way its slim lines clung to the curve of his hand, and left the useless footwear, crossing the room to the door that led to the front.

Somehow he was not surprised to be confronted with mountains of neatly folded material; they framed the doorway and made a path to the very front of the room. He stalked it unsteadily, marking but not pausing at the sudden coolness of flat stone beneath his feet.

Light shone from the front of the room as brightly as it had beat against his eyes in the back yard. He squinted and paused, just out of sight of the several people who were discussing the suitability of a particular material. From bright to dark to bright again, from bed to activity— his adjusting vision greyed in warning. Reandn leaned against the nearest pile of bolts and took a deep breath.

"Pa-farren!" The cry was youthful and loud, a warning.

Reandn's eyes snapped open, his vision filled with a charging, lanky shape. It collided with him, knocking the breath out of both of them and pushing Reandn back into the cloth bolts. They grappled, but the individual had no real strength; Reandn wrested his arms free and reversed position with the slender assailant, shoving him against the cloth, putting the nearly forgotten knife at his throat. The figure froze. As far as Reandn could tell, *every*one froze.

Reandn took a tighter grip as his knees slowly gave way, dragging them both down. *Damn.* When his vision cleared once more, he was staring into eyes as startled as his own, young and filled with the folly of impetuous action. They both trembled, one from weakness and the other from fright, locked in place until something triggered the next move.

Behind them was silence, and a hasty gulp as someone remembered to breathe. Then—footsteps coming up behind him, firm with confidence. Reandn tightened his grip again, so the boy's head was forced back, his eyes rolling as Reandn scrambled to make sense of it all, to gauge his danger. There were wizards involved, and nothing was to be taken for granted, his own safety least of all. The boy, reading Reandn's face, paled.

"Tanager," came a voice dripping with sibling disgust,

"you are living proof that boys are dumber than flatfish." Maurinne's sardonic voice broke through the tension, leaving behind it the quickly quelled whispers of the women.

"Son." The voice of the footsteps was Pa-farren. "This is a mistake. Tanager was impetuous. We won't hold your reaction against you if you release him—if you release him *now*."

Tanager was the least of his problem. Slowly, Reandn relaxed his grip, pinning the boy with his eyes alone—a clear warning. Tanager slid sideways on his knees while Reandn shifted to keep him in view. By the time the boy stood and walked on obviously shaky legs to stand beside the old man, Reandn had his first full view of the room.

The light streamed in from the open wall in the front of the shop, framed by shutters and two carefully hung samples of tunics. Silhouetted by that light were several figures, indistinguishable except for Maurinne's shorter, plumper self. And closer, enough so the light illuminated rather than shadowed his features, was Pa-farren. No one else, no one with any sort of weapon. It was only a tailoring shop, filled with people he didn't trust. Reandn sat back against his heels, the knife resting along his thigh, knowing better than to try to get up just yet.

"Tanager," Pa-farren said, resting a brief glance on the youth, "remind me to talk to you about the difference between courage and foolhardiness."

"He had a knife," protested Tanager with wounded pride. "He was sneaking in on us with a knife!"

Surprise must have registered on Reandn's face, for the old man smiled. "He *is* a Wolf, Tanager. They make no more noise than that running across cobblestones in hard soles."

"Let him speak for himself." The accusing voice came from one of the shadowed women, and Reandn squinted into the light. When the figure came forward to resolve into a stately woman he had not seen before, it was followed by two others that turned into Maurinne and her mother. "You took this man in without the benefit of consulting my husband, and see what it has brought you."

"Nothing has happened," Pa-farren said mildly.

"But something almost did," she said, not a whit put off, her manner nothing but Highborn. Reandn marked her fine clothes, and the expensive scent that drifted his way. Her hair was brown, and, to his eye, dyed against grey, but it was carefully coiffed, braided and looped in ways that showed its length. Lina and Maurinne, hovering anxiously behind, underscored the social differences with their closely cropped hair and plain, one-layer skirts.

"We don't need a man like this causing trouble in Maurant," the woman told Farren, then stared directly at Reandn. "This is a peaceful town. We don't need men like you."

"And I don't want to be here," Reandn said. Pa-farren's lips pressed together as the woman—he suspected her to be the Minor's wife—widened her eyes at the affront.

"I'm sure we can arrange to remedy that," she said, stiff dignity straightening her back. "When my husband hears of your unwarranted attack on the boy—"

"Tanager went after him!" Maurinne said, a loud voice that nonetheless went unheeded.

"—I'm sure he'll personally attend to the problems you have created. First the women's wash, bold as you please and no apologies for it, either. Now this. As long as Savill is Minor of this town, we'll not have intrusions—"

Reandn glanced at Pa-farren, finding his lips still firmly tightened. Anger, he'd initially decided, but now recognized the twinkle of humor. The wizard did not, apparently, take this woman too seriously—and neither did he. He shrugged at her, which slowed her down, and then stopped her completely with his grin, the same feral challenge that had so offended Lina. The woman's mouth shut, and then opened again just long enough to promise further attention to this matter. She swept out of the shop, snapping open a small shade parasol as she entered the sunlight.

"Wow," said Tanager. "Will you teach me that?"

"No!" Maurinne exclaimed. "He will not. You get into enough trouble as it is."

"*Farren*," Lina said under her breath, a quiet demand.

Reandn mentally pushed them away, climbing carefully to his feet, his eyes on Pa-farren. The suppressed smile that licked around the corners of the old man's eyes faded as he regarded the Wolf; the expectant expression that so irked Reandn was back.

"It's my boot knife," Reandn said. "I was only holding it—just got it out of those useless boots." He shook his head. "I'm not stupid enough to come after anyone when I feel like this."

"That I can believe," the old man said. "Tanager *was* impetuous. And you, my friend, still don't know which way stands help and which stands hinderance. Come back inside, before Jilla spreads her tale and we get customers who merely want to gawk at you. I'll try to explain things to your satisfaction, and then perhaps you'll be willing to answer my own questions."

Chapter 6

Farren left him then, moving into the back room with Lina on his heels. Tanager, reluctant, followed only at a stern word from his mother. Maurinne was left behind to watch the store, although for the most part she seemed to be watching Reandn.

Reandn climbed slowly to his feet, standing there a moment to test his legs, breathing deeply. Mingled in with the ever-present sea scent was the crispness of clean new material and the underlying smell of oily wool. The stacks leading back to the living area were just the half of it. All along the back wall, similar mounds of batiste and poplin, wool and batiked cotton rose waist high; folded neatly upon these were premade items. Next to them stood Maurinne, her formerly unabashed stare more subtle now.

He nodded at her. "Thank you," he said. "You kept that from being worse than it could have been." A little adolescent screaming during the scuffle could have escalated the encounter past reconciliation, but Maurinne had managed to defuse the tension well. The smile she gave him was startled but pleased, and then she turned away to busy herself with folding several yards of material that had already been neatly placed on top of the stack.

He returned to the living quarters on careful feet, wiser than to take his legs for granted. Waiting for him was a bowl of chicken dumplings and a circle of watchful family members. The chicken he accepted gratefully; the scrutiny he returned with skepticism.

"You haven't really met Tanager," Pa-farren said. The light tone in his voice sounded forced, Reandn thought. "His given name is Farren, but one of those in the house was enough."

The youth cast Reandn a baleful look, undiluted by adult sensibilities. His hair was slick black, and cut as short as Pa-farren's; the family resemblance was clear.

"This is Lina," Farren said, nodding at the woman, whose expression was a little more guarded than her son's, although its meaning was clear. "She's the mother of those two incorrigibles, and I'm Farren, her father. As you've no doubt surmised, we carry the tailoring of the outer edge of Maurant." He paused to finger his carefully trimmed beard while Reandn ate. He did not care who these people were. Farren prompted, "You're a Wolf. You arrived suddenly in Maurant—in the outer chambers of the woman's common bath, by the way, just as Jilla accused. And I'm sure you have a name that came along with you."

Reandn perched on the edge of the bed, balancing his food on his knees while he paused in his attention to it. "Jilla acts like she thinks she's somebody." Distraction—basic tactics when outnumbered.

Tanager laughed despite his general disapproval of Reandn, and was cut short by the quick glare of his mother.

"She married above herself," Lina said; she seemed to choose her words with care. "She's not a bad sort . . . she just hasn't learned how to carry it."

"After fifteen years, I don't look for any improvement," Pa-farren said dryly. Tanager muffled another snicker.

Abruptly, Reandn said, "My name is Reandn."

"And we're excessively pleased to learn it," Farren said, with only a tinge of sarcasm.

Reandn spared him the response that sprung to mind and instead spooned up another chunk of chicken, surprised by the sudden twinge in his elbow. The old wizard didn't miss a thing.

"Lina can get you something for that. Although you arrived here with quite an assortment of old bruises, by now you've probably discovered new pains."

Reandn gave him a sharp look, straightening the offending joint. "What do you know about it?"

"Just what I should," the older man replied evenly. "And you're going to get along here better without that belligerence. I've told you that. As to your pains . . . you've been moved from one place to another in an abrupt and unkind manner—and against your will, I'm sure, or you'd be much more pleasant to talk to. It will take your body some time to recover. Whoever sent you here must have been in a terrible hurry to dispense with the safeguards that would have kept you away from that door."

Another prod for information. What was the wizard looking for? What could Reandn know that this man would not? Ronsin had, after all, deliberately sent him here. And although Farren had done nothing that ordinarily would have earned the deep distrust Reandn had in him, it in no way changed the way Reandn felt about him. For years, Ronsin had hidden his potential deadliness behind the facade of an ineffective old man. Pa-farren, another ex-wizard, had already exposed glints of hardness beneath his apparently kind exterior, and he certainly seemed used to receiving a certain deference. There was no telling what really lay beneath that smile.

"I'll leave in the morning," Reandn said, without preamble. "I don't have enough to pay you for the lodging," more like enough for a meal and a half, "but I'll give you what I do have, and bring the rest before I leave Maurant."

"There's only one way you can repay us, Reandn," Pa-farren said without hesitation, "and that is to tell me what you know."

Reandn gave the old man a direct stare. "I can't help you."

There was silence in the little house, while Tanager looked from one man to the other, his expression wary. But Pa-farren sat quietly, his thoughts hidden behind blankly schooled features. A slight breeze stirred the air, ruffling through Reandn's hair and lifting the short strands of Pa-farren's greying blond before fading back into the hot, heavy air.

A slight twitch stretched the corners of Pa-farren's mouth, and his voice, when he spoke, was just as heavy as the air. "As you say, son. I'm sure you don't understand the gravity of this situation, just as I'm sure you intend to charge off to right whatever wrong was done you. Perhaps when you understand better, you'll be back."

"I'm not charging off anywhere," Reandn said, his voice hard, telling the old man to mind his own business. "If I had the resources to do that, I'd be able to pay what I owe you." The tug to return home, to avenge Adela—it was so strong it was almost painful. *I'll get there. No matter how long it takes, I'll get there.*

Tanager asked bluntly, "What're you gonna do now?" and then blushed, looking down his slightly crooked nose to avoid his mother's eye.

Reandn answered firmly, effectively ending the entire conversation. "What needs to be done."

That night he slept in the hammock under the porch, feeling more secure in the open air than he had in the pleasant little house. He used the quiet time during late dusk to learn the distracting sounds and smells of the area. Flowering vines and potential poisons, upwind bears and even men—what wasn't obscured by the salty, fishy harbor smells succumbed to the heady pines. The constant breeze that swayed through those same trees created a breathy, soughing undertone that would easily hide the soft crack of a twig. The only noises that came clearly through the symphony of trees were the evening birds—whose songs he didn't recognize. Reandn was out of his element.

A Wolf is a Wolf anywhere. The thought failed to comfort him. Nor did the knowledge that the next day would see him venturing into Maurant, barefoot, looking for some way to finance his trip north.

Reandn toed the ground beneath his hanging foot and set the hammock swaying. When he quit straining for the little clues hidden beneath the sounds and odor of this place, those sensory intrusions could even be considered soothing.

But they weren't enough to erase the tension within him, and the struggle of the need to be practical about moving north against the need to face Ronsin *now*. Or else how many more would the old man kill before he was stopped? Reandn had no doubt, now, of what had happened to Kavan, and Elyn—and even the long-lost Resiore boy. He just didn't know *why* . . .

Adela's fingers traced over the lines of tension by his eyes and mouth, erasing them, easing his concerns with her touch. Reandn jerked against the sudden shard of memory, memory so real he would have sworn—

Above him, the upper-story door opened with a quiet scrape, and Reandn rested his foot on the ground to stop the sway of the hammock. Hesitant footsteps sounded above him and he closed his eyes as bits of old wood and dirt fell down from the porch boards. Then came the sounds of a body settling onto the wood, and Tanager's whisper carried down to him.

"Are you awake?"

Reandn let the hammock swing again, a barely

perceptible movement. "I might be," he said. "Depends on what anyone wants with me."

"I just want to talk to you."

Well, that was better than the alternative, he supposed. "That would be easier if you were down here. Unless you don't care if everyone else can hear."

"I'm not supposed to be with you," Tanager admitted freely. "I thought I'd see if you'd answer before I put myself where I could get in trouble." He flipped over the edge of the porch and dropped lightly to the ground, a maneuver Reandn wouldn't have attributed to those coltishly awkward limbs. Then, as though intimidated by his own boldness, the boy just stood there, arms dangling in an awkward silhouette against the star bright sky.

Reandn was just about to prompt the boy when Tanager blurted, "I don't understand—" cut himself off, and finished in an abashed and much quieter voice, "any of this."

Reandn held his own silence until it became apparent no one had heard, or at least, no one was coming out to stop the clandestine conference. *Why should you be any different?* he wanted to ask. *I don't understand, either.* Instead he said softly, "What is it you think you're supposed to understand?"

"Why Pa-farren's so upset over the way you got here, instead of being glad there's magic left somewhere in the world. Why you won't tell him what he wants to know."

Reandn hiked his eyebrows in surprise, aware the boy probably could not see the movement. "You don't trust me," he said. "Why should I trust you?"

Tanager stiffened. "You had a knife," he said. "And you've been out of your head more than once."

"I'm not out of my head now," Reandn said, "and you still don't trust me. Or is that just wounded pride?

Consider yourself lucky. I could have killed you. Any half-trained Pup could have killed you."

"All right," the boy said sharply. "I was just trying to protect my family. You don't have to rub it in. It's bad enough to get beat by someone who can't even stand up."

Reandn flashed a brief gleam of a grin in the darkness. "It wasn't any better from my end, boy. I think we should call it even and quit growling over it."

"Fine," Tanager said promptly. "Then you'll talk to Pa-farren."

Reandn bit back his angry response and said evenly, "Two different things, Tanager. Just because you and I called truce of a sorts doesn't mean I'm going to trust your grandfather."

"He's a good man!" Tanager's silhouette shifted aggressively.

"Your grandfather," Reandn said tightly, "is a wizard."

Tanager's correction was automatic. "*Was* a wizard."

"There's no such thing as an *ex*-wizard," Reandn snapped. "And there's no such thing as a wizard you can trust."

"That's not true!" Tanager retorted, his adolescent voice cracking. Again, silence as they waited to see if they'd been discovered. When he spoke again, it was subdued, acknowledging the threat of Reandn's anger as well as Lina's. "And he wouldn't ask if there wasn't a good reason. If you could just get to know Pa-farren, you'd see you can trust him."

"That's not a chance I intend to take." He couldn't keep the animosity out of his voice, and he didn't try very hard. "The best thing I can do for *all* of us is to get out of here. While we're still being moderately civil to one another."

Tanager's dark figure stepped backwards, then hesitated; he wanted so badly to argue for his grandfather that Reandn could *feel* it. At last the boy opted for discretion. He jumped up to grab the overhang of the porch, drawing himself upward in a practiced maneuver that ended the conversation.

Loud and unfamiliar birds woke Reandn early, before any of the family came outside to use the outhouse. He quickly used that facility himself, and sat on the edge of the hammock—no easy task—to slice the knife sheath free of his boot. Two more laces cut from the soft uppers made ties to secure the knife at his hip, behind his regular belt knife. Then he combed his hair back with his fingers, shook the stiffness out of his shoulders, and left Farren's household behind him.

Negotiating the narrow alley between the houses, he ventured out onto the street front for the first time since his arrival in Maurant. He was the only one within sight, although he surmised the harbors would be alive early, before the rest of the populace thought to emerge from their homes. There, by the docks where the transients would abound and life was less than stable, he thought he might find his best chances of employment—although it would be little better than paid muscle, and that if he was lucky. He knew precious little about sea port life.

Sound and odor led him seaward, through Maurant. Last night, Reandn had judged the Minor—and harshly—by his wife, but as he walked through the neat edges of the town, his opinion of the man improved. The town was neat, with a minimum of trash and very little sewer odor. As he passed from Maurant's edges to the town proper, the street became cobbled, lined on either side with gutters to catch the waste water. Here the dwellings were built closely not only side to side, but back to back. It was much more crowded than his own keep-protected town, though he could see no defense precautions such as the ones devised at King's

Keep—odd considering the vulnerability of even this minor port.

The roads were level and ran in even patterns until just before the docks. Then the land sloped steeply downward, and the order of the streets disintegrated into a jumble of warehouses and dry docks. Reandn eased in against a net repair shop, where the awning hid him from the sun and a day that already promised to be sweltering; he was standing at the crest of the hill as the sun broke over a low bank of clouds to his left, trying to make some sense of order from the chaos below.

The first thing he noticed was the long, narrow port. Well fortified, jutting extensions of land dropped off from high cliffs on either side, making it obvious why Maurant's founders seemed so unconcerned about invasion. He was willing to bet those high walls held defenses that could keep any unwelcome ships at bay. There were several ships on the calm water now, sailing in from sea with flags flying high. Maybe that meant the tide was coming in, he thought, and had no idea if he was right or not.

The docks below were a confusing bustle, a dance whose steps he didn't know. Reandn crouched, resting, glancing back once to see if he still had the gawky shadow that had followed him from the tailor shop. Yes, there he was, probably secure in his little hiding place, all unaware of the edge of sunlight that caught the top of his head. He shook his head. The wizard didn't really think a Wolf could be fooled by an untrained youth, did he? Well, better to have the boy where he could keep an eye on him. Tanager's position confirmed, he eyed the activity down the hill, hoping to unravel it.

It took a very short while for him to own up to his innate distaste of water travel. The men below moved from land to ship, loading and unloading, traversing slippery planks with nary a mishap. Just watching the bobbing ships, docked in the vast horseshoe shaped port, Reandn felt slightly queasy. He was, he had to admit, a land-locked being who could not hope to fit in. There might be work for him on the Maurant docks, but he would check elsewhere first.

Beside him, a heavy wagon rumbled to a stop, drawn by two draft mules who waited patiently while the driver jumped out and hooked up the check lines; without them, the wagons would run up against the mules' haunches. Working with stock, Reandn mused, was something he could do. Of course, scrubbing pots and pans was also something in which he had extensive experience, but he had no intention of going back to it.

No, he suddenly realized. *That's not true.* He'd do whatever he had to to get back to King's Keep. If it meant working on a bobbing deck or living inside a steamy kitchen with his hands turned into prunes, he'd do it.

Reandn stood and stretched, easing muscles that still felt too weak, too easily cramped. But his stiffness was fading, and his stride was regaining some of its usual assurance; a few more days and he might forget he'd been too long abed.

Checking the heat of the cobbles with a cautious foot, Reandn pretended to ignore Tanager and set off down the hill to see what the lower end of town offered. He was bombarded by the intense sounds and smells of the docks up close; what subtlety of noise the lapping waves didn't drown out, the raucous seabirds did. The inevitable odor of dead fish turned his stomach, and it wasn't until noon that he felt the hunger of a morning without food; not long after that he started to feel lightheaded.

The docks had nothing to offer his forest-loving soul, nor his Wolf talents. Come the evening, when the air cooled, he would head back for the permanent market at the edge of town, the topic of more than a few eavesdropped conversations. Guard and caravan scout were tasks he could take on with confidence. He headed back up the hill, running from the sensory overload, and stopped at the first tavern he saw.

He couldn't read the name, of course; the sign bore a unicorn, but it was rendered in a deliberately faded manner. For several moments he merely watched the clientele meander in and out; meandering was the only activity along the entire waterfront at this time of day, and he'd about decided it was time to emulate the heat-inspired habits. Besides, even if it took his only parscores—the ones Farren had refused—he needed a good meal to fight off his wobbly knees.

Finding the tavern's patrons neither too seedy for his tastes nor too expensive for his pocket, Reandn ambled back to the closest alley, leaned against the edge of the tavern, and spoke to the air. "I'm going to be here all afternoon, so you might as well go get something to eat and tell your grandfather where I am. In case you happen to miss me, I'll be at the outer markets this evening."

From behind him, an almost sullen reply: "It was my mother who sent me."

Reandn left the corner before Tanager could muster any other argument. Immediately inside the tavern doorway, he found the reason for the absence of seedy clientele. A hulk of a man, generously decorated with tattoos, lounged against the wall, eyeing people as they entered. For the most part he ignored the customers and they returned the favor, apparently well used to each other. Reandn garnered a direct stare, and he realized anew how out of place he was here, with his leather vest and the long-sleeved shirt that now hung in his hand. Most of the men he'd seen wore short sleeved tunics over their trousers; their hair was cut considerably shorter than his own, or else worn considerably longer, and tied back. He had, at least, managed a shave the day before.

And of course there was the matter of the bare feet.

None of which he could do anything about. He gave the hulk a cool but civil nod and walked by.

Or tried to. The man's paw rested on his arm, and Reandn stopped before there was an excuse to apply pressure. "Got a problem?" he asked, too tired to truly take offense. He couldn't *afford* to take offense, at that; he had no reserves on which to call.

"You're not from around here," the man observed, as if it was significant.

"No, but where I come from taverns usually *want* their customers inside. They make more money that way. Is it different here?" Reandn asked pointedly.

"No, not different. But I'm here to keep trouble out. And you look like trouble."

Involuntarily, Reandn rolled his eyes, knowing that at the moment, he was anything but. "The only trouble here is what you're causing. So let me either in or out, and we'll both be free of it."

The man's thick eyebrows lowered into a frown. "Smarting off at me, are you?" he said, and took a step forward. He was, Reandn decided, huge. And not brimming with brains.

"Hurley!"

The man halted and straightened, quickly assembling his face into innocence. At the entryway stood a slight young woman, scowling at the hulk.

"Ania," Hurley said. "I was . . . I was just keeping this fellow from causing trouble. He, uh, he got rude to one of the ladies." His eager expression said he was sure she would believe him.

"Is that so?" she asked archly. "Well, let me tell you what *I* see. I see you harassing a stranger who looks so badly in need of Kelton's food that he can't have the *strength* to get rude. What have you got to say about that?"

"Kelton told me to keep trouble out of the *Forgotten Unicorn*," the man said stubbornly.

"All you have to do to accomplish that is stand there," Ania said scornfully. "And you know what Kelton *really* said. He said don't let any trouble in, but don't cause any, either!"

"You won't tell him?" the big man said, resentment warring with intimidation. "I gotta have work, Ania."

She sighed, and glanced at Reandn. "No real harm done, I suppose. Come inside, meir, and we'll see you fed on the house. It won't be the first such meal Hurley's cost us." She favored the man with a parting glare and led Reandn into the serving room.

He found it to be much bigger than the outside had given reason to expect—airy, with a high ceiling; what from the outside looked like a second floor was in fact just empty space. Several small dogs were placed along the walls, turning ceiling fans just like spit dogs, and they had a handler watching solicitously over them. Reandn found the handler as much an anomaly as the wide-spaced tables and shaded ceiling windows. In some ways it was a more comfortable place than the *Muzzled Fang*, despite its unfamiliarity, for here, there was too much distance between the tables to invite eavesdropping or brawling.

He chose a table near the light wood planks of the back walls and settled in, propping his tired feet on the opposite chair. There he relaxed, while his gaze idly roamed the room and located the three other exits besides the entrance.

"Come South for a visit, meir?" Ania was asking him, a question that told him well enough that the Southerners were much more used to seeing Northerners than the other way around—perhaps the by-product of being in a port town.

"Yes," he answered. "But not a long one."

"It's hot on you Northies, I know," she nodded sympathetically, adding a pleasant smile to her small, foxlike features. On Lina and Maurinne, the common short hairstyle was a practical cut; on Ania it feathered darkly around her face, adding a waifish character. "It looks like our sun's got you down, today. How about an ale? Kelton has a deep cellar with a springhouse, and I promise the drink'll be colder than you'd ever thought possible hereabouts!"

"That, and a meal—whether or not you meant what you said."

"About it being on the house?" she asked. Her fine mouth twitched, apparently at the thought of Hurley. "I meant it. We can't have people spreading word that he's causing trouble. This is our little bribe."

"Get rid of him and you wouldn't have to make it."

She shrugged. "It's Kelton's tavern, and his choice. And Hurley *has* changed things for us. He's not all that smart, and he's always looking for trouble, but used to be we'd get sailors filling their few hours of shore leave. Rough fellows. They don't come here anymore, and a lot of nicer folks do. It's a trade-off, I guess. Worth a meal every now and then. So would you like the crab soup, or the roasted flatfish?"

Reandn wrinkled his nose. "Red meat?" he requested hopefully.

Her own brow wrinkled in response. "Not usually." Then the smile came back. "Though if I remember rightly, Hurley brought in one of those little marsh deer this morning. Damone—he's our cook—can do wonderful things with marsh deer."

Reandn nodded. "See if it's available, please."

"Yes, meir."

Reandn tilted his head back against the wall, knowing it would cue her to move on, the sooner to return with the food he needed so badly. He couldn't help his stomach's rumbling oration at the smell of edibles around him, even if it *was* sea food.

The girl laughed. "Back in a moment with the ale, meir!"

True to her word, she returned quickly, affirming she'd bring the meal as soon as possible. Reandn took a sip to confirm the liquid was as cold as promised—which it was, and considerably stronger than he was used to, as well. He set it aside to wait for the steak.

Relaxed, waiting for his meal with a patience that belied his angry stomach and lightheadedness, he spent the time watching, tallying the differences between himself and the Southern natives. The less conspicuous he was, the better.

Speech patterns he could do nothing about. Southern speech was as slow and unconcerned as their habitual afternoon lethargy. It was a chore not to throw his own conversation back twice as fast as normal just to keep things moving. The men, he found, had uniformly short hair, some of it mere bristles no breeze could stir—but Adela had always cut his own hair, just the way she liked it, running long against his collar in back and shorter around his face. He wasn't ready to hand that personal task to someone else—for when Adela cut his hair, it never failed to turn into something more than a few minutes with comb and shears.

Reandn decided he'd simply stow his long-sleeved tunic and make do with the leather vest. He didn't plan to be here any longer than necessary, after all. He toyed with the idea of going to Savill, the town's Minor, but decided the risks were greater than the benefits. While the man could do little more than outfit him for his journey, he might also choose to check into Reandn's story, especially if Jilla had followed through on her promise to cause trouble. That would mean delays—and it would mean that King's Keep, Ronsin included, would learn he was still alive.

He didn't want the wizard to have time to prepare

for Reandn's return—and his revenge. For Pack First
and Pack Leader had the authority to deal out Wolf's
Justice, if the situation warranted. He'd be held
accountable, of course, and would pay heavy penalties
if he couldn't justify his actions. Killing Ronsin would
be worth it—but almost impossible to carry out once
Ronsin knew he was coming.

Reandn sighed and scrubbed a hand across his face.
He'd give anything to have Saxe sitting across the table,
his broad form solid and capable, his quick mind spilling
out solutions for the two to pick from—and his even
disposition tempering Reandn's fiery nature.

Ania brought his dinner—red meat after all—and
though he ate slowly to ease his stomach into the idea
of a hearty meal, he had no trouble putting the last of it
away. Nor did he have trouble with the thought of raising
his feet back up and spending the rest of the afternoon
in this airy, shaded place. He was even secure enough,
in this corner, to doze.

His eyes snapped open to the sight of the serving girl
sitting down opposite him, eyeing him as though trying
to figure something out. She smiled at him. "Don't mind
me," she said. "It's quiet time. I get a break."

He raised an eyebrow at her. "You didn't come to tell
me I'm taking up valuable space?"

"This time of day?" she scoffed. "Even if you were,
you look like you need the rest more than we need the
space."

"Thank you," he said. "I think."

She shrugged. "Listen, you've got to be careful in this
heat. Especially if you had a quick trip down here, and
didn't have time to get used to it on the way."

Reandn laughed outright. "Yes," he said, at her puzzled
expression, "it was a quick trip, all right. And a hard
one."

Before she could ask him the inevitable follow-up

question, he said, "I've heard there's a market at the edge of the town. Does it have stock?"

"Horses, you mean?" she asked, the expression on her face—a triangular face, with wide cheekbones and a strongly angled jawline—answering affirmative, but also showing skepticism. "But I wouldn't buy there unless you've a real good eye. It's just stock that was left behind when the owners went to sea. The good animals get shipped out with their owners."

It was Reandn's turn to shrug. "Can you aim me in the right direction?"

"I'll do better than that," she offered, her face brightening. "I want to go, myself, after Kelton shuts down for the evening. You can escort me, if you like."

Reandn scratched the back of his heel with the big toe of his other foot and allowed, "You don't even know me. Maybe I'm someone you want to be protected *from*."

Amusement filled her lively face; she smoothed the back of her dark, sun-reddened hair in a relaxed gesture. "I'll bet your *next* meal I can out-run you."

"I think you're overestimating the heat's effect on me," Reandn said mildly. "But you're safe enough. I'd be glad to escort you to the market if you'll keep me from getting lost."

"Good," she said, slapping the table lightly to seal the deal as she stood up. "Unless you've got pressing business this afternoon—and no one around here does business during the heat of the day unless it's pressing—you're welcome to stay right here. Take an evening meal, and you'll feel better. Good enough, even, to put the eye to some of that questionable stock."

Reandn raised an eyebrow. "You this nice to all the men Hurley hassles?"

"All of them," Ania said firmly. "Even the ones that don't look like they've just washed ashore after a storm." She gave him a sudden, gamin grin, and left.

Reandn could only shake his head as he watched her pass through the kitchen doorway. Then he closed his eyes again, more than willing to avoid the hot streets of Maurant. He'd try for a job at the market; failing that, the docks would be waiting for him tomorrow.

The evening meal he paid for. When he was through, Ania cheerfully gave over the customers to the other waiting girl, and led him out into the street, chattering about the spate of robberies on the evening roads recently, and how glad she was for an escort. Hurley, who'd gone off during the afternoon, was back to give Reandn an unpleasant look of farewell; Reandn returned it. He half expected to find Tanager on his tail again, but the boy seemed to have given up.

Or so Reandn thought, until they made it to the market, a mile or so from the *Unicorn*, and he discovered the boy had made it to the market ahead of him.

He hadn't spotted Tanager immediately; he'd stopped at the edge of the sprawling market, a haphazardly arranged area plopped down where one of Maurant's main roads turned into a highway. Obviously unplanned, it looked like the random results of merchants trying to avoid the pressures and odors of the dock.

At Reandn's elbow, Ania gave him a smile and sailed off into the fray, quite willing to brave the milling crowds, if not a lonely road. She'd chattered during the long walk, trying to give him an idea of what to expect at the market, and trying as well to draw him out. At first wary, he'd become satisfied that it was safe enough to coast along with Ania this evening, until he was less bemused and more directed.

For the moment he was on his own. Ignoring the lure of canopy-protected stalls that sheltered loud merchants with their claims of superior journey foods, weapons, maps, and fine luxury gifts, Reandn merely watched for a time. There were no Locals about, at least none in evidence. Perhaps they weren't needed, if all the men and women lounging around, weapons arrayed about their persons and don't-cross-me smiles on their faces, were the guards they appeared to be.

At last, above the dramatic noise of bartering, he heard the squeal of an annoyed horse. He skirted the market to track it to its source, and was rewarded with three stock dealers and a circular set of hitching rails. It was there he'd found Tanager.

The boy seemed to have no notion Reandn was there—or if he did, he didn't care. Reandn held back, keeping a stream of traffic between himself and Tanager, until he saw the boy take a coin after fetching one of the horses, tightening its girth and holding the stirrup out for the owner to mount. The tie-ups were free, but in an open market it was only wise to have a youth watching your horse and gear, for there were never enough Locals to keep a constant eye on the tie-ups. With that in mind, Reandn spotted a second child, a girl half Tanager's height, as she carefully picked her way through people and horses, leading a huge sorrel half-draft to its owner.

Reandn moved behind Tanager's back and made his way to the dealers without notice.

Two of the dealers professed, by demeanor and display of their animals, to have high-quality horseflesh. The third made no such pretensions and it was here Reandn stopped, hoping a discerning eye would catch something of worth among the culls. He had a decision to make, as well: travel light, with one horse that would wear out quickly from a heavy load and lack of grain, or buy a pack animal as well, and avoid the worry of finding food. Assessing the culls revealed nothing exceptional, and he meandered to stand between the other two dealers and listen to a few quoted prices that made him wince.

Wolf's Rights meant he could commandeer one of the horses—though no one was likely to have heard of that here. To act on it would just set waves in motion that would rock all the way to King's Keep—again, alerting Ronsin. Same with the boots, and supplies—which would cause enough of a ruckus, he imagined, to make Savill confine him under guard until confirmation of his status came from King's Keep. After all, as far as the Minors in this part of the country were concerned, that's where all the Wolves were—King's Keep.

Still, the temptation was there; his gaze roamed over the horses, sorting, choosing. . . . *No.* He shook his head, hearing Saxe's voice in his ears. *Don't commit to the trail until you've scouted out the terrain*—it was something they all taught the trainees, and something Saxe liked to say when he thought his First was letting his temper push him into precipitous action. And Saxe was usually right.

All right. He'd give himself a day or two here, until he understood the Southern way of things better, and until he got a better idea of just what kind of man Savill was. Then, if it still seemed the thing to do, he'd claim Wolf Rights. Reandn took a deep breath, convincing himself, and was just as glad when a flash of familiar color caught his eye—Ania, in the bright dress she'd donned for this outing.

Reandn lifted his hand to hail her, but she was, he suddenly realized, heading for Tanager. She waved at Reandn and turned to Tanager, resting her hand on his arm in a comfortable and familiar way. After a moment's discussion, she sent a surprised but quickly withdrawn look Reandn's way. Eventually she joined him, her expression uncertain at first but quickly regaining confidence.

"See anything you like?" she asked. Her question caught one dealer's attention, and he sidled closer, ready to jump in at Reandn's slightest sign of interest.

Reandn shrugged. "The bay looks sturdy enough," he

said. The animal lacked a little flesh but was obviously in condition. It was, coincidentally, the same horse he'd just heard quoted at over three silvers. "Too bad about that scarred hock—it's got to restrict his action. And white socks—don't like 'em. Makes for weak feet."

"The gentleman from the North knows his horses," the dealer said. He was a middle-aged man with square jaws turning to jowl, and his tone was pleasant enough. Ania moved aside to let him join the conversation, flashing a smile at Reandn as the game began. "Perhaps you'd like to try the bay. You'll find him a bold mover."

"I don't need a bold mover. I need a horse that can travel," Reandn said, focusing behind the dealer on a horse from the other enclosure.

The dealer essayed a shrug. "I was assured when I bought him that he'd come at a steady pace from Talleda. As you can see, he's still in prime condition. Of course, you're welcome to try him."

It didn't matter much. Whatever the price, Reandn would not have it, and he suddenly realized that whatever his ultimate decision, he wasn't ready to claim Wolf's Rights here and now. The dealer seemed to realize he was losing his customer, and said, "Two silvers and a parscore for that bay, and he'll hit the road running."

Reandn snorted. While he was gratified to hear the dealer drop the amount by an entire silver, he wouldn't give that price for the bay, or any other of the animals he could see here. Horses were plentiful in the South, being easier to keep on the more arable land—and they were especially abundant in a port area like this.

The dealer affected an offended expression. "That's a fair price!"

"Sure enough, but not for this horse." Reandn shook his head. "Perhaps we'll deal another day, friend—when you realize you can't get Northern prices from a man when he's in the South."

He walked away from the corrals with Ania at his side, picking her way and lifting her dress so its hem wouldn't brush against the inevitable hazards of a stock yard. Her expression was puzzled. "I don't think you'll get much better out of him," she said when they were out of earshot. "He's got plenty of people passing through here every day, and they're not able to wait for a good price."

Reandn didn't answer immediately, stopping before they entered the main body of the market to take a better look. True, there were plenty of men and women here, in all variations of groupings and social strata, and it seemed they were all readying to travel. There were also those who looked like locals, and a generous number of the guard whose ilk he'd seen upon entering the market—blatant, threatening, more often than not scarred. Unlike Hurley, these men relied on more than sheer muscle to see them through a confrontation. Reandn wondered if their presence was as necessary as all that. Finally, he looked back to Ania, who waited patiently enough, although she clearly thought he was making a mistake to pass up the bay without taking a closer look.

"The horse won't move very fast," Reandn said. "You notice the man didn't have anything to say about its hock. That scar may not interfere with its way of going, but it looks bad enough. Anyone interested in real travel isn't going to want to fool with it." He pushed his hair off his forehead and tilted his head back to catch the transient breeze that twitched through the air. "By the time I go back there and size the animal up a few more times, he'll know I'm not just taking up his time. He'll come down some."

"Hunh," was Ania's only comment.

"Did you find what you came looking for?" Reandn said, changing the subject and not caring that it wasn't subtle.

Ania shrugged. "Things come and go pretty fast around here—by the time you save the money for some little pretty, it's gone." She gave him a sideways glance from her light eyes. "Or some big pretty."

A shrug of his own. "Ania, I couldn't pay his price if I wanted—why do you suppose I don't have boots?" He extended a foot and regarded it with a frown. Tough as they were, they weren't used to going without footwear, and they hurt. "Maybe by the time I get some coins, he'll come down and we can work something out."

Ania nodded thoughtfully. "I don't see what your hurry is, anyway."

Reandn gave her a sharp look. "Tanager's a chatty thing," he said darkly.

She blinked, and hesitated, and must have decided to match his direct manner. "He didn't say all that much, actually. That you got here suddenly and that he doesn't trust you—and that you don't want to be here."

"But you came back to walk with me."

Her mouth twitched. "Tanager's a good kid. But I gather you have a disagreement with Farren, and he'd do anything for his grandfather. He's hardly impartial."

"No," Reandn said. "He's not." They were walking again, meandering. Reandn took note of a few pavilions he'd be interested in when the time came for him to leave, and puzzled again over the hard guards lingering around the wares. They were more evident, now that the crowd was thinning out. "Ania, why all these big bad guards hanging around the tents? They all look like they'd eat horseshoe nails for breakfast if they thought it'd impress someone."

"There's no need for that," she said. "People are plenty impressed already, and it's a good thing for these merchants, too. They don't live here, you see—some of them have homes the other side of town. If they were to take the time to set up and take down every day, they'd lose the best dealing hours—early morning and just before dark. So they leave their goods here, and have someone to watch them."

"Such an honorable looking bunch, too," Reandn said. "I bet anyone without one of this crew loses stuff by the cartloads."

Ania looked at him without comprehension, but added her own thought. "The horse dealer didn't have anyone there, Reandn. You might barter some of that price down with some night work. You don't have any place to stay—" and she stopped, putting a hand to her mouth.

"Tanager *is* a talkative fellow," Reandn remarked, more calmly than he expected it to come out. Ania blushed, barely discernible in the growing dusk. "But the suggestion's a sound one."

She didn't immediately respond; he could see the curiosity in her expression, and knew she was brimming with questions—*Where did you come from? Why is Farren interested in you?* And, probably, *What in Graces happened to your boots?*

"I'll make you a deal," Reandn said. "It's getting dark. I'll walk you home, and you can ask all the questions Tanager put in your head."

Ania said, "That's a deal?" Clearly she wondered what was in it for him.

He grinned at her. "I didn't say I'd give you any answers."

Chapter 7

Reandn spent the night under the trees between town and the market, and rose up soaked with dew. He found a creek and splashed his face and upper body as clean as it would get without soap, and headed for the market, ignoring his stiff body and sore feet. A clammy morning mist still hung about the land, but it was already warm enough that he once more removed his shirt.

He arrived at the market before most of the merchants. The tents and stalls were shrouded in mist, but he heard the remarkably unsavory laughter of the guards and stopped to locate them. They hung together in several clumps, and were not, as far as Reandn could tell, at all concerned about the wares they were supposed to be guarding. Nor did they seem interested in the horse that wandered the grounds, spooking at every bit of strangeness it could see and snorting at everything else. Reandn shook his head—*idiots*—and appropriated the corner tie from an unattended kiosk; he wasn't surprised when that got their attention quick enough. A short low laugh, a few mutters of agreement, and they shifted toward him. "Leave the horse be," one of them growled, a hostile suggestion.

"I'm just saving you the trouble of picking up after him," Reandn said, flipping the end of the rope in a loop to start a bowline knot. Behind him, several horses trotted into the market, their owners engaged in conversation, loud over the hoofbeats of their mounts.

The men hesitated, and then one of them shook his head; they all stopped. "Maybe you are at that," the man who'd stopped them said. "But don't make it a habit to butt in around here. We take care of things."

"I can see that," Reandn said wryly. While the first merchants efficiently turned away their cover tarps, he spoke soothingly to the skittish horse, approaching it in a game of touch-and-go. Finally he touched its shoulder, and worked his hand up its neck, scratching companionably as he went. Then the rope was around its neck, through the bowline loop, and back across its nose, leaving just enough to serve as a lead under the chin of the makeshift halter.

For a moment, the horse held its head high, air rattling through its nose. Then, decision made, it followed his gentle tug. Reandn led it through the largely unoccupied market to the stock area, ignoring the few rude remarks that followed him.

The circles of tie rails were empty, save for one hastily secured animal that tested its bonds with careful, experienced teeth. That one would need retying, or it would be the next runaway. It was easy enough to see where Reandn's stray belonged. The corral was full, the gate closed, but the horses—including the scarred bay— were milling and nervous. As Reandn watched, the dealer approached with a haltered runaway and carefully maneuvered it through a barely opened gate to join its fellows.

"One more," Reandn offered, yet unnoticed.

The man started, but his alarmed expression turned to relief when he saw Reandn holding his horse. "Ardrith's Graces," the man said, opening the gate again. Reandn released the horse, which gladly bolted to the security of its companions. "The last," the man added with satisfaction, only then looking at Reandn's face. "I knew you'd be back for that bay!"

"It seems I'm lucky he's still here," Reandn said dryly.

A frown crossed the man's square face, settling in amongst his jowl. "My father always said the trading business wasn't fun and games. I'm beginning to believe him."

"You've done well to avoid the lesson so long," Reandn said. "The guards have something to do with it?"

The man hesitated, looked away. "It's market business," he said. "Do you want to talk about that gelding, or not?"

Reandn found the horse in the settling herd. Still excited, it strutted across the enclosure with its chin tucked to its chest, grunting to itself. "Gelding, huh. Then someone left it entire too damn long. I don't suppose you know how old it was when it was cut."

"No idea," the man said, agreeably enough.

"Gonna be hard to unload him if he acts like that. I think I'll just wait for the price to go down, when you're tired of throwing hay down his belly." Reandn put a foot on the lower rail of the enclosure, watching as the horse, ignored by the others, settled.

"You came out here this early to tell me that?" The dealer looked askance at him. "I've got other matters to deal with, then. Don't need you taking up what time I have before real customers start coming around. My thanks for your help."

"It's not the only help I can offer you," Reandn said. He rested his chin on the hand that gripped the top rail and watched the horses rearrange their priorities, foregoing their fussing to crowd around the empty wooden hayrack.

The dealer was heading away when he realized what Reandn had said; he stopped short. "You don't know anything about it," he said, but there was hope beneath the hard tone in his voice.

"If you'd had a man here, like the rest of them, this wouldn't have happened."

"You volunteering?" the merchant asked dryly.

"*Volunteering*, no. I'm worth more than that. Let's say barter. My work for the bay."

For a moment, the shorter man seemed to be considering, but he shook his head. "It's tempting," he said, "but no. You haven't the faintest idea what this is really all about."

"Suppose you tell me. Then we'll decide. If I don't hire on, I'll forget what I hear."

"You'd better. It's market business." The man hooked his foot over the rail to mirror Reandn, and glanced around to see that they were still alone at this end of the market. "I think you've pretty much guessed it." The man stopped, rubbing his hand over his chin, obviously choosing his words. "The Minor knows nothing about this, and we've got to keep it that way. The men and women you've seen standing watch on market goods are far from professional guards—"

"They look like they've got more experience as the opposition," Reandn observed, glancing away from the horses to watch the dealer's face. The expression he saw confirmed his conjecture: dismay, and a certain amount of hopelessness.

"It didn't start out badly," the dealer said. "We were all losing things, just little bits and pieces. At the time we had a few men we'd all hired together, to watch over the entire camp. But it was too much of a job for them. They could stop the outright theft, but not the pilfering. That's when this man Shuyler made us an offer—if we put one of his men on every tent, he'd charge us much less than it would cost if we went out and hired each man individually. Looking back, it seems like we should have realized the deal was no good, especially when he made it plain he wouldn't be responsible for those of us who didn't participate."

"Any merchant should know a deal that's too good to be true, usually is."

"Like your offer to stand watch for me in return for a scarred up, studdy bay?" the man said dryly.

"That's no deal yet." Reandn shrugged. "Let's wait until we settle just how long I'm willing to work in return for the scarred up, studdy bay. I haven't even ridden the horse yet."

The man grunted. "The whole conversation is foolishness," he said. "But then, I'm a fool. I sent my guard packing two nights ago. He was sleeping through his watch when he wasn't borrowing a horse to spend an hour or two in the low-water section of town. I'll pay no man for a job he's not doing, but they're paying *me*, now, and will, until I use their *protection* again. I tried to hire an outsider, but they chased him off in a night. He looked to be as good a man as you."

"Maybe he was, maybe he wasn't." Reandn moved to avoid the wet questing snuffle of a mare who'd just taken a drink. He straightened her forelock and scratched around her ears while the horse dealer contemplated his situation.

"It wasn't so bad, at first," he said reflectively. "We realized what we were into a month or so after we made the arrangement. We met about it, and agreed the pilfering was less than when we had no guards at all, and that it seemed safer just to go along."

"And now it's been some time, and they're getting a little bolder. Raised their fees a few times. Grown careless about keeping up appearances." Reandn gave the mare a final pat and pushed her head away, straightening to face the dealer, whose dour expression confirmed his words. "Meanwhile, I hear robberies on the roads have increased, and the Locals haven't been able to track down any of the brigands."

"I don't know about the last," the man admitted.

"You would, if your merchants' organization was working with the Locals instead of trying to handle this on their own. Whatever problems you have with the Locals, they're under Savill's watch, and he wants this place clean. That should speak for them."

The dealer's face set in a stubborn expression. "We got into this on our own, and we'll get out of it on our own."

Too embarrassed to go to the Locals, more likely. Until things got worse—as they inevitably would.

"Now you know," the dealer said. "Do you still want to stand watch for me, for the sake of the bay?"

"Let's try him," Reandn said.

The man gave him an even, unreadable look. "There are better animals in that corral, if you don't like the bay. The deal doesn't have to hinge on him."

"I can't stay here long enough to pay for one of the better animals," Reandn said bluntly, following it up with a short, single shake of his head as the man opened his mouth. "Part of the deal—I don't answer those sorts of questions."

Nimbly changing words in midstride, the man said, "I'll get his gear."

Reandn waited by the gate while the merchant actually did quite a bit more. He forked out a copious amount of hay for the horses, who were starting to get crabby at the hayrack. He opened the little tack shed off the hay storage and propped up the awning that shaded the doorway, and then unshuttered the window. At last he emerged with bridle and saddle in tow. Flinging the saddle over the top rail, he handed the bridle to Reandn.

"There you are," he said. "If I'm to have you around my stock, I'll want to see how you handle them. So suppose you go in there and get him."

"Without boots?" Reandn said, and shook his head. The dealer eyed Reandn's feet in surprise, but this time closed his mouth on his question himself. Without comment, he grabbed the rope that hung over a post and slipped into the corral, threading his way through the horses, touching backs and shoulders and hissing reassuringly through his teeth until he came to the bay. He slid the rope around the horse's neck, high up behind the jaw, and led it out to Reandn.

The bay rolled an eye as Reandn lifted the bridle, but his mouth was full of hay and the menacing aura he was trying to project failed outright. His flattened ears only made the bridle easier to pull on, and most of his attention was on trying to recapture the hay he was losing around the bit. Reandn pressed the reins into the merchant's hand so he could saddle the horse.

Careful as he was, the bay still humped up his back and raised a threatening hind foot as the girth tightened against him. Reandn left it and moved to the horse's head, aware of the merchant's sharp eyes.

"Do you put all your hirelings through this little routine?" Reandn asked, meeting those eyes with a sharp grey gaze of his own. The horse was a test of sorts, there was no doubt about that. He lifted the bay's lips to check his teeth, satisfied to find the horse was under seven.

"No," the man said, and his smile showed crooked teeth. "Just the ones who seem to think they have mettle."

The horse pulled away from Reandn's examination; he took the reins and walked it in a few circles. "If I get up after he kicks the fire out of me, I've got mettle, is that it?" He raised a sardonic eyebrow at the dealer, eased the girth tighter, and circled the other direction.

"Keeping him from kicking you is a pretty good sign, too," the man said, not the least disturbed with Reandn's annoyance. The look on his face said he was still waiting. Reandn eyed him, and gave the girth a final tug. Then, with one last look at the unfamiliar Southern-style saddle and bit, he aimed the horse toward the road out of town, and mounted.

Whups, here we go! The horse exploded into motion, giving an exuberant crow-hop and taking off at top speed, and Reandn almost fell off out of sheer surprise at the unexpected feel of the motion. He'd been ready to sit a gallop or a bout of bucking—the dealer's face had told him that much. Instead the horse rocked beneath him, a swift rolling motion accompanied by an almost even four-beating pattern of hooves, and moving as fast as any swift canter. *What the Hells?*

But once he caught the rhythm, the movement was easy enough to sit. Reandn settled deeply into the saddle, decided they'd gone far enough, and gathered the loose reins. In response, the bay raised its head high in the air and moved even faster.

All right then. He didn't have any appointments to keep, the road was smooth enough, and the bay wasn't heading for any trees. Reandn let it run—or whatever it was doing—until its breathing grew labored. Then he stiffened his back against the horse's movement and tightened his fingers, a mere flex of the rein. Two furry black ears swiveled back to think about him.

"Easy," Reandn told the ears, repeating the reassurance in a soothing murmur. Abruptly, the bay's head came down from its sky gazing position, tucking in to its chest; still they traveled at full speed.

Might as well give it a try. . . . Keeping his voice low, Reandn asked the horse for a "whoa," and nearly went over the bay's head when it did just that. Blowing, bobbing its head and chewing on the bit, it flicked anxious ears at him while the first of the morning's traffic met them on the way to market. "I see," Reandn said, and took a deep breath. "Now we're starting to understand one another."

With the slightest twitch of his fingers, the easiest shift of his weight, Reandn suggested the horse turn around and walk back to the market. In halting steps, nodding anxiously, the horse did as requested, curling his neck up tight even though the reins were loose. "Relax," Reandn told it, and asked for a trot. To his surprise, the bay gave a weird hop and hit the same rocking gait as before—albeit at a more reasonable speed. They arrived back at the corral in a much more dignified manner than their departure, where Reandn verbally stopped the horse and dropped the reins against its lathered neck to stare at the dealer. "The first thing we do," he said flatly, "is get him a different bit. One he won't run from."

"Then . . . you want him," the man said, in flat disbelief.

"If he's shown me the worst of it, he'll do." He patted the horse's wet shoulder and straightened a bit of mane. "So, do you want to talk about it, now that I've made it back here in one piece?"

The dealer shrugged. "It's a good way to judge a man, the way he reacts to a scared horse. With his gait I didn't figure you'd hit the ground."

"I almost fell off from surprise. Never felt anything like it." Reandn dismounted and went to check the bay's mouth more carefully. The bay tossed his head away from the inspection, flinging foam and spit on both men.

The dealer made a face and wiped his sleeve off. "You *are* green to the area," he said. "And you must have come over water if you didn't run into one of these saddle horses on the trip down. They're fairly common here, and that gait's called a rack. Once you've tried it, you'll never go back to your northern-bred trotters."

"I'll have to go North to have the opportunity," Reandn said. "Which I won't be doing on this horse unless we can come to an agreement."

"Three weeks' watch for the horse," the dealer said promptly.

Reandn laughed. "You figure I won't last that long.

Think you'll get some work out of me and then hang on to the horse as well."

The man contrived to look offended. "Two silvers in three weeks is damn good pay for night watch."

I'll walk out of here barefoot before I wait that long. "Assuming the horse is worth two silvers, and the work's routine, you're right. Neither is true." Reandn gave the man space to disagree, but the dealer was silent. "I want him in two weeks, plus his gear. You bring along some of your breakfast and lunch for me, and let me sleep the morning in your shed."

"Breakfast and lunch!" the man repeated, taken by surprise at the request.

Reandn grinned at him. "Think about it, trader. If I last the two weeks, it may be enough to inspire your friends to do something about Shuyler, as well. If not, you lose nothing—but don't make this deal unless you're prepared to keep it, because I intend to leave here in two weeks on the back of that horse."

The merchant stepped back, eyeing him as an experienced man examines stock he is preparing to buy. However he'd gotten into his mess, there was no foolishness in his gaze now. "What makes you so sure you'll last even one night?" he said, apparently not impressed by Reandn's relaxed carriage and average size.

Reandn's grin turned feral. "I am a Wolf, meir. I know what I can do."

The man's gaze went to the crest on Reandn's vest, widening for an instant as he placed it; his eyes skipped over the leather lacing of rank over the crest without recognition; just as well. "So," he said, and turned away, his face thoughtful.

He looked back out into the corral, watching his threatened livelihood as it settled into patient horseflesh, stomping a leg in protest of flies here, flapping a mane there. "So," the man repeated. "My name is Bergren. I believe we've come to an agreement."

"Be sure," Reandn said. "Things could get interesting before these two weeks are over."

The man shook his head. "I'm sure."

Reandn nodded, and patted the bay's shoulder. "I'll be back this evening, then. I want this horse ready to go. Muffle his feet, and in the name of Ardrith, get me a different bit for him. A jointed bit, without shanks."

Bergren hesitated, but at Reandn's hard look, nodded. Then his gaze traveled down Reandn's legs to stop at his dusty feet, flicking upwards again, looking away to keep his thoughts to himself.

"I've just now made a deal for a horse," Reandn said, irritated. "I'll get to the boots eventually."

He left Bergren holding the bay's reins. Reandn turned back after he'd gone just a few steps—and in the corner of his eye, saw the movement by the edge of Bergren's pavilion flutter a long morning shadow across the dusty ground and slink away. *Something to keep in mind.*

"Bergren—" he said, catching the man's eyes again, holding them for a moment. "We know each other's secrets now. You let out that I'm a Wolf, and I give this whole thing to the Locals."

"I think we understand one another," Bergren said stiffly, his fingers clutching the bay's reins like a man who's waded into deep water and needs something to hold on to. He'd keep the information to himself, Reandn thought. Although for all he knew, it might not matter; Farren might even now be spreading his Wolf status throughout all of Maurant. But he didn't think so; the wizard wanted something from him, and would probably try to stay on his good side until he got it.

Reandn stopped by the pavilion as he left, casting a quick eye on the scuffed imprints in the soft dirt there. He looked at the tie circles, where Tanager was now

busy, a customer's horse at either side. But they were
the only two horses besides Bergren's, and they had just
arrived. He wondered how just much Tanager had heard.

Reandn set his feet on the road back to town, and
the dusty toes Bergren had stared at were glad it was
only a mile to the main streets of Maurant. With the
new roads he had learned from Ania, it was only a short
distance further to the *Forgotten Unicorn*, where he could
find a meal big enough to last him through the day—
for he had only a few more parscores, not even an entire
silver, to last him. Too bad he wasn't prepared to use
his stealth skills in thievery. At one time he might have,
but that was certainly before Adela had gotten hold of
him.

Adela. His steady stride faltered; he stopped in the
middle of the pine-lined road, choking in grief. *That's
enough*, he told himself. *It'll only cloud your mind.* He
had other things to do, more important things—things
that would take him back to Ronsin and revenge. It was
his own image of himself that finally bought him control—
red-eyed, unshaven, unwashed, standing in the middle
of the road with tears on his face. Big bad Wolf.

He scrubbed his face with his hands and started to
really think again. Bergren knew he was a Wolf, and so
did Farren's family. Each seemed to have their own
interest in keeping that knowledge to themselves, but
there was no reason to chance further discovery. He took
off his vest and sat on a protruding pine root by the
edge of the road, then began to remove the most obvious
clue to his identity.

It was slow, working the tip of his small boot knife
between the stitches that held the crest on. But every
tiny, carefully placed stitch of bright thread on the patch
was Adela's handiwork, and he wouldn't see it damaged.
When he finally eased the crest away from the leather,

the unweathered spot was obvious, but not so obvious as the emblem itself. In time the leather would darken and the stitch holes would close. He shoved the patch in the sleeve of his shirt and tied a knot at the wrist so it wouldn't come out. Then he pulled out the leather lacing of his rank. The holes punched for the lacing would hardly "heal" like Adela's fine stitches, but even a Local would have trouble recognizing his rank without the lacing. He put on the vest, picked up the shirt, and resolutely headed for town.

When he and his empty stomach arrived at the *Unicorn*, Hurley was back at the door, loitering into the street up to the edges of the shade. His expression upon seeing Reandn was almost welcoming, but he shook his head when it became obvious Reandn was heading for the tavern's entrance. "Not open yet."

"Then why are you watching the door?" Reandn asked, trying to keep his voice reasonable. Every smart Wolf knows that sometimes survival means not fighting at all— even a Wolf with a temper.

"You saying I'm lying?"

Reandn remembered, with an inward sigh, what Ania had said about the big man's penchant for picking victims and then picking a fight. And the grief inside him reawoke, curling into tendrils of anger and looking for outlet. "I'm saying," he replied, far too evenly, "that I'm hungry." Beyond Hurley, he could see figures moving around inside the *Unicorn*. His stomach growled. "Looks to me like you just opened up. Going to let me in?"

"I don't think I want to," Hurley said, with evidence in his expression that he'd given the decision great thought.

"Hurley." Ania poked her head out the door, apparently endowed with a sixth sense when it came time for the big man to make trouble. Her voice held the same tone the Keep Houndmaster used with misbehaving puppies.

"If you're bored I'm sure Kelton can find more chores for you."

"Leave off, Ania," Hurley said, in a dead voice devoid of reason.

Ania turned to Reandn, but hesitated, taken aback at what she saw on his face. "Reandn," she said, and her voice now held a note of pleading. "Just let me get Kelton—he can handle this. Hurley, you big oaf, why don't you just go down and pick yourself a fight on the docks? Oh, Dark Lady—" She plunged back into the *Unicorn*, probably in quest of the tavern's owner.

Saxe would have marveled, Reandn thought, that the peace between Wolf and guard had lasted this long. Sweat trickled down his back as he stood at bay in the direct sunlight; he'd had enough, on all counts. He took a step forward. "I'm hungry. The *Unicorn's* open. Are you going to let me in?"

With anticipation, Hurley matched that step; his expression was eager.

"Back off," Reandn told the big man, growling the deep notes. Final warning.

"Troublemaker!" Hurley said gladly, and lunged.

Reandn met him, ducked the grasp of two arms intent on crushing him, rammed the heel of his hand under the man's chin and slipped away. No prolonging this one, not with his stamina so low. He caught an arm as it flailed for balance, twisted it quickly up and behind, and dropped Hurley with a kick behind the knee. The crack was unmistakable, and still he used the broken arm to drive the man into the cobbles, where his head hit in a second crack, quickly muffled by the deadened thud of the bulky body against the ground.

Silence. It had taken only seconds. Suddenly the hot, quiet street had more than its share of people, and Ania was one of them. Behind her was a short, big-chested and balding man who could only be Kelton; on the man's face was an eye-rolling look of exasperation. More disturbing, however, was the man now at Reandn's side, the one wearing a crest of the colorful flag of Maurant. A Local.

But worst of all, walking up the street with a face full of curiosity, was Farren's daughter Lina.

She stopped as the Local was harrumphing for attention, took in the scene, and fixed him with a withering stare. "I suppose you're responsible for this," she said coldly.

"That's what I'd like to know," the Local said, giving Reandn an implacable stare. He was a man weathered by sun and age, with a spare frame and an expression that said he was not interested in any nonsense.

Ania frowned at the Local, but couldn't get her mouth open before Kelton, who said, "Of course he's not, meir. Of all the times Hurley's fought, you never asked before. You know he's the one who starts these things."

The man rubbed thoughtfully at the slight tobacco stain at the corner of his mouth and said, "True enough. But then again, Hurley's always won. Didn't think he'd pick a fight he couldn't win."

Kelton looked sourly at his injured employee, who was beginning to stir, huff and moan. "I'm sure the outcome was a complete surprise to him," he said dryly. "You don't suppose we could forego the usual time in the cells? He'll need some care—and you might say he's had punishment enough."

The Local's lips closed tightly over his stained teeth as he looked from Hurley to Reandn, raking the Wolf with a one-stare assessment. "I'll agree with you there. And you—" he said to Reandn, "ought to know we don't tolerate this kind of thing here. If it happens again, things'll end differently."

"Now, wait," Ania said, continuing although Kelton's hand landed lightly on her shoulder. "He wasn't at fault—"

"Never mind," Reandn interrupted, earning her startled gaze. He'd understood the message. The Local had seen what he'd done and was letting Reandn know he was not to unleash his skill—or temper—again. He met the man's narrowed gaze and nodded; the Local gave a short nod in return, and, satisfied, stepped out of the circle of people.

"I'll send Rierdon to see to him," he told Kelton. "Best bone-setter in town."

Kelton knelt at the big man's side and said firmly, "Be still," when Hurley stirred. He called after the Local, "Make sure he brings several stout men with him."

Reandn edged past his fallen opponent, out of the reach of Lina and other too-curious eyes. "Come for a meal?" Ania said, at his side.

"Didn't come for the fight," Reandn said shortly. "I'm even hungry enough to eat fish, if I'm still welcome in here."

Her mouth twisted slightly. "I told you yesterday, we can't blame our customers for what Hurley does. Or at least, I said something like that. You look better today. Did you go back to see the horse you liked?" She looked back at him as she led him inside, and laughed wryly. "Never mind. My mouth moves almost as quick as you Northies' when I get upset. You find yourself a table, and Melly or I'll be along directly to see what you want."

Reandn went to the corner he'd used the day before, found it unoccupied and sat with his back to the wall. Still, as he stared at his toes, replaying the fight in his mind—automatically preparing his defenses for Saxe— he was not prepared for the confrontation that found its way to his table.

"Brutal!" came the declaration in Lina's voice. His shirt, forgotten in the street, settled on the table in a sigh of material. Reandn slowly moved his gaze from his feet to Lina's face.

"When a man starts trouble, he's got to take what it brings him," he said flatly.

"Some are just as good at running away," she said, matching his tone. Her face was expressionless, her eyes cold.

"You've had Tanager follow me, came all the way down here, just so you could say that to me?" he asked, honest surprise coloring his voice. "Well, I hope you feel the better for it."

"I came," she said, annunciating each word clearly and inviting herself to sit at the table, "to see if you wouldn't reconsider talking to Pa-farren. And to give you these." She pushed a pile of leather under the table with her foot. "They were my husband's. Tanager wore them for a short while but outgrew them—and they're of a size with the ones you left."

He glanced under the table. "You think you can buy my answers with boots?"

Her lips pressed together in a thin line, a faint flush reddening her cheeks and forehead. "They were a reason to come and try to talk to you," she said shortly.

Reandn withdrew his outstretched feet, leaned over the table on his elbows. "Lina," he said, "I have nothing to say to your father."

"Because he was a wizard."

"I've had this discussion with Tanager," he replied shortly, "although I imagine you already know that."

"Yes, I do," she flared. "But my father is a good man, no matter what his avocation was—or is. You can't go around distrusting everyone who worked in magic. Or do you have a little fetish about other people, too? How do you feel about barbers? Or sailors?"

"I've a hard spot in my heart for men who guard tavern entrances, and pushy women," Reandn said suddenly, fiercely. She withdrew slightly, surprised, sudden apprehension on her face.

"But—" she started, and forced herself to continue, her voice low and earnest instead of filled with anger, "he's only trying to help, Reandn. And there is no magic left to fear."

His eyes narrowed. "Then how did I get here, meira?" he hissed, his hand shooting out to grip her wrist. "Pretty substantial grip for a man who's living in King's Keep, wouldn't you say?" He dropped her wrist to snatch his crumpled shirt; she drew back uncertainly as he thrust it at her, displaying the fine sewn seams. *Adela-sewn.* "How does a woman fade away to nothing but my memories, meira? You can tell *Pa-farren* I know all about wizard's magic, and I'll have no more of it!" He dropped the shirt with the same finality as he'd dropped her wrist, and leaned back in the chair, his glare defying her to answer.

Her hands shook as she deliberately rested them on the table; one finger touched the shirt seemingly despite itself. "I don't understand what you're saying," she said, her voice carefully even; her gaze flicked to his hands.

He looked down to find his thumb rubbing against the ring on his little finger. His eyes closed tightly against the sight, and against the sudden rush of emotion. *DelaDelaDela* his heart cried, sad little whispers of loss; he fought for composure. Without opening his eyes he said harshly, "You don't have to understand. Just leave me alone."

Her chair scraped as she pushed it back. When he was able to open his eyes, she was gone, and he was alone again. He saw with dull surprise that she had left the boots, and he pulled them on without thinking about it, noting their fit with only a small part of his mind. His thoughts were divided, pervaded with mourning, tangled in Lina's words.

It was tempting to think he could have an ally armed with a wizard's knowledge, someone who could deal with

Ronsin on even terms. But his distrust was real, and solid, and it hung on Pa-farren's profession that he was no longer a wizard—that magic no longer existed in this world.

For Reandn knew differently. Of all his memories from the confusing fugue state after his arrival here, one of the clearest was that moment when the pressure of magic rang in his ears. And a wizard who lied about magic could be trusted with nothing.

He wished he'd had more experience with the men of magic—he had no notion of how they drew on their skills. When Reandn was fighting, stalking, or trailing, he was there for anyone with eyes to see and understand. But Ronsin had just stood there, fingers tracing patterns in the air—first holding Adela in place, then melting her away—and then taking Reandn himself, and tossing him South. There could be no predicting what a wizard would do, and when he would do it. The very thought of facing down the wizard made a sudden chill run down his back—and then another one, when he realized that was exactly what he was fighting so hard to do.

"Are you all right?" Ania asked, arriving at the table. "Hurley didn't hurt you, did he?"

"He hardly had the time," Kelton said, coming up behind her.

Reandn took a deep breath and tried to bury his thoughts. "I'm fine," he said, and looked at Ania. "Why don't you bring me whatever the kitchen's got the most of, tonight."

"But we've got four different things to choose from," Ania protested helpfully.

"Then you choose," Reandn told her. She looked from his serious expression to Kelton's equally grim face, and forced a smile. "You'll just have to wait and see, then," she said, as she turned away from the table, leaving the two men with no buffer.

Kelton took a good long look at him, and Reandn knew what he saw. A man with long, getting-greasy hair, and a rivulet of sweat running from his temple and down his face. No doubt he had circles under his eyes and that slightly wild look that stood him in good stead when it came to backing down the rowdies.

But there must have been something else, too, for Kelton's demeanor changed subtly, his stance becoming almost imperceptibly less aggressive—though his words were hardly cowed. "I wish you'd let me handle that."

"I've never been good at letting people push me around," Reandn replied, and there was no apology in his voice.

"In another moment I would have had him in hand," Kelton insisted.

"He rushed me," Reandn said with some heat. "He wanted to do it from the first time he saw me. Did you want me to let him break a few ribs while I was *waiting*?"

Kelton gave him another long look. "You knew you could take him," he said quietly.

Reandn hesitated, not quite sure if it was a question, and what that question was. "If I didn't make any mistakes," he answered finally.

Kelton scratched his chin and looked away, glancing back as he said, "That arm's a bad break. He'll be unable to work for weeks."

"If you make it a habit to pick on strangers, sooner or later you're going to meet someone better than you. If Hurley's too simple to understand that, you should keep him on a chain."

A pause. "You may be right. But I'm coming at this sideways. In one short fight, you've gained a reputation as the man who beat Hurley. If you're going to be staying in the area, you might consider taking his place until he heals."

No. I'm not staying. But Reandn pushed away the powerful reaction and thought about it instead. It wouldn't do much for his anonymity—but he still needed funds. Working the market and the tavern wouldn't be easy, either. *Only for a little while. Two weeks at the most.* "What're the terms?"

"Room, board, and one parscore a week."

"No room, one supper a day, and four parscores a week," Reandn countered immediately.

Kelton raised an eyebrow, lowered it thoughtfully, and squinted one eye. "Three parscores," he said at last.

"And dibs on the red meat," Reandn added with finality. "And . . . I may leave without warning. It's part of the deal."

"You done something I should know about?" Kelton asked sharply.

Reandn shook his head. "No. But I have something I need to *do*."

The proprietor nodded after a moment. "Start today. We open midmorning, close around sunset, this time of year. You've got basically one duty—no one drunk comes in here, and no gangs. No whores, either."

"I expect I can handle any of those," Reandn said. "But I'll be leaving shortly before you close. I've got other responsibilities."

Kelton frowned, his mouth opening to dicker a protest.

Reandn cut him off. "It's a previous commitment. I'm standing by it." He raised an eyebrow which said *it's your move*.

After a calculated moment, Kelton gave an exaggerated sigh and nodded, touching his heart in the Northern signal of sealing a deal. Surprised by the courtesy, Reandn returned the gesture. As Kelton left for the kitchen, Reandn leaned back against the wall to pick up the threads of his interrupted contemplation. Instead he found himself wincing at what Saxe would have said about double shift guard duty. He might as well have been a Hound.

Well, it wouldn't be for long. He had only one priority now, and this was but a means to the end. Ronsin. The name rumbled through his brain in a constant counterpoint to the call of Adela's sweet contralto. He thought it likely that before much more time passed, Tenaebra would welcome them all in her realm of violent death—and the frightening thing was, he wasn't sure that bothered him.

Chapter 8

Standing watch over the *Unicorn's* entrance that afternoon was a more difficult task than Reandn had anticipated. His feet chafed in the unfamiliar boots, and the heat dragged at him. Many a patron gave him a suspicious look, and others were downright annoyed, as though finding Reandn in Hurley's spot had somehow destroyed the order of their lives. If Kelton hadn't sent him to a back room to shave and make liberal use of a basin of warm water, he supposed he would have been an outright scandal.

As the day started to cool and the customers slackened, Reandn raided the kitchen for scraps. He waited for the third quarter-bell and bid goodnight to Kelton, Ania, and Melly, heading for the outskirts of town with long strides.

The market still thronged with buyers when he arrived; the mock guards hadn't yet arrived. Bergren was talking to a young woman who held the lead rope of a goose-rumped pack horse, and driving a hard bargain, by the look on her face. Bergren's quick trader-talk didn't falter as he saw Reandn, but his eyes relaxed, and his face held relief.

The bay waited with moderate patience, tied at the outside of the corral with a loose halter over his bridle, snapping at flies—or trying to, since the lead rope brought him up short. Stomping a leg in irritation, he laid his ears back at no one in particular to let the world know he was mad. Reandn gave him a commiserating pat on the rump and went into Bergren's tack and fodder shed, where he rummaged up a couple of small canvas sacks and an old piece of supple leather. By the time Bergren finished with the girl, loosed the new horse into the corral, and caught up with Reandn, one sack held a supply of rocks; the other, a cache of sun-dried horse droppings. Reandn sat on a short basket-weave stool with his back against the shed. Bergren looked at him askance, hands on hips.

"Have you got an awl?" Reandn asked, unconcerned about his employer's expression.

Frown still in place, the merchant walked noisily past Reandn, made a great deal of commotion inside the shed, and returned with the tool. "Here," he grunted, holding the awl out next to Reandn's head. "Now, suppose you let me in on this. I'll never sell that bag in this condition."

"Probably not," Reandn agreed, placing the leather against the wood frame of the stool between his knees and applying the awl. "But it's going to help save your business, so I wouldn't begrudge its loss."

Bergren's frown made his jowls grow tenfold. "I don't see how."

"I think it'll be a surprise to them, too," Reandn said laconically, and Bergren had the sense to leave it at that. He merely nodded when Reandn asked him to take the bay to the hitching circle. A glance showed it to be much happier there, with other horses' tails at work on the flies as well as his own. Besides, he didn't want the guards to take any special notice of the bay, as they might if he stood alone outside the corral.

Reandn finished with the sling he was fashioning, and knotted the bag ties together so he could carry them over one shoulder. Checking to see that none of the market guards were around, he headed away from the market bustle and into the surrounding woods.

The heavy sack ties bit deeply into his shoulder, and he didn't carry them far. They'd be lighter soon enough. Just inside the tree line, he dropped the bags, shook his shoulder loose, and took a careful look around.

Bergren's setup was only about two hundred feet away, and deep in the evening shade from the trees he was now under. They were unfamiliar pines, decked with long, soft needles. At King's Keep, the pines had scrubby needles, sappy prickles that threatened any creature within range. These tall, straight trees were bereft of lower branches, aside from the few dead limbs that jutted out to snag the unwary. Their crowns swayed in the breeze, keeping up a constant whisper, although the air beneath the pines was still.

For that matter, that breeze somehow seldom made it to ground level in Maurant, though Reandn would have welcomed anything that stirred the muggy air.

Reandn walked part of the roughly circular market perimeter, clearing the larger branches out of his path. Underfoot, the needle-covered ground cushioned his feet, though there were plenty of dry branches for the careless to step on; he tossed aside many of these as well. At the edge of the forest were the young pines, no taller than he was; they brushed him with their long needles in a gentle caress that was almost like a welcome. Unless he moved too swiftly and left their branches swaying, they would hide him from anyone in the market area.

When he was at the edge of sling range from Bergren's area, he stopped, dropped to his haunches and stared thoughtfully at the dusky marketplace. Convenient of them, he decided, to have arranged the stock area out on a little point away from the other booths and tents. He could approach it unseen from two-thirds of its perimeter. Quietly, he made his way back to the canvas bags.

As the market emptied and the guards arrived, it quickly turned into a dark night, thick with clouds that the quarter-moon could not hope to pierce. He'd been hoping for more visibility, but then, what he couldn't see, neither could they. When darkness had fully fallen, Reandn abandoned the woods, creeping toward the horses to stand watch. It didn't take long.

Without a care in the world, two of the men fumbled toward the corral, carrying only a dim candle lamp. Reandn smiled. With the lamp blinding their night vision, there was no way they'd be able to see him. He sent a clod of manure into the bunched herd, following it up with another as the startled horses scooted around inside the corral, snorting indignantly. Under the cover of their noise he crept closer, and loosed a rock toward the flickering lamp. The yelp that rang out declared a lucky shot, and in the fuss Reandn circled back around the corral, putting the lamp in line-of-sight from the opposite direction.

"G'wan, you're in my way," one of the men growled.

"I been hit by a rock!" the injured party protested. "I think my rib's broke!"

"One of the horses kicked something up," the impatient voice said. "Just get the gate and be done with it." One of the gate bars moved, a slide of wood against wood. In quick succession Reandn sent missiles at both men, and then into the horses; they milled nervously around in the corral, crowding the gate.

"What the Hells—" His previous victim, growing angry.

"Dark Lady," swore the other, dropping the candle lamp. It broke against the ground and left them in darkness; Reandn sent a few more clods at the noise they were still making.

"What's goin' on over there, boys?" one of the other guards hailed from the center of the market. "Hurry up, will you? We got things to do tonight."

"I'm not letting these nags out—they're all riled up! Or maybe you *want* to get run down in the dark!"

"Well, Tenaebra's tits, Rulf, what're you doin' to 'em?" the voice was closer now, and Reandn tracked the man's progress by his long, lazy strides. "Why'n the Hells did you put the lamp—"

Reandn let fly, and the man found out. The commotion brought reinforcements; by now they realized they were being deliberately taunted, mocked with missiles of horse manure. When they made an effort to approach the corral, he harried them with dangerous rocks rather than the softer, insulting clods, and kept the horses stirred up. He was lucky enough to knock one of the men senseless and after that they concentrated all their efforts on finding him. The rest of the night was spent in a tiring exercise of strike and run, with the darkness lending enough cover that Reandn was never driven to flee on the bay gelding.

When dawn came Reandn was safe in the pines, and the arriving merchants discovered harried, manure stained guards who were quick to depart. The marketplace was abuzz by the time Bergren arrived.

Reandn greeted him from the doorstep of the tack and feed shed, tired but pleased with the night's work— although he held no illusions it would continue to be so easy. For one thing, the moon was waxing, and would soon make it much harder to hide. And as soon as the guards realized their torment would continue night after night, they'd start making more serious efforts to find him.

And if they did find him, he wasn't likely to survive. Dying would reunite him with Adela, but Reandn had things to take care of first. No, this would be the easiest of his two weeks work. *But then I'm on the road, and Ronsin's none the wiser.*

Bergren stood amidst the corral full of horses and the unlikely number of manure clods laying about his sales

area, and raised a begrudgingly impressed eyebrow at
the Wolf. He thrust a canvas bag at Reandn and said,
"Breakfast. Don't get it mixed up with that other bag of
yours."

Reandn just grinned at him.

In the next two nights, Reandn had injured two more
men; one, he thought, had probably needed stitches,
and had certainly been concussed. He'd have to be more
careful. For now, the guards were more interested in
maintaining what little remained of their façade as law-
keepers instead of lawbreakers; for now, they weren't
ready to break out into the obvious. But if Reandn really
angered them, they'd bring in the manpower to chase
him off—while enough remained behind to tear down
Bergren's corrals, or hamstring a few horses, driving their
point home to Bergren and making Reandn's job of
protecting the horses impossible.

Then, of course, the rest of the merchants would
understand what they'd gotten into—and would be willing
to bring the Locals in on it. Each night was a hunt, although
it was never clear who was hunted and who was prey,
Reandn did his best not to tip the scales in his direction.
It was a tricky dance, and it took all his skills to avoid
capture. As the nights grew lighter, the chase became
more intense, and even as Reandn ran himself ragged,
he reveled in it. He was stuck in Maurant, earning himself
a horse, and the harder he had to work at it, the less energy
he had to chafe at the delay. *Eleven more days*, became
his chant. And *ten more days*, looking forward *nine*.

He was stirring up a mess, one the merchants would
have been wise to go to the Locals with. Their choice.
He just hoped Bergren—and the others—realized that
the pressure he applied to the guards would find other
ways to escape when attacks on Bergren's property and
efforts to find Reandn both failed.

Standing watch at the tavern was a much more difficult job than guarding the horses. Here, he had time to think, time to chafe, and to waver over his decision not to claim Wolf Rights. Ania came out to chat with him as often as she was able, although Melly, an easily frightened young woman, tended to stay out of his way. Kelton merely respected him and left him alone. Hurley had returned to take an hour's shift in the afternoon, his arm immobilized and swathed in bandages that turned immediately dingy. The man was in no condition to take the responsibility of watching the door, but Reandn understood Hurley's need to keep a suspicious eye on his place with the tavern. Besides, it gave him a chance to eat his afternoon meal without leaving the doorway empty.

He was sitting at his usual corner table, leaning back against the light blond wood, when the day started to go wrong. Some inner warning caused him to look up, and so he wasn't taken by surprise by Farren's arrival. Reandn's greeting was a cold stare.

Farren ignored it. "May I sit?"

Behind him, Melly approached, bearing two glasses of cool water. She heard the inquiry and looked to Reandn for the answer; he gave the barest of nods. Melly left the glasses while Farren pulled out the chair opposite Reandn.

"I don't want to talk to you," Reandn said abruptly.

Farren's eyebrows rose. "Then why did you tell me to sit?"

"Because if you went to the trouble to search me out, a simple *no* wouldn't have sent you away. Not for good. I'm hoping this will: I don't want to talk to you. Not now, and not ever. Go away." He took a sip of the sweet water and carefully set the glass back down in its sweat ring, watching the wizard from beneath dark brows and wondering what was hidden behind the handsome, aging face, and the light blue eyes that watched him back. Silently, he repeated his private litany. *Not long now.*

"Do you suppose," Farren said, "That we could at least pretend to have a civilized conversation? I'm only looking for the answers to a few questions, friend Wolf. Answers it won't harm you to give."

"That would mean something if I trusted you. I don't."

Farren frowned, and shook his head. "I really don't understand why. I've done nothing to earn your enmity since you got here—I took you in when you were sick, I left you your weapons, I made no attempt to keep you there."

"I'm sure you had your reasons."

The wizard took a deep breath, and closed his eyes. Reandn, it was clear, was getting to him. "I need to know the details of how you come to be in Maurant."

"I guess you have a problem."

"It's going to be everybody's problem if you don't start cooperating with me," Farren said in annoyance. "There's no magic left in the world, yet you pop from one end of Keland to the other. I need to know how that happened." He said it like he was used to saying things and having them happen.

Reandn snorted. "No magic left?" he said, his mind full of memory—of hands holding him down while Farren's magic raged around him. "I know better. It was magic that brought me here, and magic you used on me once I got here. Lies hardly begat trust, Farren."

"I *have not lied*," Farren said, anger flaring. Eyes that had been bright now darkened in the shadow of his lowered brows. "Lonely Hells, can't you see past your own petty concerns? Someone out there has power, and I *must* find out where it's coming from!"

Power. Reandn saw Ronsin's face, heard his words. *Justice is return of power*, and power had taken Kavan and Adela away. What would Farren do with it? Reandn looked across the table at Farren, and grinned, a dangerous expression. Startled, Farren's anger faded; he seemed to be looking at Reandn anew. *Wolf justice*, thought Reandn. *That's what waits for wizards who lie for their power.*

Farren opened his mouth, protest, no doubt—but whatever he might have said was lost in the shrill scream that filled the tavern. Reandn was on his feet before the sound faded, running toward it, shoving aside chairs and customers to reach the other side of the building, and discovering the delicate balance of madness versus sanity. He came to a stop so sudden someone bumped up behind him; he ignored it.

A young man sprawled on the floor against a table leg, arms splayed—and open-throated, cut so hard the gaping edges of his windpipe jutted into air. There were three horrified people on one side of the table, where an older man clutched his wife's arm and a young woman, her sooty eyes stark against a pale face, stared aghast at the dead man at her feet. A crimson path of blood etched across her forehead, eyebrow, and cheek; more had sprayed across the blond wood walls. It dripped from the sleeve of the fourth adult, a man backed against the wall, his expression crazed and his sticky knife pressing against a child's throat—a boy with wide, terrified eyes, whose sobs were stifled only because he was too stiff with fright to draw a decent breath.

Reandn raked a calculated gaze over the man's fine clothing, over his well-made knife with jewels sparkling under the bloodied hilt. Not a professional. He took a step forward.

"Get back," hissed the killer, shifting his grip on the boy, knuckles whitening around the knife.

"Nuri," moaned the woman, reaching for the child with a trembling hand. Her husband gathered it in again, holding her tightly, protectively, but could not stop her pleading. "Koby, let him go, oh, Bright Lady, *let him go.*"

"Let him go," Reandn repeated coldly, taking another step—mostly sideways, to get a better angle, but a little distance closed in there, too.

"I've already killed once!" Koby looked at his victim on the floor with anger, mad anger. He spat over the boy's head, scoring on the dead man's leg. "Come closer and Nuri dies too!" His eyes were wild, his gaze darting from Reandn to the kitchen door, and not missing it when Reandn eased forward. "I mean it! I'll kill this one, too!"

"You're not leaving here as long as you have him," Reandn said. "You want a hostage? Fine. Take me." Arms outspread, he took another step, a deliberate one. "You have me, and you've got the only person here who can stop you. You can get away. But you try to leave with that boy, and *I'll* kill *you.*" Behind him, Kelton's heavy footsteps pounded close, came to a stop. A softer approach was accompanied by Ania's gasp.

Koby's grip tightened, so hard the boy yelped. "You'd have to go through Nuri first," he said, uncertainty touching his voice.

Reandn grinned at him, challenge. "I can do that," he said. "The only way you're safe is if you have *me.* Now let the boy go." Another step, just barely close enough to touch. "Let the boy go, Koby. Or die right here."

Koby stared at him in disbelief. Then he shoved the boy, hard, and yanked at Reandn's outstretched wrist. Reandn allowed it, let himself be pulled into Koby's grip, the blade suddenly against his own throat. The odor of blood, thick on Koby's sleeve and hand, hit Reandn's nose like a threat; the man's chest heaved with his frightened panting. In front of Reandn, the patrons of the *Forgotten Unicorn* were frozen in a shocked tableau, with Ania clutching Kelton's arm directly before him, and Farren off to the side, quiet and self-possessed.

Koby trembled behind him. "Clear the kitchen!" he shouted, so suddenly they all flinched. The man's spittle sprayed Reandn's cheek, his arm trembled against Reandn's chest and throat. Losing control. Carefully, Reandn pushed against the pressure, increasing the force gradually, unnoticed, while Koby automatically compensated.

The *Unicorn's* kitchen crew were gathered at the doorway, hesitant; at Kelton's terse nod, they dashed from the room in a flurry of skirts and flashing white limbs, Damone's heavy tread the last of them. Koby immediately sidled toward the door, taking Reandn with him. Reandn, still pushing, moving just as fast as he had to, because he had no intention of going anywhere with this man. Because—

Abruptly he reversed his hold, pulling *with* Koby's push, taking control and twisting wildly aside as the knife slid up his neck, stopping for an instant against the bone of his jaw before skidding up along his face. Warm blood coursed down his skin, accompanied by Ania's short, horrified scream and his own strangely remote thought that he hadn't been agile enough, that it was his life's blood running down his chest. Yet he pivoted, bringing himself around to face Koby with the knife between them—and now at Koby's throat.

There they trembled, inches apart, while Reandn pushed, teeth bared, mind a haze of intent. Pushed harder.

A gentle presence at his side. *No, love. Leave him.* Startled, Reandn whirled, crying, "Adela?"

Hurley rushed in, latching onto Koby with a talon-fingered grip. Reandn left them there, taking another step toward a crowd that was suddenly noisy again, talking and crying and holding on to one another. "Adela?" he whispered.

No answer. Of course not. Had he really heard her? And why was he still on his feet? He looked down at his blood-soaked vest; as much as there was, it wasn't enough to kill him.

But it could have been. Almost blindly, he found one of the pillar supports for the *Unicorn's* high ceiling. Slumping against it, he stared at the knife; its red-rimmed blade cried accusations with his own blood. *He hadn't cared.* The hand began to shake. He'd been foolhardy—Hells, he'd nearly gotten himself killed—and even when he'd thought he had, he *hadn't cared*. Reandn slid down the pillar until his buttocks hit the floor, knees drawn up before him. Ania whisked by, the sobbing, sooty-eyed young woman enfolded in her arms; her eyes were wide, looking at him with amazement and uncertainty.

I'd have been with Adela.

The scullery boys brought in buckets and mops and immediately went after the drying blood on the floor planks; it'd take sanding, no doubt, to erase the stains completely.

Together. Together in Tenaebra.

The Locals arrived and marched briskly into the kitchen, causing a short outburst from the prisoner there. Weeping, the suddenly aged woman followed the body of her older son as two Locals carried it from the tavern.

Is it really so easy to let go of this life? Does Adela wait for me, or is it priestly nonsense?

Farren paused at a distance for careful consideration, then left without speaking. By some tacit agreement, no one confronted Reandn, no one asked what the Hells he thought he'd been doing. Which was just as well, for at the moment, he didn't have an answer.

No, not that easy. Not yet. There is still Ronsin. There, he'd found his focus again. Revenge. Ronsin was still alive, and that meant Reandn still had things to do in this world.

"Reandn," said Kelton, awkwardly crouching to touch Reandn's unsullied right shoulder. "Come, Reandn. Ania will wash your face."

Without comment, Reandn followed the proprietor to the kitchen. There was no longer any sign of Koby's presence, save Hurley, who hulked in a corner looking dangerous, broken arm or not. Looking, if possible, guilty—a fact which Reandn observed but did not make sense of.

Ania pointed to a stool, beside which was a hastily cleared cook-table laden with a basin, cloths, and a jar of salve. Reandn sat, then winced as she attacked his bloodied shoulder with a wet cloth. He could only hope she'd be more considerate when she reached the actual damage. At his expression, Ania's face softened, her movements gentled.

"You don't even know what it was all about, do you," she said. He couldn't shake his head while she worked but she continued anyway, talkative in her anxiety. "Koby—that's the man who cut you—has always had a liking for Ciandra. She never thought much of him, but his boat's always been a little unsteady. When she and Nelmar announced their betrothal, I guess it tipped over. They were in there making plans for a new house—that was Nelmar's family with them. And Hurley let Koby in, knowing it all!"

"I'd have done the same," Reandn said, trying not to flinch away from her unsteady hand.

"Maybe, but you wouldn't have known any different. And I'll bet you wouldn't have let that sea-foam-for-brains Koby in here today, anyway, the way he was acting." She worked carefully around his face, her lower lip caught between her teeth in concentration, her eyes reflecting her opinion of what she saw.

"If it was really bad," Reandn said at her expression, "I'd be dead. There's not a lot of leeway there."

Ania shook her head. "That was the craziest thing I've ever seen. Surely there was another way, Reandn!"

"The boy is safe, isn't he? The madman captured and sent away? What's the problem?" But he didn't meet her eyes. She was right.

She stepped back to look at him, taking another swipe at his vest as she moved. "The problem is, I'm not sure they took the madman away."

The problem was, she was probably right about that, too.

No. He knew better. He had priorities, and preserving his life no longer seemed to be right at the top. It'd be hard for him to understand that, were he in her shoes. The real problem was . . . what about Adela? Was she really waiting for him? Or would death, when it finally came, merely be another sort of separation.

"Reandn?" Ania asked, giving him a worried look; she dug two fingers into the salve and set the jar aside. She'd finished with her unpleasant task and he hadn't even noticed. When she saw she had his attention again, she said, "This is much too awkward to bandage, though I think that spot on your jaw needs a stitch. Otherwise, it's mostly . . . well, it looks like you've been skinned, there."

Reandn lifted the forgotten knife, which was nearly stuck to his hand with dried blood. "It's dull," he said. "You could tell by the way the light shone off it." True enough, if he'd actually thought to look.

"Wish I'd seen it," Hurley said. "Got there too late."

"I'm glad you didn't, you'd have plunged into the thick of it," Ania said firmly, smearing the salve on Reandn's face—*ouch, dammit*—and stepping back. She brandished the salve pot at Reandn and said, "I want you to put this on twice a day, and don't make me run after you to do it—otherwise that pretty face of yours might scar up."

Absently, Reandn said, "All right."

"*Reandn*," Ania said, capturing his attention once more. "Are you *sure* you're all right?"

He deliberately focused his attention back to her, finding her patiently holding the pot of salve out for him to take. He took it, held it, looked at it.

She gave him a pensive look and abruptly, brusquely, turned around and shoo'd Hurley out of the kitchen, with a great deal of arm waving that seemed the only way to convince the giant she was serious.

When she came back she stood squarely in front him and took his hand. He glanced up in surprise, and she said, "Reandn. What's wrong?"

He didn't respond, distracted by the throbbing of his face, distracted by answers that he could never tell her.

She shook his hands in gentle admonishment and said, "It's true we haven't known each other very long. But I'd like to think of myself as your friend. And, friend or not, it's obvious to me that you're bothered by what's happened. Dark Lady, it'd be strange *not* to be a little shook—no matter what you're used to getting into."

"*Dark Lady*," Reandn repeated, searching her face in the late afternoon gloom of the hot kitchen.

"Did I say that?" she asked, nonplused. "Well, it's not the best language, but I've certainly heard you use it often enough. That's hardly the issue."

To Reandn, it was. "What do they believe here, in the South?"

"You mean . . . Tenaebra and Ardrith? Hardly different than you Northies, I'd think."

Never a man to put much stock in the babbling of priests, suddenly Reandn found the wondering intolerable. "Do they say that even if your death comes from the different Sisters, you can find your loved ones on the borders of the death-worlds?"

"Borders?" Ania responded with some difficulty.

"Between Tenaebra's realm and Ardrith's," Reandn said impatiently. "What do they say about that down here? What do they say about the Lonely Hells?"

Ania regained her footing in the conversation and released Reandn's hand to step back and tilt her head at him. "To tell you the truth, it's a fairly private matter down here, Reandn. We get family schooling when we're young and after that, usually discuss things with our local priest. But . . ." She looked into his eyes, and seemed to relent.

He waited, finding it absurdly important that she confirm what little he knew, the bits he had picked up from more privileged comrades who'd been schooled . . . or at least had had family interested enough to teach them. Adela had had that family, and that schooling, and had come to him with her quiet, firm faith. His most solid example, and one he now wished he'd asked more questions of.

"I think, Reandn, that if you were to go to a faith house here, you wouldn't find things so very different. Not from what I've heard you say." She smoothed the light material of her skirt, and looked away, clearly uncomfortable—evidence enough that her talk of privacy was not feigned. But she continued anyway. "I think . . . what you want to know . . . is that I have been taught the Sisters each have their own realms. Ardrith has those who leave life in sleep, in quiet sickness, and Tenaebra. . . ." she shuddered. "Tenaebra has Nelmar. And for those who deeply care for one another and die under different Sisters, there are the borders, though they can mean a long search. And," she concluded, "for those such as Koby, there are the Lonely Hells, where you may find no one. Ever."

Reandn swallowed in relief, and closed his eyes again. It was what he thought he knew, and it helped assuage his sudden doubt that he'd left behind his only chance to join Adela. And now he could mold away into old age—assuming Ronsin did not get to him first—and still, eventually, be with her again. Although he doubted this had been his last opportunity to go with Tenaebra.

But it didn't help missing her *now*. It didn't change the fact that he wanted to be with her so badly he didn't care what he might lose by leaving this realm so early.

"Suicides," Ania said, her voice scared as she suddenly took his hand again, "belong to no one but themselves, Reandn. Neither Sister will take them."

Her concern touched him. "Don't worry," he said, almost absently. "And as far as Koby is concerned . . . he's mad, you said so yourself. His . . ." he searched for the colloquial phrase she'd used, "boat's tipped over. Maybe even a goddess doesn't hold you responsible for what you do then."

He hoped it was true.

Chapter 9

The walk to the market was a long and slow one; this was, Reandn knew, going to be a difficult night. The moon, though rising fairly late, would be bright, only a handful of days from full. His face throbbed, and his concentration was nonexistent. And although soothing, Ania's salve had an annoying herbal scent with the capacity to cover potentially important odors. Freshly broken pine branches, the smell of men unwashed—staying alert to such clues had helped him through the previous nights.

His only chance of respite tonight was in the form of storm clouds moving in from the southeast, and he eyed them as he entered the marketplace, silently encouraging them.

Shuyler's guards weren't in evidence yet, at least not obviously. Still, Reandn lingered in the center of the market, tallying—*again*—the cost of the goods he would need before he left. He wouldn't have the money, that was for certain—but he'd drive the best bargains he could and then go as far as he could with what he had. Eventually, he'd wandered the length of the market to the stock area; he decided to speak with Bergren a few quick minutes and then find a place to hole up until dark.

Tanager saw him arrive; the boy's eyes opened wide at Reandn's appearance and he hastily secured the horse he was leading. He circled the horses and the intervening stock dealer in an awkward lope, coming to a stop just out of reach—he'd never gotten any closer than that, not since the incident in the tailor shop. Face flushed, he demanded, "What happened? I know Pa-farren was going to talk to you. What did you say to him?"

There was nothing to do but find it amusing; Reandn grinned, despite the fact that it hurt to do so. "Son," he said, "the way you ask that question makes me think you figure your grandfather clobbered me."

"Well . . . *yeah*," Tanager said.

Reandn shook his head, the grin was slow to fade. Of all the things that had happened today, he'd finally found something he'd avoided—to be felled by Farren's hand. Trust the wizard, no. Consider him a physical threat . . . the corner of his mouth twitched again. "You go home and ask *him* what happened. You're right, he was there. You'll enjoy hearing it more from him, I'm sure."

Suspicious and confused, Tanager cast a quick look over his shoulder to ensure there were no customers waiting. "You come in here every evening," he said. "Are you part of the night guards now?"

"What do you think?" Reandn shifted his weight to one hip in a loose-jointed way and cocked his head at the boy.

"I don't know *what* to think about you," Tanager said bluntly, and flushed again. "Pa-farren says you're all right . . . he says you make bad decisions, but you're not a bad person."

"Does he, now? Well, I doubt I changed his mind today. And you can tell him I'm not going to change. But first I'd get that sorrel before it wanders completely out of reach."

Tanager's head jerked around; he quickly spotted the loose mare. With a muttered curse, he untangled his legs, which appeared to have turned independently of one another, and loped after the horse.

"Now there's a fine boy," Bergren said from behind.

Reandn looked over his shoulder. "He's certainly concerned about his family," he said noncommittally.

"Dark Lady! What happened to your face?" Bergren circled him, towing a small recalcitrant donkey.

"A fellow went out of his head at the tavern; I took care of it. The cut's not serious."

"No," Bergren agreed. "But appears to me it could have been." His expression sobered, and too damn fast to suit Reandn. "I hope you're still in fine shape for tonight, son. There's been talk . . . and more trouble."

Only what to expect from a day that had taken the course of this one. Reandn shrugged. "We'll find out," he said. "Show me some horses, why don't you—I think I spotted one of Shuyler's men hanging out at the south entrance. Let's look convincing."

"Soon as I get this little thing tied up," Bergren agreed. "It's been somebody's pet, I guarantee. Useless creature." He dragged and cajoled the long-eared problem along with them; once at the corral, the donkey bit Bergren on the arm. The dealer instantly smacked its nose, and moved away from it with a scowl, joining Reandn a few posts down.

"Interesting looking bay you've got in there," Reandn said.

"He's spoken for," Bergren told him. "Good thing, too. Worthless piece of horseflesh." Reandn just grinned at him.

"I'm afraid," Bergren said after a moment, and his voice was heavy again, "that this has become more than just my problem. Or maybe I should say, *I've* become everyone else's problem."

Reandn nodded. "Shuyler's threatened the others if they don't get you tamed, I imagine."

Bergren put his hands on his stocky hips, and cocked a furry eyebrow at Reandn. "Yes," he said. "No big surprise to you, I can see. Well, the others got the word this morning; we spent the heat of the day trying to figure out a solution."

"And?" Reandn leaned on the top rail of the corral.

"We didn't come up with one," Bergren admitted. "All we decided was that we've had enough of this mess. Instead of pressuring me like Shuyler intended, they've decided it's a good time to do something about him. They just don't know what." He scratched the back of his neck and contrived to find something in the distance to focus on. "I, umm, allowed as to how you might have some ideas."

I'm not getting involved. "Two weeks for the horse, Bergren. I didn't promise to be everyone's hero."

"You're the only one with the kind of experience to deal with Shuyler," Bergren protested.

Reandn's eyes hardened; he gave the dealer a cold stare, until Bergren understood and added hastily, "No, no, I haven't told them where you got that experience. I may have given the impression that you've been a mercenary, but I did have to present *some* reason to endorse my trust in you."

Better a mercenary than a Wolf, at this point. "Two more weeks for the horse," Reandn repeated, trying to ignore the dark voice of his common sense, telling him the balance of the situation would never last that long, and neither would he.

"This situation won't hold that long," Bergren said, as if he'd read those thoughts. "Not unless you can protect the entire market—which," he added hastily, "no one expects you to do. But there are going to be *accidents* at other booths unless something's done—one way or the other—before then." He stared gloomily at the donkey, which was contemplatively sucking its tie rope. "Besides . . . we didn't see it before, but after we talked this morning, we more or less put things together. There's a lot of road thieving going on—one Highborn—low-placed, but still Highborn—was actually killed last week. It started about the time we made our deal with Shuyler."

Reandn watched the bay bully another gelding away from the hay rack and said quietly, "I do know of a solution."

"Well, don't keep it to yourself!" Bergren snapped.

Reandn regarded the dealer a moment. "Get the Locals in on it."

"Not a chance!" Bergren all but exploded. "I told you that when this started. We've worked hard to police this area ourselves. If the Locals come in here they'll start quoting rules at us, forcing us to their mold. Well, we like things the way they are!"

Reandn gave him a sharp look. "Do you?"

The pause was a long one. Bergren looked away, clenched his jaw, and swallowed hard. "That's our choice, then," he said. "Shuyler or the Locals."

Reandn shrugged, wrapping his arms loosely around his knees. "Only choices I see," he said. "But you worry too much. The Locals have enough to do—they may not be interested in your little corner of Keland once they get it cleaned up."

Bergren nodded unhappily.

"Maybe we can renegotiate," Reandn suggested, looking out over the busy market. Business was at its peak and not one merchant was smiling. There might be a way to cut his time here short after all. "Shuyler's gang must have some sort of ultimate safe spot, a bolt-hole—otherwise the Locals would have closed in on them. I can track it down—after all, I've got an advantage the Locals don't. I know what some of them look like, and I know where they'll be. My guess is at least one of these boys will head for the bolt-hole, come morning."

Bergren nodded cautiously. "And?"

"I track down the bolt-hole, and I give it to the Locals—

probably won't even have to bring the market in on it. Let the Locals take it from there. Whatever the outcome, once I find the den, the bay's mine. No more guard duty."

Bergren eyed him for a moment. "That might leave me here wide open."

"That's right," Reandn said. "But it's going to happen in a handful of days, anyway."

Bergren frowned at him, an expression of disappointment—and judgement. "I hadn't sized you up to be the kind who would walk out on a man in my situation."

"We've all got troubles," Reandn said, refusing to look away—as much as he wanted to avoid the judgement in Bergren's face. He couldn't blame the man—that's what a Wolf was for, wasn't it? To protect Keland's people. "Take the chance, Bergren. Give me the bay and I'll spot the gang for your Locals."

Bergren's voice was hard, his expression remote—as though in disappointment, he had somehow discarded the regard he'd had for his temporary watchman. "Two weeks. I'll go to the Locals myself. If you can track them, they can track them."

"Are you sure?" Reandn asked. "Can they do it before your time runs out? If Shuyler's gang kills me tomorrow night, you'll be unprotected. I can have them located by then."

"Graces, you're cocksure of yourself," Bergren said in annoyance.

"It's your choice," Reandn said. "We made a deal and I'll stick by it if that's what you want. But I think this other is a better idea."

Bergren's words were still biting. "A better idea for *who*?"

"For both of us," Reandn snapped. "What makes you think I'm free to stay, merchant? What makes you think it won't put someone else in danger to delay me here?"

Bergren looked startled. "I . . . never thought," he said.

"After all, you've told me so little. But . . . I guess maybe there's a reason for that. I should have suspected as much, when a barefoot Wolf showed up at my corral, wanting my scarred up, studdy bay." He hesitated. "Will you stay until the Locals make their move? Win or lose, I won't need you after that."

"No," Reandn said somberly. "You won't." He batted at a fly that fussed around his raw cheek. "If they move within a day, I'll stay. No longer."

"I guess that's as much as I could ask for." Bergren seemed reluctant to leave, and finally, awkwardly, he said, "I know about Wolf's Rights. I know you could have taken that bay any time you wanted him. I don't know why you didn't, but . . . I should be grateful to you for sticking with me through this, instead of harassing you because you won't stay longer. I'm sorry."

Reandn looked at him in surprise. "You're welcome," he said after a moment, and pushed away from the corral. "Oh, and after this is done—no one else knows my part of it."

"I figured as much." Bergren wiped the back of his wrist across his sweaty brow, and said, "I'll need some time to convince the others—this isn't a decision I can make on my own."

"I have to know before you leave tonight, or it'll be the day after tomorrow before I can do anything about it."

"I'll do my best," Bergren said. Reandn gave him a short nod and walked away from the corrals. *Do it*, he thought, and the prospect of leaving Maurant early dangled before him like a lure. *Do it, Bergren, and set me free.*

But Reandn was forced into the woods at the early arrival of some of Shuyler's men, and didn't have a chance to talk to Bergren. The thieves-turned-guards had no description of him yet, but he didn't want to give them any opportunity to form one, either. Then his respite came, for the clouds that had gathered on the seaward horizon rumbled in to unleash a hard, soaking rain, enlivened by bouts of close lightening. The rain continued through the night, and Shuyler's men didn't fight it; they stayed huddled under the awnings. Reandn suspected that they, too, were weary of the chase, and just as glad for the excuse to lay off a night.

The steady downpour eventually penetrated the thick evergreen boughs, soaking Reandn; it didn't let up until late morning, and Reandn was still damp when he arrived at the *Unicorn*. It was, he thought, a relief to feel chilled, after so many days of Maurant's heat.

Ania greeted him with one of the rough kitchen towels and the jar of salve he'd left behind, taking him into the kitchen to make faces over his injury—a procedure she repeated after he ate his noon meal. Reandn had just traded places with Hurley in the entrance dormer when he heard the sound of a one-way conversation coming toward the tavern. Nonstop, it was somehow familiar, yet he couldn't quite place it—not until right before the couple entered the dormer, and then it was too late.

A man and woman paused at the threshold, adjusting to the dimmer light within. The silent half of the couple wore a patient look; he regarded his companion fondly. But when he saw her reaction to Reandn, his expression hardened.

Jilla. It was Jilla, her hair piled up on her head—a style that somehow now contrived to look odd to him. Her dress rustled with its many fine, sheer fabrics, imitating the many-layered appearance of the Northern Highborn without putting her in a sweat bath. She looked at him, at his battle wounds, and her eyes widened; she took a small step backward. Then she looked at her husband, and her chin came up; her eyes grew scornful.

Then this was the Minor, Savill. A man barely as tall as his wife, he was compact and moved with energy. He raked Reandn with his gaze, hard brown eyes beneath brows that held a perpetual tilt of slight dissatisfaction. He might have said something; he looked like he wanted to. But Jilla took her skirts in hand and swept past with him, picking up her conversation where she'd left off.

Reandn rolled his eyes, glad there was no one to see. Personally, he didn't give scat what the Minor thought of him. But Savill had channels to King's Keep, and could ask questions that would reveal Reandn—and the very fact that he was still alive—to Ronsin. All the more reason to make his departure from this place as quick as possible, before Savill decided to be a problem.

"A word, young meir."

Or maybe it was too late already. "Meir," Reandn said politely, waiting.

Savill's eyebrow lifted at the respectful reply. Jilla most certainly had prepared him for something else. "You know who I am."

Reandn nodded. *Get on with it*, he thought.

"You will have noticed, I hope, that I oversee a large and growing town. That, as always, presents the opportunity for banditry and misbehavior."

"I haven't noticed any of those problems in great quantity," Reandn said, turning his face so its ugly wound was away from the Minor.

"I'm glad to see you've been paying attention." Savill entered the dormer so he, too, could look out into the street, though the afternoon sun had driven everyone under the protection of porches and awnings. It was a power play. *See me make you wait.* After a moment, he turned his gaze back on Reandn. "The circumstances of your arrival are somewhat confused, but it is certain they were not orthodox. Consider yourself lucky Farren has spoken of what he deems to be your good character."

Farren. Just what he needed. Did the wizard have his fingers into everything that went on in this town? Reandn said stiffly, "I usually speak for myself in such matters."

Savill's reply was sharp. "Your actions have spoken for you, instead. There's something about you . . ." he cut himself off, shook his head in a short, curt gesture. "I don't know who you are, but I know you're from the North, and pretty far north, at that. So despite Farren's opinion, I've sent a message to the Keep. If you're wanted, I'll soon know."

Reandn's neutral gaze failed him; he gave the Minor a sharp look. *The keep* could have meant anything— and should have meant nothing, to one not from the King's Keep.

"Yes, the Keep. That you know the implication of that expression only reinforces my feelings about you." Savill tilted his head back to regard the taller man in a leisurely manner. Leisurely, like a muscled hill cat about to pounce. "You're either in deep trouble, young meir, or you're a badly misplaced attempt by Northern securities to prowl about this region." His hand reached out, fingers tipping Reandn's shoulder where the leather showed brightly unweathered. "Jilla said you'd a colorful patch on you. Well, young meir, we'll soon see." Savill pushed slightly against the light patch, a warning, and a physical intrusion Reandn would not have allowed under any other circumstances. His self-control seemed to satisfy the Minor in some way, for he gave a humorless smile and returned to the interior of the *Unicorn* without further comment.

Reandn leaned back against the wall and gave an inner growl. He didn't *need* for things to get more complicated on him. But Savill had not intimidated him as much as intended; any message, sent after Jilla'd seen him if not later, had at least a week yet to reach the Keep, assuming it was going by a courier system with remounts and fresh riders. There, it would find its way to the bottom of a large pile of similarly, low-priority flagged messages. Despite Savill's concern, there was no way he could call the question urgent. Reandn would be long gone before any reply reached Maurant—and then he had merely to resolve things before Savill's probable response alerted Ronsin he was still alive.

All the same, he didn't have any intention of confronting the Minor a second time. When he saw the Minor was preparing to leave, Reandn abandoned his spot and slid into the haven of the alley beside the tavern. He leaned against the shaded wood of the *Unicorn* and let his sticky skin absorb the coolness, tracking the Minor's progress by his wife's conversation.

A scuffle to the rear of the building diverted his attention—it was a furtive sound, and he spun to face it. There, briefly framed by the *Unicorn* and her neighbor building, was the strapping, distinctive figure of a man he'd so far only seen silhouetted against the darkness by Bergren's corral.

But before Reandn could do more than drop to the balls of his feet, prepared for attack, the man left, running along the narrow alley behind the tavern. Reandn slumped back against the *Unicorn*. They'd found him. They knew who he was and what he looked like; they could come after him any time. They weren't likely to try anything in the middle of the day, but to and from the market would be an entirely different matter. He tilted his head back against the building and closed his eyes. Cornered. He might be out in the open, but he was cornered, nonetheless.

The sudden peal of Jilla's receding laugh seemed to be aimed right at him, but then her voice faded, at last lost in a tiny gust of sea-laden air. Reandn scrubbed his hands across his face and through his hair, knowing he'd just lost all chance to complete the two weeks he'd promised Bergren. He had a tracking job to do in the morning, regardless of the merchants' decision.

When Reandn arrived at the market—a long, slow mile through the woods alongside the road, checking shadows and watching his back—he went directly to Bergren's tack and hay shed. Bergren finished up with his customer and came to the door of the shed, a large, dark form blocking the sunlight.

"They're with us," he said, without preamble. "They're willing to take the chance the Locals'll haul us into town purview, if it means getting rid of Shuyler; I told them you'd do your best to keep us out of it."

"Good answer," Reandn said. "Because the rules of the game have changed."

"How do you mean?" Bergren said warily.

Reandn came to the doorway and nodded at the market entrance, where the road made a delta into the sprawling area. After a moment, the crowd thinned momentarily; it was long enough. "Even a Wolf isn't invincible, and I reckon the odds just got overwhelming for this one. See those two men, the ones just hanging around the entrance?"

"Yes," Bergren said, his tone clearly indicating he didn't understand yet. "They're Shuyler's; I recognize them."

"I was faceless before," Reandn said, retreating back inside the shed. "Their only chance was to catch me in action. Now they know me—they can go at me any time, anywhere. And some of them are archers."

"Damn," Bergren said. "How'd they pin you?"

Reandn shrugged. "It doesn't really matter. I'm just lucky I caught them checking me out at the *Unicorn*."

"I want to show you something," Bergren grunted, entering the shed himself, and going to rummage in the corner that held things he'd meant to burn and hadn't yet. He returned with an arrow that appeared to have no head. "Take a look at this," he said, holding the arrow out for inspection.

The head was merely the sharpened end of the shaft, decorated with tiny grooves; Bergren traced one with a thick finger. "For poison," he said grimly. "And sometimes, the juice of the swamp horsetail."

Reandn grimaced. He'd heard of such arrows, although they weren't common in the North. "I assume horsetail's a plant," he said. "But what about the poison? What is it?"

"Right about the horsetail. It's a caustic. The poison's commonly drawn from a snake—they're not too hard to find, if you have the nerve to milk them off."

Reandn stared at the dealer, inwardly aghast. For all his woods sense, he'd never considered poison snakes. His part of Keland was devoid of any that could inflict serious damage. He'd twice been bitten by the rock-dwelling pinsnake, and neither incident had caused him to miss a single day of patrol. The fact that there were deadly snakes in the area, and he had not known of them, made his skin crawl.

"If you happen to know what this snake looks like . . . and the areas it favors, I'd be obliged," he said, still looking at the arrow.

Bergren chuckled dryly. "I didn't mean to scare you, son. Even if you run across a swampsnake, they're basically shy creatures. They hunt mice and moles, and tend to stick to the swamplands."

Reandn took a deep breath. He smelled salve and sea, overset by pine. Unfamiliarity. He wondered if there was anything else he should know about, things they never taught in the North. He tried to tell himself it wouldn't make any difference, not if he moved out soon.

Bergren twirled the arrow, watching the play of its

grooved designs. "About yesterday . . . I'm sorry. You're right, you've been playing a dangerous game for too long already. I never thought about your other reasons for being here—and I know they must be important ones, to bring a Wolf all the way down here. I just kept thinking what would happen after you left." He gave Reandn quick glance and added, "I know, I know, it was my idea to fight Shuyler's tide in the first place. I never thought this far ahead—maybe because I never thought I'd *get* this far. I owe you thanks, instead of hard words."

Reandn looked out the door, picking out more and more of Shuyler's men—there early, and looking eager. "Don't worry," he said finally. "It'll work out. I'll do my best to keep them in line tonight, but if I'm going to be in a position to track them, I'll have to leave your stock on their own in the early morning." He shook his head at Bergren's grimace. "Don't lose sleep over it. I think they'll be good—they're turning to new tactics now." Not that their new tactics were going to be any easier to deal with. "Do me a favor, though. Leave late tonight, if you can. And stir the horses up as you go. I'll need the cover if I'm going to make the woods."

"That much, I can do," Bergren said confidently.

Fortunately, Reandn had called the game right. Although two women, their approach remarkably casual, entered Bergren's domain shortly after moonrise, it took only one lobbed stone to send them scurrying away. Now that they knew who he was, and that he was still watching, they weren't going to play the hunt and chase game anymore. He could well understand their new strategy. There was no reason for them to take any more risks; time was on their side. Or so they thought.

It was going to be up to him to change that. Before dawn, he left the gentle cover of the young pines and found a new spot by the road, less secure but ideal for the job that would follow. Shortly afterward the heavy

mist of dawn blanketed the area; by now he had learned
that the moisture would burn off in midmorning, leaving
the day bright and hot.

By then he wouldn't need its cover. With the condition
of the road, he hardly needed to stay in sight of his
quarry; yesterday's hard rain had left it as muddy as
Bergren's corral, and it was just now hardening into
ground that would make a firm track. All of the previous
day's tracks had disappeared into mire, leaving a lumpy
path, the consistency of which would be distinctly
different from the early morning tracks of Shuyler's
men and women.

As the merchants arrived, the guards left in odd,
sporadic numbers, until the man he'd long pegged as
the ranking outlaw finally trailed the others out. Reandn
waited until he was almost out of sight and eased through
the woods, ghosting the outlaw's journey.

He hoped he'd chosen the right man. Someone would
surely be reporting to Shuyler—if nothing else to tell
him that Bergren's pesky guard was still causing trouble.
There had to be a regular meeting place, a place for
instructions and post-caper gatherings—a perfect place
for the Locals to corral them.

Reandn expected it to be fully as clever as the guard
duty, which was a legitimate nighttime occupation, and
an excuse for Shuyler's men to travel the road at night,
and in numbers. If the merchants hadn't been so
frightened—or too prideful—to deal with the Locals,
this whole mess would have been straightened out long
before Reandn confronted it.

There were people on the road now, covering the noise
of his progress. The sun had fully risen, and although
his protective fog had burned off, the bright light cast
strong shadows, and made for confusing outlines in the
scrubby, road-edge hardwoods. The sun also brought
its heat, and as Reandn wiped the first sheen of sweat

off his forehead, his quarry turned into the woods on the other side of the road.

Reandn left the woods and stood in the road, considering the area. Through the trees ahead, he could see bits of straight-planed lines that belonged in no woods, and decided it was the *Edgerton Inn*, a notoriously rowdy establishment that was the center for much of Maurant's gossip. Surely, if it was the center of Shuyler's operation, word would have leaked long ago. He studied the edge of the road, finding no clear path for his quarry. Yet there was also a remarkable absence of the usual forest detritus, as though the whole area was well traveled, or kept deliberately clear. Hard to track anything in this. He started into the woods after the bandit, and saw him again just before the man ducked into the large barn behind the inn. Thoughtfully, Reandn hunkered down on his heels and waited.

After a short time, another figure came out of the building—the big man who'd found him at the *Unicorn*. The man was fingering a pouch that could have held coins or gems, his expression satisfied and unmindful of his surroundings. He blithely passed within several feet of Reandn, and went on to the road.

Time to have a look inside that inn.

The early morning crowd was a quiet one, consisting mostly of red-eyed men hunched over lumpy oatmeal. Reandn stopped at the bar long enough to order some of the same, then found himself a seat where he could turn his distinctively scraped face to the wall while marking the activity of the small, open room.

The thing that most caught his interest was the curtained-off doorway at the end of the massive wooden bar. As an age-marked woman dropped his oatmeal—and some unasked for ale to wash it down with—before him, he saw a figure slip out from behind the curtain to blend with the other patrons at the bar.

He caught the woman's wrist as she withdrew and as she opened her mouth for what looked to be a loud protest, cut her short. "Just a question," he said, releasing the wrist. She rubbed it balefully, but stayed. Reandn nodded at the doorway. "What's back there?"

She favored him with the same look she might have given any crazy man. "What do you think? We got to keep our ale somewheres, don't we?"

"Underground, usually."

"Not here," she averred. "This place's sittin' on rock, couldn't dig no cellar. What's it to you?"

He shrugged. "I'm looking for a quiet room to meet some friends, that's all."

"Well, you won't find it here," she snorted. "No one's ever accused the *Edgerton* of being quiet."

"My bad luck," he said, and shoved a coin across the table to her. She looked suspiciously upon it until he added, "I won't be expecting any change," then snatched it up and hurried away.

Reandn forced down some of the unpalatable cereal, quickly discovering why it needed an ale chaser. Fortunately the ale was a weak one, and pleasantly cool. Cellar-cool.

He regarded the mug thoughtfully, until his eye caught sight of the senior market guard, the man he'd trailed to the inn's barn. The man who *hadn't* come in the front door. Reandn hunched over his breakfast in imitation of the other patrons. Then, when the outlaw moved to the other end of the room, he left his unfinished meal and slipped out the door.

Interesting place, the *Edgerton*—the kind of place where ale cooled itself and men showed up from nowhere. Reandn thought the Locals would be just as intrigued.

Chapter 10

When Reandn at last returned to town, he headed for the bathhouse, washing away the morning's considerable sweat while he contemplated the next step in the fight against Shuyler. He knew the Local he wanted to talk to—the one who'd been reasonable over the fight with Hurley, the older man who had enough experience that he might just sit and listen to what Reandn had to say. He hadn't seen the man since that fight, although Kelton had seemed well acquainted with him. Or maybe Ania could help him.

Despite the cool bath, he was hot and sticky when he reached the *Unicorn*; the ability to acclimate to the oppressive humidity was apparently not one of his more impressive skills. *Give yourself some time*, he thought, and then laughed out loud. Exactly what he had no intention of doing, not if he could help it.

Ania was not to be seen, although Melly gave him a shy little wave from the corner of the main room, where she was wrestling chairs around. Reandn asked her about the Local, got a shrug, and headed for the kitchen, the most likely place to find Ania. It was also the most likely place to connive a few breakfast scraps out of Damone, the head cook, an older man who considered it his duty to fatten up the *Unicorn* staff.

The kitchen was full of good smells, all coming to peak for the noonday. If he could snatch a jar of preserves and some of yesterday's bread, he'd consider it a job well done.

"Ania?" he inquired of old Damone, poking at the food on the big center counter. The man was with one of the junior cooks, tutoring with fervent emphasis, his knife waving alarmingly in the air. It took a detour from the food under discussion to point out the back door, and went right back to emphasizing the point Damone was trying to make—something about scorching a sauce, Reandn gathered.

He also gathered up both the bread and the berry preserves, exiting out the back with his booty and no more notice from the bodies bustling around the kitchen. The kitchen was built in an L shape, as though someone had constructed that corner of the *Unicorn* inside out, taking a chunk from the back of the dining area. The result was a small, partially bricked courtyard with a single massive pine growing toward the back. It was quiet, and Reandn had been told the kitchen opened up into it come summer months. For now, since Ania was not immediately visible, it was a peaceful place to eat breakfast.

Reandn sat on the stone steps and retrieved his boot knife, generously spreading preserve on the bread. It was too much, of course, and ended up on his chin, threatening to fall and stain the vest—which was already marked by the blood stain he hadn't been able to completely remove. He juggled the jar and knife, the bread balanced on his knee, swallowed hastily, and caught the jam on his chin with the edge of his hand. There was nothing to do but lick it off, and that, he decided, was the best way to eat jam.

It seemed he could still connect to the simple pleasures of life, after all.

The thought startled and surprised him both. After a moment, he wiped the knife clean on the rest of the bread and tried for a more dignified posture. When someone you loved as dearly as you loved your own life died, was it all right to sit in a quiet courtyard and revel in the sensation of filling your belly with good food?

To his relief, Ania gave him something else to think about. Her voice came from the cool alley around the corner. A murmur at first, it rose in clear irritation. "I'm *not* going to suggest he stay. Why should I? This isn't his home, and it doesn't suit him. He wants to leave, and I don't blame him!"

The voice that answered was more discreet, or perhaps more fearful. Ania's was the next Reandn heard clearly.

"*You* say it's important. I don't see how it could be. *Honestly*, Tanager, if it wasn't for Pa-farren, I'd not answer a single one of your questions."

Reandn froze, unintended eavesdropping suddenly turned serious, and the food suddenly nothing but a cold lump in his stomach. Tanager's attempts to keep tabs on him were old news, but through Ania? Savagely, he thrust the knife in his boot and stood. Wolf-silent, he moved to the alley entrance, his expression dark, making no attempt to hide his presence.

Tanager was facing him; the boy gulped audibly, and Ania looked over her shoulder, paling. "I told you it would come to no good!" she hissed at the boy. Tanager mutely took a step backward.

How many others had Tanager talked to about him? Suddenly, coldly, Reandn realized the boy would have given very little thought to Reandn's situation or safety, not as long as he was intent on helping his grandfather. When he spoke, his voice was deep in its lower register. Dangerous. "You told the market guards they could find me here, didn't you."

"Me?" Tanager squeaked.

"Did you think to wonder why they didn't know already? Did it occur to you that I might have my own reasons for remaining nameless to them? That I've been watching Bergren's stock *against them*?"

"Against them?" Tanager repeated faintly, so surprised he forgot to continue his retreat. "But . . . but they said they wanted to talk to you, to find out if you would fit into their organization."

"You did tell them," Reandn said, as surprised as anyone at the calm in his voice. The meddling grandson of a wizard. That's how they'd found out, after all his days of evading them. "They're trying to kill me."

"Ardrith's Graces!" Ania said, as Tanager's eyes widened, his face stark white against his black hair. "*Git*, Tanager, while I try to straighten this out." The boy hesitated, and she said sharply, "*Go!*"

Tanager ran, his limbs moving with unusual coordination and speed; he looked back over his shoulder as he reached the street, and then bolted.

"He didn't mean any harm, Reandn, you know he didn't."

"But he's caused it," Reandn said, finding his hands clenched, the anger building. Tentatively, Ania touched his shoulder; he shook her off, explosive, and turned on her. "And you! There's not much I trust in this Lady-forsaken town, but you were one person I thought I could!"

She flushed. "I didn't . . . I didn't think I was doing anything wrong."

"Spying for my enemy?" His voice was cold.

That stopped her short, and put puzzled lines on her foxlike features. "Enemy?" she said. "Pa-farren is no man's *enemy*."

Pa-farren? The man had *every*one thinking he was nothing more than a grandfather. "The man is a wizard. I want no part of him."

Ania lowered her voice, moved closer again—though clearly not certain about doing it. "Wizard once, yes," she said. "But no more. Since he came here, Farren has been a man like you or Kelton—and that was *years* ago, right about the time I was born. But he still knows the Highborn ways—the Minor counts on him for advice in dealing with King's Keep. Before you came, he used to eat here all the time, and he's never done a thing to hurt anyone. How can you speak so badly of him?"

"I said he was a wizard. I didn't say he was stupid. If he was, I wouldn't bother to worry about him. If he's done good for the town, Ania, it's for his own ends."

"That's absurd!" Ania cried, hands suddenly on her hips, no longer trapped in her shame at what he'd called betrayal. "What makes you such an expert on wizards, when things magic no longer exist in this world?"

"What makes *you* such an expert on magic, to think that it no longer exists? How do you think I got here, Ania, from the North, unprepared for your climate and ways? Did Tanager ever mention that, ey? That I came from the hands of one wizard, into the hands of another? Farren may have managed to befriend an unwary town, but he'll get nothing from me."

Ania's cheeks were flushed, her eyes bright with tears of frustration; she obviously couldn't make sense of his words, so perhaps Tanager had been discreet— *astonishment!*—with the circumstances of Reandn's arrival. "*Ohh!*" she exclaimed. "You're as thick as dock scum at low tide!" Her hands flew up to cover her face. She took a few deep breaths, carefully wiped her eyes, one after the other, and said, "Is there no convincing you, you have no enemy in Farren? What has he done to you, aside from being who he is?"

"He spies on me," Reandn growled, knowing that the man's greatest weapon, past his magic, was the image that he was not worth any worry. Just like Ronsin. "And he uses my friends to do it."

"I did no *spying*. I answered a few questions!" Ania

said, the angry lift coming back to her chin. With visible effort, she lowered it. "He's only worried about you, Reandn. He's afraid you're headed for trouble. You've already got the Minor upset over something."

"I *am* headed for trouble," Reandn said. He watched her a moment, seeing nothing in her face but honest emotion, and clear lack of understanding. She had no idea why he was so concerned, that was obvious enough. And he didn't doubt that she'd only done as she'd said. She'd been used by the wizard, and not been in league with him. He took a deep breath. "Let's drop it. I know you didn't mean any harm. Just . . . no more. My business is my business."

"All right," she said quietly. "I . . . I'm sorry, Reandn. I never would have . . . purposely . . . I mean—"

"It's all right, Ania," Reandn said.

She hesitated, and then nodded, and left without saying anything more.

He was left in the small courtyard, alone. Alone, and filled with tumultuous conflict. He wanted revenge, he wanted the Keep safe from Ronsin, he wanted Shuyler's men off his back—and most of all, he wanted Dela by his side. And at the moment, he couldn't do anything about any of it—which didn't stop the desires from driving at him until Reandn thought he'd have to run in circles, just to be doing *something*.

He settled for appropriating the lid of the rain barrel and propping it in the lowest broken stubs of branches of the pine to use for a target. The sound of his well-balanced boot knife thwacking into the wood was deeply satisfying, and, despite the elbow ache that had never disappeared after his unconventional travel, his accuracy did not suffer. He was absorbed in the exercise, gladly allowing it to occupy his thoughts, when a figure stepped out from the alley and stood, legs braced, watching him.

Reandn completed his throw and walked up to yank

the knife free before acknowledging the Local. The man waited for him at the tavern, and mutely held his hand out for the knife. His face showed no threat, no anger— in fact, there was little of anything revealed in the seamed features. After a brief hesitation, Reandn reversed the knife in his hand and passed it over hilt first.

The man hefted it and glanced at Reandn. "Nice," he said. "Not fancy. Well made." He handed it back the same polite way he'd received it.

Reandn tucked the knife away in a gesture smooth from repetition. "I want to talk to you about the roadway troubles you've been having."

The man grunted. "You one of those fellows who believes he can walk into a place and fix all its woes?"

"No," Reandn said, grinning at the man's forthright attitude. "But maybe I can help you fix this one."

The Local stared at him a moment longer, shifted the small wad of chaw in his cheek and spit. "Name's Cyrill."

"There are conditions on this," Reandn said. "I can show you the gang's bolt-hole, but I don't want to be in on the catch. That, and no one else in the Locals knows I'm the one who helped you."

Cyrill squinted and cocked his head. "Sounds like a man who don't want to be found," he said, as though a disinterested observation.

Reandn grinned again. "It does, doesn't it. You interested?"

"Town's my patrol, not the roads. Suppose I could pass it on. Though," he added skeptically, "I'm not sure you know all that much. Talking 'bout a gang—there's never more'n a few men mixed up in the robberies, and they're happening on all sides of Maurant. There's never been anything to suggest it's all one bunch of men."

"Their leader's a smart one," Reandn said. "And your Locals have a big disadvantage. You're not in cooperation with the market."

"'The edge of town market?" Cyrill asked, and snorted. "That's by their choice, son. They're scared to death that working with us'll put 'em in the town proper—think we want to boss them around." He shook his head. "We got enough things to watch over, with the stuff that goes on at the docks."

"I think the merchants are changing their minds," Reandn said, and briefly told the man about Shuyler's racket there. Cyrill's expression grew less skeptical and more attentive.

"Savill's got a pretty good Local organization here," Reandn finished thoughtfully. "I figure the only reason you haven't had much luck stopping the road trouble is that they only strike in twos and threes—easy enough to hide your trail with so few, especially if you split up and meet later. This morning I followed one of their men to the barn behind the *Edgerton*. Interestingly enough, he showed up in the inn, without making use of the front door. When I asked, they said they had no underground rooms, but their ale is too cool to be stored above ground. I think there's a basement, and that barn tunnels into it."

"In my dreams," the Local scoffed, but after a moment of silent thought, he mused, "It'd be a *bandit's* dream . . . a steady supply of ale, a cool place to meet, a quiet way to get there. Even a place to get a handy horse. If one of us did check at the *Edgerton* after a robbery, there'd be nothing to find, not if they had the door well hidden. You can't search a room that isn't there." After another moment he added, "The place *does* have a rough reputation."

Then he gave Reandn an annoyed look and said, "You've got me pretty near convinced for a man who hasn't said much about it."

"Facts can do that to you," Reandn said. "The only other thing I've got to say is that if you're going to act on this, I wish you'd do it quickly. They're on my trail as much as I've been on theirs, and I'm not going to be able to dodge them forever."

Cyrill spat again, absently; his expression was appreciative of Reandn's understated plight. "You don't want to be known about these parts," he commented, "you might try getting in a mite less trouble."

"I could do without it," Reandn agreed. "When can you get back to me on this?"

Cyrill nodded, almost to himself. "This afternoon," he said. He shifted his weight, readying to leave, but stopped. "It'll be hard to keep you out of it."

"Do it," Reandn said, uncompromising.

The pause before Cyrill's nod was barely noticeable. "This afternoon," he repeated, and left.

Reandn spent an uncomfortable day in the portal of the *Unicorn*, sure that every shadow held at least one of Shuyler's men. If he'd actually spotted one, he might have felt better, since his imagination was supplying him with powerful enemies. He knew he was behaving like a Yearling, but the truth of the matter was that his involvement with Bergren—which had started out as an attempt to find transportation to Ronsin—might very well prevent him from ever reaching the wizard.

In the late afternoon, Cyrill returned to remove some of his uncertainties, nodding affirmatives at him before he ever came within speaking distance.

The man's expression, however, wasn't as positive. Reandn greeted him with a slight upward nod of his chin, inwardly wary, and met him at the alley entrance.

"What you told me fit into what the wide patrols already knew," Cyrill said without preamble, as they drew close to the wall to avoid blocking traffic. "They're not going to waste any time acting on it, either. They're setting up a snare—a Highborn target too ripe to ignore, one that'll take a lot of men to handle. We've already let the word slip out—Savill's moving his daughter's dower tonight."

"Savill?" Reandn asked sharply. "The Minor?"

Cyrill shrugged. "They called him in on it as soon as our Leader heard the news. He wouldn't ask anyone else to risk losing their valuables—y'see, we're going to let the gang have them. We'll have a little welcoming party at the inn and the barn." Cyrill's sudden grin deepened the lines running down his browned face. "Ought to be quite a show."

It would, at that. After a haul such as the one the Locals were presenting, no bandit could bear to seek safety far from the goods. There was always the chance his cohorts, unsupervised, would squirrel away precious bits and pieces for themselves. He nodded absently, still thinking about Cyrill's initial demeanor, the tension on his face as he'd approached the tavern. "What else?"

"That's it. Simple plan, less to go wrong." But Cyrill's gaze slid away from Reandn.

Reandn studied the Local, and his eyes narrowed. "What else?" he repeated, voice sliding down.

"Savill," Cyrill said, and studied the opposite wall for a moment. "He's a sharp man, that Minor. He knew my information came from someone seasoned. Struck him odd that such a person wanted to stay out of the doing of it."

"You told him," Reandn stated flatly, looking out into the street as if expecting to see the Minor, flanked by Locals, coming up for another *chat*. He took a deep breath. Suddenly Maurant felt very crowded.

Cyrill gave a firm shake of his head. "Didn't do it," he said. "Told him I didn't know your name—it's only the truth."

Reandn's deep breath came out slowly, but he couldn't

relax. "He knows your posting, though. He'll find out the tavern's in your territory. . . ."

Cyrill was nodding, reluctantly. "Son," he said, "you make me some nervous. I've given my word to keep you out of this, when it's obvious you're running from something. Now, hold on—" he said, when Reandn stiffened, and pinned him with cold grey eyes. "I'm not asking you for details, but it'd be some help to this old Local's conscience to at least know it—whatever you done—isn't any worse than these fellows we're after are up to. Then it'd be easy to consider it a kind of a trade."

Alarm faded to mild amusement. "Then sleep well tonight, Cyrill," Reandn told him. "My worst crime is that I'm on my way somewhere else. But I *don't* want to be slowed down—and I get the feeling any interest from your Minor will do just that."

"He's thorough," Cyrill agreed. "Likes to sink his teeth into things he figures don't fit his ways. Don't suppose you'll take offense if I say you don't fit, not a bit."

That earned a genuine grin. "I can't swim, I can't sail, and I don't like fish," he agreed. "I'll be gone soon. I don't care what you tell him after that, if he worries you over it."

Cyrill moved back out into the doorway, sliding his thumbs into the belt that cinched his sleeveless tunic. "I'll let you know how it comes out," he said, stepping into the street.

Reandn watched him go, and began making travel plans.

Chapter 11

As the shadows grew long and the evening cooled, Reandn left his post and sought out Ania. She was with Melly, nibbling on leftovers in the kitchen while the cooks banked the stove fires and Damone filled the scraps plate in the center of the table. Reandn picked out a slice of gravy-soaked bread and mutely pointed a finger at his scabbing face.

Ania wiped her hands on a wash rag and shook her head. "I ought to make you find a mirror and do this for yourself," she complained, and winked at Melly.

The shy girl gave her a smile, and said, unusually bold, "If it wasn't him it'd be some stray cat you found at the docks. And I think he's cuter, don't you?"

Ania snorted. "Not than that pretty little calico I had last time. And she was better natured, to boot." But the glance she gave him, as she dabbed at his face, was uncertain. She'd avoided him since their morning confrontation, and clearly worried about it now.

"Being contrary is one of my better qualities," he informed her, and waited until she caught his eye. After a moment, she relaxed, and returned to her administrations. "Ow!" he yelped.

"Sorry," Ania muttered, biting her lip in concentration. "It's just because it's healing. It looks awful, but really it's doing well, if you don't count this spot." She lightly touched his jawline.

"Then we won't." He waited for her to cap the little jar and held out his hand for it.

She exchanged a quick glance with Melly, but did not give him the jar. One of the scullery boys jostled her, unnoticed; she looked at Reandn, a suggestion of a frown wrinkling the space between her brows. "You wouldn't take it unless I wasn't going to put it on any more," she said. "You're leaving."

Reandn didn't respond immediately; his hand fell back to his side, and he shrugged.

Melly shook her head, quiet regret in her voice. "She doesn't like it when she loses a stray before it's healed."

Reandn almost laughed, knowing there was more hurt in him than Ania could ever heal. But he saw she was truly distressed, so instead slowly shook his head. "I'll probably be gone tomorrow, and I'd thank you if you'd tell Kelton; I haven't seen him."

Ania looked away, her lips thinning. "I've already told him you probably would," she said. "After this morning. You're so private, and I know I offended you badly. Please don't go just because of me. I won't be talking to Tanager anymore."

"Ania," Reandn said, gently admonishing. "You take too much on yourself." She wouldn't meet his eyes, and Melly cast quick, anxious glances between the two of them. "I've got places to go, and things to take care of. Nothing to do with you." Gently, he took the salve jar from her hand. "If it hadn't been for you, I'd never have made it past my first afternoon here, and I'm grateful. I don't want you thinking any differently after I go. Strays like to be remembered fondly."

Her smile was somewhat tremulous, but it was genuine. "All right," she said. "You've got pay coming to you. If you wait, I'll get it." She walked briskly out the back door, headed for Kelton's house and his private workroom.

In the quiet, wondering way of someone who isn't

used to speaking their thoughts out loud, Melly said, "I'm sorry you're going. She don't take on strays all the time like she said—not men, anyways. But right from the first time she saw you, she . . . Well, she likes you. We both do," she added, and then fled.

He hadn't expected it to be hard to leave them, too, as much as he ached to be elsewhere. But he wiped the thought off his face before Ania returned, all brisk and business.

"The week's pay," she said, dropping the coins into Reandn's hand. "And don't you dare forget to take care of that face. *And* don't get yourself into any *more* trouble like it. And—"

"And I'll wash behind my ears every day," Reandn interrupted smoothly, but amended it to, "Well, most days." He tucked the coins away, checked the seating of his boot knife, and adjusted his half-chap around it in preparation for skirting the road—and any of Shuyler's men—on the way to the market. If all went well, the market would be sparsely guarded tonight, and he would have an easy time of it.

Ania tried an unsuccessful smile at his attempted humor. As he straightened, he said firmly, "Ania, I mean it. Forget this morning. Just remember you've been a friend when I needed one." He waited for her nod, hesitated, and gave her a quick kiss on the cheek on his way out the back door.

Once outside the *Unicorn*, he paused, flexed the tension out of his shoulders—as if he could shrug off the people he was leaving behind—before striking out for the market. At last, time to move on. *One more night*, came the litany.

And this time, he smiled.

Although he had to avoid two of Shuyler's men waiting for him on the road to the market, the night went easily for Reandn. The few market guards stayed in a group, drinking and loudly bemoaning the fate that left them out of the big road job. They aimed coarse comments at Savill for being stupid enough to move the dower after dark. Reandn prowled in the woods, too uneasy to sit still, even though his movement increased his risk. When it came right down to it, he was just as unhappy as they to be left out of the evening's action.

When morning came and the guards left, he went immediately to Bergren's shed, prepared to ride out no matter what had happened to Shuyler's men and Savill's dower. The merchants themselves were tardy; Reandn had no doubt they were waiting somewhere, together, for the results of the Locals' work. He'd wait for Bergren, he decided, and that was it. What supplies he could afford were bought, and he'd just have to manage as he went along.

He picked through his chosen equipment, checking straps, cleaning the bay's bridle, and finally getting out the horse itself for a good grooming. He was picking out a front hoof when a hesitant woman's voice on the other side of the bay said, "Reandn."

He dropped the hoof, wiped his hands on his thighs and found himself looking over at Ciandra, the young woman whose betrothed had been killed in the inn. There was no sign of an escort; the morning mist was still thick, and the heavy dew had soaked the thin cloth shoes Ciandra wore. She looked just as pale as the day her betrothed had been killed, thoroughly unprepared for her environment and the task she seemed to have taken upon herself.

"Do you remember me?" she asked anxiously.

"Yes, of course." He trailed a hand along the bay's side and rump as he passed behind it, and watched her a moment; she hesitated, forming and abandoning several words along the way. "You don't really look like you want to be here, Ciandra. How can I help you?"

"It . . . it's the other way around, I hope. I came to warn you." Another hesitation, and then she plunged into it. "You've got to leave Maurant."

For a moment Reandn could not quite reconcile the words with the messenger. She saw it in him, and abruptly offered explanation. "Jilla made a condolence call at our house last night," she said. "She isn't very fond of you. Of course she talked about—about what happened that day. She was very pleased to say that Savill's just heard from King's Keep."

He gave her a sharp look. *Already?* No, it was too soon, at least for any response to Savill's query about him.

"It was the regular monthly dispatch, just gossip, usually. She often shares it with us. Things like the Keep wizard's left for Solace to take retirement, the Resiore Highborn are still causing trouble over a missing boy, that sort of news. But there was also something about a missing Wolf, and some sort of killing spree." She looked at him, her eyes taking in his features. "They don't know if the Wolf is dead or not—they don't even know if he was responsible for the killing—but they want him back. He . . . they said he was just above average size, with dark blond hair. And . . . and grey eyes." She looked at his, and if she lacked confidence, she at least showed no fear of him, or of the reaction that must have been showing in his face.

They don't know if I'm responsible for the killing? How could that be? And a quiet little voice in his mind said, *You found the Resiore boy's trail—and lost it. By the time anyone else got to the area, it was completely muddied up—no way to know for sure it'd been like that from the start. You reported the hole in the pond ice, which delayed serious searching. It was your boy Kavan who went missing next—and your wife. And* probably much easier to believe he'd done it and fled, than to imagine a Wolf First being taken down as easily as a child. *Then they still don't know about the magic.*

Ciandra caught his eye again. "They named you, Reandn. Savill's coming for you."

Reandn was still a long moment. He pushed a hand through his hair, caught on one last, finally reassuring thought. *Ronsin hasn't killed anymore at the Keep or they'd know it wasn't me.* But once the wizard reached Solace, he'd have countless opportunities. "You seem to be pretty well informed," he said to Ciandra.

"I told you," she said, "Jilla was at my house last night. It wasn't hard to get her to tell me everything she knew."

"I don't imagine it was," Reandn said, suddenly feeling weary. "Do you have any idea just *when* Savill is going to come for me?"

"He'll be waiting for you at the *Unicorn,*" she answered soberly. "Where you won't have any woods to get away in."

Then he still had some time. Savill wouldn't send the Locals out to the market until after Reandn was late in town; even then, the men might stall some if Cyrill put in a word for him. If he left within the hour, he'd have a good start on them—though it looked like he wasn't heading back for the Keep anymore. *Solace. How far away is it?*

A rustle of Ciandra's skirts made him realize he'd been silent for some moments, one hand absently smoothing the bay's thick mane. He looked at her again. "I don't think it would do you any good to be found alone out here. I'll take care."

"I'm not alone," Ciandra said, smiling for the first time, though it quickly faded. "Nelmar's family—and his younger brother Nuri—were there last night, too. It was his idea to warn you, but . . . he just couldn't quite face you. It's what he saw, I think."

"I don't blame him. But go. I won't be here long, myself."

She gathered her skirts to raise them above the usual obstacles in a horse yard, yet couldn't quite seem to make herself leave. Her expression was uncertain, as though she herself wasn't sure what she wanted, but Reandn, more familiar with the aftereffects of violence, knew she was looking at a link to the last time she'd seen Nelmar alive. Once she left, once he was gone, there would be one less tie to her happiness with the dead man. He absently rubbed the ring on his little finger. "It'll be all right," he said gently. "Go, Ciandra."

She blinked, and gathered herself. "Take care," she said, and walked quickly away.

Reandn returned to grooming the bay with a vengeance, and saddled him, leaving the girth loose and the bridle slung over the saddle while he made last minute adjustments in the arrangement of the sparse items in the saddlebags—a hammer, an extra shoe for front and back, and horseshoe nails, under all the grain he could fit into the roomy bag. The other side held trail rations he'd picked up the evening before, all but depleting his supply of parscores. This journey would be made with just enough to keep him going; he only hoped the bay would hold up as well.

Finally, the merchants arrived, every single one of them, clumped in a jubilantly noisy group. Reandn didn't have to guess which way the night's work had gone; he breathed a sigh of relief and tightened the cinch another pull. The bay swished his tail and gave a quick sideways nod, not quite daring a nip, lifting his hind leg just an inch before putting it back down. Reandn gave him only a small part of his attention as he watched Bergren separate from the gaggle of men, his face all exhilarated relief.

"We waited together all night," the merchant said. "Got the word only a short while ago—from a fellow named Cyrill. They're," he nodded at the other, "all pretty pleased with you, son."

"The Locals did the work," Reandn snorted.

"You know better. And even if you don't, I hope it won't keep you from accepting their thanks."

Reandn shook his head. "I'm on my way out, Bergren, and I can't waste any time about it."

"You'll want to take the time for this," Bergren said, taking Reandn's arm and leading him away from the bay. "Their thanks are a little more substantial than words."

As it turned out, there were plenty of words as well, enough so the delay was nerve-wracking. The bay irritably allowed a full load of supplies to be balanced over his loins and shoulders, until loose straps tickled his flanks and he scattered the merchants with half-hearted bucking. Bergren declared it a good test for the security of the load, and, finally catching the extent of Reandn's concern, shooed the other merchants away. Reandn was settled in the saddle when Bergren returned, alone.

The horse trader looked up at him for a long moment, apparently turning over words in his mind. Finally he put a hand on Reandn's leg, choosing that silent communication of thanks over all the possible words. Reandn hesitated, brought his fist to his throat in the Wolf's salute, and turned the bay's head away from Maurant.

As a protest to all he'd put up with, the gelding stuck his nose in the air and took off at full speed. Bergren's laugh fell quickly out of earshot, and Reandn couldn't help a grin of his own, just as glad to be moving. The bay tilted his head slightly to keep an eye on his rider, his nose pointed up in case Reandn tried to stop him with a jerk on the reins. "Skygazer," Reandn said, sitting the rolling gait as easily as the pleasure of a good canter. Sky the gelding gave a moist, noisy snort and left Maurant far behind them.

Chapter 12

So Ronsin had left for Solace, just as he'd mentioned to Adela. Not so surprising, as she'd said—originally a retreat and education center for working wizards, it was now a center for learning in all fields, especially the medical. No doubt Ronsin had many colleagues there, still bemoaning their loss of status when the magic had faded away.

It had happened gradually, at first. Spells misfiring, powerful wizards unable to access the potent spells they'd once wielded with ease. By the time Reandn was a child, there was very little left, and then, one day when he was thirteen, it vanished completely, from one hour to the next.

By the time it happened, the wizards had been limited to minor magics, simple things like wards against biting insects and protection spells; they'd always made Reandn slightly queasy, and he hadn't found it difficult to avoid magic altogether. Abandoned, his days full of fighting for his most basic needs, it'd simply never been a part of his experience. Now, in retrospect, he knew the loss of magic, and of the creatures of magic—from chameleon shrews to the coveted, elusive unicorns—was a small price to pay, if it meant eliminating threats like Ronsin.

But after seventeen years of searching, Ronsin had somehow gotten his magic back. And he had to be stopped. *Which means me. One man on an insecure horse, on his way to Solace.*

Solace was small but well traveled, bursting with intellectual activity, and located in the rolling, forested hills of southeastern Keland. Even without initial guidance, Reandn had no trouble keeping to the right roads. Once he'd aimed himself in the proper direction, the occasional inquiry at roadhouses along the way kept him straight, and let him know he had about two weeks of travel at his very slow pace.

Far too much time. Plenty of time for Ronsin to pick up, in Solace, with what he'd left off at King's Keep. But Sky, carrying Reandn and provisions, could move no faster. Sky was not a mount Reandn would have wanted on patrol. He was sensitive, like Willow—but unlike Willow, he had plenty of history behind him, and took careful handling to avoid triggering another run-away. But he was willing to work, and could pick up a medium rack that was easy on both horse and man, keeping it up for miles.

Each morning, accompanied by the orchestration of almost-familiar birds, they started in the gloom of the dawn for the best travel of the day. In the heat of midday, Reandn pulled off Sky's bridle, replaced it with a halter, and hobbled him so he could pick and nibble at the road's edge, where tall trees on each side of the road lent them shade, and Reandn could nap. After a while, when he couldn't stand the inactivity any longer, he would amble down the road on foot, leading Sky. It wasn't until late afternoon that they picked up a steady pace again, and traveled into darkness.

What he dreaded most was stopping for the night. When Sky was taken care of, and some semblance of a meal eaten, there was nothing to occupy his mind but the things he least wanted to think about. Adela's birthday coming up. Their anniversary, not long after that. The thousand little things about her that he missed. He tried, instead, to worry about the things that he at least had a *chance* to do something about—like how he'd manage more grain, once his supply ran out. He'd been miserly with it, grazed the horse for as many hours as he could—but Sky was losing weight, and Reandn didn't have enough money to buy grain all the way to Solace.

Well. He'd use Wolf Rights if he had to. Out on the road, he was likely to have more problems enforcing Rights than worries about his activity reaching the Keep or Ronsin. And once in Solace, all he had to do was find the man, and then one well-placed knife in the dark . . . it would be an execution, the Wolf Justice Ronsin had sneered at as he destroyed Reandn's life.

He'd traveled for a week when he found the road to Solace—it was well marked with a freshly painted sign—but almost as an omen, Sky took one step upon it and tripped, catching his front shoe with his hind toe and tearing it off his foot. He stumbled awkwardly for a few steps and stopped.

Reandn swung down and retrieved the twisted shoe from the road behind them. "Good job," he told the gelding, who stretched his neck to sniff at the offending metal. Reandn sighed when he saw the foot it had been on; well-clenched nails had torn chunks from the hoof wall, making the reset a tricky task. Reandn resigned himself to digging in the saddlebags after the nails and tools, and tied Sky to the nearest tree.

Sweat dribbled off the end of his nose as he replaced the shoe. He was soon shirtless, driving each nail with a care he didn't usually take, breaking the sharp ends off with a twist of the hammer claw and settling for clumsy clenches he hoped would hold until he found someone with a complete set of tools to do the job right. Sky was docile throughout the process, which Reandn was thankful for, although he did wish the gelding would stand on three legs instead of using Reandn as a prop for the fourth.

By the time he had finished, Sky looked rested and pleased, while Reandn felt like a Yearling during the first days of training. He tucked his vest through the back of his belt and tightened the horse's cinch, turning back the way they'd come. The road crossed a stream less than a mile back and Reandn intended to wash up and make camp for the night there. Sky was delighted when the saddle came off, and expressed himself with a snort-filled exhibition of rolling. The comical sight was almost enough to make up for the delay—and so was the extra time Reandn had to devote to a decent meal.

But when night fell and he wrapped his light blanket around bare shoulders to keep the insects off, things changed. Sleep came fast, and plunged him into the void he thought he'd left behind at Farren's house—the tangle of mismatched senses, swirling impressions of danger, nauseating memories of pain. Coherent thought was impossible, but he knew, he *knew* what had happened— *the madness is back—*

He fought it, holding on to his need to complete what he'd started, to find Ronsin and avenge Adela, to make sure he could no longer tear people apart with magic. But Reandn's mind was shredding in the ethereal torture chamber Ronsin had introduced to him, and he couldn't claw his way free.

No. Adela's voice was clear and firm, and not to be denied. In the background, Reandn heard something he'd only heard once or twice before—the sound of Kavan laughing. Joyful, childish laughter, a balm. Then Adela's voice again, whispering, *You're safe, love.* He clung to the feel of her, burying the confusion of his senses in the one thing he knew best. *Hold on to me,* she said, and he did, until suddenly she was gone, and the disorientation was gone as well.

Reandn started awake. The blanket was twisted off his shoulders, and sweat dribbled down his temple and chest. *Damnation, that was real.* Too real. Enough to make him tremble, to stick in his throat where his breath came quick and hard. After a moment, he climbed to his feet and moved unsteadily to the gelding. The horse was large and solid in the darkness, and Reandn put his arm over the animal's withers, glad for the company. Sky dozed without concern, tangible evidence that the night held no threat for either of them.

But as Reandn steadied, relaxing against the horse's bulk, he realized he was working his jaw, working to ease the discomfort he had not felt since his arrival in the South. Since he'd left Ronsin behind. . . .

Magic. He lifted his head, as though he could scent the magic on the wind; and the memory of his dream tugged at him. *Magic.* It roamed the night, and he had no defense from it. And there was only one person who could be wielding it. He took a deep breath, stroking the bay's neck with a resolutely steady hand; soon, the magic faded. *Get used to it,* he told himself. Ronsin would have magic when Reandn finally met up with him; Reandn would have to deal with it somehow. He rubbed his thumb across the gold on his little finger, drawing strength of purpose from Adela's ring. *I will not fail you.*

Eventually, he retrieved the blanket, propping himself up against a tree near Sky. The horse had turned to a lazy browsing, wrapping his lips around leaves and pulling until they tore off, grinding steadily at the mouthful he was accumulating; occasionally he stopped and gave a sleepy sigh, content and secure. Perhaps it was catching, for when Reandn fell asleep, it was deep and sound, and had no vestige of magic at all—only the soft brush of a presence that was Dela.

When he woke it was late in the morning, and Sky was jerking restlessly at his tie rope, eyeing the travel-diminished pile of gear and supplies within which sat his grain.

Reandn groaned and pulled the blanket over his head, theatrical reluctance to face the world. When he rose, he hurried to feed the horse and himself, even though it was really too late to make any time before the heat struck them. As he saddled the horse, commotion at the roadway made him pause, and the thick trees revealed just enough for him to make out the approaching wagons of a trade caravan.

Sky arched his neck at the scent of other horses, then lifted his head high and curled his lip up, finding the odor of a mare in season. "Quit that, you're a gelding now," Reandn said sharply, but not without sympathy. He hoped the caravan would go straight on and leave them the road to Solace; he was not interested in dealing with a frustrated horse who didn't yet realize he was a gelding. He gave the slow moving conglomeration of wagons and riders plenty of time to make it past the turn-off before he ventured onto the road with his prancing horse.

Sky wanted to run, to catch up and flirt with the mares; they compromised with a high-stepping rack that would have been lovely to watch and even nicer to sit if, for the first time, the scarred hock hadn't interfered with the gelding's animated movement. They had a brief fight when Sky refused to turn toward Solace; Reandn took it as good sign that the caravan had indeed gone on. After they'd whirled a few circles and raised a little dust, the horse heaved a sigh and moved reluctantly down the side road. Reandn gave him a pat and let him walk out the angry sweat he'd worked up.

"That was quite a show."

Reandn stiffened at Farren's unexpected voice; Sky stopped short, hopeful at any sign they might indeed follow the caravan mare. Farren was standing in the trees by the side of the road. Just standing, as if he'd been there for days, waiting for Reandn to come along. Tanager was sitting a short distance away, his back up against a tree and a small pack mule tied behind him. Reandn didn't say anything for a long moment, as he thought of his dreams from the previous night, and the magic he'd felt. Finally, coldly, Reandn said, "Farren."

The wizard nodded, and said nothing. There was no sign of magic—at least, not now. It occurred to Reandn that Farren wouldn't realize that Reandn could sense the use of magic; Adela and Saxe certainly hadn't, and even Ronsin had seemed surprised. He gave a grim little smile. "And what in the Lonely Hells are you doing *here*?"

"Following you, of course," Farren said. "There's no use at all in denying it. I told you before—you have something I need. I need it too badly to just let you go."

Reandn gave a short laugh. "However you found me—" *magic* "—you're still on foot. I've got a horse. You're not likely to run me down."

Farren tilted his head. "Yes, and quite an animal he is, in his moments. But now that we've met up, I hope you'll consider traveling together."

Reandn gave a bark of laughter. "You're one of the things I'm leaving behind." He twitched his legs against Sky's sides and the horse ambled forward, taking only one wishful step toward the caravan's road before turning toward Solace.

"We found you once," Farren said. "And we know where you're going." Reandn froze, but did not turn. "Well, we have a good idea," the wizard said, qualifying his words. "Bergren said you'd asked for direction this way. So you go on, son. We'll see you in Solace."

Reandn hesitated, looked over his shoulder. If he left the wizard behind, Reandn would never know just what he was up to; it might very well simply be more trouble than having Farren close by. And if the old man continued to keep track of him with magic, Reandn would always be plagued with that feeling behind his jaw, that noise playing at the edge of his hearing.

His dilemma must have shown, for Farren said quietly, "We're not here to hurt you, son. I only want some answers. They're important enough that I can't let you walk away—although I don't mind telling you, Lina just about had my hide when I said I was going to follow you."

"You got here with the caravan," Reandn guessed.

"They left Maurant the same day you did. I'm surprised we caught up with you."

"Sky threw a shoe." It might as well have been a conversation between two farmers at a pulling contest. Reandn sighed, took up the reins. *Better to keep an eye on him, if he's going to follow me anyway*. And he had no doubt the wizard would. He'd come half the distance already. A touch of his calf, and Sky moved out, bobbing his head impatiently in commentary at the human's indecision. They moved away from the two figures— but they moved at a walk. Behind them, Tanager scrambled to his feet, dragging the mule along as he took to the road with his grandfather.

The slow pace was monotonous, and the stress of having the wizard with him was wearing even without magic. Tanager's chatter was almost as bad; he never seemed to notice he was the only one making any significant noise. The group walked right through noon, although Reandn led the gelding for an hour or so, and by the time early evening arrived, he was more than glad to see a modest inn nestled among the trees.

Over the past days Reandn had passed plenty of similar establishments, and ignored them—they offered little more than a roof and marginal food. Tonight, however, he needed a blacksmith, and he had no intention of making camp for three people. He left Farren and his grandson at the inn and followed the innkeep's directions to the small village, not so far away, that held the closest blacksmith.

When Reandn went by the inn the next morning, he found Farren and Tanager waiting for him—Farren patient, Tanager bored. Reandn hadn't had any intention of deliberately stopping for the two, but he didn't bother to argue about it when they fell in beside him. After an hour or so of walking, Farren mentioned, as offhandedly as Reandn figured it was possible, that he'd seen Sky didn't have enough grain, and he'd bought some.

Reandn stopped the horse and looked down at Farren. Tanager lagged behind, leading the mule, and not paying much attention to anything at all. "You're really going to follow me all the way, aren't you," Reandn said flatly to the wizard. "Even if I leave you behind, you'll keep right on coming."

"I have friends in Solace," Farren said. "I have no doubt I'll find you again when I get there. Knowing Teayo alone will probably do it, the way that man works."

Of course he had friends in Solace. Just like Ronsin would. Reandn looked away from Farren, off into the woods. He didn't have any doubt the wizard meant what he said, and could carry it out, with or without friends. He could, after all, always use magic. He didn't seem to have as much as Ronsin, but Farren had shown up on the heels of the magic Reandn had felt, and that was no coincidence. He spent a moment weighing the aggravation of having the wizard at his side against the freedom to travel more quickly—but of having to deal with magic in his head while he did so. After a moment, he abruptly dismounted.

"Might as well do this the smart way," he said, in response to Farren's inquiring look. "Load your mule with my extra gear, and we'll see if Sky will carry double."

After an anxious moment, Sky decided he would indeed carry Tanager and Farren together—as long as the newcomers didn't so much as touch the reins. The gelding was glad enough to follow at Reandn's shoulder as they walked the packed dirt road. Tanager rode with his grandfather—Farren was, after all, not a large man, and while Tanager had more in the way of arms and legs, it was all gawk and not much flesh yet. No one suggested that Reandn might ride double with anyone. By switching frequently, they kept up a stiff pace.

It worked for a day and a half, which was longer than Reandn had expected. It was evening, and they were all tired; Reandn was sitting atop Sky with a loose rein, scanning the woods for a place to stop, when their uneasy truce came to an abrupt halt. Suddenly magic was back, subtly thrumming through Reandn's head and building to quick fury.

He spun the surprised bay in the road, blocking Farren's path; his voice growled low. "Stop it."

Farren came to a standstill, startled. "Excuse me?"

"I said, *stop it*." Reandn crowded the wizard with Sky, forcing him several steps backward. Sky's eyes rolled white, and his nose went straight in the air, torn by the commands to do this forbidden thing, this pushing the human.

"I heard you," Farren said irritably, snatching his foot back just in time to getting stepped on. "But I don't know what you're talking about!"

"The magic," Reandn said, waving a hand at his ear as though that would make sense to someone else; Sky gave half a rear, balking and close to blowing up. "Turn it off *right now*."

Farren shook his head, looking baffled, still backing away. "Reandn . . . I haven't used magic for over half your life span. And even if I *was*, there's no way you could *know*—"

"I do know," Reandn said grimly. "I've told you you can't lie to me about it."

Tanager shoved himself between Sky and his grand-father; the horse reared high, and Reandn gave rein, legging the horse forward to land just beside the boy. "Are you *stupid*?" Tanager shouted, brave if not wise. "There *isn't* any magic. That's why we have to find out how you got to Maurant!"

By the time Tanager's words had died away into a silence which tingled between Farren and Reandn, the magic had died away as well. Reandn heaved an inward sigh of relief; Sky settled, just as relieved. "Keep it that way," Reandn said coldly, and turned Sky back down the road, unwilling to listen to any argument from the wizard or his grandson.

By tacit agreement, neither mentioned the incident, although Reandn caught the wizard looking at him, contemplating him—and never minding that Reandn usually caught him at it. Reandn warred constantly with the desire to leave the wizard behind—but it also occurred to him that he could use Farren for his own means, as well. The man knew the city. He knew the people. He probably wouldn't deliberately give Reandn information that would help him track down Ronsin, but Reandn thought he could glean some nonetheless.

Several days passed without incident. Their path curved between rolling hills, wavering between due north to northeastward; when afternoon came, the broad leaved trees filled the world with stark changing shadows across and around the road. One minute staring into a shadow, the next blinking against sunlight—Reandn was almost glad when it was his turn to walk, so at least those shadows did not sway with Sky's movement. He led the mule, silent, listening to Farren's responses to Tanager, and watching the horse for signs of fatigue.

Tanager was talkative this afternoon, constantly

leaning against his grandfather's shoulder to share some observation or another, his excited anticipation at seeing Solace unjaded by the fact that he and Farren were unwanted company. The youth had taken off his short-sleeved tunic, and it dangled from one hand to tickle Sky's flanks.

Should I warn him? Reandn watched bay horseflesh twitch irritably beneath the tickling shirt. He could, of course, just let the inevitable explosion happen . . . *No. Not fair to the horse.* "Tana—"

Magic hit him, a surge of it. Struggling, Reandn pushed his way through its effects, but not through the rage it produced. He growled, *"Farren."*

Farren had already turned the bay sideways in the road, one hand reaching back to shush Tanager, although the gesture looked strangely protective as well. "Graces," he breathed, his head lifted in intense attention, "You're right, Reandn. Someone *is* using—*look out!*" Even as he spoke, the insidious flow of magic ceased. Farren's hands rose, fingers moving, lips twisting around mumbled words.

Reandn followed his gaze into the sun-and-shadow striped woods, crouching, hand already closing over his boot knife. It wasn't until the woman moved to notch an arrow that her brown and green mottled clothes turned into a distinct human shape among the leaves. Reandn brought his knife up and threw as she drew the bow.

"Don't kill her!" Farren cried, too late to stop the flash of Reandn's knife. "We need to know—"

Reandn ignored him, snatching Tanager's shirt and wringing it through the air, bringing it against Sky's rump with a loud *smack*. The gelding bolted away at full speed, head in the air, not to be stopped. The mule stared in stupefaction and refused to follow.

Reandn dropped the shirt and ran into the woods, stooping just long enough to retrieve both his knife and the dying woman's bow and quiver, his gaze darting from shadow to shadow beneath the trees. When there was no sign of movement, he slunk further into the woods and climbed a beech that took him far off the ground, and offered several sturdy forkings to place his feet in.

Once there he set an arrow to bowstring and waited.

The woods were silent, aside from the harsh, sporadic warning cries of several birds. Reandn was as motionless as his tree save for his eyes; he searched the woods, step by step, tree by tree. The arrow rested against the bowstring, smooth tipped, grooved and glistening; he gave an internal grimace at the sight of it.

A drop of sweat tortured and tickled the end of his nose; he refused to be distracted, not until he was certain the woman was alone. When something to his right rustled, he twisted to face it, drawing the bow in the same motion. A small, pale man was aiming at him; Reandn let the bowstring roll off his fingers, ignoring the arrow that thunked into the tree trunk.

As the man fell, a sudden solid blow thwacked into Reandn's bicep from the opposite direction; a grunt of surprise and he was falling, losing the bow on the way. He hit the ground with a partial roll, but by then the only thought in his mind was stopping the burn from his arrow. His scrabbling fingers found the shaft and closed around it, yanking hard, not even thinking of the damage he might be doing—but the headless arrow wrenched free and he flung it away. On his knees, hunched over the fierce agony in his arm, he looked up just in time to see the flash of a short curved saber aimed at his head.

Again he rolled, jerking out of the way as the saber flashed by his head and struck solidly into dirt. The man tugged it free as Reandn rolled to his knees and scrambled across the ground, filling his hands with humus and debris and flinging it in his adversary's face, snarling a savage threat as he bowled into the man. The saber flew far to the side and Reandn, pain-robbed of anything but base instinct, had killed his attacker three different ways before he even noticed.

He threw himself away from the dead man and lay panting on the ground, trying to think, too full of pain and adrenalin to manage it. He didn't notice danger until booted feet filled his vision; gulping for air, he turned onto his back to stare helplessly up at the grinning face of yet one more foe. A brutal knee came down on Reandn's throat, another jammed against his chest. He struggled, floundering, one arm useless and the other hand pushing futilely against the knee that cut off his air. He twisted his legs underneath himself, vainly trying to cast the man off his chest as his strength fled and his world darkened.

Suddenly he could breathe, and air whooped through his bruised throat—until the dead weight of the other man fell across his chest and he was fighting to be free of it.

Someone heaved the body away. "Are you all right?"

It was Farren's face, wavering in his vision; Reandn would have attacked on principle if his body had still been listening to him.

"No, I see not," the older man muttered to himself. He took a firm hold of Reandn's burning arm, ignoring Reandn's yelp of pain as he peered at the wound. "Sorry, son," Farren said absently, frowning. "What made this?"

"D-damn," was all Reandn could gasp in reply.

"Tanager, bring the waterskin," Farren called over his shoulder. He left Reandn curled around his tortured self, and rummaged in the battleground around them.

When he returned his face was grim. He knelt, one hand on Reandn's shoulder in a gesture that was oddly comforting; the other held an odd-shaped rock on a thong, which he set aside as Tanager thundered up beside him.

"What happened?" the boy asked breathlessly.

"It appears someone was looking for our friend," Farren said, prying Reandn's fingers away from his wound and liberally splashing it with water. Reandn groaned with the cold relief, though deep inside his arm it still burned like fire. But it was enough of a surcease so he could pull himself together, calm himself and start to function again.

"Better?" Farren asked.

"How the hell did you stop that horse?" Reandn said, rolling over to get his knees beneath him; with a helping hand from Farren he was able to sit back on his heels.

"I didn't," Farren said, a twitch at the side of his mouth. "He stopped on his own when I headed him for a tree. Got here just in time to keep that big fellow from squashing you." He nodded his head at the prone figure, which had a short, curved blade sticking out the back of its neck. "There seemed to be plenty of weapons lying around."

"You shoulda' seen him!" Tanager crowed. "Pa-farren went right after—"

"If you'd stayed where you were told, *you* wouldn't have seen anything," Farren said sharply. "This is no game, Tanager. Someone was looking specifically for Reandn, *and* they used magic to find him." He nodded at the stone.

"But they didn't get him," Tanager said, obviously as much objection as he dared.

"Not yet," Farren said, giving Reandn an anxious look. "How do you feel now?"

"You couldn't do it," Reandn said fuzzily, staring at the older man. "You tried to use magic before I spooked Sky, and it didn't work, did it?"

Farren said gently, "I've told you all along, I couldn't. It was a reaction of habit, and it lost us precious time." He frowned at the bodies scattered around them and said, "I wish we'd been able to save at least one of them. We need to know who sent them."

"I know who sent them," Reandn said, squeezing his eyes shut, concentrating, trying to drive the pain deep into the back of his mind where it could not distract him.

"Tanager, help him up," Farren instructed abruptly. "There's a village half a day's walk from here. If we're lucky, Teayo still doctors there."

"Do you want me to wrap it?" Tanager suggested, nonetheless following instructions. Almost against his will, Reandn found himself on his feet, suddenly viewing the world from a strange, detached point of view. His fingers tingled numbly.

"Let it bleed," Farren said grimly. "It's the best chance to get the poison out."

Caustic and poison. Bergren had warned him.

His legs mutinied, or maybe they now belonged to someone else. As he set one clumsy foot in front of the other, it was only the two men on either side of him that kept him upright. The first time his knees gave way, he sparked into a semblance of his usual vigor. "Damned magic," he panted, as Tanager, taken unawares, also went down. The second time it happened, it no longer seemed to matter. Sky loomed in his vision and with much pushing and grunting he was suddenly atop the horse, who moved apprehensively beneath his unsteady load.

Farren's words came to him remotely but slow and distinct; the wizard put a hand on his wrist and squeezed to get all of Reandn's limited attention.

"Hang on, Reandn. I think I can get you to good help. But you've got to do your part."

"It doesn't matter," Reandn said, speaking in that same distinct manner past a tongue that seemed . . . fuzzy? "Dela's waiting for me." In fact, there she was, standing at Sky's head, although the horse was walking and she was not. She was in a thin summer dress, one of the ones he had bought for her in town not because she needed it, but because she liked it so much. She smiled at him, and her lips said *I love you*, and she was waiting for him.

Then pain lanced through his entire left side, and he yelped in surprise, shattering the vision. He lurched and would have fallen if someone's hands had not caught him.

"It'll be all right, son." Did he know that voice? "Tanager, help me up behind him. We'll never make it walking—I'm going to have to leave you behind. Take the first left-hand turn you come across, it'll be clear enough. If you go too far you'll run into Little Wisdom, and someone there will know the way."

"Yes, Pa-farren." The other voice sounded uncertain but unprotesting. In a moment, a weight settled behind Reandn and two arms encircled him, straightening him as he listed left.

"The first left-hand turn," the voice behind him repeated. "Teayo's surgery. Got it?"

If there was an answer, Reandn did not hear it, too enveloped in his own little world, which was made of oddly echoing hoofbeats, Adela's sweet voice, and an occasional groan that seemed to fill his head until it oozed into the outside world as well. Beat beat beat . . . beat, the even-stepping rack marred only by the scarred hock of a studdy bay who for once went calmly and steadily with someone else's cautious hand on the reins.

Touched By Magic

Chapter 13

Kacey was alone and glad of it. It was the chance to catch up on the distasteful chore of late spring cleaning. Her father was seldom any help when it came to the practical aspects of his healing practice, and Rethia was off gathering herbs, as usual. Kacey wiped her hands on well-rounded hips and then pushed her brown curls out of her eyes, deciding that after the sickroom windows were washed, she would relax. Only after she cranked up a sloshing bucket of water and hauled it to the stone side of the deep well, splashing her brown galatea trousers, did she hear the unusual pattern of hoofbeats coming up the long wooded lane to the house.

She spotted the horse while it was still well down their lane, and knew right away someone was in trouble. The sweat-darkened bay carried double, and the extent and duration of his run was written in every move—the lather dripping from his chest and flanks, the rapid huff of air from his pinked, extended nostrils. He finally stumbled to a stop directly beside her; his head dropped almost to the ground.

The man in front was the problem; at first she thought it had something to do with the ugly scrape running up his jaw, but she quickly realized that was a healing wound. The man in back, smaller, older, struggled to keep his companion upright as they shifted with the bay's halt; his voice brusque and demanding, he said, "I must see Teayo."

Kacey balanced the bucket on the well's edge. "He isn't here. I'll have to do." Peering up at the listing passenger, she discovered at last the water-diluted blood stains on his left arm. His shaggy, dark blond hair hung over a pale, sweating face. An undeniably handsome face, Kacey realized suddenly.

But that thought lasted only a moment, and then stolid, sensible Kacey took over. "Get him in the house," she said. "And then you can see to that poor animal."

"I was really hoping to find Teayo."

"What you've found is me. You don't have to stay."

The man poked his beard out at her and his brows drew down, but more in puzzlement than anger. "Good Goddess, Kacey, is that you? Surely there aren't two women in the world given such a tongue."

She nodded an impatient *yes* and said, "It would be a shame if your friend died right there after you nearly killed that horse to get here. Do you want me to help, or not?" Strong words, but they startled the man out of his hesitation, and he wordlessly headed the animal for the house, a huge, timber-beamed dwelling that held both Teayo's home and his infirmary.

Kacey left the bucket and walked swiftly in front of them, pushing through the door at the end of the house, turning to hold it open. "Here you go—*whoops!*" For as the silver-bearded stranger slid down the horse's rump, his friend tumbled off the side. Kacey grabbed him halfway out of the saddle; the horse grunted and straddled his tired legs against the off-balance load. Together, gracelessly, Kacey and the stranger hauled the injured man into the house and dropped him on the closest cot;

he might as well have been dead meat, for all the reaction they got out of him.

"Heavier than he looks," Kacey panted. *Solid*. She immediately began cleansing the arm wound—for boiled water and cloths were never far away in this room—but after a moment she hesitated, looking from the neat round hole to the patient's unconscious, sweaty face. Its edges were red and swollen, irritated more than they should have been. "This isn't a bad wound," she said carefully, her stubby fingers touching the arm. "Not enough to put down a healthy fellow like this."

"It was an arrow," his friend said, looking suddenly older than Kacey had first thought. She motioned for him to sit on the next cot. "We were attacked on the road . . . I'm certain it had been dipped in something."

Oh, no. Kacey closed her eyes and sighed, dropping the cloth back into its bowl. She snaked an ankle behind her to hook the small wooden stool she knew was there and sat heavily.

"Unless you know . . ." she started, but trailed off and shook her head. There wasn't much they could do about poison even if they *did* know which one it was. Her patient stirred suddenly, and she glanced down, finding his eyes half open, dull and vague. But they suddenly snapped into focus, a clear dark grey that made her blink. He looked at her, and gave a feral, challenging grin; Heavens knew what he thought he was looking at. Only years of experience got Kacey to the sheathed knife at his side before he did; she tossed it to the floor with one hand and held his shoulder down with the other, but the surge of aggression left as quickly as it had come. He subsided with a groan and she raised a wry, inquiring eyebrow at the older man. "Used to some action, isn't he."

"He's very good at watching out for himself," the man said, then added dryly, "Usually."

Kacey balanced her words carefully, striving to sound

matter-of-fact. "Too bad he wasn't more careful this time. This looks like a snake venom reaction, and there's not much I can do for him. I think they used caustic, too, but that's just meant to be a distraction in case the first arrow doesn't slow him down enough." She gave the still figure another searching look. Yes, solidly built, but lean enough. His leather vest had soaked up too much sweat, both man and horse, and there was an old blood stain on it, beneath the healing wound on his neck and jaw. He did, in fact, look like he was good at taking care of himself. She wondered what had happened this time. "Someone must have wanted him very dead. Most of the time, these roadmen just use the caustics. That way, even a nick gives them distraction to do their job and run."

"Not distraction enough. He killed two men," said the companion, almost absently.

Her eyebrows went up again. "So? Well, then, maybe he'll have enough fight left in him to beat what's in his system, especially if the arrow came out quickly. Maybe if Rethia gets back soon. . . ." Until then, some drawing poultices, and they'd have to try to get an infusion of snakeroot down him. She stood, already choosing herbs in her mind. Definitely some hopvine, for that inflammation from the caustic. And for the snake venom symptoms . . . pink yarrow tea, to combat the lethargy and depression of body; bluemint would help that, too. Sometimes snakebite victims fell into convulsions—bluemint would do for that, with some ghost flower added in.

Not that it would taste good, mind you, or guarantee survival. But it would help.

She suddenly realized the older man was looking at her, and his expression was just as . . . *demanding* as it had been when he rode up. As if he expected things to happen because he thought they should. "And who is Rethia? Has Teayo had another daughter, without the benefit of a wife?"

Her eyes, set wide in a square face, narrowed. "That's about enough of that," she said. "It's time for introductions, I think!"

The man blinked. "You haven't recognized me yet," he said. "It's true you were only fourteen or so, and that there was more blond than grey in my hair—"

"That was a long time ago," Kacey interrupted. "Surely you won't hold me to a child's memory."

He shook his head. "I was a wizard in those days, Kacey, and your father and I occasionally worked together. My name is Farren. Then, I spent most my time in Solace. Now I live in Maurant."

Kacey searched her memory, and was rewarded with very little. At that age she had been growing into womanhood, and realizing that she was *not* going to grow out of her plain features and less than lithesome body. It had made her rebellious . . . and preoccupied. She shrugged at him, but did address his previous question. "Rethia wasn't with us then."

"And you said . . . she might be able to help Reandn?"

Reandn. So that was his name. She looked thoughtfully at the light, unweathered spot on his vest—that thing was going to come off right away, to see what a good scrubbing could do for it—and wondered what kind of declaration the missing crest had made about him. "It's just Rethia's way," she said. "She's . . . good with the sick. Your friend's best chance is that she returns—and soon."

"And what are the chances of *that*?" Farren asked dryly.

Kacey shook her head. "I don't know. Rethia is . . . Rethia. She doesn't always notice the passing of time. She's probably gone to the village school to watch the children. If he's—" she nodded to Reandn, "—lucky, she'll be back when school's out."

"She teaches?"

"No," Kacey smiled. "She just watches them. They fascinate her."

Farren shook his head. "I look forward to meeting her. Until then . . ."

"I'll do what I can," Kacey said firmly. She winced as her patient groaned. The snake venom wasn't all that painful, but the caustic was a different matter. "Also . . . I can dose him for the pain, but that can be risky on top of the poison."

Farren closed his tired eyes. "I've watched him go through too much already."

She tried not to imagine their ride here, or how far they'd had to come, as she left the bedside to prepare the drought. At the worktable in the front inside corner, she dribbled a viscous syrup into a small wooden bowl. She sweetened it generously with honey and mixed it well. Now to hope he had a sweet tooth. . . .

It was not, however, too difficult to get him to swallow a spoonful. By the time she'd prepared the poultice and left the other herbs simmering in the kitchen for an infusion, it was evident just from the muscles around his eyes that he felt relief. She sat with him a while, then, with Farren still watching from the cot on the other side. Eventually, her patient cracked open drowsy, large-pupiled eyes to look at her. "You came back," he said, taking her hand. She was astonished at how the look on his face tugged at her.

But she was used to playing along with such delusions, and she shot Farren a silencing look. "Of course I came back," she said, closing her fingers reassuringly around his. She wasn't expecting his strength when he drew her closer, was too astonished to react when he pulled her down and kissed her, with intimacy and passion.

She goggled wide-eyed when he let her go, barely hearing as he said, his voice low and rough, "Wait for me, Dela."

"I will," she managed, the back of her hand to her mouth. She ran her tongue around the inside of her lips, tasting the sweet medicine. When she looked at Farren, she could not decipher his expression.

"And what's that supposed to mean?" she snapped.

He blinked at her, and nodded at her patient, asleep with contented if wearied features. "Not so defensive, Kacey. You've eased his mind."

"Who," she said, finally daring to really look at him again, "is Dela?"

"I'm not sure," Farren said, working his shoulders back and forth. "You've assumed us to be closer than we are, when the truth is, he's just been putting up with me." He watched Reandn a moment. "Someone he cares deeply about, obviously. If I were to put together a few offhand comments I would say his Dela is dead, and recently so. He was in a rage about something when he entered Maurant. Bottled up, impossible to reach. . . . I think, if I knew more, I could have handled him much differently. Maybe even gotten through to him."

Kacey wondered if Reandn had reacted any better to the hint of command and demand in Farren's voice. She doubted it. "Maybe you'll have a second chance," she said, privately tasting again of the sweetness in her mouth.

"Sky!" Farren said, suddenly sitting straight upright.

She stared at him, puzzled, wondering if it was some regional curse.

"The horse," he explained, rising hastily. "I left him standing and he's probably stiff as a board—if he hasn't keeled right over."

"There's a small barn out back," Kacey said. "Or do you remember? Nothing's changed."

"I remember well enough," Farren said. "I'll be back when I'm convinced I haven't ruined him."

So, for a while, Kacey was left alone with her patient, and with her thoughts. She studied the man, his features, the way his brows and lashes were darker than his hair;

she remembered the wild, panicked look on his face, then the longing. The man had not responded to *her*; she knew better than that. Even without Dela on his mind, whoever she was—or had been—he'd hardly be interested in solid old Kacey.

And the last thing she would ever do was show him— assuming he lived through this—what he had done to her with that one kiss.

Farren was still in the barn when Rethia appeared in the sickroom doorway. There she paused, silently taking in their new patient from beneath the fringe of her thick, fair bangs, absently standing on one leg to scratch her calf with the other foot, rucking up the skirt of her lightweight kirtle, taking her time. Kacey, knowing her ways after so many years with them, did not offer any information until Rethia walked to the foot of the bed and glanced at her.

"An old friend of Father's brought him. He needs your help, Rethia, he's been hit with a poisoned arrow. But be careful—he was violent when he first got here."

"Sweet syrup?" murmured her foster sister, moving alongside the bed, where she sat down opposite Kacey and considered the man.

"As much as was safe. I wish it could have been more. He's also had infusions of bluemint, ghost flower, and snakeroot."

Rethia reached to touch the wounded arm but abruptly drew back. "Kacey," she said sharply.

Kacey leaned forward on the stool, seeing what her sister had sensed—that the man's lethargy was more than just the syrup's effect, much more. Kacey grabbed both his shoulders and shook him. "Don't you dare! I thought you were a fighter!"

"No," Rethia said. "He's not even *trying*." She reached past Kacey's grasp to touch the punctured arm.

Reandn erupted in unexpected fury.

Kacey hit the floor, gasping for breath, utterly confounded, her cheekbone smarting from his fist. She had enough presence of mind to kick the yet nearby knife skittering away before she lunged to her feet and rejoined the fray, just in time to see him hurl Rethia to the end of the bed, where she landed with a soft whimper of lost breath. Who'd have thought he had such strength left? A second ago she'd been convinced he was but moments away from death.

"Good Goddess!" Farren cried from the doorway, his eyes fastened on the berserker who'd been nearly comatose at last sight.

"Which one?" Kacey asked grimly, aiming for heaving shoulders and settling for a death grip on one arm. With all her weight attached, he could no longer swing it around with such force, and the other arm was not working properly despite his efforts.

"Whichever one I can get!" Farren said, plunging into action. He found the shoulders she'd missed and looked helplessly at the legs which were about to carry them all away.

At the foot of the bed, Rethia got to her feet, her face distressed, her eyes glued to Reandn. "Oh, no wonder!" she cried, and slid between Kacey and Farren to briefly run her hands over Reandn's ears. "There, there," she said soothingly. "It's all right. Easy, now."

Just like you'd talk to a horse. But Kacey was not the least surprised at its effectiveness. Reandn lay back, his chest heaving from exertion—that would be the snakebite, affecting his lungs. In a moment she was able to release her grip; she sat back to rub the shoulder she'd landed on.

"What did you *do*?" Farren demanded breathlessly, not confident enough to relinquish his own grip.

"Spoke to him. . . ." Rethia said distantly, gentle fingers

traveling over the wounded arm. "Felt for him . . . his ears went peculiar, you see."

Farren looked at Kacey as if she could explain the enigma of Rethia. Kacey shrugged. For years she'd watched her foster sister find and ease other people's pains. She couldn't—and didn't have to—understand how it happened, nor did the family talk about it much. It was a quiet fact of life, and when it bordered on the miraculous, they were careful to downplay it for the sake of Rethia's quiet soul.

So Farren's look went unanswered, and neither sister concerned herself about it. "I'll stay with him tonight," Rethia announced, unaware of Farren's scrutiny. "He's so upset . . . I think he could use the company."

"You think he'll be all right, then," Farren said, disbelief evident.

Rethia lifted her head to meet his eyes. Kacey watched, seeing once more a stranger's reaction to Rethia's exotic and wonderful eyes, large eyes of the brightest, clearest blue rimmed with deep brown—eyes that had once been only blue. "I don't know," she said, as oblivious to Farren's reaction as Kacey was aware. She put a comforting hand flat on Reandn's chest, her fingers rising and falling with his breath. Then she frowned, taking her gaze from Farren and settling it on Reandn's face. "If only . . ." she said, completing the phrase only in her head, immersed in her patient.

"If only what?" Farren said after a moment, his hand tugging slightly at his beard in what Kacey interpreted as an out-of-sorts gesture. *Here* was someone who was totally unaffected by his apparent expectations that people respond to him.

"What?" Rethia looked at him again, then to Kacey, to see what this man was talking about.

Kacey stifled a smile. "Rethia," she said, diverting them both from the futile attempt to straighten things out, "this is Farren; he used to be a wizard, and says he's worked with Father. This," she nodded downward, "is Reandn. They were attacked on the road."

Rethia nodded, paying little attention to Farren. If there was a fault to her way of healing it was her tendency to get over-involved. It was she, Kacey thought with a sudden jealous pang, who would attract this Reandn away from his problems with the unknown Dela—if anyone could. Her features were even, set with precision, and if her mouth was a little small and her nose a little long, her eyes more than made up for it. Her medium length hair—thick, fair blond—came down in heavy bangs that brushed against her eyebrows and often hid the full impact of her eyes. Kacey looked down at her stubby fingers and sighed.

Farren caught her eye and tipped his head toward the doorway. Kacey was not slow to catch his meaning, and preceded him outside. "What about it?" he said abruptly.

Kacey gave him a not-to-be-questioned look. "Time," she said. "We'll have to wait and see. We'll keep poulticing, and we'll dose him as long as he'll swallow it. We'd do better if he'd try a little harder." But she thought about Farren's earlier words. *He's been through enough already.* She wondered what that meant.

Farren looked down the road, and spoke almost as though she wasn't there. "He's too important to lose."

Kacey was about to ask what *that* was supposed to mean when they simultaneously spotted a tired figure dragging along the road, leading a mule.

"Tanager!" Farren said. "Graces, he must have run half the way."

Kacey rolled her eyes. "*Two* patients," she said, noting in the boy's approach the kind of lurching motion that meant he'd been running in the sun too long.

Tanager arrived winded and tired but apparently not

in need of extra care; Kacey watched him carefully until she was realized that the gangly movement was merely Tanager being fifteen and not a sign of heat exhaustion. After a slow, cool glass of water and time under a shade tree beside the house, his face lost its ruddy flush and he began to ply Farren with questions about Reandn's condition. Farren, Kacey noted, withstood the barrage better than she would have.

Finally, she'd had enough—the moment came as Tanager asked—*again*—to see Reandn. She ignored Farren's wince as she stood, her hands on her hips. "Your grandfather has told you," she said with what she thought was restrained authority, "that Reandn's as good as he'll be for some while, and you'll learn nothing more by going in to gawk at him. My sister is with him and she works best alone, and I don't want to hear anything more about it!"

Even as she wondered at Farren's mildly amused reaction, and took in Tanager's obvious sulk, she discovered she'd been caught—again—with her temper showing, and by the only man who had a say in such things. Her father.

"Displaying a little hospitality for tired travellers?" Teayo asked from behind her.

Kacey's hands fell to her sides, briefly inanimate, as she turned to face Teayo. "I didn't hear you coming."

Teayo climbed down from the sturdy two-wheeled cart that bore his considerable weight, and, eyebrows raised, said, "I'm not surprised. You were making too much of your own noise."

"She was sorely tried, Teayo," Farren said, rising to his feet.

Kacey watched with satisfaction as her father's attention diverted to Farren, his round, bearded face slacking for an instant in surprise.

"Farren?" he said, then, more confident, "*Farren*. You

old finger-twister. Why in the Hells has it taken you this long to visit?"

Farren gave a short shrug, and said evasively, "Hard to come back here, Teayo. Too many memories of what I can't do anymore."

Teayo drew up his considerable chest and breathed noisily out his nose. "Hmmph. Well, yes, there's that. Then why *now*, hmm? Certainly not for the loving attention of my daughter."

Kacey tried to hide her frown, without much success. Tanager opened his mouth to contribute, seemed to consider the measurable bulk of the man before him, and sank back against the tree to take a gulp of water. Kacey, pleased to have him silenced at last, was more willing to face her father. "They have an injured friend, Father. Rethia's with him."

"Ah?" Teayo said.

"Tanager, as soon as you get your feet under you, take the mule and meir Teayo's horse to the barn—and check on Sky while you're at it." Farren ignored the boy's open mouth of protest, and after a moment, Tanager got to his feet, wearing the expression of a martyr. Farren accepted Teayo's helping hand and stood as well, brushing bits of bark from his short-sleeved tunic. "You're going to find this interesting, Teayo," he said, as they started toward the house. Kacey walked on the other side of her father, an ear attuned to the new things she suspected she would hear. "But I want you to know right off it's probably dangerous."

"I was always an easy scare, Farren," Teayo said with a snort, stroking his dark beard at its grey corners. "What are you harboring in my house, eh?"

Farren's blue eyes crinkled in brief amusement. "Don't put it off so lightly. Neither of us are as young as we were, and the last time we dealt with magic, I had my own to counteract it."

Another snort; Teayo stopped short to face his friend. "I was going to say there's no such thing loose in the world anymore. But . . . perhaps I'll listen to you first." He glanced at Kacey, an expression that was meant to quell her protests at this talk of magic. But Kacey, too, was listening, and that alone was enough to get her father's attention.

Farren took a moment of thought, rubbing a thoughtful finger along the slight crook in his nose. "Here's the quick of it. A month ago a man arrived in Maurant, obviously by advanced translocation. Lina helped him through it, and he was lucky enough to come out of it with his wits. But he doesn't trust me, he's nursing a grudge, and he's absolutely convinced there's still magic being used against him. I followed him when he left for Solace—"

"Poor old finger-twister. The lure of magic, eh?"

"Not just that, Teayo. Reandn's a King's Wolf and that speaks for many things. I don't have to know why he ended up in Maurant to know there's trouble behind it. If some maniac has magic, something's got to be done about it." He took a deep breath and found Teayo's dark brown gaze; Kacey was able to look straight at his piercing blue eyes without notice, and found a conviction she couldn't doubt. "I'm almost certain this person has killed, probably more than once. He or she has a weapon no one is watching for—or has a defense against. I've been trying to gain Reandn's confidence, but it's been useless so far. Now he's been tracked by magic and ambushed on the road, and I need him alive to have any chance to straighten this out."

Framed by beard, Teayo's lips pursed; he switched his gaze to Kacey.

"Poisoned arrow," she said. "In the arm. Not a bad wound, but he's definitely got swampsnake venom in his system. They used caustics, too. He's had infusions, is about ready for fresh poultices, and I gave him half a dose of sweet syrup for his weight. Rethia's with him now."

"How long?"

Kacey and Farren exchanged a glance, neither sure who the question was directed at. Farren ventured, "It happened half a day ago. We've only been here a short while." He took a deep breath. "I don't want you to forget the danger in this. Someone *is* after him." He lifted a dull, thong-hung stone from his belt and let it dangle. "They used this to find him. They can probably do it again. But—"

"But you want this fellow alive," Teayo said. "Did you really think I'd toss you out? You don't have enough words to scare me into that, wizard. Let's go look at this man."

As soon as they entered the house, Kacey saw that Rethia had not been wasting her time alone. Reandn's arm was already bound with a fresh drawing poultice, and Rethia hummed over him now, unaware of the bangs in her own eyes as she gently petted back sweat-damp hair, the whole of her concentration centered around the man who but for the slightest rise and fall of his chest could be dead.

Some of that lassitude was the drug, and Kacey mentioned quietly, "He was violent before the sweet syrup, father. I think it's passed now, but . . ."

"If he gives us trouble I'll sit on him," Teayo said, standing back to appraise what he saw.

"Graces, Teayo, you'll surely kill him that way," Farren muttered.

"Hmmph," Teayo responded, but moved in next to Rethia without responding. She looked up with a quick smile of greeting, and returned her attention to Reandn. Teayo did little more than finger the bandage, lift an eyelid, and check the heartbeat at Reandn's throat. "Good," he said, earning another smile. "You'll stay with him?"

"Tonight," Rethia said.

"I'll make sure you have what you need," Teayo said, nodding. "Don't tire yourself, and I'll be home tonight in case he gets fussy again." He turned to Farren, maneuvering his bulk deftly between the beds. "I've got some good smoked ham waiting for a cold supper, Farren. I'll bet you and your boy are hungry."

"Now that you mention it—" Farren said, but his last words were all but drowned out by Tanager's startled remark from the doorway.

"That's it? That's all you're going to do?"

Teayo raised tufted eyebrows at the boy, whose stabling chores had been done with suspicious speed. "What would you suggest, boy? That I sit here and hold his hand? My daughter's already doing that. I can boil up some healer's potions, but my *other* daughter's already done *that*. The only other remedies for the swampsnake poisons are time and luck. Meanwhile, I do not intend to starve myself or your grandfather for the sake of looking useful."

Tanager looked like he wanted to protest but did not dare; his dark eyes were riveted on Reandn's form, far too still, on the cot. Rethia turned to give him a brief glance with her brown-rimmed eyes, and Tanager flinched away from the oddness, the touch of . . . *something* there. Just like everyone else, Kacey thought. She wondered if Tanager had ever seen someone so gravely ill, and for the first time, felt sorry for him.

Farren, apparently, felt the same. He put a hand behind the boy's neck and said, "All of a sudden it seems more serious than when you were watching in the woods, and saw your old grandfather get in a lucky blow, doesn't it?"

Tanager nodded, looking again at the bed. "It . . ." he said, barely audible, "I . . . I figured he'd be fine once we got here."

Farren ruffled his grandson's sweat-grimy hair. "Maybe

he will be, Tanager. We'll just have to wait. But there's no reason not to fill our bellies while we're doing it."

"No," Tanager said, sounding unconvinced. He followed mutely when Teayo led them through the sickroom and into the house proper.

The meal was a slow process during which Kacey finally heard enough reminiscing to enable her to place memories of Farren, and the time he'd spent in this house combining spellwork with her father's healing to combat malicious magic-working. Tanager fell asleep during the discourse; they left him in the common room while Teayo took his turn at the dishes and Kacey, accompanied by Farren, took a cut of ham and some bread to Rethia.

Kacey hesitated in the doorway, softly clearing her throat to let Rethia know she was there. Farren's breath tickled her ear as he crowded her to look in; his reaction wasn't quite as blasé as hers when he saw the younger woman cutting Reandn's shaggy hair with a small pair of shears. The noise that gurgled in his throat made Kacey turn with a frown.

"Don't even come in here if you're going to make noises like that."

Carefully, Farren said, "He's proven to be a very private person. I'm not sure how he'll react to that . . . intrusion."

"He needs the touch," Rethia said softly from the bedside, where she stopped her careful work.

Farren walked past Kacey, and she followed him to Rethia's side. "Is barbering on the duty list of a medic?"

Rethia gave him one of her pleasant smiles. "If it makes him feel better, yes."

The patient in question *did* look much better, Kacey thought, her gaze taking in Reandn's features and trying to decide what made him so attractive to her. She'd always been drawn to larger men, big framed men who echoed her father's build before he'd gathered weight. This man was leaner . . . but there was strength in his clean-cut frame. And his eyes . . . their intensity drew her. Kacey shook her head minutely, thinking of his hands pulling her down, only hours before. Rethia looked up from where she knelt to brush the last of the loose light hairs from the pillow, and her expression was sympathetic.

She always knows. Crossly, Kacey straightened her shoulders, gave a glance to make sure Farren hadn't noticed her thoughts, and quietly set the wooden trencher on the worktable behind her. Past the table were two sets of floor-to-ceiling shelves, and what was left of last year's herbs. Drawers under the table held preboiled bandages and wraps, along with a few precious suturing needles. The bottom drawer, least used, held disturbing memories along with the more gruesome tools of their trade. When those implements came into play, not all of Rethia's caring or Teayo's skill ensured successful treatment.

Kacey rounded the table to poke around in the upper drawers, making a mental list of the replacements they would need. It was sufficient to distract her from the thoughts she shouldn't have been bothering with. It was a familiar chore, sitting on the stool to make careful notes, glancing up to the row of cots stretching down the long wall on her left. The opposite wall was full of more windows than any one wall had a right to, but they kept the place cheery even in winter. Between them were several small heating stoves and a few more storage shelves. Kacey reminded herself to give them a good inventory, and make sure all the organic material remained unspoiled.

Farren, thankfully oblivious to Kacey's internal conundrums, eventually entered the room and bent to look more closely at Reandn. "When do you think I can talk to him?"

"Why, any time you want," Rethia said.

Kacey ducked her head and stared hard into an open drawer of bandages, trying hard to not smile at Farren's bemused silence.

"When," Farren finally asked, his patience exaggerated, "will he be awake?"

A glance from the corner of her eye showed Kacey the flicker of annoyance on her sister's face. *Then that's what you should have asked*, it meant. Aloud, she said, "Not before tomorrow morning, not the way he was dosed. Even then . . ." And, her attention back on Reandn and the one last hair she picked from the pillow, her voice trailed off.

After a another moment of covert observation, Kacey saw Farren, brows drawn, open his mouth and start to form the word "What?" but he was a fast learner, for he closed it again without asking.

"He'll be groggy for a while," Kacey supplied quietly, "and weak. I hope you weren't in any hurry."

"I'm not," Farren said, leaving the bedside to watch her short, quick fingers sort through the drawers. "I can't speak for him, though."

Kacey shrugged. "He won't have much choice." She closed the last drawer with her knee and turned back to her list. Farren stood by her side, but it was Rethia and Reandn he watched. Kacey was frowning at an inkblot when Farren's voice intruded again.

"How *did* you acquire a sister?"

She glanced up at him, then deliberately penned out one more item while he waited. "It's not that great a mystery," she said. "The rest of her family died in a night fire when she was six. She fell out of the loft window trying to escape, broke her leg, and came here. I was fifteen at the time." Eighteen years ago. Hard to believe so much time had passed. "Father wasn't about to give her up; she always needed . . . a gentle hand—and even more so after . . ." She stopped. They'd never quite figured out what had happened that day, only that something *had*.

Farren nodded, ignoring her unfinished sentence. "I can see she's . . . unique." At his waist, his fingers ran up and down the thong that held the dull stone he claimed was magic. "Very preoccupied. With what?"

Kacey shrugged and set her list aside to dry. "Thoughts," she said. "Why the roses have thorns, how hard the wind is blowing—or how to make Reandn feel better. If you think someone used that stone to find him, why don't you just get rid of it?"

"Hmm?" Farren looked down at the unremarkable object. "Oh, I think it's been discharged. But if it hasn't, and its owner tries to use it again, I might be able to get some taste of the magic."

"It sounds like you're playing with his safety." *And ours.* Kacey crossed her arms and waited for him to deny it.

"If he doesn't make it, this is my only remaining link to whoever is looking for him. To whoever has the magic." His voice gave a nod of regret to her accusation, but no sign of doubt. For a quick moment, Farren frightened Kacey. All at once she understood his priorities, and saw the kind of determination that, were she Reandn, she might have chosen not to trust, either.

Chapter 14

Reandn was floating and ungrounded, and he did not care for it. He preferred a solid base to his world, while now he could barely feel the bed he rested on.

A bed. Not the woods, not on Sky, tilting back and forth, lost in a swirl of numbness and pain. A bed. He wondered where, and thought, angrily, about the last time he had woken from sickness and discovered himself in the hands of a wizard. Nothing had changed, for he was certain . . . nearly certain . . . he had felt magic here, as well.

Wherever *here* was. It smelled innocuous enough, sharp herbal scents and strong soap, with good kitchen smells layered thinly on top. Reandn cracked his eyelids open, but found he barely knew more than before because his gaze kept wandering around without permission.

There was a woman sitting on the bed next to his, he saw that much. At least, he was fairly certain it was a woman. He got an impression of clean facial lines and deep set eyes nearly obscured by a thick fringe of fair hair. There seemed little to threaten him here; he closed his eyes, staring at lids upon which even the patterns of darkness wandered. A cloyingly sweet taste clung to his tongue and he wondered what he'd been given. It even occurred to him to wonder why he was alive. Hadn't he been poisoned? Hadn't he seen Dela, waiting for him?

Go away, he thought wearily as the blond woman sat

215

on the edge of his bed. The movement brought back
the pain his thick thoughts had hidden.

Her hand touched his cheek; in her throat was a soft
wordless expression of sympathy. Just what he wanted.
He opened his eyes and said as distinctly as possible,
"Go away."

The response was quiet laughter, pricking him into
the effort of focusing.

"What the Hells are you laughing at?" he inquired
crossly.

"It just struck me funny," she replied, still sitting on
the edge of the bed, a more definite version of what
he'd seen before. "How do you feel this morning?"

Like I should have died and somehow forgot to. But
since he hadn't, then it was time to find out just what
had happened, and whose hands he was in this time.
"That depends on where I am."

"You're in Little Wisdom," the young woman answered
promptly. "Or, close to it, anyway. My father is a healer,
and so is my sister. And me," she added in an afterthought.
"I stayed with you last night. My name is Rethia."

"Farren brought me?" Reandn asked, finding a vague
flicker of memory to draw on, Farren, his arms around
Reandn, clucking encouragement to Sky.

"Yes."

An ambush . . . magic, and poison—and an interminable
ride on smooth-stepping Sky. Magic. There had been
magic, and it hadn't been Farren's. Was Ronsin near, or
was there more magic in this world than anyone seemed
to realize? A sharp throb from Reandn's arm took away
his trail of thought; he blinked, and realized he'd drifted
away for a few moments.

Above him, Rethia frowned. "It's not safe to have any
more sweet syrup just yet," she said regretfully. She laid
a hand on his arm above the wound for a few moments.
"That's better," she said, even as he realized the pain

had receded, at least enough so he could think past it again. Her careful hands moved to the bandage around his arm, and started unwrapping it. Reandn could have sworn he smelled garlic. They had put garlic on his arm?

"Still among the living?" Farren's voice from behind and to the right made him realize, for the first time, that there was a doorway there, one that led to other rooms. Farren moved into the room to stand by the bedside, looking down at Reandn, who didn't much like it, and then glancing over at Rethia. "We *can* relax, now, can't we?"

Rethia worked at removing the dressing, carefully unrolling it, lifting Reandn's arm as she unwrapped each pass around it. Farren had to clear his throat before she looked up. "Oh," she said. "Yes, I think so. It'll be a while before he feels well, though, so I hope . . ." Her eyes drifted back to him and for the first time Reandn became aware of their stunning coloration.

"Hope what?" Farren said, a trace of impatience in his voice.

"Hope? Oh," she said, and straightened her shoulders, looking, for the first time, like she'd been up all night. "He won't be traveling for quite a few days."

But Reandn had slowly been adding up the clues before him. She'd been up all night, no doubt caring for him. Farren's question—*we* can *relax now, can't we*—the kinetic memory of jerking an arrow out of his own arm, and Bergren, explaining the arrow poison to him. And most of all, filling his mind's eye, Adela, waiting for him. She had been *waiting*. Reandn's good hand shot over his body to grab Rethia's wrist, all the strength of his weak body in those five fingers; she gave a quiet gasp of surprise. He tightened his grip in emphasis, and her great blue-brown eyes centered on his face, jolting him as he looked into them for the first time. His voice was a harsh whisper. "You kept me alive, didn't you? It was *you*."

Her eyes flicked away, up to Farren, and then to her imprisoned wrist. "Yes," she said, and her expression was reassuring. "But you'll—"

He shook her arm, silencing her. "You should have let it be."

She twisted her wrist away, and he couldn't sustain the strength to hold her. "I was right!" she cried, stumbling back from him, distress in her voice. "You *weren't* trying."

She ran around the bed and past Farren, into whatever room lay behind him. Reandn didn't understand what she meant, and didn't try. He closed his eyes and thought about Adela, disappointed, waiting for nothing. But it was all right, he told her silently. He still had Ronsin to find. He just needed to heal, to divest himself of this ex-wizard; he'd been wrong to think they could travel together. Whether or not he had magic, Farren was a liability, and Tanager was twice one.

A new voice startled him out of his thoughts; it was a woman's voice, beside him, and full of scorn. "It's not our habit to just *let it be.*" She waited for him to open his eyes, and then set down a food-laden lap tray, standing back to regard him with her arms crossed.

He stared back, wondering who *this* woman was. Plumply full-bodied where Rethia was slender, dark instead of light, dressed in practical trousers and a short-sleeved tunic, she looked like her feet were firmly on the ground. Amazing, Reandn thought. He'd only been awake for a few minutes, yet he'd already managed to earn this woman's ire—even if he wasn't sure exactly why.

He shouldn't have worried. She didn't hesitate to tell him, her dark hazel eyes smoldering. "We'll help just about anyone, but we do have rules of courtesy. For one thing, if someone stays up all night to save your life, you don't complain about it. That girl worked hard for you."

He just looked at her, knowing he had no chance against her, tired just by being in the same room with her energetic bearing.

"Hmmph," she said. "Eat that. Whether or not you want to." She circled around behind Farren, out of Reandn's narrow field of view; he thought she was probably still in the room somewhere.

After another moment's consideration—and a prompting pang from his stomach—Reandn eyed the tray. It was sitting on his stomach, and there was no way he could pull himself to a sitting position beneath it. To his surprise, Farren leaned over and lifted it for him. Then, awkward with his right hand, Reandn managed to spoon up most of the stew. At least there was a damp cloth on the tray to clean up after his clumsiness.

Farren didn't speak until the food was almost gone. Then he sat on the short padded stool beside the bed and said somberly, "We need to talk."

"I have the feeling this is the beginning of a conversation we've already ended," Reandn said shortly. As if he was supposed to trust the man just because he *hadn't* used magic at the ambush.

Apparently so, for Farren gave his head one short shake. "Things are different now. You've seen I have no magic to use, while I've seen someone else does. I've also watched you identify it before even *I* could feel it. I need to understand what's happening if I'm going to help stop it."

"I didn't ask for your help."

"That's very gracious, to the man who saved your life." The woman's sardonic voice had lost none of its bite. Reandn looked past Farren and found the worktable beyond him; behind that he found the yet unnamed face that went with the voice. It was an oval face, plain aside from expressive hazel eyes, and it reflected none of the plumpness of the body below. Brown hair hung in soft curls and just brushed her shoulders, swinging with the motion as she worked with mortar and pestle.

"If I'd been on my own, I wouldn't have been caught unaware, or on foot," Reandn told her, his voice just as sharp as hers. She stopped her work long enough to raise eyebrows of doubt.

"Reandn," Farren interposed, "if I let you and Kacey get started at each other you'll wear out before I get a chance to hear what I need to know. Please. We'll begin with the simple part. How do you know about the magic?"

Reandn let the spoon rest in the shallow bowl in his lap. Did it really matter if the man knew *how* he could tell, once he already knew Reandn wasn't to be fooled over the matter of magic? He said simply, "I can feel it. Can't you?"

Farren closed his eyes in relief at the sudden cooperation. Behind him, Kacey wrapped her crushed herbs in a loosely woven cloth and dipped it into a steaming mug. Then she leaned on her elbows to watch.

"All right," Farren said. "How do you feel it? What made you so certain I'd used magic on you after your . . . arrival in Maurant?"

How did he feel it? Because it disrupted his entire being, nothing less. Reandn flashed back to the spot in the woods where the Resiore boy's trail disappeared, and worked his jaw just at the memory. He thought of crashing to the floor in front of Saxe in the ready room. He remembered the fear when magic rushed through his system, disabling him before Ronsin, destroying Adela.

And then he swallowed hard to open his throat and said, as near as casual as a voice could get, "Mostly in my ears, or maybe it's in my head." *A hundred echoing bees flying around inside his mind.* "It's a rush of noise. I don't know why I can hear it and others can't. And if it wasn't magic I heard in your house, what was it?"

"I'm not sure," Farren admitted. "Unprepared trans-location is a terrible shock to the body as well as the mind. It was necessary for Lina to dose you—so I've no idea what you thought you might have heard."

"Did hear," Reandn growled.

"Dosed him?" Kacey said, bobbing her seeping herbs up and down in a thoughtful gesture. "What medicines, Farren?"

Farren shrugged, twisting on the stool to address her. "I'm not sure. Pain medicines, something to keep him sedated until his body got a chance to sort things out. Nothing an ordinary household would have any trouble obtaining."

"Probably something like this," she said, lifting the herbs from the mug before she brought it around the table for Reandn. "Here," she ordered. "Drink it all. And if your ears ring, don't go tossing us around the room again—it's just the herbs. That's probably all it was at your house, Farren, especially if she was brewing it thick." She looked down at Reandn, who'd made no attempt to pick up the mug, and gestured impatiently at it. "It's only something to take the edge off that arm. Now that you've driven Rethia away, you'll be feeling it more."

That made little sense to him, not that she seemed to expect it would, or to care that it didn't—although, he realized, it was already true enough.

He'd have preferred it to make sense, and he'd have preferred that this woman didn't seem so prepared to pick a fight with him. Arms crossed, Kacey stared down at him, a scowl growing in her eyebrows and spreading to the face below. "Drink it."

With a glance at Farren—whose amusement he didn't appreciate—Reandn took a first, bitter sip and couldn't help making a face. But he drank the rest of the tea without further fuss, deciding it was worth it to escape her glare, even if it didn't ease his arm.

Farren gave him that time, and the moments afterward to close his eyes, waiting and hoping the herbs would take effect. Kacey returned to his side, removed the tray, and pulled another stool out to sit by his arm, stingingly aromatic poultice and bandages in hand.

"It *is* garlic," Reandn said without thinking, looking at her. He thought he saw a hint of a smile.

"Among other things," she said. "Probably not necessary anymore, but it's good to draw the snake venom out."

"Sounds like allergies," Farren said, continuing with his own conversation. "It's been so long . . . I should have realized."

"Allergies?" Kacey repeated, saving Reandn the trouble. "What—?"

"What Reandn just described to me. Allergies to magic weren't all that common even when magic was strong, but every once in a while, someone would crop up with it. The very sensitive usually died before anyone recognized what was happening—after all, the reaction is mostly internal, and not as easy to recognize as a rash or runny eyes. But when a sensitive child *was* recognized in time, they were cherished and protected." He looked at Reandn, a smile playing about his eyes. "If you'd been born into magic, Reandn, you would have spent your life among the Highborn, serving as a detector of sorts for people who were neither talented nor sensitive to magic, and who had no other way to know if malignant magic was in use."

Reandn blinked at him, but spoke more to himself than the wizard. "That's what it was," he murmured, thinking of all the times his body had tried to tell him about Ronsin. "All that noise in my head—"

"That's what Rethia said," Kacey offered suddenly, obviously voicing her thought before she had time to order the words. "About your ears, I mean. When you started in on us."

Reandn raised a brow. "When I did what?"

"That's right," Farren said, but it was to Kacey he spoke. "He reacted much that way at home, once, as well. Does it bother you that much, Reandn? Or is it what you saw that magic do?"

Reandn's gaze snapped to the wizard, his heart struggling between anger and anguish; his rough voice filled the room without raising in volume. "You ask too many questions, wizard."

Farren held his ground, his own eyes cool, his face unreadable. "And I don't get enough answers," he said quietly. "Haven't you figured it out yet, Reandn? I'm on your side. But I can't continue to blunder along. I've got to know what's going on before I can put a stop to it."

Reandn pulled away from Kacey as she finished her work, twisting to face the wizard, his voice hard. "I'm a Wolf, Farren. Letting you travel with me was a mistake, magic or not. From here I go on my own." *Ow, dammit.* But not today. Not for a few days. His arm throbbed under the taut new bandages; he closed his eyes against it. *Not today. But soon.*

"Be still," Kacey said quietly, matter-of-factly. "Try to relax. The tea will help in just a moment—and you've still got venom depressing your system. Don't push it." As if she could read his mind. Rethia certainly seemed to be able. "And you, Farren. I know this is important, but I think you'd better try another time."

"That's all right," Farren said, scraping the stool back, his voice rising as he stood. "It looks like I have time to work with, at least for a while."

His footsteps took him out of the room, and Kacey's softer tread followed, then hesitated. Her hand fell down on his good shoulder with a more comforting touch than he would have expected, given the antagonism she'd shown him from the start. "The worst of it's over," she said. "It'll get better soon."

He hoped so. For as soon as he was able, he was shaking himself free of Farren to go after his prey.

He was with her, the bright-eyed, dark-haired woman who fit so well against his body; she warmed him, body and soul. Her fingers traced his spine, her breath was hot against his neck, and she laughed with delight at the goosebumps she caused. He threw his leg over her thighs and tangled his fingers in her hair, kissing her. Starting with her mouth, moving to the sensitive skin of her neck, his free hand caressing her bare shoulder, her breast, the gentle swell of her lower belly. They spoke their own language, now, of quick breathing and throaty noises. Skin on skin as she rolled on top of him, settling down on him with a mutual gasp of pleasure—

Gone! She was gone, and cold grey deafening magic surrounded him instead, mocking him, tearing at him. Panting, he fought to regain his love, to help her, refusing to believe she was truly gone. He couldn't think, couldn't breathe, couldn't move—

Suddenly the eyes looking down on him were startling blue and brown, the hair that brushed down to tickle his face was thick and light. With a great gasp, a drowning man reaching precious air, he flung aside the visions. His hands were around her upper arms, fingers digging into soft flesh. He gripped all the harder, clinging to the sight of candlelight flickering off her brow and cheek, dimly illuminating the lines of her shoulder and the bed beside him.

"You're awake now," she said, somehow knowing that that was the question raging through his drug and pain befuddled mind.

"Am I?" he demanded in a gasp. Her hands were on his shoulders and he felt a tingle there, and it spread to his ears in the too-familiar feel of magic. "Am I?"

"Yes, of course. You're at Teayo's now, remember? You've just had a bad dream."

"Are you magic?" Sweat dripped down the side of his face; he gripped her with his eyes as much as his hands.

When she laughed, it was light, and held nothing more sinister than amusement. It made the candlelight seem brighter, and Reandn blinked, relaxing his hold. The magic still sang through his blood, but all at once he realized there was no malice in it.

"You *are*," he said, and she laughed again, shaking her head.

"Only if there is magic in caring, Reandn." She used a damp cloth to wipe away his sweat, and he submitted to it like a child with a dirty face. "Feel a little better now?"

He looked around the room, empty but for himself, and saw, barely visible in the light of the stubby candle on the worktable, that the woven cover on the bed next to him was rumpled only at the head of the bed, as though someone had been curled up, sitting, watching.

"Why?" he asked.

It should have made no sense to her. She sobered and said, "Because it's what I do."

"After what I said this morning?"

She sat quietly, without response.

"I'm sorry about that," Reandn admitted into the silence. "I didn't mean to hurt your feelings."

Her eyes flashed up from the cloth in her quietly folded hands. "You didn't."

Slowly, he relaxed from the grip of his visions. "You were upset."

"Yes . . ." she said, looking away again. She took his hand in both of hers in an absent, familiar gesture he couldn't bring himself to ruin, although he didn't welcome it. "I . . . just can't understand . . . I mean, the wind, and the way it sounds in the trees, or the way the air smells after rain, and the clean rustle of hay in the stalls—you want to run from all that. It . . . yes, it upset me."

His first reaction was to laugh: she sounded like the few Ardrite priests who bothered to invade the barracks, looking for converts, and for someone to give an hour's work to some particular House of the Sister. But he stopped himself, for he saw she was sincere. Carefully, he said, "It's not quite that way . . . I'm not running from anything." Was he? "It's just there's something else I miss more, and there's only one way to fix that."

"I see," she said, and absently—although he was beginning to suspect she always knew just what she was about—worked his injured arm slightly at the elbow, just enough to flex at the torn tissue without pulling it. He offered no resistance, and noticed that it no longer creaked with the effects of what Farren called translocation. "And what makes you think she would want you to give up all the things of this world now, when you will be with her in the end regardless?"

He stiffened in surprise, in the automatic stirrings of anger. But astonishment won out, and as she released his arm, never having tried to force it once he took control, he said roughly, "How do you know so much?"

Her shrug diffused the mystery. "Farren's been guessing about you since you popped up in Maurant. Kacey said when you came in, you . . . reacted to the poison, thought you saw someone else. I've seen loss before. I know it. You carry it with you like a shroud."

He gathered it about him now, a thing of familiarity in this strange Southern place with its magic and the creature of precise and quiet beauty that sat on the edge of his bed. It shadowed his eyes, set his jaw. She saw him close up and drew back away from him, so that despite her unchanged position she might as well have been sitting across the room.

"Just think about it," she requested. "You know her

best. Is giving up what you have here, now, what she would ask of you? Or is it patience she wants?"

He swallowed hard, and looked away, staring in a most determined way into the darkness. A muscle along his jaw clenched, faded, and trembled into shape again. Rethia moved over to the other bed, and tucked her knees up under her chin, smoothing her skirts into decency. After a moment she leaned back against the headboard, and shortly after that, to all appearances, was asleep.

Reandn stared into the darkness for a long time.

Kacey was satisfied with what she found that morning, Reandn's second new day with them. Rethia was asleep on the bed beside Reandn's, which meant she was perfectly secure in her patient's well-being. Reandn slept heavily, his breathing deep and regular, his color good, his face relaxed. Even the scabby swath along his jaw looked better today. She squelched the urge to touch that face—it was too unprofessional—and settled for heaving a sigh. Soon he would wake, and despite healing, would be in need of more bitter tea. Now, with the poison out of his system, he had only to rest, recover from the shock of it all. The arm would heal quickly and as far as she could tell, he hadn't even lost all that much blood.

The sound of a yawn took her eyes away from Reandn. Rethia sat, stretching, rubbing her eyes in a childlike gesture.

"Good morning," Kacey said.

Rethia closed her eyes and took a deep breath, inhaling the scent of the morning. "Yes," she said, and smiled, looking at Kacey. "He'll be all right now."

"Looks that way," Kacey agreed. "I hope he was civil to you this time."

"He never meant to be rude." Rethia left the bed,

pausing for a quick glance at her patient. "He's hurting so much inside, I don't think he knows when some of it leaks out to other people."

"You sound so certain." An instant of envy gripped her, that her sister could so casually, so quickly, know this man that well. But it was something Rethia'd always done, and likely always would.

Rethia shrugged, but then her expression turned distant as her attention went inward, her body standing idly in front of the workbench. When she came back out she frowned, and said, "He said I was magic."

Kacey stiffened slightly, remembering the revelations of the day before, how Reandn could feel such things. Then she remembered the tea and relaxed. "He was full of bitter tea," she said. "It bothers his ears a little."

Without argument in her voice, Rethia said, "He seemed very certain."

Kacey saw only that it disturbed her sister to think it might be true, and, in fact, more than Kacey would have guessed it would. "It doesn't matter what he thinks," she said, a little more harshly than she'd meant to.

Rethia twisted to look back at him. "No, I suppose not. Are there biscuits this morning?"

"Yes," Kacey said, unflustered by the sudden change in subject. One grew used to it.

"Tell Father I've taken my breakfast to the clearing, please?"

Protest was generally useless. "I will, if you promise not to fall asleep up there, and stay until we rush up to see if anything's happened to you."

"Promise," Rethia said over her shoulder on her way out. Kacey had the feeling it would happen anyway.

She broke the herbs and bark in the pestle and returned to the cooking room for boiling water. She was fiddling with the bobbing herb bundle of the steeping tea when Reandn woke.

"Where's Rethia?" he said, groggy, pushing back against the pillow to sit. "When did you get here?"

"A little while ago. Rethia left to get her breakfast— she's got other things to do, you know, than hold your hand all day."

"Damn," he mumbled. "Slept through it."

"Slept through it? You're going to sleep through a lot of things for the next week or so, so I'd get used to it."

He grimaced and said, "That's a habit that could get me killed."

"So, apparently, is revenge." She regretted the words as soon as they left her lips; he gave her an incredulous look, anger simmering close to the surface. Deliberately, he closed his eyes and tilted his head back against the wall.

"I'm not ready for this," he groaned to no one in particular. "I think I'll go back to sleep. Maybe you'll be gone when I wake up."

The words *I'm sorry* somehow got stuck in her throat. He said nothing more, and didn't move, except to shift his arm in seek of ease. She suddenly remembered the tea, and quickly removed the herbs. It would be strong, all right. She wondered if it was strong enough to take away the sting of her words.

"Here," she offered, coming around the table, mug extended to him.

He cracked open an eye. "Graces, are you going to scald me with tea, next?"

"Drink it," she responded, exasperated, her sympathy melting away. It disappeared entirely as she recalled Rethia, on her way to the one place she unerringly fled to when upset. "Why'd you have to say that to her? Tell her she was magic?"

He had the tea; he drank half of it in one gulp in lieu of answering. For a moment he just waited, his face tight; she saw him subtly flexing and relaxing the arm. Then, just before she took a deep breath to repeat herself, he said, "I don't remember last night very clearly. If I told her she was magic it was because I believed it."

"Don't you ever think before you say something? Are you *trying* to hurt the woman who saved your life?"

"Goddess, Kacey!" He opened eyes that looked hunted. "Don't you ever let up? *Anyone's* touch would seem magic next to your bedside manner."

"I'm just looking out for her!" Kacey said defensively. "I don't want you telling her tales about magic again, you hear?"

That was when the grey eyes grew hard, and his expression cold. "Taking your orders is not the price I'll pay for this care," he said. "Damn, woman, leave me alone."

He downed the rest of the tea with a grimace, and placed the mug carefully on the little stool that still sat by his bed. Then he closed his eyes—closing her out. Kacey watched him for a minute longer, wondering how the conversation had gotten so out of hand. She decided it was back at that kiss, back when she had resolved he'd never know its effect on her. No doubt she'd accomplished that goal already. With an inward sigh, she collected the mug and returned it to the kitchen.

When she came back to the sickroom, he was gone.

Reandn walked slowly across the short, grassy distance between the house and barn. Behind the barn, behind the goat pens and the cow that seemed to wander freely yet not away, there were woods. The same woods lined the narrow lane that led to the main road into Little Wisdom, and crowded up against the house. If it weren't for the chickens, the peace would have been absolute. Even with the cackle and fuss of the birds, he'd been able to take the deep mental breath he needed. Now he took a deep breath of another kind, groping for the wall of the barn, holding himself upright until the world steadied. From the darkness in the back corner, Sky nickered a greeting.

"Nice to hear you've missed me," Reandn said, chancing another couple of steps. He didn't let his weakness bother him, knowing this excursion could do him far less harm than another day of laying in that long, bed-rowed room, easy target for haunting memories.

Sky was a dark blob of a bobbing head in the dim light of the barn, the details of his long black mane and fine-boned head gradually becoming evident as Reandn moved closer and his eyes grew accustomed to the light. He breathed softly through his teeth in greeting; Sky snorted once, withdrew his head, and then reappeared, having made the decision to be petted.

"Not much for being closed in, are you?" Reandn asked the horse, noting that the animal had plenty of hay and water, if not the sunshine and open space he preferred.

"Somewhat like you, it seems."

Reandn spun around, a mistake that sent him reeling into the stall door. "Farren," he said flatly.

"I don't know how you wiggled out from under Kacey's watchful eye," Farren said, silhouetted in the sunshine outside the barn. "I doubt it will be considered wise."

"Is that supposed to matter?"

After a pause, Farren said, "I suppose not, not to you. Only one thing matters to you, I think—getting to the one that hurt you."

"He's hurt plenty of other people, too," Reandn said. "He's got to be stopped." His thumb brushed against smooth gold on his little finger.

"Fine. I agree. I always have. I don't understand why you aren't willing to let me help."

Reandn sighed. "He's the one with magic, Farren. Not you." That much, he did, finally, believe. "I don't see how you can do anything but make me more obvious."

The light-lined shoulder rose and fell. "I know the ways of magic. That has to count for something. And I know Solace." A brief silence fell, until he added, his crisp words falling quietly between them, "Or maybe I'm just as selfish as you. You want revenge, and cloak it in the welfare of others. I can do the same. I want what I had, Reandn. Maybe just a taste, maybe not even that much. But I can't *not try*."

"Then I was right all along. Just a wizard who wants his magic back. Then what'll make you any different than the man who holds it now?" Reandn asked bitterly, wishing that he could know, just *know* beyond doubt, that he could trust this man.

Another silence from Farren, who took the time to fully enter the barn. When he spoke again his delivery was remote, unlike the almost intimate confession of his need for magic. "You were still a youth when we lost the magic. I'll bet it was never even strong enough to bother your allergy."

Reandn pushed Sky's nose away from where it questingly nipped at his bare shoulder, and leaned more heavily against the stall framing. "No," he said, not bothering to hide the fatigue in his voice. "Not much."

"Do you really think it was a bunch of wizards running around, pointing their fingers at people and causing trouble?"

"It wouldn't surprise me," Reandn said heavily.

"Let me see," Farren said. "From what I know of the Wolf Pack—and what I've seen of you—I'd say Wolves can move quickly and quietly, track down prey, and fight when they find it. I guess that means you spend a lot of time attacking people and taking what you want."

Reandn scowled. "You know better than that."

"Then because a man or woman has aptitude and training doesn't mean they have to misuse their abilities?

That, in fact, like you and your Pack, some might choose to *help* others with their skills?"

Reandn snorted, and shook his head. "You're good, Farren. You are good. But almost anyone can be a Wolf. How many wizards do you know?"

"You'd be surprised," Farren countered quickly. "I live as a tailor now. Don't you suppose there are others out there, tanning and grinding meal and farming? Don't you suppose that even some of your Wolves would be capable of harnessing magic?"

Reandn just stared at him, flabbergasted. It could be that common? So many, all with the power to do as Ronsin had done?

"What I'm trying to tell you," Farren continued, unaware, in the gloom of the building, of the effect of his words, "is that while very few people can attain the level of translocation, there are enough solidly skilled people *of conscience* to police the use of magic. If we can affect magic's return, Reandn, the world isn't going to erupt into chaos."

"I'm sorry, Farren," Reandn said tiredly. "You may think you can follow me to this wizard and figure out his magic, but when I find him, he's dead. Him and his magic with him."

Farren stood for a moment, the set of his jaw revealed in the outline of short cropped silvery beard that picked up even this dim light. Stiffly, then, he turned and walked away. In the slanting light entering the barn, dust motes fell and gathered on the ground. Sky gave his stall door an irritable kick, and Reandn thought about being alone, about Rethia upset and Kacey angry, and the temporary, tentative association with the old wizard possibly shattered. Quietly he longed for a time not so long ago when even a man who was a loner among Wolves could find companionship and, if needed, backup. With a deep sigh he straightened against the support of the stall, tucking his thumb in his belt to support his pain-shot arm. He ran the other hand across his eyes, rubbing hard. He'd been on his own before, and he could do it again. But somehow those days seemed long ago, and not half as hard to live with.

He had only a moment for his thoughts before another silhouette blocked the light of the entrance. This one didn't hesitate, but came right in, resolving into the shape and features of Rethia.

"Come with me?" she asked.

"Where?" he asked, taken off stride by her straightforwardness, looking for the turmoil Kacey had said he'd caused.

"To my meadow. It's not too far." She took his hand and made as if to lead him out of the barn, although he didn't move.

Reandn couldn't help his snort of amusement. "And just how far do you think I'll get? Remember, I'm too big for you to carry." Even as he spoke, he became aware of a warmth that filled him, taking the wobble out of his legs and some of the wooziness from his head.

"You'll be all right," she said blithely.

He shook his head—*I doubt that*—and followed the tug on his hand. "I'm turning back if it's too far."

"It won't be," she reassured him, and, apparently certain he would follow, released his hand. She took him into the woods behind the barn, where they struck a clear, oft-used trail. She walked no faster than was comfortable for him, and he was surprised at how much of the rolling ground they covered.

They were still on the trail when Reandn pulled up short, alarmed. Though his ears were relatively unaffected, he could still feel it. A tingling vibration flowed along his limbs, resonating uncomfortably in his wounded arm. Rethia stopped too, came back and took his hand again.

"No," he said. "I'm not going any closer." It wasn't

the same feeling of Ronsin's magic, but it was here
nonetheless.

Still clasping his hand, she moved closer to study him.
"Do you feel something?"

"You already know, don't you?" He couldn't quite bring
himself to tear his hand away, for there was no malice
in her face, just a hint of distress—as though she was
torn between dread and hope.

She looked away, or, more than that, her gaze moved
inward. "I wondered," she said, and then hesitated,
tugging his hand slightly. "Will you—"

"No," he said, more firmly than he'd intended, as he
reclaimed his fingers and stepped back from her. Her
genuine dismay was an argument he found hard not to
listen to, and that made it as threatening as the magic.
Without another word, he turned and left her, blundering
back the way they'd come.

Chapter 15

Reandn stumbled back down the path, fighting the urge to turn away from Teayo's home, away from the temptation of trusting those who welcomed magic. But by the time he reached the barn again, all he could think of was the bed he'd occupied for two days already. Just outside the sickroom door he stopped, drew a few deep breaths, and steadied himself. He entered the house more deliberately, but no less intent on the bed; he barely registered the small form in the second bed.

Kacey stared at him, her brows beetled together, her lips drawn thin in an expression that only emphasized her round jaw. But that silent response was her sole comment as he sat heavily on the bed, toeing off his boots and bringing his legs, one by one, to stretch out before him. She stuck her hands in her deep, baggy trouser pockets and merely stared.

Determined not to start trouble, he said evenly, "I had to check my horse."

"I thought as much," she said, though it sounded too casual to him, as though she hadn't thought anything of the like, but had been worried instead; she didn't meet his eyes at first.

But then, her expression clearing, she caught his glance and nodded at the bed beyond him. He suddenly realized he *had* seen someone in that bed, a young someone. Looking small—and like he wished he was smaller—

lay a miserable huddle of boy with one leg splinted awkwardly out in front of him. "This is Braden," Kacey said, her voice overtly cheerful. Underneath he heard the edge of irritation that was reserved for him. "He's just discovered why his father said to stay away from their stallion."

"I want to go home," the boy said, an almost inaudible plea. Tears gathered and hung, ready to spill over.

Reandn stared, instantly reminded of Kavan when he'd arrived at the Keep—although there had no longer been a home to return to, and Kavan had known it. There had been nothing but dark, miserable eyes set in a frightened face, and then Adela, quickly gathering the boy up.

Reandn's first impulse was to turn from the memories, and the boy, as well. But . . .

"I want to go home," the boy repeated. Sobs were definitely imminent.

"And leave me without a roommate?" Reandn widened his eyes in dramatic dismay. "I was getting lonely."

"I *want* my mam," Braden insisted, growing bolder.

Kacey shook her head. "Not for a day or two, I'm afraid. You know it's breeding season; your mam and da are awfully busy now, and there wouldn't be anyone to watch you. Here, we can get you water when you're thirsty, and tell you stories at bedtime. You're having a real adventure."

Not to be mollified, the child shook his head. The waiting tears spilled over and ran down his face, and his voice trembled. "I don't wanna have an adventure."

"Then you shouldn't have gone into that horse's stall," Kacey said, firmly but not without sympathy. "But you did, and here you are, so we have to make the best of it. It won't be so bad, Braden—I know your favorite foods, and it's not often you get sweet potato and gingerbread on the same day, is it?"

A silent shake of his head admitted the truth of that, but his face said it didn't make any difference.

"Well," Kacey said with a sigh, "You won't get it if I don't make it, so you'll have to be on your own here for a while. If Rethia were here—" she shot a covert glance at Reandn and finished, instead, "You call me if you need anything, Braden. I think you'll find you're a little sleepy, though."

Braden's head followed her as she walked around the beds and out of the room.

"I'm not sleepy," came his stubborn little voice after Kacey was gone. "My leg hurts. Why should I be sleepy?"

"Because it's convenient," Reandn said dryly.

The boy's response was a startled look; he hadn't expected an answer. Nor, at his age, which looked to be around six, could he comprehend the one he had gotten. "What happened to you?" he asked guilelessly, easily distracted.

"I—" Reandn started, then hesitated. "I got bitten by a horse," he said, managing to look embarrassed.

"Me, too!" the boy said, delighted at the common bond. "I mean, it was a horse that done this."

Reandn cleared his throat and said, "It was my own fault. I was warned the horse was dangerous, but I wanted to see it."

"Yeah," the boy commiserated. "And then they all made you feel really stupid, I'll bet. Like you done it on purpose."

"Well," Reandn said thoughtfully, crossing his legs, "the worst part is, they were right. I should have known better. But it would have been nice if everyone hadn't *said* so."

Sagely, the boy nodded. "And you got left here, just like me. Like nobody cares . . ." His face began to crumple again.

Reandn took a deep breath. "I *was* lonely at first—

but then I realized they didn't have any choice. And Kacey helped me when my arm hurt, so now I'm glad I'm here."

"But," the boy said moistly, swallowing hard, "didn't . . . didn't your brothers get real scared at night, with so much room in the bed?"

Reandn couldn't help his smile. "Maybe they did," he said carefully. "Tonight, if you think *your* brothers are lonely, we can talk about it. You think that might help keep you from worrying?"

Braden sniffled. "Dunno," he said, but the tears had stopped.

Reandn couldn't help the yawn that slipped out.

"Maybe she was talking to you," the boy suggested. "You look tired. I'm not."

"Maybe to both of us," Reandn replied, easing his arm into a more comfortable position. "I'll bet your leg doesn't hurt as much now, does it?"

Braden shook his head, and fingered the sheet beneath him.

"Good." Reandn brought a knee up to steady himself against the headboard. "You won't mind if I take a nap, then?"

Another head-shake. Reandn closed his eyes, wedged comfortably into an upright position. Several minutes later he opened them again, and found, not unsurprisingly, that the boy had already fallen asleep. Kacey's potions were hard to fight, whether you were child or adult. He closed his eyes again, satisfied. No need for everyone here to feel alone.

Kacey, with Tanager in tow, left the kitchen for the sickroom. The youth had pestered her all day about seeing Reandn; her father and Farren were riding the surgeon's rounds together, talking over times old and new, and she'd had no authority to appeal to when her own endurance against the boy's pleas wore down. So with an admonishment to watch his tongue and his place, she put him to work, carrying the food tray to her patients.

She'd half expected the steamy odors to have alerted the two before she got there, but they were both asleep. Braden, worn from the accident and the stress to his small frame, had succumbed completely to the weak draft she'd given him. Reandn looked like he'd been sitting, but at some point had half fallen over into an awkward arrangement of limbs.

She considered him a moment, eyeing the strain on his face, and decided that although she'd needed to create some distance between them, at some point it had become counterproductive to her healing duties, making him confused and defensive. Kacey couldn't blame him— only from her vulnerable point of view did it make sense. But from what she'd learned, he had enough to worry about without having to deal with her as well.

Behind her, Tanager cleared his throat. "It's heavy!" he hissed.

Kacey nodded at the worktable. "Put it there," she said. "And sit down behind it. Give him time to wake up." She rubbed her kitchen-sweaty face against the shoulder of her tunic. Then, since Reandn hadn't woken and didn't seem liable to, she sat down on the edge of the bed and touched his shoulder.

His eyes opened, yet befuddled. "Damn," he said. He'd slept through her arrival again, she realized, and didn't like it.

"It'll take time," she told him quietly. "I've brought the evening meal. Hungry?"

In his drowsiness, he seemed to have forgotten they were barely on speaking terms. "Do I get sweet potato and . . . ?"

"Gingerbread," she supplied. "It's hard to make enough for just one, you know."

He sat, grimaced, and stretched what he could. "Poor kid," he said, glancing over at Braden. "I don't think he's ever slept in a bed alone before."

"With the size of his family, I imagine you're right," Kacey agreed. She hesitated, and added, "I heard you talking with him. Thank you for making him feel more comfortable here."

He shrugged one-shouldered. "He's a kid, and he's upset and hurting. He just needed someone to understand."

She hadn't expected him to be good with children, somehow, but instead of saying so, she nodded at Tanager to bring over the food.

"No," Reandn said. "I'll eat at your workbench, if you don't mind." He didn't seem at all surprised at Tanager's movement, although she'd taken for granted that he wouldn't have been alert enough to notice the boy. Apparently he wasn't all that debilitated after all.

Tanager moved aside for him, then proceeded to hover while Reandn played fumble and catch with his right hand—obviously a lefty, Kacey thought. Several annoyed glances from Reandn did nothing to warn the boy he was intruding, and just as Kacey was about to diplomatically suggest he at least move back, Tanager said, "I just wanted to see if you were feeling any better."

"Yes, I am." Reandn's voice was hard and flat, another clue Tanager ignored.

"Are you going on to the city?"

A nod, a wise sideways glance at the boy. "You here to champion your grandfather again? How noble, how learned, how helpful?" Now this was the sharp-tongued, aggressive Reandn Kacey was, somehow, already used to.

Startled, Tanager drew back, then drew himself up to bristle. "If it wasn't for Pa-farren—"

"I wouldn't have been in a position to be ambushed," Reandn finished for him. "I'd have been on horseback and I wouldn't have stayed long enough to take an arrow. So don't try to tell me how he saved my life."

"You'd have run?" The surprise was enough to turn Tanager from his original purpose.

"If I said no, you'd be talking to either a liar or an idiot." With a sigh, Reandn poked around the slab of ham on his plate, and turned to the gingerbread. Kacey gave herself a mental smack and reached over the table, teasing the shallow trencher closer so she could cut the meat. Men. Always too proud to ask. When she returned the plate, meat neatly cut, he speared a piece without comment, glancing a clear grey thank-you in her direction.

"That scrape'll be healed soon," she said, looking at it.

He ran his hand along the pink skin on his face, fingering the dark line of scab where the cut had gone deep. "The sooner the better. I might as well wear a sign on my back as march around with this."

"It's an odd wound. How . . . ?"

"It doesn't make sense," Tanager interrupted, earning one of Kacey's scowls; it faded as she realized he wasn't really changing the subject, but in fact, almost answering her question. "You'd go up against a madman for a little boy but you wouldn't try to get the men that were after *you*?" He wore the frown of a youngster chewing over unfathomable adult ways.

"A madman, was it? Somehow I'm not surprised," Kacey snorted. But he'd done it for a child, and from the looks of it, nearly died as a result.

She wished he'd gotten it in a tavern fight instead.

Reandn closed his eyes with exaggerated patience. "One on one is something I can handle, Tanager. But when there's magic gathering, and you can't see the source, what is there to fight? *This* time it turned out to be men. Next time, I hope I won't be there to find out."

Tanager was silent for a moment, though his face was

beginning to flush again. His mouth twisted to one side as he said, almost sullenly, "You're always so certain there's magic around. I think you're just scared, and using magic as an excuse."

Kacey winced. Reandn's ham halted midway to his mouth; he looked up from under dark brows as if to convince himself he'd heard right. "If you think I'm too weak to whip a senseless man-child, I'd think again," he said clearly.

"What did I tell you when I said you could come in here?" Kacey said, her hand clamping over Tanager's arm, getting his attention and a surprised little expression. "I surely didn't instruct you to start a fight!"

"But—"

"Tanager," Reandn said bluntly, pointing the short, split-ended eating knife uncomfortably close to the base of the youth's neck, "I'm sure you came in here to *help* your grandfather. But you're just making me mad. Quit worrying at me like some dumb pup. If you have something worthwhile to say, I'd be glad to discuss it."

Tanager stared wordlessly at the knife a moment, until Reandn set it casually on the edge of the plate and nibbled at the gingerbread.

Kacey helped herself to a chunk of the fragrant bread. "Besides, Tanager, if you'd been paying any attention at all, you'd have heard that Reandn has what your grandfather calls an allergy to magic; Father thinks so, too. Which means he *can* tell when there's magic in use."

"Imagine that," Reandn said. "Damn, this is good bread."

Kacey shrugged off the compliment and checked over her shoulder to see Braden was still sleeping soundly. "Farren said it's similar to the way some people sneeze when they get a nose full of flowers. I'd never heard of it, but who cares, when there's no magic around? Besides, Farren said it was very rare."

"So I'm just lucky," Reandn said dryly. He shook his head at some internal commentary Kacey would love to have been able to hear, and his expression darkened.

"What?" Kacey said, when his attention remained inward and didn't seem liable to return to the conversation. She had the feeling that the answer would give her the key to this man, to understanding the depths of his reactions. "What's wrong?"

He seemed to shake himself, then regarded her with a little frown. "If only I'd known," he said. "I'd have been able to figure out what was happening. If I'd been a little smarter . . . a little faster . . ."

"Tell us, why don't you?" Farren invited from the doorway.

Kacey cursed the old wizard's timing; Reandn's head snapped around, his face gone cold and hostile. She sent Farren a glare he ignored, so she snatched the tray from the table and took it and Braden's meal over to the boy. As she woke him, reassured him, and showed him his favorite foods, she eavesdropped shamelessly.

"You're pushy, Farren," Reandn said. "Suppose I tell you, right now, who this man is, and what he's done. What would you do about it?"

Farren leaned against the door frame and scratched his beard. "To tell the truth, I've been working so hard at getting through to you that I never thought past it."

"You could go get him," Tanager offered, as if he really believed it was that simple. Kacey stole a look at his face. Yes, adolescent boy—as usual, with answers to everything.

"On whose authority?" Reandn asked.

"I'm not unknown in the city," Farren offered slowly; Kacey thought it was the first time she'd heard him talk *to* Reandn, instead of trying to talk him *into* something. "But I can see I'd have to get some backing before I did anything. Of course, if this person truly has magic, it will be difficult to apprehend him regardless of legalities."

"My grandfather was—*is*—important," Tanager said, his courage returned in the moments since he'd looked down the blade of the knife. Kacey, having settled Braden and gotten him started on his meal, eased into place behind Tanager. "If you think *he* can't get this man, why do you think anyone'll listen to *you*?"

Farren raised his fine silvered eyebrows, inviting Reandn to answer, even as Kacey elicited a yelp from Tanager with her expert pinch. "Rude!" she hissed in his ear.

"You've said worse to him!" Tanager hissed back, aggrieved.

Reandn paid no attention to them. He grinned, an unusual expression that looked more like a defiance than humor, and said, "Pack First has the right to mete Wolf's Justice."

"So," Farren's breath escaped through pursed lips. "Savill was right. A Wolf with fangs."

"Damn right. By the time he knows I'm there it'll be too late. Can you say as much?"

Farren shook his head, rejecting the argument. "This was my city, once. And I *do* know how to wield magic, which makes me the expert when it comes to predicting what your renegade might do—or even when it comes to telling what he *is* doing. I'll know where to find him, too. If you've made it to Pack First, you ought to know better than to refuse an advantage like that."

"And him?" Reandn jerked his stubble covered chin at Tanager.

"I go where he goes," Tanager said quickly.

Farren gave his head one firm shake. "Not this time, son. You'll stay here until we're through."

"I'm just as useful as a one-armed man!" Tanager cried.

Kacey wasn't sure whether to admire the boy or just lose her temper. He never knew when to quit.

For once, Farren seemed inclined to agree. "Tanager," he said, "I seem to remember a boy who rushed a stranger in our shop front and almost got himself killed. That same boy, only days ago, ran back into the thick of a sword fight, and again could have been killed—if, in fact, there had been anyone left to fight. Someday you'll have judgement, and then I'll take you into situations where you have to use it. Until then, you'll have to use mine, and *it* says you stay here."

Instead of protesting, Tanager looked at Reandn's arm; Reandn raised an eyebrow at him, amusement in his grey eyes. Probably, Kacey thought, Tanager was remembering that moment when he'd stared in at Reandn, on the edge of death, and recognized how quickly it could happen—and that he himself was just as mortal.

Farren caught the direction of his gaze and interpreted it differently. "We'll be here, as well, until that arm heals. Believe it or not, sometimes your old grandfather can work these things out without your help."

"Father invited you to stay," Kacey guessed.

Farren smiled agreement. "As if he would ever turn anyone away."

Kacey snorted. "You're right, there." She retrieved Braden's half-finished mug of milk and took it to the workbench, elbowing Tanager aside to get at the sweet syrup. A careful measurement, a brisk stir, and Braden would sleep the night comfortably. The boy took the mug back with a wrinkled nose of suspicion, but, after a cautious sip, fell back to his gingerbread without comment.

"There, see?" Kacey said. "You should have been as good a patient, Reandn."

"Sorry," he said, with a quick grin, a real one this time. "I've been scrapping so long I don't know what to do with myself if I don't have the chance."

Maybe, Kacey thought, in the aftermath of that grin,

it would be safer to go back to being obnoxious to him.

Farren cleared his throat. "Reandn, regardless of your opinion of me, you'll be here a few more days. I suggest you use the time to rethink your plans. You may be your Pack First—or, at least you were when you left King's Keep—but arriving unheralded in Solace with charges of magic may be more difficult to back up than you think. Don't cut yourself off from my help just because you don't like my motives." Farren nodded at Tanager, who reluctantly followed his grandfather out of the room.

"When can I go home?" Braden asked loudly in the silence that followed the wizard's departure. Kacey gave a short laugh.

"You are persistent," she said. "Not for a few days, baby. Give yourself a little time to feel better."

"I feel fine *now*. Thank you for the nice meal," he said in a clumsy afterthought.

"You probably do. That's because I have some medicines here that your mother doesn't, and because I'm very good at giving them. That's why your parents brought you here."

"I'm bored."

This time Reandn laughed as well. "Give him a few moments," Kacey said quietly. "That sweet syrup'll send him back to sleep."

"I don't doubt it," he said.

"How about you? Would you like some more of the tea?"

Reandn flexed his arm slightly, made a face at it. It was a goofy gesture, and Kacey stifled a giggle. "I'll get you some," she said. "After all, when there's poison and caustic involved, it's no simple thing. You need to give it—"

"Some time," he finished for her. "I know, I know. The problem is, I may not *have* the time."

She didn't understand that; she didn't think she had to. Maybe later. "I'll be right back."

The kettle was on the cook stove as a matter of course, and it only took Kacey a moment to fetch it and a clean mug. She brought a candle lamp as well, with a mind to the impending darkness. When she returned to the sickroom, Braden had fallen asleep, and Reandn sat upon his bed, his eyes open but distant, and his dark brows drawn down over them, unhappy.

"Hurting?" Kacey guessed, and set down her goods to scrounge up the needed herbs.

"Thinking," he said distantly. "Just between the two of us . . . this is one Wolf First who may have a little trouble calling on his influence. At least, until I get things straightened out. Although Farren probably knows that, considering his friendly relationship with Maurant's Minor. And I can't afford to go to the Locals for help in finding Ronsin . . ."

"You think Farren might be of some help to you, then."

"Yes, dammit. But I just can't trust him—he's a wizard."

"My father is not in the habit of developing friendships with scoundrels," Kacey said dryly, pouring the steaming water.

"People change over the years. And Farren has made no secret of the fact that he wants to talk to Ronsin— he wants to rediscover magic for everyone."

"If this one person has found it, it does seem reasonable that there's more about," Kacey said, bringing him the mug. She sat down on the padded stool by his side. "You can't blame him for wanting it."

He gave her a sharp look. "You sound like—" but broke off, taking a convenient sip of the tea, his eyes running from hers with such sudden pain that Kacey didn't think, just reacted.

"What did he do to you, Reandn—this nameless enemy of yours? Where did you get such a thirst for revenge?"

For a moment he looked like he might answer. And then he looked like he wouldn't, sitting there, the pain in his eyes coming through so clearly Kacey was almost sorry she'd asked. Finally he said, very low, "Adela." He cleared his throat and added, only slightly louder, "My wife."

"Oh, no," she said, just as softly.

"It was the Keep wizard—a harmless old man. He started with a young fosterling," Reandn said, his face at first still and expressionless. "Then a boy from the kitchen. And Kavan, his own apprentice, and . . . someone I was very fond of. Then Elyn . . . all the time, my ears giving him away, and I didn't figure it out. Not until it was too late. I got there . . . he had her . . ." A muscle in his cheek jumped. "He took her away from me." His hand clenched around the ring on his small finger, and then, abruptly, he scrubbed his other hand roughly across his face. "Yeah, well," he shrugged. "I'm going to kill him."

"I'm sorry," Kacey whispered, and it sounded worthless. She sat in silence for a moment, wanting to reach out to him. Instead, knowing better, she stood, rested her hand on his shoulder for the briefest moment. "The rest of the household'll be in the common room for a while. You should join us, when you feel up to it."

He nodded without looking at her, and she left the sickroom, first returning the kettle to the kitchen and then wandering out toward the common room, through which was her own modest sleeping room.

Deep in thought, dividing her concern between Reandn and Rethia's prolonged absence, Kacey almost didn't notice that the conversation ceased when she walked through the short hall and into the main room. Tanager sat on the edge of a stool by his grandfather's chair, while Teayo resided in the stuffed chair by the cool stone hearth, and it was Tanager's guilty expression that piqued her suspicion.

"Well?" she said, looking at her father.

"Kacey," he greeted her. "We're just discussing some

of Farren's alternatives. And I have to repeat, Farren, that I don't think you'll get any cooperation from this man, considering the grudge he's carrying around."

Tanager looked more stricken with every word that was said, and Kacey watched him, growing more and more suspicious—he'd been up to *some*thing, even if she didn't know just what yet.

"Maybe I should just go on into the city," Farren said thoughtfully. "Now that I'm fairly certain it's Ronsin who's caused all this trouble, I can make some discreet inquiries."

"How'd you get his name?" Kacey asked in surprise.

Farren raised a silvered eyebrow at her. "I've been in Maurant, not dead. If it was the wizard from King's Keep, that would be Ronsin."

Tanager's guilty look suddenly made sense. *Eavesdropper!* Kacey advanced on him in a flurry of angry steps and hauled him up by the shirt. She didn't realize that her other hand was fisted behind her, not until Teayo rumbled her name in a surprised imperative. She gave the hand a brief, startled glance, and shoved the youth away instead of using it; he stumbled and sat heavily on the stool, and she stood over him, shouting in his face. "You were *listening!* You had no right! You creepy little *sneak!*"

Farren straightened, bringing both his feet flat to the ground with a considerable thump; his face was stern. "You led us to believe you were in on this conversation, Tanager."

"N-not exactly," Tanager said, suddenly facing the unpleasant prospect of his grandfather's anger. "I . . . *heard* it."

"Sneak!" Kacey snapped.

"Hush, girl," Teayo said, not without understanding.

"I thought you had to know!" Tanager protested.

Farren's voice was grim. "And are we ever to convince

Reandn we are not the enemy if we don't treat him as a friend?"

"What's more important?" Tanager cried. "Getting him on our side or getting the job done? You *know* he's going to do all he can to kill the magic when he finds it!"

Farren eyed his grandson with disapproval. "That may well be. But you passed on a private conversation, and you owe him an apology for that."

Tanager moaned, "He'll *kill* me."

"You'll deserve it," Kacey spat. "It's no wonder he doesn't trust you—he's trying, but he won't, once he finds out about this. Or weren't you there when Reandn said it might be best to work with Farren after all?"

Tanager slunk down to the stool. "No," he said in a low voice.

"Son," Farren said, "There are important things happening around us, and there's no more time for you to fiddle with growing up. We can*not* afford any more of your impetuous acts. Is that clear?"

Stricken, Tanager seemed to shrink within himself. "I . . ." he mumbled, looking down at his toes, "I was only trying to help."

"I know," Farren said. "I think that's the worst of it."

"So?" Teayo said with a harrumph. "Where's this leave you, Farren? Does it change your options?"

Slowly, Farren shook his head. "No. We still need someone to scout around Solace. I won't create half as much stir as that former Wolf First—he can't draw on his connections, and he knows it—although for what it's worth, I have no doubt his involvement with the Keep deaths is an innocent one. And as I'll share everything I discover with him, I don't think he'll have as much call to anger."

"He's going to be angry, anyway," Kacey pointed out.

"I suppose he will," Farren agreed, "At this point, there isn't much I can do—short of walking away—that will make him ha—" he cut himself off, glancing sharply at the fireplace mantle. His hands, Kacey noticed, rose to make a quick dictation of movement, freezing in mid-gesture; he looked down at them, frustrated and angry.

"What is it, old finger-twister?" Teayo asked, and it was *his* alarm that raised Kacey's own hackles.

"That stone!" Farren jumped to his feet, closing on the mantle, staring at the ensourceled rock there in a moment of intense concentration. He shook his head sharply. "I can't do a thing with it—get a mallet, Teayo!" And he scooped up the stone by its thong and took it outside at just under a run; Teayo, his large bulk moving faster than Kacey had ever seen, ran for the barn. Kacey and Tanager crowded together in the doorway, enmity forgotten as they stared out into the starlit yard, trying to discern what was happening. Teayo, a large dark figure against the grass, met Farren in front of the well. Almost immediately, Farren's voice rang out in sharp command. "Get back in the house—cover your eyes!"

Tanager would have lingered, but Kacey had no desire to brook that voice; she pulled him in by the arm and slammed the door closed with her back against it. Her eyes were closed as she heard Farren repeatedly order her father to move back, but the sudden, soundless flare of light that followed bullied its way through her eyelids with ease.

"Damn!" Tanager cursed beside her, his hands going to his eyes. "Can't see a thing!"

"It's dark anyway," she flung over her shoulder as she pushed him out of the way and ran out the door. "Father? Farren?"

"Did I tell you it was safe to come out?" It was Farren's voice, and it led her to him, faint though it was. In the darkness she found him, rising slowly from the ground. Teayo was at her shoulder in a minute, reaching over to steady his old friend.

"Did you cover your eyes?" the big man demanded. "I'll be upset with you if you've managed to blind yourself, wizard."

"I put my arm over them," Farren said, far too calmly. "I hope it was enough."

"And was it worth it?" Teayo said, helping Farren to his feet. His voice was not gruff enough to match his words.

"Pa-farren?" Tanager called, worried, stumbling toward them, one hand still rubbing at his eyes.

In the cheerfully lit doorway behind him, Reandn appeared at a dead run, half skidding, half tripping to a stop. "Farren!" he cried. "There's magic—they're back! Watch yourself out there!"

Farren's voice rose, still firm and calm, to ease the alarm. "No, they're not," he said, allowing Teayo to lead him toward the house; Kacey took his other arm. "We just saw to that."

"You—" Reandn said, and moved aside so the little procession could enter; he peered out into the yard, and Kacey realized he was carrying his knife. "What in the Lonely Hells *was* that?"

In the light, Farren's grey-shot hair and beard were clearly scorched; it ran across his cheekbones and blistered his lips. His blinking eyes watered and squinted, and Teayo immediately told him to close them. "Sit, keep them closed, and be still," he ordered. "I'll be back in a moment, and we'll see what we can do."

"What happened?" Reandn repeated, surveying Farren and his blinking grandson. He looked ready to attack anything that moved wrong, and Kacey found herself moving with slow precision, not wanting to be the one that triggered him.

"Stupid," Farren muttered, then spoke more clearly. "When you were attacked on the road, those men located you with a spell set into a stone. I should have destroyed

that stone . . . but I'd hoped it could somehow help us
find the perpetrator—that I might be able to draw on
its source of magic. I couldn't."

"That's what I felt," Reandn said, relaxing only a touch.
"The stone." He looked at the wizard, his gaze stopping
at the man's uncontrollably weeping eyes. "And you—?"

"Smashed the stone. There was, indeed, power left
to the spell."

Tanager, his blinking finally slowed, said, "That's what
we saw? What was *left*?"

"Yes. I only hope I released it quickly enough, that
Ronsin was not able to pin a direction on you."

"Ronsin," Reandn said flatly. He gave Kacey and
accusing look, and she directed his gaze to Tanager with
her own, not for a moment willing to assume the boy's
guilt.

But Teayo returned before Reandn could react,
shouldering him aside to reach his patient's side. "A little
salve," he mumbled, almost cheerfully, "A nice cool
bandage across your eyes, foolish wizard. I think we can
fix you up." He glanced up and behind him, at his
audience. "You children get back, go on. Time for talk
later."

Kacey plucked at Reandn's arm and at his clear
resistance. "I'll tell you," she said, a whisper, beneath
Tanager's protests that he wanted to stay. "Come on, to
the kitchen."

With a last sideways look at the scorched Farren,
Reandn acceded, following Kacey a few steps toward
the kitchen. Tanager hesitated, not sure which course
was the safest. He settled with peeling off through the
sickroom and presumably to the barn. Kacey let him go
without comment. *Best just to get him* out *of here.*

"How'd they find out who I'm after?" Reandn demanded,
as soon as they were in the kitchen.

"Tanager, of course," she said calmly. "Listen up a

minute." Distraction, that's what she needed. Besides, she had her own worries. "Rethia's not home yet. Whatever you said, you upset her good. I can't remember another time she stayed gone this late, though to be honest, I wouldn't put it past her, which is why I'm giving her till morning." Reandn just looked at her, the demand in his eyes not easing a whit. Kacey swallowed. "If she's not back by morning, we're going looking—you and I. It'll be good for you."

Reandn nodded; it didn't look like he was really paying attention. He repeated darkly, "Tanager."

"Yes, Tanager," Kacey said, trying to keep her voice light, and turning a suddenly critical eye toward Reandn. Here, in this cleanest room of the dwelling, his dirty hair and the accumulated sweat of effort and illness suddenly struck her as beyond acceptable. Besides, sometimes concentration on the mundane was a useful thing. "And Farren really gave him a mouth switching for it, too. You know, you need a bath," she said bluntly. "Just happens I have water heating."

He stared at her, and inside she flinched, wondering if she'd stepped over yet another one of his lines—and then he laughed. Not a big laugh, but humor, all the same. "A bath," he said. "I guess I do."

"All right," she said, as if she'd never lost confidence. "There's a small room off the end of the kitchen, you see the door? I'll bring you the water. *And* I'll tell you what else you missed. But I won't scrub your back." *Oh, Graces, how had* that *slipped out?*

He laughed again, and Kacey blushed.

Chapter 16

Reandn woke with a start, then froze, completely disoriented, knowing he was not in exactly the same place where he'd spent the last few nights. He raced through his senses, taking in the smell, the sounds, the feel of the bed against his back. It was early morning, from the light against his lids, and if there was someone else in the room aside from the small body next to him, they weren't about to give themselves away.

Then that small body gave a small sigh, and abruptly Reandn recalled where he was. Braden's bed. The boy had made it through half the night and then awakened, homesick, frightened, and inconsolable.

At least, until Reandn joined him.

And now the six-year-old had somehow managed to take up most of the bed and light covers, even though the weight of his splinted leg anchored him firmly in place. Reandn didn't find it difficult to ease quietly off the bed—he was halfway there already.

He stretched hugely and opened the door to let the faint morning breeze run over his face and through hair that was noticeably shorter—Rethia's ministrations, he'd been told, and pushed away a wistful memory of Dela doing the same—and now clean, thanks to Kacey's blunt shove toward a bathtub the evening before. His arm was stiff and painful, but he felt truly awake, as if he'd been in a daze for the past few days. Awake, and ready to turn back to the reason he was here in the first place. Ronsin.

But he was no longer the only one who knew about the wizard. Thanks to Tanager, Farren knew, too—even if he didn't know the details. Another complication, when all Reandn wanted to do was leave complications behind and go for the clean, simple kill. Momentarily, his jaw tightened, but it was too early in the day to give in to anger. He let the breeze take it away, and turned his thoughts to Rethia. If she'd returned during the night, he'd missed it. And if Kacey was truly worried, she'd want to start looking early. Reandn gave the barn a thoughtful look and idled over the decision to saddle Sky.

Behind him, there was the slight scuff of a bare foot against the plank floor, a whisper of material. Kacey, he thought, or Rethia, returned.

But it was Farren who greeted him when he turned.

"I guess it's true," Farren said. "You can't sneak up on a Wolf."

"Why bother?" Reandn said, frowning. A good mood could only be pushed so far.

The older man shrugged. "An old man's games. Teayo sent me back to wait for him—he wants another look at my eyes." His face glistened with ointments at the reddened highlights on cheek and brow, and over his eyes was a light layer of gauze.

"Does he think they've been damaged?" Reandn stepped closer, looking more carefully at what the released magic had wrought.

"Who knows," Farren said, and smiled. "It's hard to decipher *harummph* sometimes. Myself, I'm not too worried. They're only insulted. A little sensitive to light." Then the smile disappeared. "It's enough to keep me from rushing off to the city, which should please you no end."

Reandn didn't even try to hide it. "Like you, I'll take any advantage I can get."

Farren hesitated, and Reandn felt the blue eyes searching him, even through the gauze. "I have to apologize about that," the wizard said. "I wanted to know how the man had made you an enemy—and I'm glad I do—but I'd have preferred to find out some other way. And, Reandn, I am truly sorry about your wife."

"You believe it, then. That the man has killed with magic."

"I always *did* believe there was magic afoot. It was the only way to explain your arrival in Maurant. I don't know how Ronsin accesses the magic, though—and that's all *I've* wanted, right from the start."

As if Reandn could possibly want to help another wizard find magic. He took a deep breath, but said none of the things that immediately came to mind. There was no reason to cheapen the sincerity of Farren's sympathy. And for the first time, it occurred to him that perhaps the wizard could help. There were questions he had, final doubts about what Ronsin had done to him—and to Adela. His voice hitting grit but remarkably even, he said, "There are some things I have to know. Maybe . . . you can help me."

"If I can," Farren responded, his voice just as even, as if he knew that even the faintest sign of triumph at this request would destroy any chance at working with Reandn.

"I don't understand what happened to Dela. And . . . I don't understand why he didn't do it to me, too." He swallowed, amazed it could hurt so much, physically, just to say a few words. "Ronsin had us both, but he killed—" He worked his jaw and tried coming at it a different way. "But he sent me to Maurant."

Farren asked gently, "What makes you so sure he didn't merely send her elsewhere, as well?"

Reandn shook his head, even though he longed to be told he was wrong. "Four gone before her, and no reason at all to send any of them away; besides, none of them showed up elsewhere. No, he was killing people, although I don't know why. And then . . . there was the way Dela just . . . faded. She had metal on her, the binding of a book and her ring. They were left behind." Just like the boy's unicorn halter. "But the ring—and my knives— came *with* me." He stopped, seeing it again in his mind, and recalling with clarity the awful recognition of Adela's *not-being*. "I felt her *go*," he added softly. He didn't mention that he'd seen her since.

Farren shook his head, his brows drawn above the gauze and his expression troubled. "I'm afraid I *can* help you make some sense of that," he said. "And I'm sorry to say you're right. Your wife—and the others, if Ronsin used the same technique on them—are indeed gone."

Reandn looked away, out the door and into the fresh sunlight splashing long shadows across the generous space between house and barn. He'd known it. He'd never doubted it. So it shouldn't feel this way to hear it from someone else. It *shouldn't*.

After a moment, Farren spoke again, his voice taking on an impersonal note, as if he understood it was the only way to get them past this moment. Behind the gauze, his blue eyes were closed. And for the first time, his words lacked a sense of dominance, the authoritative note that so easily sent Reandn's hackles up. "Everything in our world is filled with a certain amount of power; it is that which binds us together, and which makes a rock a rock instead of sand. Some things are more tightly bound than others—metal, for instance. When this power is . . . stolen, the binding is gone and the object disperses." He paused a moment, waiting, giving Reandn the chance to ask questions. But Reandn said nothing. "Unbinding is a difficult spell for even the highest caliber of magic-user. The site and the wizard must be properly prepared. Ronsin apparently decided he didn't have the time to waste with you."

Reandn shook his head. Trust a wizard to turn such a straightforward thing as killing into complexities of magic. "There are far simpler ways to kill," he said dryly.

"I doubt his goal was the *killing*. I think he was bringing in a harvest."

For a moment the words made no sense. A harvest, from death? From unbinding, as Farren had called it? Or was that *it*? "The binding power," he said. "He was taking their binding power and using it for himself, wasn't he? That's where he was getting his magic."

The answer was not immediately forthcoming; the wizard's watering eyes opened; he turned his back on the sunshine. Eventually he shook his head. "Not initially. It takes magic to set up any major spell, which means he has indeed found another source. But he must have been supplementing that source. That spell is . . . prohibited."

"Of course," Reandn said dryly. And if a wizard was disinclined to follow the rules, what would stop him then? *But why Dela?*

No, he knew the answer to that. She had figured out what was going on. She had believed in the magic long before Reandn. "He must have had time to set up the unbinding spell . . . and then I showed up."

"The energy from her death would have left him well able to deal with you, not that he appears to have put much thought into what he did. No doubt he found you very threatening."

"With good reason," Reandn said, and showed his teeth.

But Farren wasn't paying attention; he was still following the logic of Reandn's arrival in Maurant. "I doubt he had any idea where you'd end up—though there used to be a translocation station near where you arrived."

"And the ring? She left it behind, but it came with me."

"Metal is held together too tightly to succumb to the same spell that will unbind flesh. You end up putting more into it than you get out." Farren took a deep breath, shook his head; one hand came up to lightly touch the protective covering over his eyes. "He must be stopped. If he's continuing to perform such high-level spells, I'm surprised he's been able to hide it for this long."

"Maybe he hasn't," Reandn suggested, a touch of revenge-lust creeping into his voice. "Maybe we should find out if any one else is missing."

Farren's face was as grim as Reandn's voice. "I'm afraid I think you're right."

Kacey offered her mare a nubbin of dried winter carrot and reached for the bridle looped over a corral post. The horse—it was more of a pony, really, a saucy, sturdy black mare that suited her perfectly—opened her mouth for the bit and then shook her head, snatching the throatlatch buckle from Kacey's fingers. "Be still," she told the creature. It'd be easier to do this if she wasn't also watching Reandn from the corner of her eye, ensuring herself that he really *was* ready to return to a more normal routine, and the activity he obviously craved.

He was in the barn, dealing with the leggy bay horse that had saved his life. She winced as his arm gave way, thumped the saddle on the back of his bay and sent the creature skittering reproachfully across the aisle. Reandn followed with a curse, then lifted his voice to something she was *meant* to hear. "Maybe we should have checked this out with Sky first. Maybe this wasn't such a good idea after all."

Kacey gave him a wicked little smile. "*Maybe* we've been pampering you long enough. Besides, you're the one who's in such a hurry to go places." She leaned against the corral and waited for him, gently pushing away the mare's nose as it quested for the rest of the carrot in her pocket. *Besides*, she said to herself, *you're the reason Rethia's stayed away so long*. The ride might very well be a strain on him, but if Rethia wasn't in her meadow, it would be time to worry, and Kacey wanted all the help she could get in finding her.

With a grimace, Reandn maneuvered the bridle into place and tickled Sky's lip. The bay flicked his ear in annoyance and took the bit. "Try not to look like you're enjoying this," he grunted, glancing in her direction.

She made no attempt to straighten out her expression, but bypassed a smart remark in favor of another topic. "Rethia's meadow isn't too far from here. Just a bit too far for you to walk." *Now what did that expression mean?* Quick amusement, here and gone, swiftly replaced by something grimmer; it made no sense and Kacey decided to ignore it. "I have a few other places we can check, but if we haven't found her by then, we'll have to go into Little Wisdom and notify the Locals." She sighed. "I bet after all this worry, we'll probably find her asleep inside a ring of happy little wild animals."

"I'm not sure that would surprise me," Reandn admitted. He smoothed Sky's thick black mane where it had tangled in the laced leather reins, and led the horse out of the barn to where Kacey waited by the open corral gate. "Otherwise . . . sounds like this could be a real adventure." Then he gave the gelding a wary look, although it seemed calm enough to Kacey, and muttered, "Just mounting this horse after three days in a barn is going to count as adventure."

On second look, it did have a bit of a roll in its eye, and its ears did flick about a little too rapidly. Reandn double-checked Sky's girth, gave Kacey a look she didn't quite fathom, and mounted, a swift and graceful move. The minute he settled into the saddle, the gelding's nose shot into the air. His haunches trembled, his eyes rolled, and with a sudden, peculiar hop-start, he bolted.

Astonished, Kacey cried out after the pair. She'd thought the ride would do her patient good, but not on a *runaway*, good Gracious Goddess! She quickly mounted her mare, who seemed delighted at the unexpected entertainment. "Yes, yes, go," Kacey muttered to her, not concerned that the mare cantered off while she was still fussing with the reins. They were partners, she and the little black horse, and knew each other's ways.

Reandn and his crazed gelding were out of sight when Kacey reached the main route to Little Wisdom. Kacey stopped the mare, considered the winter-ravaged dirt road, and finally found a fresh mark where the gelding's toe had dug into the hard surface.

She cantered the mare onward and found them almost right away, halted, with the bay pawing at the ground; oddly enough, the reins were hanging loose. She managed to keep her expression neutral until she closed the distance, but then had to laugh. His expression was such an odd mixture of affection and annoyance, and his hand stroking the horse's shoulder gave away which emotion was winning. There was even a little amusement lurking in his grey eyes. It was, she thought, one of the first times she'd seen it; it overrode the grim lines of pain and worry that usually resided there, and made him look suddenly younger. Even the scar on his jaw was nothing, next to the grin he flashed her.

"Sky has his own ideas about the rules between horse and rider," he said.

"Very impressive," she told him. "I like to warm a horse up a little, myself."

Reandn shrugged, and grinned again. "We have an agreement about that, but sometimes he forgets."

"Now that you've got him stopped, do we dare try again?"

"I think the worst is over. Besides, we must be halfway there by now."

She shook her head, laughed again. "Just about—you're lucky, you picked the right direction. It won't take long. I bet we can even keep up with you."

"Let's see," Reandn suggested, and Sky moved out in a much more deliberate version of his slightly skewed four-beat rack. Gamely, Kacey's smaller mare leaped to keep up, while Kacey's loose trousers caught the wind and her hair, flushing her cheeks.

"Don't forget you don't know where you're going!" she called ahead, in case that might make him slow a little. It didn't, though; the bay's black legs flashed through a splash of sunlight in the road and took Reandn out of sight around a curve.

Kacey leaned forward and clucked to the mare, who took the same curve at top speed—and found the bay's rump suddenly filling her vision. Kacey shrieked without thinking and drew the mare up hard, sending her to the side of the road in a stiff-legged stop. "Reandn!" she gasped in protest, and then suddenly found herself fighting to keep her seat as the irritated mare pulled a series of crow-hops. When Kacey had the little horse under control again, she turned back to Reandn, who had said nothing, and only then realized why he'd stopped so abruptly.

They weren't alone. The road before them was filled with men and women on horseback, at least thirty of them, still settling their horses in the aftermath of their own hasty halt. The woman in the lead stared at Reandn with astonishment on her face and Kacey clamped her mouth shut on her questions, knowing, somehow, that this was not the time to interfere. Quick glances racked up the similarities between Reandn and the woman— and indeed, the entire group. Their vests were cut like his, only with a bright patch on each shoulder, and laced leathers of rank much like the more complicated pattern of holes on Reandn's. Their shirts were white broadcloth with loose sleeves—most of them rolled—and they looked identical to the one she'd washed for him.

And then Kacey saw Rethia, riding double near the back of the group. Her sister slid down and ran to Kacey's side, offering not a word of explanation, not even a contrite glance. She and Kacey both watched, riveted by the tension, as the woman in the lead stared at Reandn, hesitant, her broadly spotted white horse jigging forward ever so slightly. Emotions chased across her face, working from disbelief to hope, and finally she said, barely audible, "It's you, isn't it."

Reandn seemed hardly less astonished to find the woman in his path, and his nod was minute, a mere dip of the head. "Faline," he said. "What're you—"

"By Goddess, Danny, I can't believe it. It's *you*." She shook her head. "We thought you were dead!" Behind her, horses moved restlessly, and harsh whispers—clearly contentious—mingled with the sound of shifting hooves. Faline gave them all a quick, hard look, which silenced them, and called, "Dismount!" as she herself swung down from the flashy pinto. Uncertain, Kacey moved her mare closer as Reandn, too, dismounted.

"I guess I've been close to dead a couple of times since I last saw you," Reandn said, "but so far I still seem to be here." He nodded at her shoulder laces. "Made Second?"

She nodded, hesitant, and looked down for a flick of a heartbeat. Then she raised her head and turned upwind so the breeze would clear the fine strands of short brown hair from her face. "Ser is First now," she said resolutely. "We thought . . . well, we hoped, but there wasn't much to hope *for*. Both you and Adela, gone. Just like the others." She straightened suddenly, a hopeful look in her thin face. "Does that mean Dela's—"

"No," Reandn said, probably more sharply than he'd meant to. "All the others are dead. I just went on an unplanned trip south."

She didn't bother to hide her confusion. "I don't get it, Dan. Where did you go? *Why?* Don't you know what it did to Saxe? And that Hound friend of yours *still* hangs around trying to convince us you're alive, and that you had no part in the—" She broke off abruptly, awkwardly, then said with some exasperation, "I know you're a loner sometimes, but—this!"

Reandn shook his head, and looked, suddenly, tired. "It's a long story, and none of it was my doing. What about you? What's Pack Second doing out near Solace?"

"That's short and easy," she said. "I'm on my way to Solace. They sent a panic-flagged request for special enforcement. Seems they've had a couple of unusual deaths."

Reandn's jaw set, a sign Faline seemed to recognize and respect, for she didn't push him, but waited quietly. After a moment, he said, "I think you and I are on the same trail, then. Come with me, and I'll give you my side of it—and there are some people you need to talk to."

His voice held an easy authority that made Kacey wince, and wonder if he'd forgotten what the woman had said. Someone else held Reandn's rank, now.

But Faline nodded, and mounted again; her patrol followed her lead. Kacey took her foot from her stirrup so Rethia could use it and her supportive arm to climb up and sit on the short-backed mare's rump; Sky, thank Goddess, did nothing more than toss his head when Reandn mounted. The entire group rode at a subdued walk, casual conversation conspicuously absent. What talk there was seemed to shoot between the riders in quick, emphatic bursts of feeling. They had opinions about something, it was clear; that they knew better than to express them openly was just as certain. Kacey spent the time casting surreptitious glances at Reandn, who had so casually fallen back into his role as Faline's superior officer; she suddenly felt she didn't know him at all. There were things happening here, and things not being said, that everyone but her seemed to be aware of. She took comfort in the warm clasp of Rethia's hands at her waist, and the familiar movement of the mare beneath her.

It was a long walk home.

Faline sat in a modestly padded, straight-backed seat; Reandn leaned against the doorway to the great room. He'd seen Kacey doing needlework in that chair, her legs curled up beneath her, her feet tucked under the old quilt that was now slung over the back of the chair.

But Faline sat stiffly in the middle of it, her wiry form leaving plenty of room on either side of her. Her tea sat untasted, perched on her dusty knee; Kacey had brought the kettle and a few fine teacups, and then dragged Rethia off to the back of the house. Outside, the noise of the Wolves' conversation rose and fell, bordering on rowdy. Tanager was helping water the horses and from the sound of it, they were telling him some tall tales.

Faline ignored them. She was eyeing Farren, and her expression was patent disbelief; when she glanced at Reandn, it changed to . . . he wasn't sure what. He was only sure he didn't like it.

"Just can't believe us, is that it?" Farren said, cutting off Reandn's equally blunt reaction.

"What makes you say that?" Faline said, coolly non-committal. She rotated the mug in a series of tiny circles, tight, controlled movement, typical of the energetic patrol leader—especially when she didn't like what was happening.

"Your age," Farren told her. "You can't be much older

than Reandn. There wasn't much left to magic when you were growing up—certainly not enough to do the sort of thing we're talking about."

Faline leaned back in the chair. To all appearances she had relaxed, but Reandn knew her better than that. "My inexperience with powerful magic has nothing to do with it. The story you two have put together is just plain implausible. When Ronsin left the Keep for Solace, he was a pitiful old man—losing Kavan was hard on him, and losing Adela was the end of it. He gave up on magic and went to see about teaching botany with some of his old associates." She shook her head. "I simply can't believe he had the strength of will to plan and execute the things you're claiming he's done."

"He's convincing," Reandn growled. "If not by his magic, how do you suppose I made it to Maurant, stayed there two weeks, and then traveled here, in the space of time I've been gone?" He felt his temper slipping to the edge, but pushed it back. She was facing a situation it had taken him weeks to absorb; it was no wonder she balked.

Faline looked him square in the eye; her jaw lifted—a touch of contention—though her voice remained even. "I don't know that you *have* been to Maurant, Dan."

The room fell silent with sudden, open tension, and then Farren made a disgusted noise, slapping the arm of his wooden rocking chair. Reandn stared at Faline, and felt the anger gathering; his voice was dangerous. "You think I'm lying?"

"No," Faline said, relief in her face at that honest answer. "But I think you've been through a lot, whatever it was. And I'm not sure what it's done to you."

"I'll tell you what it's done," Reandn said, igniting the tension as he pushed off the doorway and descended upon her, leaning down to cage her in the circle of his arms, white knuckled hands gripping the sides of her chair. The tea slid off her lap and onto the floor in a crunch of delicate pottery, and she flinched at the look on his face. But it didn't last long, as her own anger rose, and glared back up at him. "It's turned me into someone you don't really know. There are only two sets of rules in this world that matter right now—the ones Ronsin is making up for himself, and the ones I'll live by until I kill him, and rid this world of magic once and for all." She frowned, shook her head, and started to argue, but he cut her off. "I *will* kill him. I'll kill him for Elyn, Kavan, and two boys I never met. And I'll kill him for Adela. Wolf's Justice."

She didn't hesitate; her words held an almost physical slap. "And if you do it without proof of his guilt, you'll answer to *King's* Justice—if I have to take you in myself." They glared at one another a moment, and if she was intimidated by the way he loomed over her, it didn't show. But she was the one who broke away, flicking her gaze down. When she looked up again, her expression changed, and her voice held regret. "Please don't make me do that."

Reandn gave a short laugh. He said softly, "What makes you think you could?"

"Please," Farren said. "This is getting us nowhere."

Reandn didn't move, kept Faline's gaze trapped with his, two hardened Wolves facing one another down. Once again, she was the first to look away, and this time her light brown eyes did not seek his again. Still, her voice was unyielding as she said, "I'd hate to have to find I could, Reandn."

Reandn straightened, stepped away from her, the anger fading as he realized the inevitable tragedy of such a confrontation. No matter who came out on top, they would all lose.

But it wasn't enough to make him back down from revenge, from taking care of Ronsin. There was more

at stake here than his own losses, past *or* future. He
scrubbed his hand through his hair, turned away from
her, just as abruptly turned back. She was reaching for
the broken cup and saucer, her face impassive, piling
the shards in a careful stack beside her foot.

"Look into it, Faline," he told her flatly. "You don't
have much time."

Faline didn't answer.

Farren quietly cleared his throat, reminding them both
he was still there. "You may indeed doubt us," he said,
his expression leaving no doubt as to how this irritated
him, even with his piercing eyes hidden behind the
cheesecloth gauze. "You're not sure of your First, and
you don't have any reason to trust me when I confirm
his story, at least the parts that include Maurant. Fine.
There's still nothing to keep you from taking what you've
heard and acting on it in a manner you find acceptable.
Check on Ronsin, ask around. See if those who
disappeared weren't at least seen talking to the man. If
you've nothing else to go on, why turn away a possible
answer? We may be looking at the world from a different
angle than you—crazy, you think—but that doesn't mean
we're not right."

Faline laced her fingers at her lap, regarding the old
man steadily. "I never said they'd disappeared. I said
they were dead."

But Reandn caught the note of surprise in her voice.
"We're right," he said, certain of it. "That's why the Locals
have given up on it. No bodies, no evidence, no way to
figure out who's behind it."

It was her turn to look irritated, as she gave a short
nod. "All right," she said. "I'll give you that much, and
I'll keep what you've said in mind. But Dan, there's
something you should know." She sighed, and rubbed
thumb and forefinger across her brows. "Goddess, this
is getting complicated. Look, there's been plenty of talk

about what happened to you. When you and Adela disappeared in the same night, on the heels of Elyn, there were two camps about it. One said you were dead, along with all the others. And then there were people who thought—"

"Who thought I did it," Reandn said, finishing it for her when she hesitated. "I heard. Or rather, the Minor's wife heard from the Minor, and after that, it was just a matter of time before everyone else knew, too." Farren made a noise that sounded suspiciously like an amused snort. "I killed all of them, my own wife at the last, hid her body, and made it all the way down to Maurant without being seen." He held up his hand, his voice turning sardonic. "No, no—don't remind me. We don't know that I've *been* to Maurant."

Faline's lips pressed together in clear exasperation. "You better take this seriously, Dan. Because half the pairs in my patrol are fighting over it, and I can't swear which way they'll settle out. And because I'll *have* to send a rider back to the Keep to let them know you're here."

Of course she would. He should have thought of that immediately—not that it would have made any difference. "What do *you* think, Faline? Did I do it? Did I kill those boys? Did I throw Kavan's body somewhere to rot? Did I watch the life drain from Dela's eyes?"

She watched him; her eyes had taken on a suspicious glint. "No," she whispered. Then she cleared her throat and said, "We'll be housed with the Locals in Solace, if you need to find me." She nodded at Farren, shoved the pile of teacup shards aside with her toe, and left the house. Just past the doorway she hesitated, her straight shoulders dropping slightly—but in the end walked on without looking back.

Farren said nothing. Reandn sagged against the door frame, his eyes closed; he listened to the patrol's conversation fade as Faline arrived at the well, the snorts of mild protest as horses were mounted, a few good-byes to Tanager. Then the Wolves left him behind with no more farewell than the sound of hooves on dirt, muffled by numbers into a low-key clatter.

He could have been with them. Back in the Pack, once more the best among the elite.

But he'd chosen his trail. He could no longer afford to be restrained by the rules that made a Wolf the King's man instead of his own, no matter what the price in the end.

Chapter 17

Reandn took the cup of blackberries Kacey offered him as lunch, gulped a mug of her bitter tea, and headed for the barn, crunching the infinite tiny seeds of the berries between his teeth. Kacey, who'd been lurking close enough to the common room to hear most if not all of the exchange with Faline, was obviously interested in talking about it.

Reandn was not. And since Sky seldom asked him questions—not to mention that brushing and currying were just the consistent, low-effort motions that would get the blood moving in his stiffening arm—the barn seemed to be the place to go.

He scattered chickens between the house and the log barn with his long, swift stride, stopping once to look at the woods that folded around the physician's household. It was the woods he really wanted, but *his* woods. And *his* life. Both, he suspected, were something of the past now.

The barn was a cool cave of shade in the midday heat. Although this area did not seem as warm to him as swampy-aired Maurant, it was still warmer than any Keep resident had to deal with until much later in the season. Spring, they called it, but their gardens were already planted and the earliest crops were in harvest. The leaves had even lost their early yellow-green tint; they rustled dryly against the side of the barn where it backed up into the woods.

Reandn grabbed the brushes and opened the stall door;

Sky gave him a wary look. "No worry," Reandn told him. "You're through working for the day. Let me get you cleaned up and I'll even turn you out in the corral with that black beast of Kacey's. She'll teach you some manners." He chose the stiff brush and began at the gelding's neck, where the winter hair was coming off in copious amounts. Northern horse, still adapting to Southern ways.

As was he. He'd have to be careful when he rode into Solace, he realized. The last thing he needed to do was make enough of a stir so Ronsin was alerted to his presence. No, he'd have to go in quietly. He'd learn everything he could about the city. He was a Wolf and Solace would be his hunting grounds—just as Ronsin would be his prey.

Faline wouldn't like it. She might even try to make good the promise to take him in. Reandn rubbed troubled eyes, knowing he had to avoid a confrontation with her at all costs. Evade her, and the Prime would eventually give orders to forget about his cold trail. Harm her and he'd be labeled as rogue as Ronsin; even Saxe would hunt him down.

He decided to give her a day or two to sniff out the city. She'd be there ahead of him even if he left within the hour, so there was no point in rushing. Give her time to gather some of the facts, discover she couldn't dispute anything he and Farren had told her, and she might change her mind about what was and wasn't appropriate justice. Reandn's thumb gently rubbed Adela's ring, surprised at the thrill that skittered down his spine at the thought of revenge.

Just another couple of days. And then, even if he survived—for there was no telling what magical counter-strike Ronsin might have ready—he would at least have the consolation that Adela's murderer was dead and languishing in the Lonely Hells.

Reandn brushed gently over Sky's bony knees, thinking

about Farren. Now that the old man knew as much as he himself, Reandn wasn't certain it was wise to let him go unwatched in Solace. Some stumble, a comment fallen on the wrong ears, and his advantage of surprise was gone. But despite the wizard's reasonable claim that he could be of some help, Reandn couldn't risk that Farren would somehow alert Ronsin to Reandn's presence in his efforts to reclaim magic. He especially couldn't risk having Tanager along—Tanager, who would do anything for his grandfather, no matter what the consequences— merely because he never thought about the consequences until it was too late.

Sky sighed, a content sound, as Reandn brushed the sweat-stiff hairs of his back. "Enjoy it while my arm lasts," Reandn told him, stopping the rhythm of the brushing to flex his arm several times. It was not happy.

"Reandn?"

Rethia. He was surprised she wasn't asleep somewhere; she'd looked drawn and pale this morning, and plenty tired. Now she was walking into the barn, and when she was close enough to escape the silhouette effect of the bright entrance, he could see she looked no better than before; even her thick, bright hair was out of sorts, her bangs mussed and long strands of hair, escaped from her braid, framing her face.

"I thought I might find you here," she said.

"You look like you should be in bed." He didn't really want to talk to her. Given his penchant for saying just the wrong thing without a clue, he might just drive her out to the meadow again. Or maybe she'd drive him somewhere, instead.

"Probably I should," she admitted. Her striking blue and brown eyes were red-rimmed, and her slightly long nose had a moist look to it, as if she'd been crying just recently. Well, then, she was *already* upset. He shook his head; he'd probably done that, too.

"How'd you come to be with Faline this morning?" he asked, bending to carefully brush Sky's belly, and giving the horse a warning tap on the rump when one hind leg lifted, thinking about protest.

Her gaze wandered away, slightly unfocused; for a moment he didn't think she was going to answer, and he wondered why she'd been looking for him in the first place. But after a moment, she said, "I was in the meadow and I thought I heard you on the road, so I went, and there they were. It must have been her I felt. She's a lot like you."

Reandn tried to unravel the meaning behind this and gave up. Half the things she said didn't make sense to anyone but her anyway.

Then she looked at him again, and the perpetual vagueness in her expression was gone, replaced by a sharp gaze he didn't even know was in her repertoire. "I want to talk to you—about the meadow, and about what you said the other night, when you asked if I was magic."

"I'm sorry I said it," he told her. "I didn't do it to upset you . . . I was drugged, and I wasn't thinking very clearly."

"That's exactly why I know it was the truth. Or at least, the truth as you saw it." She gave him a wry little smile. "Though I get the impression you tell the truth as you see it any time you open your mouth."

He stopped, resting the brush on Sky's rump to stare at her, trying to decipher the intent behind *that* one. He was beginning to realize there was more to this woman than he'd given her credit for.

Sky shifted beside him, pushing his arm into an awkward and painful angle. He removed it with a grimace, rubbing it, and as absently as ever, Rethia reached out and took his hand, petted his arm, and released it. She was at it again; the faint buzz in his ears was no trouble, and quickly faded, but he'd have recognized it anywhere.

His pain, of course, had receded. He caught her eyes, kept her in close with his gaze. "*That's* why I said it."

Her odd brown-ringed blue eyes made no attempt to evade his own. "I think you may be right," she said. The tip of her pale braid had fallen over her shoulder and she fingered the bluntly cut end. "I never paid any attention before . . . it's just been the way things are. But you made me think." She gave him a sly glance. "And you didn't suppose I did a lot of that, did you? Thinking."

Reandn left the brush sitting on Sky's rump and leaned back against the stall. Sky gave a lazy sort of snort and resumed picking at his hay, apparently convinced the grooming was over. "You think your own thoughts, Rethia. I just don't suppose they're much like anybody else's."

She smiled. "Perhaps they're not. But it never occurred to me to wonder why, and now I *am*. I even think I know."

And she thinks it has something to do with me? As if he didn't have enough to deal with.

Rethia didn't seem to notice his reaction. "When I was a little girl, I went missing for a day. They found me that night in my meadow. Father was upset, of course."

"No more than Kacey, I'm sure," Reandn said dryly. But he might as well have been talking to himself, for Rethia was caught up in a world of memory.

"I told him I'd fallen asleep; I certainly didn't remember anything else. All these years I thought I was telling the truth, but when you said . . . when you called me magic, when you ran from the meadow . . ." She hesitated. "Have you ever seen a unicorn, Reandn?"

He shook his head. "They died with the magic, Rethia."

"I have," she said firmly. "A whole herd. They're beautiful, not what you'd think. They're wild, and dangerous. They scared me, at first."

Reandn pushed his fingers through his hair and got

it off his forehead. "Rethia," he said, "I don't think you were born when there were still enough unicorns here to make a herd. I don't think *I'd* been born, then."

"Listen to me," she said, with a hint of impatience. "After you said what you did, I had to go think, and I went to my meadow. And I thought of the things I've done, the way I can ease your arm and the way Kacey gives me all the sickest children to care for, and how they get well when she seems to think they shouldn't, and how you're allergic to me—though I stopped most of that." She gave him an earnest look, far too earnest, as far as he was concerned. He didn't want to be part of this. "I never *tried* to remember that day before, Reandn—I never knew there was a reason. But last night I *did* try, and I found the unicorns waiting in my head. They were the last. They came to my meadow and they talked to me—they *changed* me—and then they went away. And the next day, the last of the magic was gone." She shook her head. "I've known it all along, without knowing. They were the keepers, you see. They *were* the magic."

"If you say so," he shrugged.

"Don't treat me like a child," she told him, giving him a look that bordered on disgust. "They *were* the magic, and they left. But . . ." she frowned, trying to frame the words. "They didn't go away without leaving a key."

"You," Reandn said. "Or you want to think so."

The quick flash of her gaze was filled with totally unexpected pain, and then she tilted her head down so all he could see was the impenetrable fringe of her bangs. "You can't know . . ." she said, and her voice was thick; a tear fell to the thin blue cotton of her kirtle, leaving a dark spot over her breast. "The things they said to me, *felt* at me. There was a walnut-colored unicorn, with the longest mane . . . he was huge and he could have killed me so easily. Instead he got inside my head, and then hid from me in there. All this time I didn't know, and now—now I can't stop remembering!" She turned from him, covering her face with her hands—not crying, as he'd expected, but obviously struggling hard to keep from it, to pull herself together.

"Rethia . . ." Reandn said, and reached a hesitant hand out to her. He almost withdrew again, not ready to offer that kind of contact to any woman, but Adela's command was as clear as if she'd been there. *Comfort her*, said her voice in his head, so his hand fell gently on her arm and gave it a little squeeze.

"I know how to get rid of it," she whispered. "But I need your help—you can feel if the magic's getting stronger. If I'm a key, I want to find the lock. I want to ask them back."

Stunned, Reandn let his hand fall slowly back to his leg. "If you're right, then you'll bring back magic as well."

She looked at him, her eyes full of sincerity, and premature gratitude. Their bright-dark strangeness caught him as always, but didn't keep him from hearing, "Yes. Help me bring back the magic."

Chapter 18

Reandn stood by the well in the front of Teayo's house and poured another bucket of cold water over his head, raising goosebumps on his chest and arms as he washed away the day's sweat-glued dust. He dropped the bucket back into the well and let its own weight pull it down, listening to the slow creak of the rope. One more pail might do it; he gave the handle a push and the rope spooled out with more speed.

Dusk had arrived and was giving way to darkness, hiding him from the casual glance. The household had been thoroughly involved in itself and its duties when he left it; even Tanager had been set to chores. That suited Reandn fine. Stiff, more tired than he liked from the day's activity, and still touched by enraged astonishment from Rethia's request, he wished the cold water could wash away his thoughts as well as his sweat.

The bucket hit water and slowly settled; Reandn held the crank to keep it from sinking too far and then forced his sore arm to work, bringing the bucket upward again. There was no more time to pamper it. With Rethia determined to bring her own magic into the world—and he couldn't discount the possibility, couldn't discount anything right now—his options were gone. Ronsin had to be dead before she had the chance to accomplish her goal.

Reandn set the bucket on the thick stone edge of the

well, thinking grim thoughts about trying to stop Rethia. With or without Ronsin, the thought of magic in the world appalled him as much as ever—but Rethia didn't think about the dangerous side of her magic. She thought about healing people and seeing unicorns again—getting them out of her head—and never about the kind of wizard who would kill children for power. She knew what she wanted, and whether she received Reandn's help or his hindrance, she wouldn't be deterred. If he was lucky, she simply wouldn't be successful—but if she was right, and she *was* some sort of key, she was more likely to succeed than not.

Which left only one way to truly *stop* her, and the fact that the possibility had even run through his head was more than he could deal with. He dismissed the whole subject by dunking his head in the bucket, scrubbing his hands across his face and hair.

Someone's there, coming up behind—

Reandn flung his head back, spraying water, and reached for his knife, squinting against the water that still dripped in his eyes—but even water-blurred eyes could make out the light of the mirrored candle lantern moving toward him; it paused several yards away, running up the knife blade and sparking off the droplets of water on his lashes. He couldn't tell who stood behind it, but lowered the knife with a sigh anyway. Someone from the house, of course.

"Touchy, aren't you," Kacey said.

Kacey. He returned the knife to its sheath. "I can't wait to get back to a place where people know better than that," he grunted, turning his attention back to the bucket and the small sliver of soap borrowed from the house.

"You might want to get used to it," Kacey said, coming the rest of the way to set the lantern on the well. "From what your friend said today, you won't be very welcome at your keep if you go ahead with this . . . plan of yours."

"If you came out here to make that plain to me, there's no point. I heard her and I understood her." He lathered his face and reached for his razor, but not before flicking the lantern shutter closed. Light leaked out around the seams of the shiny tin, no longer enough to disrupt his night vision.

"Actually, I came out because I thought you might like some light, but I see I was mistaken." She made as if to pick up the lantern, but hesitated. "No, that's not entirely true," she added reluctantly, then deliberately changed the subject *again*. "If you shave in the dark, you won't see what you've missed."

"I don't have a mirror. Why should I care if it's dark?" Reandn frowned briefly at her, then decided her eyes wouldn't be adjusted enough to see him. Shrugging inwardly, he set the blade against his face.

"If you let me crack the lantern open a little, I'll do that for you."

He lowered the straight blade to look at the dark form of her, skeptical; it didn't seem characteristic of her and was therefore suspect. Besides, somehow the thought of acerbic Kacey with a sharp blade at his throat made him feel a little too vulnerable.

"Cut yourself, then," Kacey said, and her voice sounded more stung than acerbic, now. She reached for the lantern.

"No," Reandn said, setting the razor on the well. "It's just . . . been a while." No one but Adela had done this chore for him in years—and with her, it usually turned into more than just a shave, which was why he always did it himself if time was short. But Kacey, he realized, probably shaved many of the men in the clinic, and trimmed her father's beard as well. And Kacey, he also realized, this time with a little start, was also trying to give him a peace offering of some kind. "If . . . you don't mind," he told her, sounding as awkward as all hells.

If she thought so as well, she said nothing about it. She put her back to the waist-high well wall and hopped up to sit on it, then leaned over to unshutter the lantern. "Razor," she said briskly.

He made a face of trepidation, and she snatched the proffered blade from him with a frown. "This would be much easier if you were sitting down inside," she said. "Now, hold still."

"I came out here so I wouldn't be inside," he reminded her, holding still indeed as the sharp blade came in contact with his face.

She grimaced. He hoped it wasn't because of something she'd just done; she was following the line of his short sideburn. He raised his eyebrows in question.

"I know you did," she said. "And I came out to tell you I'm sorry."

"*You're* sorry? For what?" He drew back to look at her.

"I said hold still!" she commanded, planting her hand firmly on the top of his head. "You're not making this easy. Any of it. Because of what your friend said today . . . because of what's happened to you, and . . . mostly because of what Rethia asked of you today. She really doesn't know what she's asking, you know. She doesn't."

Quietly, he said, "None of it's your fault."

"I can be sorry it's happening, can't I?" The annoyance on her face did not extend to her steady hand. Scrape, scrape, and wipe against her skirt.

Hot and cold Kacey, one moment mixing teas for him, the next aiming a scathing look in his direction. That she'd come out here to be with him was as significant as anything she'd done before. And, as usual, equally as puzzling to him. No matter what she scolded or how she comforted, he had the feeling he'd never seen her true self. "Yes," he said, when no longer concerned for his upper lip. "You can. Thank you."

Silence from her, as she concentrated on her task. Voices from the house drifted down to them; Tanager's, in a complaint that broke from low to high and then stopped in the embarrassment of it. Teayo, some typically hearty response. They had, he thought, no real inkling of what this day had wrought.

More footsteps behind him, and although Kacey's gaze flicked out and then back to her task with no alarm, he could not help but stiffen.

"Oh, stop," she said, impatience coloring her words. "Do you Wolves really have to be like that?"

"It's Farren." The old man's voice was quiet, understanding. Reandn made a face, taking the chance as Kacey looked down to wipe off the razor. "If you're *all* going to come out here, maybe I should go back up to the house."

"I wouldn't. Tanager still hasn't accepted that he won't be going into the city, at least not at first."

"And you?"

"Another day or so," Farren said quietly. In the pause that followed, Kacey guided Reandn's head to the side and tipped it back to carefully shave around the fresh scar there. A few last strokes of dark stubble gone, and Reandn was free to turn to Farren. The old wizard's beard gleamed in the candlelight, and his face still glistened with ointment. "What now, Wolf First? Will you wait for me, so we can look into this matter together?"

Reandn's first impulse was to argue. He squelched it, nodded his thanks to Kacey, and took back his folded razor. Then, with unfeigned reluctance, he said, "You could probably find out where he is without causing as much stir." Not true. With Faline's patrol in Solace, Reandn was no longer without cover for his stalk. "But if you want to learn anything from him, you'll have to be quick enough to do it before I kill him."

Farren didn't hesitate. "I've a few more days to work

with you on that one," he said. "Maybe by then your Faline will be closing in on him."

The worst possibility of all, if he wasn't there to watch her back. Faline didn't believe in the magic, nor in Ronsin's strength. If she went to investigate, she wouldn't take any of it into account; she'd be unprepared, and unprotected. There would be only be more deaths, and Ronsin would be gone again. "Maybe," he said. He combed his fingers through his hair, let the wet length of it fall below the nape of his neck. Farren regarded him searchingly, and when he turned away, he seemed convinced, satisfied that Reandn would travel with him into the city, although the words had never been said. Hoping, perhaps, that what they'd been through together had created enough regard that Reandn would wait, and did in fact want the wizard's help.

Rethia wanted him to stay and help her find magic. Farren wanted him to provide access to Ronsin, to help *him* find magic. And Reandn had the best reasons in the world for shutting magic out of Keland. He shook his head. *Sorry, Farren.*

Kacey was silent, watching with him as Farren's silhouette in the doorway announced his arrival back at the house. Reandn almost forgot she was there as he took in the night smells, the earthiness that came with a heavy dew. For an instant he could convince himself that he was home, enjoying a quiet moment alone at the beginning of a night patrol. A night of working with the men and women who respected him, and believed in him, and then in the morning, Adela's scent in his bed.

Kacey took a deep breath and the illusion shattered. He turned to her—almost turned *on* her—nearly overcome with the loss of it all.

"You left your gear on the cot when you got your razor out," she said, and her voice sounded odd, like there was a small hurt thing hiding in her throat. "There's a patch there. I was wondering if you'd like me to sew it back on your vest."

She knows. She knew he had no intention of waiting for Farren. She knew he'd accepted that he might die. And her words had not meant what they'd *said*, at all. They'd meant *I wish you wouldn't go* and *I'm worried about you* and worst of all, *I wasn't shaving a patient. I was shaving a man.* Hot and cold Kacey, trying to run from the mistake of caring for him with the cold, and trying to make up for it with the warmth.

Reandn felt his chest go tight, his voice grow distant. *There isn't enough here for me—there certainly isn't anything for you.* "Thank you," he said. "But if you leave the needle and thread, I'll do it myself."

She sat there a moment, clearly understanding the rejection. Then she hopped off the well wall and picked up the lantern. "Just don't break the needle," she said, her voice not quite up to the asperity the words demanded. "Good ones are hard to find, you know."

Reandn watched her go, thinking of her steady, sturdy fingers against his face, and wondered, quite suddenly, whether it was the last shave he'd have. To stop Ronsin, to be with Adela again—it was worth trading whatever he might have left waiting for him in life. *It was.*

But he stayed out in the cooling darkness until all the lights in the house had been doused, wondering if betraying Farren and Rethia, true to themselves only when they had their magic, would be as hard to live with as the pain that choked him now.

Kacey found her needle and thread on her workbench, neatly laid to the side where she would be sure to see it. Nothing of Reandn's was left in the sickroom, not the saddlebags under the bed, the densely woven shirt he'd often slung over the iron headboard, not even a wrinkle in the bed sheets. There was no sign he'd ever been here, except for the small knot in her stomach.

Thank goodness she still had another patient, at least for the moment. "Eat slowly, child," she told Braden, who was gulping down his breakfast as fast as he could swallow. He paid her no attention and she added sharply, "Slow down or I'll take it away and feed you like a baby."

More canny than alarmed, he instantly slowed his pace. It gave him enough time between bites to say, "I'm going home today. When's mam gonna be here?"

"When she gets here," Kacey replied, less than charitably. She pulled the sheets off Reandn's bed with one efficient, practiced move that had only a hint of savagery to it.

"He said he had someone to find," Braden told her, taking a break for a swallow of milk. He left a rim of white around his upper lip and Kacey eyed it meaningfully until he gathered up the napkin and wiped it off. "I wanted him to stay and eat with me. He said you'd understand. I don't. Why'd he have to leave before breakfast?"

Because I'd be here, Kacey almost said, but knew she'd only have to try to explain it to the boy. So she said nothing instead, standing at the outside door with the bundle of sheets in her arms. There was no movement within the barn.

She thought about the previous evening, when he'd known. When she'd succumbed to the knowledge that he would be leaving soon. She'd gone out to be with him, to touch him, one last time. Maybe it hadn't been fair, hiding beneath brusque old Kacey, Teayo's daughter, or concerned, apologetic Kacey—Rethia's sister. But her hopes had gotten too loud and he'd seen them, had realized she was there as Kacey herself. She grimaced at the memory of how he'd shoved her away, without ever moving a muscle.

To think she'd earlier apologized about Rethia, who

didn't truly understand what he'd been through. How much worse was she, who understood, and then still pushed?

She set her jaw against the feelings, even knowing it just emphasized her rounded chin. Was it wrong to have her own hopes and wishes, even when she knew they were but fantasy? Couldn't he have given her that one moment of nothing more than two people alone in the quiet darkness? *Stupid*, she chided herself. She was blunt and independent, sturdy and plain—and at thirty-four, already well past the age of marriage. Her lot would be with one of the few local farmers, probably a widower, not with some roaming, grey-eyed wolf. Especially one that would shortly be either dead or outlawed.

She looked down at the innocent bedclothes in her arms, which she had twisted and kneaded into a tortured tangle. Might as well heat some water for washing, and she never *had* finished cleaning the windows in this room. Kacey felt a definite bout of cleaning coming on.

Rethia's earnest voice, breaking into a comment of Farren's, waylaid her in the hall as she passed the main room. She left the bedclothes in a bundle by the door and leaned on the door frame, blatantly listening. Farren nodded at her.

"What you've told me is quite incredible, Rethia," he said. Rethia took it straight-backed and undeterred, perched on the edge of a cushioned stool. Farren, in the comfortable chair Faline had occupied the day before, seemed to tower above her.

"But you believe me, don't you? Reandn did, and it upset him."

"I imagine it did," Farren murmured with a smile. His face wasn't quite as red today, and there was a spot on his forehead that was peeling like old sunburn. His watery eyes blinked more often than normal, but were as bright and perceptive as ever.

"Why?" she asked earnestly, leaning forward to look up at him from beneath her thick forelock of hair. "It's that other man he's so angry about, not me."

Farren's correction was gentle. "It's that other man's *magic*, Rethia. It's what *anyone* would be able to do with magic. If you were anyone but who you are—"

He didn't finish the statement, but when Kacey exchanged glances with him, she thought she knew the direction of his thoughts. Reandn was a driven man, and a dangerous one.

But Rethia was driven, too, battered by memories of an afternoon in her meadow. Maybe Farren didn't know her well enough to see the shadows in her eyes, but Kacey did. She came the rest of the way into the room, standing by the side of Farren's chair so she could watch her sister. Rethia paid her no attention; she was focused on Farren. "But Reandn believed me. Do you?"

Farren's smile was meager. "I have a disadvantage, Rethia. I've lived in the time of unicorns and chameleon shrews and great magics. I've handled my own magic, and I was an expert. No one in that time ever suggested that magic was connected with the unicorns."

"But unicorns are magic," Rethia protested. She'd said the same to Kacey when she'd returned with Faline's patrol, and Kacey had done her best to keep Rethia from going to Reandn with it, and failed. So Reandn was gone, chased off by demands from all of them—Farren, wanting things done his way, Rethia, reaching out for magic, and Kacey herself—reaching out for Reandn.

"So were the shrews, and the flying lizards," Farren told Rethia, playing the role of a teacher who didn't imagine there were answers other than his. "There were plenty of creatures who disappeared when the magic left, simply because they couldn't exist without it."

Rethia's bright and dark eyes held deep offense. "Farren," she said distinctly, "the unicorns *are* magic.

When they left, they took the magic with them. I need to know why they left. You don't have to believe me, you know," she added suddenly, "as long as you help me anyway. You want your magic back, and I want the unicorns. What do you lose by pretending I'm right long enough to help me?"

Farren raised a thoughtful eyebrow at her. "Nothing," he said after a moment. "All right then. Why did the unicorns leave? If I had to say, I'd guess because they were hunted." He settled back in the chair and nodded. "The hunt pressure was definitely on the rise. Not for the kill, mind you. But for status, to own and pen. Though no one ever kept a unicorn long, not with the strongest corral or the trickiest gate. Even so, they grew scarce. And the rarer they got, the more they were coveted." He looked back at Rethia and repeated firmly, "That would be it. We hunted them."

"To pen them?" she cried, aghast. "Why? What pleasure could there be in looking at a *penned* unicorn?"

Farren shook his head. "You'll have to ask someone else that question. It was a pursuit of the Highborn. We wizards were always too busy to pay attention to such pastimes."

"Maybe if you'd paid attention, you wouldn't have lost your magic," Kacey observed.

Farren thoughtfully rubbed a thumb along his lower lip. He didn't answer Kacey, but stood, and held out his hand to Rethia. "Come, child. You're right; there's nothing to lose. Let's go take a look at your meadow."

Sky racked on in a steady gait, his back rolling beneath Reandn's seat. Occasionally he talked to himself, snort-snort-snort, under his breath, as if he'd thought of something particularly interesting. The sun heated up the day, and Reandn kept them in the thickest shadows by the side of the road; so far, they remained in deep woods, with only the odd cleared field and homestead here and there. At this moderate speed, Sky was nearly tireless, and had chewed up ten of the twenty miles to Solace before Reandn took him down into an extended period of walking. Only ten miles behind them; it somehow seemed much less significant than the ten miles left to go.

The one bad thing about the bay's easy to-sit-gait was how free it left Reandn's thoughts. Rethia's intentions haunted him with a sense of impending failure—even if he took care of Ronsin, the threat was not over. He had the feeling she would not give up on her quest to revive Keland's magic, and worse yet, he thought she'd probably succeed. After all, she alone in this world had her own magic. Not stolen, like Ronsin's.

He didn't even want to think about what would happen if she brought the magic back while Ronsin lived. And what about the others? Farren claimed that the magic-users policed themselves, and it looked like Reandn was going to get the chance to find out.

Unless, of course, the return of magic killed him outright, considering his reaction to Ronsin's use of it.

Keep thinking like this and you'll lose before you even start. Ronsin. Adela. Concentration, that's what he needed. Plan.

With his shirt sleeves rolled up and his vest in the saddlebags, he could enter the city without the gate guards making any comment to Faline about the late-arriving Wolf. Once inside, the vest and its newly reattached patch would make his job easier. And once he had Ronsin in front of him . . . two knives and his hands were the only weapons he'd need.

Sky snaked his neck to the side to snatch forbidden leaves from the abundant brush along the road. Reandn twitched the reins in rebuke and the horse stuck his nose in the air, lip extended and quivering, eye rolled

back to his rider. "Oh, stop," Reandn told him, unimpressed. The horse bobbed his head down and began
gathering the leaves in past his bit. They'd have to stop
soon, Reandn decided; the horse deserved a few minutes
of browsing.

He yawned, once again reminded by his body that it
still fatigued far too easily . . . or was it something else?
He was, he realized, working his jaw, trying to pop ears
that were in no need of it. *Magic*. He stiffened, and
Sky stopped in response.

The feeling strengthened, tingling down his spine in
a lively dance completely unlike the magic he'd felt from
Ronsin. Rather than crawling, it tickled along his skin,
and though he knew it was miles away, he couldn't help
but look back down the road toward Little Wisdom.

Rethia, it seemed, was making good her words. She
was trying to bring back the unicorns—and from the
feel of it, she was on the right trail. Reandn spat an oath.
She should have waited until Ronsin was dead. Instead,
she was about to provide the man with an unlimited
source of power to abuse. He wondered if he could get
back to the meadow in time to stop her, to at least gain
the time to deal with Ronsin. Why hadn't Farren stopped
her? *Because he's like the rest of them—besotted with
the thought of getting his magic back*.

Then *he'd* have to stop Rethia. Losing a day on Ronsin's
trail was nothing compared to the trouble he'd have if
he didn't. He turned the bay around, and put him into
a rack, faster than was wise, slower than he wanted. If
only he got there before she succeeded . . .

And then magic struck him, familiar, harsher magic.
Leaden, uncompromising, it dragged against him, past
him. Not at him. Ronsin, working his own magic
somewhere, powerful magic, for him to have felt it this
far out. *I'll come back for you*, Reandn promised him,
pushing through the dizziness, the disruption in his head.

After all, if there was forever to be magic around him, he had to learn to live with it.

The very thought made him nauseous. Beneath him, Sky moved with mincing steps, too sensitive to ignore his rider's distress. Ronsin's oppressive wizardry built and then crescendoed, exploding around Reandn, who gritted his teeth and closed his eyes and patted his horse. Then, as abruptly as it had started, it faltered, fading to a mere whisper.

A whisper that now came from Little Wisdom.

He'd followed Rethia's magic.

Reandn closed his legs around Sky's barrel, turning loose the horse's speed. The miles that had seemed so few only moments before now loomed between him and Rethia's meadow.

Kacey stood in the doorway of the sickroom and waved as Braden shouted good-bye to her *again*. He was propped on a throne of blankets in the back of his mother's cart, moving away at a steady trot. Even with the padding, she knew that by the time he got home, he'd be glad for the one last dose of sweet syrup she'd sent along. Another shout; he seemed determined to see just how far away he could get before she could no longer hear him. She dutifully waved.

When the cart rounded the curve in their lane, moving behind the trees, she turned back to the sickroom. Empty. The entire house was empty. Well, there was plenty to do. She didn't need anyone else around to keep her company.

She pulled the sheets from Braden's bed and started a mental inventory of the medicinal plants that ought to be ready to harvest. That was Rethia's job, the gathering; it always had been. The thought of Rethia made Kacey's mouth twitch in irritation. She and Farren should have waited for Teayo before charging off to the clearing; he was due home at midday and the delay could hardly have made a difference. Kacey had no idea what Rethia and Farren truly thought they'd be able to accomplish, but it'd been quite a while since they'd left; she'd really expected them back by now, and didn't know whether to take their absence as good or bad.

At the least, they should have waited for Braden's departure, so she wasn't left behind. Just because she was Kacey, practical and dependable and always the one to make sure there was food on the table, didn't mean she wouldn't have tried whimsy on for size if it meant a chance to see a few unicorns.

It was her own fault. She'd waited to be included instead of asking. She took the sheets back through the kitchen to the washing area and dumped them on top of the bedclothes from Reandn's bed. At the sight of them, she scowled again and kicked them against the wall. "Ha," she said loudly to the sheets. So there.

He'd left her behind too, without even so much as a good-bye; Farren, it seemed, would be paying the bill, and even Kacey had to agree that seemed fair, now that she knew all the circumstances. When she'd checked the barn, the bay's stall was cleaned and ready for the next visitor; Farren's mule had given her a baleful eye and she'd stuck it out into the paddock with her mare. Didn't seem fair to leave it in there alone.

The house seemed too quiet. Where were the damn chickens, anyway? She left the laundry where it was and went back out to the barn, out to sit with the black pony mare, who had always been a good companion in her own right.

The mare was in the enclosed dirt paddock behind the barn, ignoring the mule and stretching her mobile lips under the fence for the tufts of grass that were just out of her reach. She abandoned the effort when she saw Kacey, and came to stand by her. She didn't nuzzle or nudge, nor did Kacey make a great fuss of petting. They just stood together, and Kacey found her a soothing tonic for nerves that were usually well buried.

After several moments, the mare pricked her ears forward and lifted her head. Without alarm, she flared her nostrils to take in the wind, inspecting the area—sensing something, curious, but finding nothing to focus her gaze on. Behind her, up against the barn, the mule snorted. And then Kacey felt what the mare must have sensed, an odd bobble in the breeze, like a heat wave coming off the road. It happened again, then once more; the mule kicked at nothing and the mare rushed him, chasing him away from the barn; she came trotting back to Kacey, her ears swiveling tight circles. Searching.

There it was, a series of stutters in the breeze, and something that tickled Kacey's nose so she and the mare both sneezed at the same time. Kacey gave the horse an astonished look, and wondered out loud, "You don't suppose . . ." without finishing it, because suddenly she *did* suppose. Rethia. It had to be. Rethia was finding the magic.

By Ardrith's Graces, she wasn't about to play this game any longer. Braden was gone, and Teayo could read a note chalked on their slate—Tanager, who was with him, would be livid to learn what he was missing, but that was no fault of hers, and no reason she should sit here at home, missing it too.

Mind made up, she found she couldn't move fast enough. She ran back to the house and scribbled her note, then returned to bridle the mare. The sturdy little creature was easy to wrap her legs around and she didn't bother with the saddle. She wanted to be part of this, *now*, before it was too late. Before it had already happened. The mare caught her feeling of excitement and jigged down the road until Kacey let her canter. They both knew the way to the clearing, though a larger horse wouldn't have managed the path through the woods. On the mare she merely lay herself across black withers and ducked her head, watching the path move quickly beneath flashing dark hooves.

When they hit the open space of the clearing, the mare stopped of her own accord. Kacey slid to the ground, pulling the bridle off, knowing the mare would wander home. Then, taking a deep breath, she stood at the edge of the woods and looked into Rethia's world.

The clearing danced with ripples and glints of light, visible bobbles of breeze and errant gusts that tugged at Kacey's brown curls and loose shirt. At the center, where Rethia sat, things were calmer—though it seemed to Kacey that her sister and Farren, who was standing behind her, were less than distinct around the edges.

She took another deep breath and thought for the first time about the possibility of danger, then stepped into the clearing to let the ripples wash around her. Nothing. She felt nothing other than the tiny tickle inside her head that she had already grown used to. But *something* drew her closer; another step and Farren saw her. He held up his hand to stay her where she was, but the blue spark of his eyes was smiling; he gave the slightest of nods.

She's doing it. Kacey stopped as directed and watched Rethia; even though they were half the clearing apart, with ripples in reality between them, there was no mistaking the quiet exultation on her sister's face. *She's doing it*, Kacey thought again. She had tapped into magic, pure and clean and light, and she was about to change Kacey's world. Kacey sank down to her knees to watch.

The mare came up to stand behind her, and eventually wandered away to nibble at the grasses; Kacey barely noticed her. Ants found her ankle and crawled circles on it; Kacey brushed at them and then forgot them. The direct sunlight burned against her face, beading sweat on her upper lip; Kacey tilted her head to put her eyes in shade. And she watched. Kacey-Of-No-Patience sat entranced, all her brusque practicality forgotten, watching the magic grow over time she didn't notice passing.

Rethia seemed *elsewhere*. Her eyes were closed, a slight smile curved her lips. While sweat dripped down the side of Kacey's face, her sister's remained dry, her paler skin unflushed by the sun. Her hair stirred in the currents of magic she moved around herself, lifting, floating as though she was underwater. She took no apparent notice of the passing moments.

Farren was the one who started the world moving again. In a sudden movement that startled Kacey out of her wonder-filled stasis, he whirled, his expression alarmed. Kacey felt nothing, saw nothing—until *there*, just to the left of her—a sudden flash of darkness surrounded a blazingly bright silhouette of a man. Kacey fell backwards with a gasp of pure astonishment, but he didn't even notice her. As the darkness oozed away, as the bright light faded, his features resolved into that of an ordinary, aging man.

He looked at Farren and Rethia, and his face was triumph and death.

Chapter 19

Sky's stentorian breathing and his slightly off-rhythm hoofbeats were the only sounds in Reandn's world; the blurred passage of the roadside trees his only anchor. The strong odor of overheated horse steamed up at him from the foam on Sky's shoulders; what had taken leisurely hours to ride out was less than one at this forced pace, but both man and horse were paying for it. Reandn rubbed his already soaked, rolled-up sleeve across his stinging eyes, futilely trying to blot up salty sweat. *If you don't rest this horse, you'll kill him.*

But he couldn't. For though the feel of Ronsin's magic had faded after his translocation, it had then grown again—brooding, waiting, already bolstered by what Rethia was offering. A vulture, ready to turn into a malevolent bird of prey. Reandn's imagination and fears rode beside him, and allowed no leeway, no rest for the laboring bay.

The magic thickened, floating at the edge of his eyes, rushing through his ears, tightening his chest. He'd never actually made it to Rethia's meadow, but he didn't need landmarks to guide him there now. When he came to a clear footpath branching into the woods, the weight of magic there marked it as the path to take. Sky, brutally exhausted, plunged into the woods, breaking aside branches with his head and chest—until he ran blindly into a tree too big to yield to him, jamming his shoulder into bark. Reandn flung himself off the bay and ran on; he was breathing as hard as Sky, running on wobbly legs and not sure if the roar in his ears was pounding blood or magic.

The vulture waited.

Be careful!

Reandn stumbled, blinked. Who'd said that? Dela? Here, where the magic was strong, had he heard Dela? *You're a Wolf. Act like one.*

Maybe it had been Dela. And maybe it was just his own common sense, stopping him from charging right out into the clearing that was just ahead of him. Reandn threw himself down to the cool ground, and forced himself to assess what he saw there. His breath came hard; as he rubbed his brow against his upper arm, blinking painfully to clear the stinging sweat, he began to understand it was not only physical exertion. It was the magic, playing around him, disrupting all the rhythms of his body.

Breathe. Slowly. *In, out.* The clearing held four people. *In, out.* Rethia, absorbed in herself, showing no signs of outward awareness. *In, out.* Farren, his face grim, his attention divided between Rethia and the intruder. Kacey, on the ground and closest to Reandn, clearly terrified of Ronsin, awed by her sister.

In. That was better. *Out.* His body's successful fight to reassert itself gave Reandn leeway to think. There was magic about, but Farren hadn't used it to drive Ronsin away—and Ronsin hadn't used it to eliminate Farren. They appeared to be thwarted, unable to call on their magic, until Rethia finished . . . whatever it was she was doing.

And then all Hells would break loose. Ronsin's smug expression told him as much, as did Farren's tightly worried eyes. It did not escape Reandn that Ronsin had been practicing his art of late—while Farren had been tailoring clothes. From their expressions, both wizards were well aware of the fact as well.

But Reandn didn't need to call on any magic. His was a physical world, and it was right at hand. His breathing was as normal as it would get while he bore the strain of magic, and while his ears were too full of magic to hear, he knew well enough how to be silent without them. Not that it appeared to matter—neither of the wizards had looked his way, and his arrival had been far from subtle. Distracted by the noise of magic? For now, that was *his* advantage.

Still prone, he began to work his way closer to the clearing, reaching down to draw his boot knife. He only needed to get close enough for clear aim; he didn't care if the man never saw him. This was not an honor fight. It was execution.

As he moved closer, using Kacey's form for cover, she stiffened, turning. Reandn gave a quick shake of his head. *No, Kacey, I'm not here. Don't give me away . . .*

She didn't. Quickly, she looked away, fixing on Ronsin instead. Her shoulders trembled; Reandn suddenly wished he could reassure her.

He didn't have the time to think about it. The little black mare, unconcerned with magic and wizards and the potential arrival of unicorns, was picking grass on the other side of Farren; now she lifted her head with interest and nickered. Behind Reandn came the growing noise of something stumbling through the woods. *Sky*.

If the horse came into sight, Ronsin would know someone else was here.

Reandn gathered himself behind Kacey. Pushing her down as he rose, he cocked his arm back, his eyes centered on Ronsin's chest—

Sky staggered between them, momentum building as his front legs gave out while his back legs continued to propel him forward. His sides thumped erratically, spasming, telling tales of imminent death. Ronsin's gaze shot toward the horse, and then beyond, to Reandn. As the horse fell between them, Ronsin smiled. He lifted his hand, gave a preemptive gesture.

Magic enfolded Reandn, squeezing him hard. The blade slipped down in his fingers and his hand clutched convulsively around it, a cut he could barely feel past the chaos in his body. Kacey, sprawled at his feet, glared at Ronsin and shouted, "Let him *go!*"

Ronsin's scorn made his opinion clear; Reandn was no threat to him. He flicked his fingers dismissively. Reandn dropped the knife, gagging as the magic left him. But when he fell to his knees, he groped among the long, flattened grasses of the meadow until his blood-slicked fingers found cold hard metal, the movement hidden by the twitching bay body of his horse. He stabbed it into his boot top as Kacey helped him up, and they stood together, neither of them steady, one of them terrified and the other almost helpless. *But not quite.*

"Don't do anything foolish," Farren warned the smaller wizard, moving between Rethia and Ronsin. "Strong magic will destroy what she's trying to do—and probably destroy her, too."

Ronsin crossed his arms and raised an eyebrow. "Do you think I'm going to interfere with this girl?" he asked, truly astonished. "You know how badly I want magic, Farren. You want it as much as I or you would have attacked me when I arrived, Tenaebra take the girl." He gave Rethia a thoughtful look; she remained oblivious to him, oblivious to all of them. Her lips moved, forming soundless words, and her eyes followed something only she could see. "I don't understand what she's up to . . . but I can tell well enough what it means to me."

Reandn wondered if he could goad the wizard into attacking with magic, into ruining Rethia's efforts—and wondered if Farren's words were true, that it might ruin

Rethia as well. "She's doing it," he said flatly, looking at Farren, and Kacey's grip on his arm tightened. *Tell me she's not doing it.*

But Farren nodded. "I've no idea how long it'll take—or if this is only a temporary gate that will close when she comes back to us."

"What if she never comes back?" Kacey said fearfully.

"Then she'll join the others who've died from magic," Reandn said harshly. "Kavan. Adela." He moved forward a step, disengaging from Kacey. He couldn't let the magic return to Keland.

"They died for a cause," Ronsin said, the indifference in his voice licking against Reandn's ears, against his pain. "For the ultimate cause. They were nothing but stepping stones, an insignificant forfeiture."

Reandn closed his eyes against the rage. *Anger loses the fight.* The knife was back in his boot. He was so close he'd hardly have to aim, and after that, it wouldn't matter, not as long as Ronsin's goaded, magical riposte also destroyed the gate Rethia had opened. Ronsin, dead—the magic, gone for good. And Reandn, with Adela at last.

But the magic buffeted him, made it impossible to clear his thoughts, made each breath a strain that never brought in enough air to satisfy his lungs. His knees wobbled, and on sudden impulse, he let them go, hitting the ground hard.

"Reandn!" Kacey cried, crouching next to him, her arm wrapped around his shoulders. She looked up at Ronsin and snapped, "He wasn't doing anything—leave him alone!"

"Sorry, my dear," Ronsin said. "It's not me. It's your sister's doing, I'm afraid." His voice sounded smug. "Now that *is* justice, Reandn, don't you think? In the end, I don't have to lift a finger to take care of you."

Reandn's hand found the knife again, withdrew it, and

reversed his hold on it. *Don't crowd me, Kacey—don't get in my way.* He was going to have enough trouble keeping his balance, moving fast . . .

And then he felt the assault of the magic actually lessen. He looked up in surprise, saw Farren's satisfaction and knew the wizard was somehow shielding him. Trying to shrug off Kacey's arm, he took a deep, satisfying breath, straightened, and threw—but not before Kacey's hold got in his way, spoiling the throw.

Kacey backed away with her hands over her mouth as the knife struck Ronsin solidly in the arm. "I'm sorry!" she cried, as Ronsin whirled away from Rethia with an outraged cry, facing Reandn straight on.

"Fool!" Ronsin clutched his arm, fingers wrapping around the knife, jerking it out. He threw it to the ground with contempt. "Did you really think I couldn't kill you without stopping the magic? You, who react so strongly to it? All I have to do is direct it *through* you."

Reandn froze—ready to die, ready to be with Adela— but not ready to do it for nothing, to leave this job so completely unfinished, a failure. He glanced at Farren, moving nothing but his eyes, and found his confirmation in the grim expression there.

Ronsin laughed, a sudden, quiet and bizarrely *happy* sound. It was the last thing Reandn heard. The magic rushed through him, knocking him flat on his back. His eyes found Kacey's and widened in the astonishment of the power that gripped him, tore the strength from his limbs and spasmed his lungs. He tried to rise and failed, felt Kacey's hands at his shoulders and chest, her cheek by his mouth to search for his breath. His vision greyed and the agony of airless lungs rose to drag him into darkness.

But not a darkness unaware, nor a darkness alone. Even as he was taking stock, discovering there was no pain—not from his arm, his sliced hand or the stress of trying to breath, he opened inner eyes and found the warm brown gaze he had missed so much.

"Dela," he whispered, and held out his arms. When she came to him she filled an empty space inside, warming places where he hadn't even recognized the chill.

Danny, she whispered into his ear, raising hairs along the back of his neck. That was all, and it was enough; it said anything he could ever want to hear.

He ran his hands down her back, following the curves he knew so well, holding her tightly against him. His senses were filled with Dela, and it was ecstasy. "You've been with me," he said. "I've heard you right along."

Her laugh was more a feeling in his chest than a sound in his ear. *I could hardly do otherwise, love. You held on to me so tightly . . . and I, to Kavan.*

He raised his face from where it was buried in the hair at her neck. "Kavan? You've found him here? I can see him?"

Not . . . just yet. She kissed him then, intensely and almost . . . desperately. *Whether you know it or not, you're holding on to life just as tightly as you've held on to me. Else I would have had you earlier . . . by knife, by arrow . . . You've left things undone, I think.*

"I tried," Reandn said, hearing the anger in his own words. Suddenly they were apart, and he'd turned his back on her. "I tried to stop him, I tried to stop the magic. There's nothing more I can *do*."

Your friends are fighting hard to save you. Her hand settled gently on his shoulder from behind, ran down his back. *See?* Both hands snaked around his waist to clasp in front of him, her head resting on his shoulder from behind.

He started as he realized what, somehow, she was doing. She'd brought him back to the clearing, and together, they stood beside Sky's body. The magic danced around him without affecting him, without doing so much as stirring his hair. Before him was his own sprawling body, with Kacey crying uncontrollably on his chest. Farren stood protectively over Rethia—still apparently oblivious to it all—his jaw set, his eyes tight with grief. Grief over Reandn's death? Reandn just blinked at the older man, taken aback. He'd been a tool, he thought, something to lead Farren back to magic. Not a friend. Not someone the wizard cared about. He saw resolution on that silver-bearded face, as well. Ronsin was still alive, and Farren would do his best to change that—although he, too, would certainly die in the trying.

Ronsin stood apart from them. His face was distorted in pain and anger; blood ran freely down his arm. Even injured, he looked younger than Reandn had ever seen him, vibrant and strong, soaking in the magic—nothing like the aging-wizard facade he'd presented at the Keep. Just how old *was* the man? And how much longer would he live, if Reandn didn't somehow kill him in this clearing?

Farren gave a sudden, startled step backward as, without warning, Rethia stood. She stood, and she stepped up to Sky, and she looked Reandn right in the eye. "We need you," she said. Behind her, Farren looked alarmed and befuddled. "They won't come into Ronsin's magic."

Adela tightened her arms around his waist. *They need you.*

"I won't leave you," he repeated fiercely. Desperately.

I was the one who left you, she said. *I went into that tower, and I knew better.* She moved around to face him, raising a hand to lift the hair over his forehead, pushing it tenderly to the side. *I love you. I'll always love you. But I'm through with life; this is where I am, now. You're not. Do you think I want you to give up on your time there?*

"I'm not going to lea—" he said, stopping short as his eyes fell upon Ronsin. The swirling magic was growing, spreading out from Rethia to lift the wizard's long thinning hair in its currents along with hers. Rethia's bangs blew aside to reveal her ever-startling eyes, and they were expectant, eager. Farren tensed, subtly gathering a wall of power that showed only in the wild rippling around his head. His fingers moved, limbering, remembering.

Life waits for you, Adela said, moving close to him, her fingers spread across his chest. *Take it. Breathe it in.*

Only Kacey seemed oblivious to the spreading changes in the clearing; her face was in her hands, and her shoulders still shook with sobs. She smeared a hand across her eyes, resting it on Reandn's unmoving chest. And then she looked up at the wizard, and her puffy eyes narrowed. Unnoticed, undistracted by the magic that had the rest of them entranced, she searched the ground around Reandn, and when she stood, her face red and distorted, she had a handful of rocks.

"Let him go!" she shrieked at Ronsin, unleashing a rock in his direction. It pinged off the wizard's shoulder, startling away his control over the magic that was killing— *had killed?*—Reandn, and Kacey quickly followed the rock with another. "Let him *go!*"

"Dela, no!" Reandn said, appalled to see this strange, timeless place waver around him. "Not without you!"

"Let him go!" The phrase became Kacey's mindless, bared-teeth litany, backed with rocks and shaking loose Ronsin's control, shaking loose Reandn's hold on Adela.

I'll still be here, Danny, Adela said. *Don't give things up for me. Live. Be the man I fell in love with.* She kissed him, and he closed his eyes and thought of nothing but the way her lips felt against his, moving with infinite tenderness. Nothing but the way her body pressed against him, warm and intimate, as familiar as his own. Nothing but the way her scent filled his nose, the feel of her hair tangling in his fingers. Nothing. . . .

No! He took a great whooping breath and air rushed

into starved lungs. Magic still beat around him but no longer through him; his hair stirred in it as he rolled to his stomach and lifted his head. "No!" he cried out loud, astonishing Kacey, startling everyone but Rethia. He pushed himself off the ground and rushed forward, clawing his belt knife free. When he crashed into Ronsin it was only momentum that drove the long blade into the man's chest. They fell together, a tangle of arms and legs, until Reandn rolled away, battling to reorient himself, sobbing with pain and weakness and effort.

There was to be no respite yet. Sudden hoofbeats shook the ground and he forced himself to his knees, swaying, afraid to try for his feet. Tears and sweat tracked down his face but his eyes were alert and focused as Kacey rushed past the dying wizard to wrap her arms around Reandn, fierce in relief. The shape of her arms and body was alien after the familiarity of Adela.

Hoofbeats. Rethia's face was lit with joy, and she cried, "Look, Kacey!"

They came from nowhere, misting into shape, thundering around the clearing. They were flashing bays and too-bright-to-bear chestnuts, stark black and riddled-with spots, their horns blue-black and pearl and flaming orange; despite their numbers they galloped nimbly around the clearing without stepping on the fallen. Farren and Rethia stood in the midst of them without apparent fear, and the stream of galloping bodies split around them, horns bobbing low to honor Rethia.

Kacey hid her head against Reandn's shoulder as the unicorns brushed close and charged away, not quite touching the huddled pair; they dashed around the clearing, turning it into a dance comprehensible only to themselves. Finally the dust of their run gritted Reandn's eyes closed, and he dropped his head, resting it against Kacey's until the beasts were satisfied with their celebration and charged out into the world with their magic.

In the quiet, Rethia spoke, and her voice was breathless. "I know. It's all right."

Reandn looked up, blinking, to see what she meant. Before her stood the walnut-brown unicorn she'd described to him. It stretched its neck, dark muzzle briefly touching her hair, taking in her scent. After a moment it snorted and stepped back, executed a neat turn on its haunches, and walked away from the clearing.

"Reandn," Kacey breathed, her voice hoarse. She tugged gently at his shoulders, turning him. Behind them, Sky grunted; his legs flailed. He came up to rest on his chest like a dog, his ears twirling around and his expression dumbfounded. Reandn stared, but before he could truly comprehend, Ronsin groaned. *Alive!* Reandn pushed Kacey away, scrabbling in search of his lost boot knife.

The wizard no longer bled. Reandn's belt knife was in the grass at Ronsin's side, unsullied. The arm wound, previously a gaping cut below the man's tunic sleeve, was hardly more than a pink mark.

"Reandn, no!" Rethia said, as Reandn's hand found and closed around the knife. Holding Farren's hand, she moved between Reandn and Ronsin. "This is how they want it, Dan," she said. Something in her eyes was less remote than it had been. "Don't worry. It's safe."

"How can it be *safe* as long as there's magic for him to play with?" Reandn spat, discovering his voice was as hoarse as Kacey's.

"No magic," Ronsin said, sitting, as befuddled as any of them. His hand went to his chest, ran across the rent in his brocaded tunic. "It's gone. How can that be? I felt it—it was *here*."

"It *is* here," Rethia agreed. "The unicorns are back, and there's magic in the world again. Is it not so, Farren?"

In response, Farren surrounded her head with a rainbow of butterflies; they fluttered and clung to her hair. She laughed, and he admitted, "Showy, but they make their point."

"No," Ronsin said, horror on his face. "I can't find it. I *can't feel it.*"

Rethia looked down on him, then reached over to give her sister a hand up. Kacey took it, and held it even after she stood, staying close. When Reandn rose, he stood apart, warily eyeing the old man who had made himself an expert at feigning loss of magic, his every drained muscle gathered for attack.

"You'll never have magic," Rethia said, when the old wizard's gaze, pleading and almost panicked, settled on her. "They decided Reandn's sentence was too easy, so they brought you back and built a wall around you."

"Your unicorns have a well-developed sense of justice," Farren said dryly. "I hope they won't mind if we take him along and give him to the Wolves."

Reandn ignored him, watching Ronsin instead. "Revenge," he said, taking a deep breath, telling himself it was enough. "The magic's back, Ronsin, and you'll never have any of it." It *was* back. Though the air had cleared considerably since the unicorns' departure, no longer rippling through the air, it yet sung in Reandn's ears, an almost subliminal reminder.

Rethia looked at him. With Farren at one side and Kacey at the other, she looked to where he chose to stand alone and said, "She was beautiful, Reandn. I'm so sorry."

He tried to respond to her, but couldn't find any words. The ending he had fought for was no ending at all, but the beginning of a thousand new fights against a thousand budding Ronsins—while the original lived on, and Adela and Kavan were still gone.

He turned to Sky. The horse greeted him with a confused and anxious nicker, and Reandn mounted and rode out of the meadow.

❖   ❖   ❖

The silence, Kacey thought, was deafening. Above the trampled ground cover, dust floated in the sunlight, shafting through the woods on the new paths created by the charging unicorns. She closed her eyes on the scene before her, but could still see it clearly. Farren stood breathing in the magic, his color high and his eyes bright, infused with magic for the first time in seventeen years. Ronsin still sat on the ground, a dark complement to Farren's quiet euphoria—his clothes bloody, his flesh healed, but his soul defeated. And Rethia. Kacey knew she'd always remember Rethia as she looked after the unicorns, tears tracking through the dust on her face but her striking eyes focused and sharp, knowing exactly who she was and what she'd done.

As for Kacey . . . she guessed she was still Kacey. Not suddenly gifted with magic, not deprived of it . . . she even supposed she'd eventually use it, in one form or another, to supplement her herbs and knowledge. But right now, she was feeling a little too battered to care about it at all. Reandn was gone, sick and hurting. And her mare was gone, no doubt carried away by the excitement of it all; she hoped the horse had simply returned home, and wasn't off following any damn unicorns.

Rethia's hand squeezed closed on hers. "It's all right," she said. "It's going to be all right." She wiped a fresh tear from her eye, smearing dirt on her face. Kacey couldn't take it; she unrolled her sleeve, pulled the cuff over her hand, and wiped away the dirt on Rethia's face as best she could. Rethia let her, even contributing another tear or too as she said, "Weren't they beautiful?"

"They were wild, and dangerous," Kacey disagreed, fighting to keep the tremble out of her voice and her hands. She stepped back from her sister.

"That's part of their beauty," Rethia said. Her hair was in complete disarray, and she pulled the tie from her braid, shook it out, and retied it in a thick tail at the nape of her neck.

Kacey shook her head. "At least it's over."

Farren said, "No. I'm afraid it's just the beginning." He extended a hand to Ronsin and helped the man to his feet, relieving him of Reandn's belt knife, which he gave to Kacey. There was no doubt on Ronsin's face; he knew he was a prisoner despite the overlying civility of Farren's manner.

Kacey looked at the knife, numbly wondering what she was supposed to do with it. She could hardly return it to Reandn—she had no idea where he'd gone. "What do you mean, just the beginning? You've got your magic back—isn't that what you were after?"

"Oh-h, yes," Farren said emphatically, almost endearingly so—although endearing wasn't a word Kacey would have thought to apply to the demanding wizard before now. "But, Kacey, there's a whole land of people who never felt magic before, and never expected to."

"I don't feel it now," Kacey said, feeling stupid instead.

"Most people won't," Ronsin said miserably. He no longer seemed like the enemy, or like anyone important at all. He was an old man who needed to comb his hair and mend his expensive, torn tunic. "But there will be those who do . . . the ones with potential. It's going to hit them hard."

"All right," Kacey said, feeling snappish all of a sudden. "So it's not over. I don't much care." She looked around the clearing until she spotted her bridle, and scooped it up. "I'm going to find my horse, and then I'm going to find Reandn. *Someone* ought to make sure he's really all right." All this magic in the air, and even if she couldn't feel it, she knew *he* certainly was.

"You're right." But Farren's expression was reserved. "Don't expect too much from him, Kacey," he warned. He looked at Ronsin, who was so obviously less than what he had been when the magic caroused the clearing, and shook his head, an unintentional comment. "We'll walk with you. Your mare's probably at home, anyway."

"Fine," Kacey said. "But I'm not wasting any time about it." With no more ado, she set off at a brisk pace, swinging the bridle by her side. Rethia ran a few steps to catch up with her and Farren was content to fall behind, his prisoner walking alongside, fettered only by his own defeat.

"I expect he hates me, now that I've brought back magic," Rethia said, her voice sad but holding no regrets. Her hair was already coming loose from the tie, and she tucked it behind her ear. "I wouldn't blame him."

"Rethia, *no*," Kacey said, and then reconsidered. In the end she said it again. "No. He'd have stopped you if he could, but . . . he understood. I think that's why it upset him so much when you told him you were going to do it. He knew that you could—and that you couldn't *not*."

Rethia said, "I didn't know, before. Or maybe I knew, but I didn't really understand—how important it was to him, and how good his reasons for feeling that way were. Not until I saw them together. And he came back for me, as much as anything—to do something about Ronsin, even though it meant the unicorns would come." She shook her head. "And when they did, they saved Ronsin's life! It won't be easy for him to come to terms with all that."

Kacey just looked at her a moment, deciding whether to ask what Rethia was talking about—saw *who* together?—and settling on later. She said, "The unicorns saved Sky, as well."

"And you saved *him*. I wonder if he knows it. He was there, but I don't know if he realizes."

Kacey offered her a patient but skeptical look. She wasn't used to hearing her sister talk about other people, and what they might or might not feel. "Of course he was there, but he was unconscious. He'll never know."

In response, Rethia's expression was surprised, and she opened her mouth—but didn't voice whatever thought she'd had. Instead, after a moment, she said, "He *should* know. You deserve that much." This time Kacey gave her a sharp look, but Rethia just shrugged. "It's true," she said. "You do. And more."

Kacey suddenly wanted nothing more than to sit down and have a good, exhausting cry—as if she didn't feel exhausted enough already, and stuck walking this road in the late afternoon heat, sweat coming through her light tunic and dust and grime sticking to her face and hair—but she didn't give in to it. She swallowed hard and felt her stubborn look settling on her face, and the set of her jaw change to what Teayo had always called the mulie-face. The day wasn't over yet. When it was . . . well, then she could have that cry if she still wanted it.

The little group walked in silence. Kacey scanned the roadside for her mare, and was the first to see Teayo's cart coming toward them, the horse at a brisk trot, Teayo up front and Tanager at his side—and the little mare tied behind. Hot and tired as she was, she broke into a run herself, nearly throwing herself at the stopping cart so she could reach her father's legs. Teayo leaned down to put his solid strong arm around her, comforting her like only a father could. "And what have you children been up to?" he asked as Rethia reached them. His voice was light, but Kacey heard the concern in it. She leaned into his arm.

"Unicorns," Rethia answered happily.

"So the note said, but I didn't make much sense of it. You, Farren—don't you know you're supposed to be wise enough to keep my girls out of trouble? And who's *this*?" Teayo jutted his beard at Ronsin; his expression was not welcoming.

"Unicorns?" Tanager said, startled. "You mean you were after magic? And you left me behind?"

"You weren't there to leave behind," Kacey said irritably.

His comeback was instantaneous. "If you'd told me what you were going to do, I'd have stayed—"

"Not *now*," Farren and Teayo chorused at their respective charges. Kacey felt like sticking her tongue out, but refrained. She might as well *pretend* she had some dignity, no matter what she knew she looked like.

"It's a long story, Teayo," Farren said in the aftermath of obedient silence. "It suffices to say your daughter found her unicorns, and with them came all the magic we've been missing. For now, we're tired and just want to get home—although Kacey has it in mind to find Reandn, and I think it's a good idea. Did you see him?"

Teayo shook his head, a short, distinct movement; he glanced, concerned, down at Kacey, which surprised her. She hadn't realized just how keen those healer's eyes were. Farren said, "He probably saw you first. In any event, I suspect he's gone south, at least until he can pick up the first side road west."

"He can't—he shouldn't," Rethia said. "The magic will get to him."

Farren and Teayo exchanged a look that alarmed Kacey; it was grim agreement, and resignation. Farren said, "Soon enough, there'll be others who can help him—perhaps. But for now . . . I'm afraid she's right. We're lucky she can help him at all. I suspect it's got something to do with the fact that while I—and other wizards—need to invoke magic to protect him, Rethia—as far as I can tell—has somehow *become* magic. There is no gathering of magic when she works, aside from what she brings with her. The unicorn's touch—"

But Kacey had heard enough. She moved abruptly away from the cart and shrugged the bridle off her shoulder and down into her hand. "I'm not wasting any

more time, then. I don't think he'll play Wolf on me."
At least, she hoped not. She had a pretty sharp eye, but
she had the feeling that she'd never come close to finding
him if he didn't want to be found.

Mercifully, they made no more comment, but set about
finding the right arrangement that would fit them all
into the small cart. Teayo's voice rumbled behind her, a
comfortingly normal sound, as she bridled the mare. "One
more up front here—come, Rethia, you're nice and
skinny—and you gentlemen may arrange yourselves
behind."

The ado that went with loading the cart was just
background noise as Kacey stepped from the hub of the
cart wheel to the mare's back; she was riding away when
Farren's call stopped her.

"Don't try too hard, Kacey," he said, understanding
coloring the words. "Plant the seed and let it be, if it
comes to that."

Kacey nodded without turning around. She understood.
It had to be Reandn's decision—even if that decision was
to ride away from the only people who could help him.

Reandn sat a dozen yards off the road, under the
symmetrical, spreading branches of a maple. Sky was
tied to a low branch on the other side of the tree, his
coat dully white-tipped from the sweat of the morning
run, dried foam crusting his lips and ground-in dirt
marring his hips. Frisky and cheerful, he was totally
unconcerned with his body's failure and revival; instead,
his attention was riveted on the leaves that were just
out of his reach, and he was patiently, craftily exploring
different angles to crane his neck to snare the foliage
with his mobile lips. Reandn gave him an annoyed glance.
Unlike Sky, he was overwhelmingly aware of his sharp
aches, the blood still oozing down his fingers, and the
sun in his eyes; he'd only ridden a short while before

the feel of magic buzzing through his skull overwhelmed him. A little rest, that's what he needed; time to get used to the magic, and to take back a little of what this day—these *weeks*—had taken from him.

Instead he sat here trying to shove the events of the morning to the back of his mind. But flashes of his struggle to live, kill, and die were hard to keep away, and he longed for Adela's warm touch. Reandn yawned again, trying to pop his ears free of magic—there were already tears on his face from the spate of yawning he'd indulged in since stopping here—and concentrated on the smooth coolness of the bark at his back, at the sounds of Sky's tail swishing angrily at flies, and on the quiet grinding of the gelding's jaws . . . he must have reached some of those leaves, after all.

None of it kept him distracted from the fact that not only was Ronsin still alive, but Keland—as well as neighboring Taffoa and Rolernia, as far as he knew—was now immersed in uncontrolled magic. And—the thought he veered away from, flinching outwardly as well as in his mind and heart—Adela was well dead, and seemed to have accepted it completely. Accepted their separation, for however long it lasted. Maybe to her it wouldn't seem long. To him it was already an eternity.

Behind him, Sky gave up on the leaves, nibbled a little tree bark, and subsided into a hip-shot stance, his tail the only remaining active part of his body. Magic dragged through Reandn's thoughts like a farrow through the soft spring ground, and he wondered, suddenly, if he fell asleep here, would he wake up again?

Not that it mattered either way. He was far too tired, too worn from chasing Ronsin halfway to Solace and back, from dying—and from coming back to face what Rethia had wrought. Unicorns. He snorted, and fell asleep on the damp ground, his face against the dirt.

❖   ❖   ❖

"Reandn."

Kacey's voice. Soft, worried, barely audible above the magic. Presumably her hand on his back. He turned over, his first mistake—what had he done to make himself so damned stiff? "Hunh," he said, propping himself up on his arms. "Damn."

She crouched by his side, her face smirched with dirt, her soft curls tangled, and her expression worried. "Are you all right?"

"Goddess knows," Reandn said. It meant nothing, was pure evasion. She knew it, of course.

But to his surprise, she didn't push. Instead she reached out and brushed a small twig from the corner of his mouth. "You've got leaf prints on your face," she said. Then, hesitantly, she said, "Will you come back to the house with me?"

He didn't say anything. He didn't think anything, either; he seemed to finally have found that blankness of thought he'd sought earlier.

"I think you should," Kacey said, carefully, lowering herself to the ground. "I'm worried about you, and Rethia can help the allergy. Besides, I'd like to bind that hand." The last was a little bit of asperity, trying to come through with limited success.

Reandn looked at her a moment, and took in the extent of her worry, from where it hid behind her hazel eyes and put the slightest of furrows between her brows. "You shouldn't care about me," he told her, words that came out without thought, and possibly some of the truest words he'd ever said to her.

Her worry fled, to be replaced by . . . irritation, he decided, but he wasn't sure at whom. "I do a lot of things other people think I shouldn't," she said, and looked away. "Don't worry about it."

"I guess I do," he told her. One more reason not to go back to Teayo's.

She glanced back at him, then shook her head, as though to herself. She pulled something out of her belt— his knife—and put it on the ground next to him. Then she climbed to her feet, cleared her throat, and said, "I was thinking about making gingerbread tonight."

He just looked at her, surprised that she was simply going to walk away, when she so obviously wanted to argue him into returning. "Kacey . . ." he said, searching for some words that would help her understand how confused he was, how far he was from knowing what he really wanted to do.

"I happen to think you'll die out here, without someone to do something about the way magic hurts you. I don't want that to happen, but . . . I'm tired. I want to go home and sit in the shade of my own yard. You know you're welcome."

She tugged her tunic back down into place, and reached for her mare's dragging rein. She just stood there for a moment, looking up and down the road, long enough for Reandn to finally realize she was looking for something to help her reach that bare back. She *was* tired, then. But she'd come looking for him anyway.

Stiffly, he got to his feet, dragging himself against the tide of magic. Moving out to the mare's shoulder, he bent to offer his hands as a stirrup. "Can't miss out on the gingerbread," he told her. "Will you wait until I get Sky sorted out?"

She shifted on the mare as Reandn went to tighten Sky's girth and remove the tie rope. "I'll wait," she said.

Chapter 20

Kacey brought him to a quiet house, and the slate message that the rest of the inhabitants were in Little Wisdom—except for Tanager, who was on his way to Solace to fetch Faline. Reandn hoped Teayo and Farren came back from Little Wisdom without Ronsin, because he knew he wouldn't simply let the man go a second time.

He sat on the edge of the bed in the clinic he'd come to think of as *his*, his elbows on his knees and his hands dangling between them, feeling drawn and worn and as thin as Adela had looked when Ronsin stripped her of her body's essence. Off the kitchen, Kacey was heating bathwater, and after a while she came and stood in the doorway, so he got up and followed her.

A bath—the water turned grubby and still Kacey took her turn after his—and a weak draught of bitter tea, and Reandn stretched out on top of the bed, wearing his single pair of extra trousers while the rest of his clothes soaked. He fell asleep quickly, of course, with the magic coursing through his head and tightening his chest, while Kacey waited for Rethia to come home, hoping out loud—and fiercely, as was her way—that her sister could do something to ease the way the magic ate away at him.

He woke once, to find Kacey standing at the window and looking into the fading light of evening; she told

him to go back to sleep, barely turning around to say it.
So he did.

"Reandn."

The voice barely penetrated the depths of his exhaustion,
and he ignored it. A light touch, scented with spice, tickled
in his hair on both sides of his head, and suddenly the
weight on his chest floated away, and the noise in his head
faded. He snapped his eyes open. Rethia, of course.

It was daylight, which astonished him. Sun splashed
over the worktable and left a warm rectangle of light
across his lower legs. Another hot day—though *that* no
longer surprised him.

Rethia pulled over the little stool that perpetually
kicked around between that first bunk and the worktable, and sat. Her face was still smudged with dirt,
much as it had been when he'd last seen her, although
it did appear as though someone had tried to smear
some of it away. Under her sleeveless kirtle, her light,
loose tunic was torn where sleeve met shoulder; he
thought he remembered that, too. She looked tired,
and it showed around her eyes more than anywhere
else. If he'd had to guess, he would have said those
somber brown and blue eyes held regret, but that
seemed unlikely, considering what she'd done. *Help
me bring back the magic*, she'd said, then gone and
done it on her own when he refused.

Slowly, Reandn sat up to face her. "Thank you," he
said. "Care to make that permanent?"

She shook her head. "I don't know if I can. There's a
lot I don't know about this new world we're in, for all
the unicorns told me." She looked away, and dipped her
head; when she turned back, her gaze was protected by
thick blond bangs. It took her a moment to frame her
words, and Reandn could see her trying. "Ronsin," she
said, stopping to start again. "I hope you understand . . .

the unicorns exacted a much more severe price from him than you would have had him pay."

He didn't even have to think, and his words came out hard and low. "He hasn't really paid until he's dead."

"He'll die someday anyway," Rethia said. "Until then, he's isolated from the magic that's been his obsession—while everyone else revels in it."

Reandn remembered Adela's gentle lecture on that very subject. *Try to understand him. Think what it would be to be taken from the Wolves*. He smiled, an ironic quirk of his lips. Considering he'd been living by his own laws these last months, he didn't think he'd have to *imagine* what it would be like. His life with the Wolves gone, and Adela gone, and the slow torture of magic all around him . . . He took a deep breath, latching on to sudden hope. "Will they stay this time?" he asked. "The unicorns?" After all, what was to keep them from leaving again?

"I think so. We know, now—we've had the chance to figure out what it's like without them. They'll have the respect—and the peace—they want. They missed it here, you know. They found another place, an in-between sort of place. But it wasn't like Keland."

Hope died as fast as it had risen. Unicorns, here to stay.

"I saw her, you know," Rethia said suddenly, and Reandn knew she was talking about Adela. "I saw you both. I know you didn't want to leave her, but I'm glad you did."

Reandn's eyes narrowed, but he'd learned enough not to ask *how*. Instead he shook his head. "Kacey's doing. Kacey and her rocks."

Rethia gave him a clear, quick look, and then hid behind those bangs again. "Not all of it, Reandn. You don't believe it now, but I think some day you will."

Reandn shrugged. "It makes little difference now."

"It will," she repeated, and got up, her movements filled with deliberate care as she left the room. She was as tired as he was, Reandn realized. She, too, was paying a price for the return of magic.

At least she'd *volunteered*.

Stop it. Bitter little thoughts like that weren't going to get him anywhere. Reandn scrubbed his hands over his face, his fingers tripping over the scar on his jaw. Still soft and tender, a reminder of how much had happened in such a short time.

Enough of that, too. After a moment, he convinced his body—which felt it deserved another week in bed—to take charge of itself and get to its feet, and aimed for the privy beside the barn. Then, since he was there—and there seemed to be very little else happening, which made him think no one else was around—or perhaps simply not awake—he went in to check on Sky.

The gelding was cheerful and alert and even inclined to act a little studdy with the mare stabled across from him. Reandn found Sky's brush and turned the horse into the dusty little paddock to work off some of his energy, ducking out through the three-plank fencing to cross his arms on the top plank and wait. Sky made only a few circuits of the paddock before coyly sidling up to Reandn to lip at his hair.

Reandn regarded the horse, who had been stiff-haired from old sweat when he'd been put up, and looked none the better for having rolled in his stall overnight. He climbed back through the fence and applied the stiff, pig-bristle brush to his mess of a horse, while the mess stretched his neck and wiggled his lips in ecstasy.

When he'd worked long enough to be sweating freely in the noonday sun—for that's how much of the day had gotten away from him—movement at the corner of the barn caught his eye. Farren, he saw, quickly enough, and—he straightened, stared at the second figure. *Faline*.

He wasn't particularly interested in talking to either of them. Sky snorted impatience at the flies and slapped his side with his tail; Reandn turned back to him. The horse really needed a bath of his own. "Any decent-sized streams around here?" he asked Farren, without looking up as the two stopped at the other side of the fence.

"Not too far," Farren said. Faline said nothing, the audible *nothing* of someone who just doesn't know what to say. After a moment, Farren added, "It's a pity he can't comprehend what was done for him."

Reandn shook his head, not turning around. "I think not, wizard. He's generally on the edge of sanity as it is."

"He's not the only one right now," Faline said. She sounded relieved, as if she was glad to have found something to say at all. "Most of my patrol's running themselves ragged, trying to keep things under control in Solace. The only good thing about the way magic came back is that despite the number of people who can feel it in some way, there aren't all that many who can *do* anything with it yet."

"At least in Solace, you have a significant number of mature individuals who do understand what's going on, and can help you with the transition," Farren said. "I suspect some of the other cities are having a rough time."

"No doubt," Reandn said dryly, flicking a fly away from his nose as he bent to Sky's stomach.

Behind him, Farren's voice gathered enthusiasm. "In a week, we'll have the beginning of the network back. Then priority messages will fly back and forth with little delay—we'll get things sorted out."

Reandn carefully brushed the tender skin behind Sky's elbow and said, "I shouldn't be surprised to hear of such a thing," but shook his head anyway.

"Surprised that we use magic for the good of everyone, you mean?" Farren said, his voice unusually bitter. Reandn didn't answer; eventually the ex-tailor added an apology. "I know, son. You've had a poor introduction to my craft. Believe it or not, some aspects of life will now be quite a bit less complicated."

Reandn snorted. "I can imagine." But he knew the wizard was right. Keland, slowly deprived of magic, had drawn into itself. With the breakdown of easy communications, the cities had become isolated from one another, and too far away. What had been a solid structure of governing under magic had begun to stagger without it—leading to southern cities who no longer recognized a Wolf when they saw one and northern regions like the Resiores, whose resources were so vital but whose people no longer identified with their own king.

Keland would have recovered, Reandn felt. Would have adapted, given a crisis or two to drive it. Could have done without magic indefinitely. His silence said as much to Farren, and said it loudly.

Reandn moved around the gelding's hindquarters and worked his way down Sky's leg without further comment from either the wizard or Faline—although she had something to say, all right, or she wouldn't be here. When Reandn finally stood, he blew a drop of sweat off the tip of his nose and gave the horse a nudge to send him on his way. He tossed the brush through the fence and ducked through to join Farren and the patrol leader; they watched Sky amble around the enclosure, finding the horse easier to look at than each other.

"How did he do it? Is he talking?" It was what Reandn had wanted to know all along, and he couldn't quite keep that fact out of his voice.

"He's talking, all right," Farren said.

Faline snorted like someone who'd been forced to listen, and was fed up with it. "He's being held in Solace . . . eventually we'll get him to King's Keep for a full justice hearing. Under law, Hawley can easily have him put to death—although scuttlebutt is that he's apt to honor the unicorns' decision—Ronsin has to know that. But he just keeps talking—*bragging*. He's condemning himself. We could never have proven anything otherwise."

"Bragging about his work is all he has left of it, and his accomplishments *are* astonishing," Farren said. "He started with a regimen of meditations, attuning himself to the weak forces of the short-lived things of this land. It's something anyone could train themselves to do, with or without magic around to assist."

"Plants," Reandn said, recalling the abundance of greenery Adela had pruned and watered.

Farren nodded. "Eventually he learned to use those forces in lieu of magic—just for the smallest of spells— which allowed him to take even more. As he gained strength, he went from using plants to small animals, then small children—and finally adults, never leaving any evidence of his crimes." He offered Reandn a wry smile. "It was him, of course, who sent those brigands to ambush you, using the stone he'd created to find you. I don't suppose he counted on a Wolf with allergies."

"No," Reandn agreed in a murmur. He leaned against the fence, feeling somewhat small and tired now that it had all been explained. It was the last tie to his old life, and it released him into the new. There was no longer the least excuse to keep him here—or *any*where.

His silence seemed to be the opening Faline was waiting for. "I need to talk to you, Dan. You're the only one who's been in on this thing from start to end, and I've got a report to send to the Keep."

"Not doubting me so hard anymore." What was meant to be a question came out as a bitter statement.

Faline regarded him for a moment from serious brown eyes, her expression an odd mixture of regret and resolution. "I stand by it, and you know why. You'd have had the same reservations, in my position."

She was right, and he knew it. But though she stood there, honest and ready to face his anger, she somehow seemed unfamiliar, and not the same woman he'd sparred with in the practice yard, and whom he'd ranked these last four years since his promotion to Wolf First, and hers to Third.

It's not her, he realized. It was him. She was what she'd always been, a Wolf Patrol Leader. But he was something different, something changed by grief and magic. So he was the one who looked away, into the cool shadows of the barn. "You're right," he said. "I'll tell you what I can, as long as I'm here."

It was only when he said it that he realized he had no intention of staying. Faline gave a little frown, as Farren looked sharply at him and said, "You have plans, then?"

"What about the Keep?" Faline asked, hard on Farren's heels.

"I . . ." Reandn paused a moment, then shook his head. "I'm not going back there," he said, and knew it was true. He'd never be able to return to that life, not in the same keep where he lost Kavan and Adela. He'd left it behind when he opened his eyes to Maurant, surrounded by half-dressed women and his boot stuck in wood.

"Your Prime may still consider you a Wolf," Farren suggested, but carefully.

Reandn shrugged. "I'll always be a Wolf." He'd told Adela the same once, and he'd been right. Being a Wolf was what he was. But he was a Wolf on his own, now, someone who would never fit in the pack again.

Faline's frown turned into a scowl, but Farren spoke up again, cutting her off as though he hadn't noticed she was about to say something. Reandn knew better.

"I'm going to be here a while," he said. "Teayo and I

have some ideas about reintroducing magic to Keland's people, and it'll take some time to work them up and present them. But Tanager needs to return to Maurant."

"Good idea," Reandn grunted. "Better do it before Kacey kills him."

Farren nodded, his expression wry. "My thoughts exactly. I need someone to take him, and to take a letter to Lina. You'll need a few days to recover, of course, but I was hoping—"

"Tomorrow," Reandn interrupted. The last thing he needed was enough time to really *think* about what had happened here. It would be raw enough, telling the tale to Faline. "Let him know. We'll ride out tomorrow."

Farren blinked, but recovered quickly. "I guess I'd better start writing that letter, then."

Tanager, riding a borrowed patrol horse, was a sullen companion, and more of a burden than a help when it came to the chores of travel. Once or twice a day, Reandn reminded himself that he'd been *glad* for the distraction of this job, although it was turning out to be less of a distraction and more of an irritation.

But as they neared Maurant—and as Tanager realized he would be in some demand as the only one in the town to have been anywhere near the events that had changed their world—the boy grew easier to live with. A chance remark or two revealed his anticipated glee at the effect of his new status on Maurinne.

Lina greeted her son with a cry of joy, and then turned on Reandn, demanding to know of Farren, certain without being told that the older man had been involved in the return of magic. Reandn merely handed her the letter, staying only long enough to reassure Lina of Farren's safety and to hear Maurinne's claim she'd seen a unicorn. When he left it was with new packs slung over the spare horse's saddle, crammed with supplies, and clothing to replace the tattered uniform he still wore—as well as a return letter for Farren. That he'd have to return to Little Wisdom was not unexpected—if not for Lina's letter, and the return of the patrol horse, then for Rethia's healing, as the magic made inroads on his body again.

The return trip was leisurely. The days had crept well into summer and even Sky's unicorn-gifted vitality wilted at the noon heat; Reandn did most of his traveling in the early morning hours and into evening darkness. Once or twice he felt magic at work—more than the hum that was building in his head—and he was careful to avoid it. It was past high summer before he rode back into the familiar territory surrounding Little Wisdom.

Undoubtedly, Faline expected him to check in with her; but she was probably in Solace. Farren was likely to be there as well, helping old city structures to re-emerge to accommodate the return of magic. He'd need to see them both—but he couldn't simply ride by Rethia to do it, not with his chest tightening up now and again, and the way every step seemed to have turned into an uphill process lately.

Besides, he wondered how the ever-practical Kacey was dealing with the changes that had no doubt turned her life as topsy-turvy as his own.

Farren, at least, seemed to be about; as soon as Reandn took the turn toward the Teayo's house, he felt the stirrings of increased magic. He popped his ears—or tried to—and set his jaw, and rode toward it. Thankfully, it soon stuttered, then ceased altogether. He was still savoring the relief of it when he rounded the bend in the lane and the house came into sight. Sky felt his tension and stopped, while Reandn stared narrow-eyed at the number of horses tied at the front corral posts along with Teayo's hitched cart horse. They were good animals, patrol quality. But the horse at the end of the line was unsaddled, a grey horse whose build and stance sparked an unreasonable flutter in Reandn's chest.

Sky hop-started into a fast rack at the sudden squeeze of Reandn's calves, taking him past the house and straight to the corral. He dismounted and left Sky and the pack horse ground-tied, swiftly reaching the creature who had been Adela's special pet.

The horse nickered at him. *Willow*. Older, filled-out, minus his gangly demeanor, but no less bright in his dark eye, ever cocky in the carriage of his neck and head. Adela's Willow. He let a hesitant hand fall on the horse's back, while Willow craned his head around to sniff Reandn up and down, whuffing quick little breaths that practically demanded to know where Reandn had been. Reandn had not even begun to think of the ramifications of the horse's presence when he heard footsteps behind him.

He didn't turn around right away. He knew that tread, someone he had missed yet wasn't sure he could face. So he merely stood there, the hand on Willow trembling just enough to remind him he wasn't in complete control.

"Danny."

It was Saxe, indeed, and Reandn slowly turned to face him. He found the Pack Leader's brow creased, his eyes troubled. Just as uncertain as Reandn. And then, recognizing the misgivings in one another made it suddenly all right, and Saxe snatched him up in a bear hug that squeezed the breath out of both of them. Just for an instant, and then they were grinning idiotically at one another.

"Lonely Hells, Danny, you had us half worried to death," Saxe said, his grin fading to a more serious expression. "You don't have to tell me about it. We've got the whole story from Faline."

Reandn shook his head. "No one will ever have the *whole* story, Saxe. That's mine alone."

This time Saxe's grin was bereft of true humor. "And

well it should be. But I mean to tell you, pup, you've been the talk of the Highborns' spring fetes. Half of 'em had the killings pinned on you and the others stayed in their rooms the whole season to avoid whatever monster had *gotten* you. I can't believe we didn't see the connection to Ronsin, when the disappearances stopped once he'd slunk away to Solace." He eyed the puckered pink smudge on Reandn's arm and then tilted his head aside to examine the short, healed but livid line on his jaw. "Collecting scars, hmm?"

"Jealous?" Reandn said, allowing the handling.

"I feel nothing but pity for any man who has to listen to ballads about himself."

Reandn winced. "I don't plan to be in the circles where such things are sung."

"Ah." Saxe nodded. "That brings us quite nicely to the very reason I'm here, Dan."

A dark brow lifted. "Does it?" Reandn asked. He stroked Willow's side. "Your horse, now?"

"You're sidetracking." But Saxe gave the animal a rueful look and said, "No. I led him here. You and Dela saw a good horse in him, but no one else's been able to find it. He was on his way out when we got Faline's first message." He scratched his head and added, "The wizards are doing the priority messages now. Most amazing thing. Anyway, I brought him here. I thought you might want him. The one you've got looks borderline sound, I see."

"Sky?" Reandn said in surprise. Aside from his one-hop start, there'd been little to remind him of the horse's scarred hock. "He goes well enough," Reandn said, but was forced to add, "once you get the hang of him."

"Uh-huh," Saxe said knowingly. "Take Willow anyway. You'll need to build up your stock again."

Reandn was silent for a moment. Then, voice low, grey eyes regretful but holding Saxe's gaze, he said, "I don't think so. I don't belong in the Wolves anymore, Saxe."

Saxe snorted. "Is that why you're wearing that shabby old vest? You don't want to be one of us any more?" His frown was one of annoyed disbelief.

"Not *don't want*. Can't." When Saxe opened his mouth, Reandn cut him off. "For one thing, Saxe, you've replaced me. I'm not interested in hanging around the bottom ranks to take orders from some patrol leader who knows half as much as I do. For another thing, I . . . can't go back to the Keep. Not yet." One glance at Saxe's face told him his old friend understood exactly why. Reandn shrugged, and put a lighter note into his voice. "Besides, Faline must've told you that magic doesn't sit well with me. Too much of it will—and almost has—killed me. I won't be spending much time in keeps or cities any more."

"I thought your young friend fixed that," Saxe said doubtfully.

Reandn shrugged, moved away from Willow to relieve Sky of his saddle, slinging it over the fence and then moving it down from Willow when the young horse started to lip at the hanging ties. "She did. It didn't last."

"Well," Saxe said, untacking the patrol horse and following Reandn's lead as he led Sky to the paddock gate and turned him in to the small area, "don't give up on us yet. The Prime, the Pack Leaders and the King have been discussing things since we sent Faline out— once we heard the sort of resistance she ran into. People don't *know* us any more, it seems, and we need to do something about it. I think you'll like what we've come up with."

"I'd like dinner," Reandn said. "Can you come up with that?"

Saxe gave him a smug grin, and did just that. After helping Reandn settle his two horses, he led the way back to the house, through the sickroom and straight into the kitchen. There the room's occupants sat and stood around the rarely used table—a few vaguely familiar

Wolves, Faline, Farren, Teayo and his daughters. Kacey looked up and her faint tan darkened with a deep blush; Farren smiled a greeting and Teayo waved a chicken leg. Rethia outdid them all, by rising from her seat and placing her hands behind his neck. "Welcome back," she said, and gave him the gift of a smile and peace within his head.

"Thank you," he said gravely, while Saxe looked on in puzzlement, and then nodded at Kacey.

"You look near as bad as the last time you dropped in on us," was Kacey's typically brusque response. She tilted her head to appraise him more carefully. "Maybe not quite. A wash and change of clothes might do you."

"I'd welcome either," Reandn allowed. "But not until I've had food."

"We saved some for you," Rethia said, not appearing to notice how her words startled him.

He shot her a good hard look, and said, "You *saved*—"

"I had a spell set up to let us know when you arrived," Farren interrupted. "We knew you were close, yesterday— that's when we brought your Patrol Leader and that grey horse in from the Keep—though why the horse had to come, I don't know. Preparing it for translocation wasn't easy."

"The horse had to come," Saxe said, unperturbed by the wizard's comment or the way Reandn practically turned on him.

"You came by *magic*?" Reandn said, thinking only of the agony of confusion such travel had caused him, and the weeks of near insanity.

Saxe shrugged.

Farren looked annoyed. "As I said, Reandn, properly prepared, the wizard's road doesn't cause the harm you suffered."

Reandn gave him a cold stare, deciding the weeks with magic had certainly done no harm to Farren's commanding attitude. "And I told *you*, I don't trust what a wizard says."

Kacey stopped them before it went any further. "Sit," she said. "And eat. And you, Farren—leave him some peace while he does it."

"Hard to get a word in edgewise around here," Saxe observed dryly.

"I'll eat, you talk," Reandn said, ignoring Farren's disgruntled look as he snagged a spiced drumstick. A mug of cool tea appeared in front of him and he ate without searching for a chair, having had quite enough of sitting in the last month. But the ride had been good for him—distracted him, even while giving him time to think—although he was still working on conclusions.

One thing he knew. Saxe had been right to point out that he still wore his vest—it was time to take it off for good.

"Are you listening?" Saxe asked, his voice suddenly sharper—and enough to recapture Reandn's attention.

Reandn swallowed chicken and said, "No, I guess not."

Saxe rolled his eyes. "Show some respect, will you? I'm still your commanding officer."

Reandn raised an eyebrow of disagreement but left it at that. Kacey and Faline watched with attentive silence, although Rethia seemed to have wandered off into thoughts of her own. Teayo had pushed away from the table and was gathering his things, muttering something about visiting Braden, who had fallen from a horse. Farren looked like he figured he already knew what Saxe was going to say. It was all very familiar, somehow. Some things, one could count on.

Saxe cleared his throat. "I told you that there've been discussions at the Keep. The gist of it is, we've—the Wolves—allowed ourselves to become strangers to the general population."

"There weren't many people in Maurant who were familiar with Wolves," Reandn agreed.

"We've got to do something about it. The Northern hills are talking trouble again—they have no intention of letting the Keep resume the direct administration we employed when we last had strong magic. We've got to get people used to the idea of the Wolves' authority, before we have to send out Dragons."

"And have you thought about my suggestion you create a new rank of peacekeepers to deal solely with magic?" Farren interjected.

Saxe waved off the interruption. "Later, Farren. It's got nothing to do with this." Undismayed, Farren tipped his head in acknowledgement and the promise he would bring the matter up again.

"And how do you plan to reacquaint an entire country with something they've chosen to forget?" Reandn questioned.

"Remote Patrol," Saxe said, his hazel eyes carefully studying the former Pack First. "Just one, to start with, to see how it goes. Work the kinks out. We're not sure how big an area such a patrol would cover, or the exact procedures. We thought you'd want to work that out yourself."

"Remote Patrol," Reandn repeated.

"Instead of patrolling over one shift, your pairs would go out for a week or so at a time, then report back to you. If you hit a trouble spot, it would be your discretion—you'd either notify or augment the Locals." Reandn's face was unreadable, and Saxe added, "Autonomous patrol, Danny. Can't imagine you could ask for anything more than that."

"The patrol's ready?" Reandn asked suspiciously, beginning to believe in a future again, yet wary of believing—of *wanting* something that wasn't there.

Saxe nodded; Faline's comment reinforced him.

"They've been with my people," she said. "We're camped out of Solace."

"I told them not to make you put up with being near the city," Kacey said. "It's hard enough to catch you civil, never mind when there's magic about."

Saxe snorted and unsuccessfully tried to hide his amusement, although at Reandn's frown, the pack leader managed to clear his throat and straighten his face.

"You sure you want me to do this?" Reandn asked. "Listen to what Kacey just said. I'll have to track wide of anywhere there're people with magic. I'll probably have to stay close to Little Wisdom, unless—" he looked at Farren and Rethia, "you two can figure out a way to take care of this allergy."

Farren shook his head. "I doubt it, son. It's intrinsically you. Any spell strong enough to work would kill you before it cured you. I'd hate to risk even using a protection spell, with the strength of the reaction you have. I'll give it some thought—but for now, best you don't stray too far from here."

"Reandn," Saxe said, his voice sliding into the no-nonsense command tone that Reandn had responded to for too many years to ignore now. "If ordered, would you come back to the Keep?"

Reandn pushed his plate aside and met Saxe's eye straight on. "No."

"Then I suggest you think hard about the offer I've made." He sighed, and dropped back into being a friend. "Some things are in the blood, Danny. You've lost so much already—don't push this away, too."

No one said anything, though it was plain they all wanted to. Kacey's anxiety shone in her eyes, and Reandn was sure it was killing her to keep quiet.

"Yes," he said.

Saxe blinked. "Yes."

"Yes, I'll lead your patrol. Yes, I'll spend my time

teaching this part of Keland what a Wolf is. Yes, I'll be your experiment." Pretending indifference, Reandn picked up his mug and studied the pattern of the condensation dripping down its side.

It might have been his imagination, but he thought the entire room heaved a sigh of relief; Saxe ducked his head to hide a grin Reandn saw anyway.

Faline leaned against the table and nodded. "Good," she said. "Having a second patrol in with mine has been a handful. Especially since half of them were in your old patrol and they feel unnaturally obliged to defend your honor against the passing remark."

Reandn gave her a satisfied, quirk-mouthed smile. "It's the Wolf in them," he said. "It's hard to get rid of."

The Beginning

Rethia watched Reandn eat, missing entirely the conversation that flew across the table between the three ranking Wolves, reunited. She thought about the day of the unicorns, when he'd been so raw with anger and pain. While she'd been communing with the wild spirits of unicorns—over several hours, she was told, although it certainly hadn't seemed like more than a few minutes—Reandn had faced the man who'd killed his family. And he'd faced the woman he loved, seen her satisfied to be where she was, and not interested in sharing that place with him, not ahead of his time.

Just like she found herself coming up with the odd unexpected thought or magical innovation that came from that timeless time with the unicorns, Reandn was obviously still bumping up against his inner scars. They left him sharp-edged, aloof but always ready to lash out; she saw it now, as his friend Saxe posed some question to him—an instant of hope, quickly shuttered with disbelief. His were not the kind of scars that would disappear, but perhaps over time they might fade.

That's what Kacey was hoping, anyway, although Rethia thought her sister had come to terms with her emotions. She was certainly much more relaxed around Reandn, as though she'd realized she, too, had to go on with her life, and had tucked her feelings away as potential for the future.

Rethia's thoughts wandered to the soft, spice-scented breath of a walnut-colored unicorn as it blew puffs of air in her face, taking in her own scent. When she *tried* to remember the exchange of thought between them, she couldn't. But if she came on it sideways, and just let it happen, sometimes . . . sometimes she could get a glimpse of the strange and wondrous ethereal world they'd made their home.

Finally, belatedly, she realized Reandn had spoken to her. "What?"

"I said, come outside with me for a minute." He gave her a quick smile, as much of one as she ever saw from him—this time, it was acceptance of her nature, and the remote reflections that she got lost in. She shrugged at him, and stood; she was long through with eating, anyway. Kacey gave her a look, a request; Rethia responded with a quiet shrug, and her sister joined them.

"I'm not through with you yet," Saxe warned as Reandn's hand settled gently on her shoulder, guiding her out of the room.

"I'm not going anywhere," Reandn said over his shoulder. The other man may have been his superior officer, but it seemed to Rethia that Reandn was making his own decisions here. She preceded him into the sickroom, and let him take the lead outside.

"Why is it you don't have a horse?" he asked without preamble. Rethia hurried to keep up with his long stride, trying but unable to understand why he would ask. A glance at Kacey netted only a shrug—her sister seemed uncharacteristically quiet after the banter of the kitchen.

Eventually, when he looked back at her, she said simply, "It's hard to pick herbs from horseback."

"I have a feeling that you're in for some traveling," he said. "People are going to want to talk to you."

"Then they can come here," she replied, unable to imagine any great number of people wishing to speak with her.

"The wizards in the city will probably want to talk to you, to pick your brains about the unicorns. The Highborn will want to talk to you just to be able to say they have. You don't want them coming here, Rethia." He stopped suddenly, and turned to face her. "You want to keep this place your own. Don't let them steal your privacy, or your meadow—or even who you are."

Trying to understand, she searched his clear grey eyes, but he was already turning, taking her to the barn and the line of horses there.

"This," he said, stopping by the lightly dappled rump in the line, "is Willow. Saxe would say he's mine, but he was really Dela's. He needs someone to love him like she did. Will you take him?"

Take Adela's horse? Rethia just stared at him, and then stared at the horse. It was a gelding, not too large, but sized well enough for her long legs. His legs were sturdy, his neck fine, and most of all, his eyes looked at her with a quick, sensitive gaze. Adela's horse. She looked at Reandn—Danny, Adela had called him—and knew she'd never find the words to acknowledge the magnitude of this gift, or the deeper gift it represented.

He didn't hate her for bringing back the magic. He understood she'd had no choice, that she'd been, in her way, just as driven as he. She moved up to the horse's head, stroking the broad plate of his jaw. "Willow," she crooned, and his ears perked. His nose quivered; clearly he expected a treat. Some horses seemed to know to expect that from her.

Reandn hesitated, then gave the horse a few gentle pats on the rump—the good-bye kind. He looked, for a moment, indescribably sad. But then he straightened, closed in on himself, and closed her—and everyone else—out.

"Oh, Dan," Rethia said, easily drawn in by his grief. "There's another side to endings, you know. They can turn into beginnings." If he had not come here, had not been hurt, would she ever have been goaded into realizing what lay within her?

He gave her a sharp look, a clear warning not to lay platitudes on him.

"Adela didn't want you to come back here just to mourn her for the rest of your life. *'Life waits for you,'* she said," Rethia told him, pushing on through his astonishment. She lay her cheek up against Willow's, watching Reandn with an oblique gaze. He, as much as she, had been touched by magic, and now other people would stand off from him and wonder what went on in his fierce, private thoughts. Very few would have the chance to find out, as she had. Very few would know just how much he had lost. But . . . *Live*, she thought at him, and said it again, out loud. *"Live*. It's not so bad."

He looked away from her, out across Willow's back. Rethia doubted very much he was actually *looking* at anything, but she thought she knew what he was seeing. Then he glanced at Kacey; it seemed almost like a question. Kacey merely smiled back at him—not blustery, not curt, just the sweet smile she seldom shared. But it clearly held no answers; she was leaving them up to him.

Reandn turned back to Rethia, searching those strikingly odd eyes of hers, giving her the direct contact so many others ran from. After a moment, he gave her a wry, quirky little half-smile. Pure Reandn. "If there's a beginning here for me, I'll find it."

"I know," she said, and smiled through those magic-touched eyes.

Author's Note

Authors take their neonatal ideas, massage and plump them, weave in subplots, and turn them into books. Along the way we grow to believe in our characters, and sweat and grow and cry with them. There are very few things as satisfying as typing the last few words of a book, and knowing you've told the story as best you can.

But then comes the important part, the reader's part. That's who we're writing *for*, after all. Long after I write those last words in *Touched By Magic*, I'll wonder how they affect the people they're meant for . . . which is why my postal and current E-mail addresses are at the bottom of the page.

Doranna Durgin
PO Box 26207
Rochester, NY 14626
(SASE, please)

d.durgin@genie.com

To Read About Great Characters Having Incredible Adventures You Should Try ✒ ✒ ✒

BAEN

IF YOU LIKE...YOU SHOULD TRY...

Norse Mythology...
The Mask of Loki by
Roger Zelazny & Thomas T. Thomas

The Iron Thane by Jason Henderson

Sleipnir by Linda Evans

Puns...
Mall Purchase Night by Rick Cook

The Case of the Toxic Spell Dump
by Harry Turtledove

Quests...
Pigs Don't Fly and *The Unlikely Ones*
by Mary Brown

The Deed of Paksenarrion by Elizabeth Moon

Through the Ice by Piers Anthony & Robert Kornwise

Vampires...
Tomorrow Sucks
by Greg Cox & T.K.F. Weisskopf